Torchship Pilot

Karl K. Gallagher

This is a work of fiction. Names, characters, businesses, places, events and incidents are either the products of the author's imagination or used in a fictitious manner. Any resemblance to actual persons, living or dead, or actual events is purely coincidental.

Published by Kelt Haven Press, Saginaw, TX.

Cover art and design by Stephanie G. Folse
      (www.scarlettebooks.com).
Interior art by Michael van Slyke, Archangel Arts
Editing by Laura Gallagher.
Audio Recording by Laura Gallagher.

First edition, revised.

To Fencon, a place of community and inspiration,

To all the volunteers who make it happen,

And especially to Ed Dravecky III,
now at the eternal con

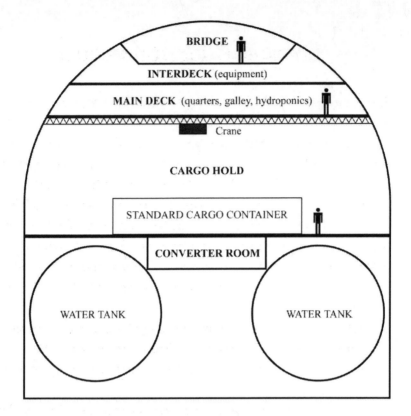

Cross section of 25m freighter.

Chapter One: Homeward

Fragment of FNS *Terror*, Bonaventure System, acceleration 0 m/s^2

Michigan Long floated through the corridors of the wrecked battleship. Her spacesuit was recycling the smell of her own sweat into her face. Even in free-fall, hauling out survivors was heavy work.

At a bend in the corridor she braced against the bulkhead. Spreading her hands flat on the wall let her sense any vibrations from survivors banging on their compartments. She was listening for survivors. Not resting from the effort of maneuvering in free-fall. At least the wreck had enough spin to let her rest against the wall instead of having to brace herself.

She felt some vibrations. Not the bang-bang-bang of someone trying to attract attention. This sounded like someone working.

Her radio was set for the standard suit emergency frequency. She called, "Anyone out there?"

"Oh, thank God. I thought we'd been abandoned. This is Chief Donner. Who are you?" The signal was clear. He had to be less than fifty meters away.

"I'm Mitchie Long. Where are you?"

"Corridor Twelve-Golf-Five. It's blocked. I've been trying to get through."

"On my way. Anyone with you?"

"About a dozen back in the compartment. I'm the only one with a suit. We need to find survival bubbles for the rest."

"That's going to be tough. All the ones I've seen are full. Let's clear the block first." She'd also seen plenty of spacers who couldn't find a bubble fast enough as their ship was torn apart.

The Fusion Navy might skimp on safety gear, but they labeled everything clearly. Finding 12G5 only took a couple of minutes.

The blockage filled the corridor. A molten penetrator had passed through, liquefying structures as it went. The strands of steel alloy surrounded the hole in the bulkhead, looking like a spider web made of icicles.

"That you, Long?" transmitted the chief.

"Yeah. I see the problem. Hold on, I saw something back there."

A cross-corridor had twisted and warped in an explosion shockwave. A thick spar was lying to one side, held in place by the wreck's spin. She hauled it to 12G5.

Some shoving forced it through so Chief Donner could grab the other end. Then they could combine their leverage on the icicles.

After breaking four of them Donner said, "That's a start on a hole."

"It's big enough," said Mitchie. She squirmed into the gap. The coverall she wore over her pressure suit snagged on a spike. Tugging it free cost a slice in the heavy fabric. It wasn't the first one she'd gotten on this mission, but at least her suit didn't have any holes in it.

"Big enough for you," was the chief's greeting on the other side.

Mitchie thought it was a fair complaint. He was almost two meters tall. In gravity she wouldn't even reach his chin.

"That ain't a Navy suit. What ship are you from?" demanded Chief Donner.

"I'm off a freighter passing through the system. We were called in to help look for survivors." Which was true, if incomplete. Telling him she'd had a part in destroying his ship wouldn't help the immediate situation.

"Your accent is funny. What's your home planet?"

"Akiak."

"A Disker!"

"Yes, I'm a Disker." Mitchie kept her voice calm and friendly to de-escalate things. "The Disconnected Worlds won the battle. We're doing search and rescue. You're going to a prisoner of war camp, which is better than staying here."

"Like hell." Donner pulled a pistol from the holster on his belt.

Mitchie kicked off into the corridor behind him. As she bounced off a bulkhead she considered the decision. Going back through the hole would have been too slow. Pulling her own pistol would have left them both bleeding out through holes in their suits. And trying to attack him bare-handed was ludicrous. So this was the best option.

It just wasn't a good option. The corridor made a right angle just ahead. A bullet smashed into the bulkhead ahead of her, sending sparks and bits of metal flying.

She bounced through the bend and despaired. The corridor went straight for a hundred meters with no cover.

There was a hatch. If it let into a compartment with cover she could fight it out there. Or she could use the hatch itself as cover.

Mitchie twisted the dogging wheel with one hand while the other gripped the edge of the hatch, ready to pull it open. The wheel released the hatch just as Donner came into sight in the bend.

The hatch pulled out of her grip. Air pressure flung it open against the stops, hiding Donner from view. *Oh, crap. That was a pressurized compartment*, Mitchie thought in horror.

Escaping air pushed on Mitchie's suit with screams and the roar of wind. A Fusion spacer slammed into her, his limbs flailing in panic.

She grabbed the edge of the hatch with one hand. The other shoved on the spacer, trying to push him back into the compartment so the hatch could close. More people bumped into him, pushing back.

Vibration stung her fingers as a bullet struck the hatch. She pulled harder but an arm was caught against a hinge.

The roar of air became a whisper and then vacuum silence. Mitchie cursed in frustration but none of the dying spacers could hear her.

Another bullet struck the hatch. She pulled herself into the compartment, shoving aside more warm bodies. A table was mounted on the floor, now a tilted wall with the wreck's spin. Mitchie wedged herself behind it and waited, her pistol aimed at the hatch.

Chief Donner broadcast a string of curses over the radio. She didn't answer. When his helmet poked through the pile of bodies she fired. He twisted to try to spot her. She kept firing until he was still.

Mitchie thought, *This war became brutal fast.*

TWO MONTHS EARLIER
Planet Pintoy, gravity 9.4 m/s^2

The elevator opened into a round lobby. No hallways, just four doors. This floor of the skyscraper had big apartments. Captain

Schwartzenberger started checking the names on the doors. Mitchie and Guo gently guided Alexi out of the elevator. One of the advertisements fascinated him. Guo had to hold a duffle bag in front of it to block his view before he'd shuffle along to their lead.

"This one," said the captain. The door was marked FRANKOVITCH in old-fashioned static letters. When Alexi was in front of the door Schwartzenberger pressed the notifier.

The security system must have warned of people approaching. The door flew open. "Bozhe moi, Alexi! How long have you been on planet? Why didn't you message me?" Alexi's sister was equally blonde and almost as tall.

Alexi slurred out, "Hi . . . sis."

"Are you all right?" Ms. Frankovitch looked at Schwartzenberger for the first time. "Is he all right?"

"I'm afraid he's on some very powerful medication, ma'am. I'm Alois Schwartzenberger, captain of the analog freighter *Fives Full*. Alexi was a crewman on our last voyage. This is my pilot Michigan Long"— Mitchie offered a friendly smile—"and engineer Guo Kwan. May we come in?"

"Yes, of course. Please, call me Donna."

A few minutes later Alexi was seated on a couch staring at a fish tank. She'd forced a cup of coffee into everyone's hands.

"Now," said Donna. "What happened to my brother?"

Captain Schwartzenberger took a sip. "He had a psychological breakdown under the stress of a very difficult mission."

"How stressful?" asked Donna.

"We took a load of Pilgrims to Old Earth. We were attacked by AIs, holed by a meteor, and ran short of food. Long hours of work and complete isolation. There was also . . . did Alexi ever talk to you about what your grandfather hid when fleeing Eden?"

"Oh, do not tell me Alexi talked you into doing his stupid treasure hunt," scoffed Donna. "You looked so sensible."

Schwartzenberger waved to Mitchie. The pilot produced a small box covered in tacky "Happy Birthday" film. She'd chosen it to make any watching criminal think it had to be worth less than twenty keys.

Donna took the box with a doubtful expression. Opening it revealed a necklace. A dozen rubies formed a triangle hanging from a gold chain. She pulled a datasheet from her pocket and tossed it on the coffee table. "Grandmother's wedding portrait," she ordered.

By the time the crumpled wad had unfolded itself into a smooth display it had found the picture. A young woman, gowned in the swooping excesses of late 22nd-century fashion, wore the same ruby necklace.

Donna collapsed into an armchair. "Bozhe moi. You found it."

His eyes still following the fish, Alexi said, "Found it."

"How much was there?" asked Donna.

"Two containers," said the captain. "Ancient art, fuel metal, stable transuranic elements, jewelry. Tons of stuff. We're not sure what we can sell it for yet. Tens of millions of keys at least."

She clutched the necklace tighter. "Do you need to sell this?"

"No. That's part of Alexi's share. The deal was that he'd get twenty-five percent of the value before expenses."

"I'd think he'd be happy now. He's been lusting for that his whole life." Donna studied her brother's blank expression.

Schwartzenberger hesitated, not sure how to explain how things went wrong.

Mitchie sat down next to Donna. "He was, at first. But then he became terrified of losing it all. Started acting paranoid. Accusing us of trying to steal the treasure."

Mitchie continued, "He assaulted one of the crew, then ran off to the hold and started shooting at my husband." She looked over at Guo. "Fortunately he missed." Guo smiled back at her. "We restrained him and locked him up. Weeks in solitary confinement didn't make him any happier. The Navy evaluated him and prescribed a calmative."

"So he's gone mad," said Donna.

"The Navy psychiatrist thought being in a familiar environment with people he trusts was the best therapy," said Captain Schwartzenberger. "Do you think you can keep him here and get him professional care?"

"Of course, he's family. I don't know how we'll afford that but we'll manage."

"You won't need to worry about that," said the captain. He fiddled with his datasheet.

Donna's sheet lit up with a message. She gave permission for the deposit to go into her account. The amount drew Russian curses from her. "That . . . that will pay for many doctors."

"It's Alexi's pay for the Pilgrim trip and his share of what we've sold so far. We'll send more as we can. It's going to take a while. We don't want to attract attention from the Fusion."

"No," agreed Donna. "They'd grab it all if they had an excuse."

"The art is the hardest to sell," said Guo. "Proving it's authentic requires telling the whole story."

"You'll need to set up a business we can transfer funds to," said Schwartzenberger. "Paying you directly will get noticed. Now that we've paid off Alexi we won't have an excuse to make more direct transfers."

As Donna and the captain discussed the details of money laundering Mitchie walked over to Guo.

He stood behind the couch, ready to deck Alexi if he overcame the medication. Guo wrapped an arm around Mitchie and pulled her close. "I wasn't your husband when he shot at me," he whispered. "And Abdul wasn't one of the crew, just a working passenger."

"Nitpicker," said Mitchie. "I knew you were going to say that."

The cuddle broke up when Schwartzenberger finished his deal with Donna. Guo put the duffle bag on the couch by Alexi. "This has his clothes and effects," explained the mechanic. "This pocket has the medication. There's a week of it left."

The captain got them out the door with minimal farewells. The elevator was waiting for them.

After the doors closed on them Guo said, "I feel bad not saying goodbye to Alexi."

"He wouldn't have registered it," said the captain.

"Still, we owe him a lot. Maybe I'll write him a thank you letter after he recovers."

"So he'll know where to send the assassins?" asked Mitchie.

***

Michigan "Mitchie" Long had spotted a pattern early in her Intelligence training. If a tradecraft technique had a cutesy name she hated it. They always went for the flamboyant, exactly what she didn't want while trying not to be noticed.

She'd tried to arrange a data drop-off with her Pintoy contact. Instead he had asked her to do a pick-up using "Posing with Pigeons in the Park." If she had to go for a walk in a park this was a nice one. Walking paths made a figure eight around two lakes. Her datasheet played music. She kept a good grip on it. Dropping it should look like an accident, not be one.

Singh had the feather in his hat at the right angle to mark himself as the contact. She'd recognized his profile from farther away than she'd seen the feather. He was familiar from the year they'd spent training together on Bonaventure. Since the point of "Pigeon" was for them not to interact at all she ignored him.

Actual pigeons clustered in front of the park bench as Singh tossed them another handful of breadcrumbs. She hoped they had some fear of humans left. If they stayed in her way they could ruin the drop.

The birds flew off when she closed to kicking range. She scanned the remaining breadcrumbs looking for a datacrystal. It was supposed to be in the center of the path where she could drop her datasheet and pick them up together. Nothing.

Singh stood up, leaving the breadcrumb bag on the bench. He fell into step with Mitchie. "Hey, while you're in the neighborhood, could you give me a lift home?"

Mitchie ground her teeth. *You frigging idiot, screwing this up won't get you flunked, it'll land us both in a Fusion interrogation cell.* She said calmly, "I thought another friend was taking you home."

Singh shrugged. "I don't like the way he's been drinking. I'd feel safer riding with you." The code word "drinking" meant his main contact was dead or detained.

Keeping her poker face took work. Mitchie had made contact to put her data on the battle over Demeter in a secure delivery route. Being asked to pick up his data instead was annoying but part of the job. Bringing Singh onto her ship . . . seemed like a good way to get Fusion Counter-Intelligence's attention.

"Don't you still have work to do here?" she asked.

He kept his eyes straight ahead. "Well, yeah, but ever since, you know, it's been a lot harder to get anything done."

Obviously he was referring to when a Fusion warship nuked the town of Noisy Water on her home world. It destroyed a conference of scientists pursuing research forbidden on Fusion worlds. The Disconnected Worlds imposed a blockade in retaliation, and tensions were still increasing. More counter-intelligence activity was probably part of that.

She decided to pass the buck. "It's not my ship," said Mitchie. "I can ask the captain if he'll take you. He's not eager to do me favors though." Which was true. Schwartzenberger hadn't enjoyed finding out his new pilot was an undercover operative, even if her reports had been good enough to earn him an appointment as a naval reservist.

"I'll make it worth his while," said Singh. "I want to get off this rock before it gives me a drinking problem."

"No promises."

***

Alois Schwartzenberger sat in the swivel chair, watching silently as the metallurgist collected data. Dr. McClendon had moved the sample to the spectrometer. He'd started the process hiding annoyance under a polite mask, just going through the motions. Now he was nervously double-checking every step.

McClendon fiddled with the spectrometer display until an array of lines appeared on the lower half. A minute later the machine dinged. More lines flashed onto the upper half. The sets matched precisely. McClendon collapsed into a chair. "You're right. It's ansonium."

Schwartzenberger didn't answer. The metallurgist needed to adjust to the idea before they could talk money. He'd have to convince someone much more important to agree to the amount of money this would cost.

"Where the hell did you get forty-five grams of it?" demanded McClendon.

"I don't have to say," answered the captain.

The other stared at the wall. Schwartzenberger spotted flickering in his pupils as McClendon's implanted HUD flashed up data. "You've been in AI-controlled space. All the way to Old Earth."

"The Navy inspected and cleared us. There's no data in that sample."

"Did you find it along the way?" asked McClendon. "Or did the Pilgrims give it to you as hazard pay?"

Okida, the middleman who'd arranged this meeting, had faded into the corner while the analysis was done. Now he felt the need to protect his percentage. "The origin isn't the important point," said Okida. "You've proved it's real ansonium. How many uses are there for it?"

"Hundreds," said the metallurgist. "Maybe a dozen truly profitable ones. We're only set up to do half of those fields. We'd need a three month trade study just to narrow down the options."

"If Amalgamated isn't a likely user, who should we be talking to?"

"Oh, no, no, we'd use it, I just don't know what's the best option. Doping nanochips maybe. How much do you want for it?"

Schwartzenberger and Okida had rehearsed this part. "One million keys," said the captain.

"Oh, I can get you that."

"Per gram."

"That's just—are you serious?"

Okida said calmly, "I'm sure some other outfit would pay that much or more. But they'd have to find an analysis lab we and they can trust. Time-consuming. Your advantage is that you don't have to waste our time."

"I can't sign for that kind of money," said McClendon.

"But you know who can."

***

Three hours later Schwartzenberger and Okida walked out of Amalgamated Foundries' building. "No hard feelings about the three percent?" asked the captain.

The middleman laughed. "My punishment for being greedy. 'Five, or three and I'll give you five thousand keys up front.' I thought I was taking advantage of you being a reckless optimist. And it's still the most I've ever made for one day's work."

Schwartzenberger endured a hug. "You spend some of your share on something fashionable," said Okida, tugging on the spacer's jumpsuit.

"It's comfortable."

"It's noticeable. A Disker shouldn't try to be noticed these days." From some Fuzies 'Disker' would have been an insult. From Okida it just meant he was from the Disconnected Worlds.

"I'm leaving as soon as the deal's done." Amalgamated was concealing its payment by overpaying *Fives Full* to haul some material. The logistics VP had promised to find an innocuous load by tomorrow.

"Go straight home, my friend." Okida walked briskly away.

Schwartzenberger patted his cargo pocket to make sure the tens of millions of keys box was still there. The day was lovely, sunny with just enough breeze not to be too warm. He strolled down the sidewalk toward the spaceport.

Two-thirds of the way there he had to stop. A line of people was blocking the sidewalk. They didn't move at his "Excuse me." He tried to see what they were staring at but just saw more of a crowd. Possibly another of Pintoy's stipend kids was preparing public art. Elbowing his way through them would earn Schwartzenberger a fine for Anti-Social Contact and accumulate points toward being banned from the world. He decided to wait.

A few minutes went by without any visible performance or a shift in the crowd. The sidewalk on the other side had more traffic than normal. *People must be bypassing the obstruction.* He opened up his datasheet and ordered a local search to see what was going on.

The hot subject was "Disker." He brought up the chatter. His skin prickled as he read it.

"Look at him, standing there like he owns our world."

"Probably looking for security holes."

"Or stealing our tech for their AI developments."

"Bastards shoot holes in our ships and act innocent."

"Wish we'd nuked the whole planet, not just one town."

"Think he's working for a Betrayer?"

"How long until he realizes he's trapped?"

"You can get away with all sorts of stuff as long as you don't physically harm him."

"The best trick is to get him to punch you. Then it's all self-defense."

"Shouldn't let the damn Diskers on our planet."

Schwartzenberger looked up from the sheet. A second line of people had formed behind him. He ran out into the street.

Traffic was heavy but the autocars stopped clear of him. Schwartzenberger's datasheet squawked with traffic fines. He tried running down the middle of the street to get around the crowd. Two drivers slid their cars gently together to block him. He dashed into a gap on the far sidewalk. Some of the pedestrians formed up in lines to block him.

He tapped the emergency code into the datasheet.

"Public Safety Services, how may I help you?"

"Hello, my name is Alois Schwartzenberger, I am being harassed by a large number of people."

"Let me see if any Safety Officers are near—oh. Are you sure there's a problem?" Her voice had changed from cheerful to harsh. His identity must have come up on her display.

"They're deliberately keeping me from moving. I'm feeling threatened."

"Crowds blocking you happens to everyone. It's one of the prices of living in civilization. Just wait a bit and I'm sure you'll be on your way." The Public Safety dispatcher ended the connection.

While he'd been talking the lines had spread out onto the curb. Now they were only separated by the trunk of the tree casting gentle shade on the scene.

Schwartzenberger fought down his fear. He had to find a way out. Taking someone's clothing was "mischief," not assault, by Fusion law. If he bruised someone resisting they'd beat him senseless. There was no way he'd keep the box of ansonium.

He called a cab. The datasheet displayed a countdown to its arrival.

The lines were closing in on him. Everyone faced away, still pretending they weren't paying attention to him. They'd take a step backward when he wasn't looking.

A low fence guarded the tree's root system. Captain Schwartzenberger took three fast steps, put a foot on top of it, and pushed off hard. He grabbed a branch and pulled up hard enough for his feet to clear the heads of the line.

Not installing an elevator in the cargo hold had been stinginess, not virtue. But all the hours of climbing the ladder to the main deck on high-grav worlds paid off now. He dropped to the road as the autocab came to a stop and popped its door open.

Schwartzenberger fell across the seats and pulled his feet in. "Close the door and drive!"

"Driving westbound, sir. Do you have a specific destination in mind, sir?" asked the autocab.

"Spaceport. Landing pad twenty-two," said the captain as he squirmed back upright.

"Arrival in seven minutes, sir."

"Good." He took the datasheet out of his pocket. It informed him that a two thousand key fine for arboreal vandalism had been added to his other infractions. Checking the buzz showed the mob had dispersed. No one hated him enough to risk the wrath of the cab company.

Schwartzenberger started dictating a message to Okida. "Hi, buddy. I'd like you to do a renegotiation for me. Take an extra percent for it. Knock a tenth off the total price. I want it half as cash, half as export-level goods. Have them hire me to take the load to Bonaventure and I'll keep it as the other half of my payment. Like you said, just go straight home."

***

Shi Bingrong, the First Mate, leapt to her feet as Schwartzenberger entered the galley. "What the hell happened to you?" she demanded.

"It's nothing."

"Your hands are bleeding," said Bing.

The tree bark cuts had broken open again on the ladder up from the hold. "Just climbed a tree to avoid a crowd who took a dislike to me. Anyone else noticed Diskers getting worse treatment here?"

Billy the deckhand said, "I've been getting thrown out of clubs just for being one."

"Some," said Guo. "The local Confucian Revival groups split on Fusion-Disconnect lines. But it wasn't anything overt, just people only socializing with their own."

"Heck of a thing for a philosophy that preaches social harmony," quipped Mitchie.

Guo shrugged. "If it was easy, we wouldn't need a movement to work on it." He turned back to the captain. "Why do you ask, sir?"

Schwartzenberger winced as Bing applied antiseptic. "Some locals tried to throw a riot in my honor. I'm wondering if it was random or if someone set it up to get the loot off me."

Mitchie extracted the key details from him and spread out her datasheet. "It wasn't newsworthy. I'll dig into the buzz."

Bing's datasheet announced a container had arrived. She headed down to sign for it. Billy followed to handle loading it into the hold.

Ten minutes later Mitchie pushed the datasheet away. "Started with two guys who noticed you on the street. They got into a positive feedback loop of making nasty remarks and drew other people in. Both on stipend, no criminal history. They're three degrees of separation from a bunch of Amalgamated employees, but so's most of the planet. If someone arranged it he did a very professional job of covering his tracks."

"So we don't know."

Mitchie shrugged. "It's enough money to justify arranging something. But it's not that unusual behavior." She looked around to make sure the purely civilian members of the crew were still gone. "Speaking of the money, did you get any in advance? I got a note from DCC asking me to pick up some parts."

"No," said Schwartzenberger. "I wanted to keep the deal simple."

"Okay. I won't mind telling them no. They act like it's their money."

"About that." The captain hesitated. "I got a copy of the DCC regulations from the consulate."

"Oh?" asked Mitchie. The tension in her voice made Guo look up from his book.

"There's specific rules on undercover agents keeping profits from their operations. Anything over your military pay is supposed to be turned in. Sorry."

Mitchie remembered screen after screen of forms she'd had to sign off on. Halfway through she'd stopped reading them. Then she started cursing.

Guo put a hand on her shoulder. "Hey, we can live nicely on my share." The curses dropped in volume.

"Don't make people think she's just marrying you for your money," said Schwartzenberger.

"No worries, sir. Right, *baobei?*"

Mitchie looked up at Guo and smiled. "I'm only marrying you for your money." She kissed him firmly.

"See?" Guo said to the captain. "It's true love."

Captain Schwartzenberger kept his mouth shut.

Mitchie changed the subject. "Oh, sir, I ran into a, um, professional colleague of mine. He's worried about conditions here and wants to hitch a ride home. He might bring the wrong kind of attention down on us though."

"We'll take him," said the captain. "*Any* Disker who wants a ride out of the Fusion, we'll take."

"There might be a lot of them," said Guo. "The Council of Stakeholders just announced that because of the blockade against the Fusion Navy they've expelled all the observers from Disconnected Worlds and ordered them out of Fusion space."

Mitchie said, "That's politics. Nothing to do with working stiffs like us."

"Our turn may be coming."

Corcyra, gravity 17.2 m/s^2

Mitchie decided the best thing she could do for the ship was make sympathetic noises while the captain ranted. Which he'd been doing ever since they left the Corcyra Groundport Administration Building.

"They're not even trying to be consistent," continued Schwartzenberger. "If we're such an unregulated danger to public safety, why are they letting us have a fully fueled ship right by their capital? It's just another excuse to lock us down here. Fine, they're pissed about one of their destroyers getting blown up. I didn't do it. I ought to be mad at them for destroying two of the blockade ships."

Mitchie murmured agreement as she followed him up the ramp to *Fives Full's* airlock.

Bing was in the cargo hold, restowing some of the safety gear that had been strewn about by the latest inspections. "How'd it go?" she asked.

Captain Schwartzenberger lay down on a crate, trying to catch his breath from climbing the ramp in high gravity.

Mitchie answered her. "Complete waste of time. They ran us in circles around the building. Nobody's willing to admit to issuing the grounding order in the first place." She sniffed at the air, then took a deeper breath through her nose. "Have you guys been welding or something?"

"Something," said Bing with a smirk. "Talk to Guo."

A clang made Mitchie look up. The elevator basket had been attached to the crane and positioned by the top of the ladder. Billy had just tossed something into it from the main deck hatch. She decided to go see Guo's project.

Mitchie eyed the elevator basket. It would be so much easier than climbing the ten meter ladder in this gravity. But the captain kept doing it the hard way, and she was damned if she'd look weak while he was watching.

The rungs were close enough together that she'd take every other one when she was hurrying at normal acceleration. With Corcyra nearly doubling her weight she didn't even think of skipping one. She didn't lift her feet to alternate rungs. She put both of them on the same rung so she could rest for an instant between steps. *No wonder the other Fusion worlds didn't slow down our paperwork. They wanted us to get here so we'd be stuck in the worst gravity well around.*

The climb was easier near the top. As the hull curved in the ladder followed so she didn't have to haul herself straight up anymore. Still, she was thrilled when Guo stuck his hand through the hatch and pulled her up to the main deck. He gave her a quick kiss – she was panting too hard for anything more. Instead he wrapped an arm around her shoulders as she sat with her feet dangling out of the hatch.

When Mitchie's breathing was almost back to normal, Guo pulled her to her feet. "Come on," he said. "I want to show you something."

She followed him through his – their – cabin hatch. "Oh, my God! It's huge!" No groundhog would agree with her, but for a spacer, both the room and the bed in it were astoundingly big. The bulkhead between Guo's cabin and the unused one next to it had been cut out. The air still stank of welding gasses. "Where did you get that bed?"

Guo had a grin as big as the bed. "We were getting a fresh food delivery. The chandlery has everything in stock so I just added a couple of things to the order."

Mitchie flopped onto the bed. The mattress held up her back as firmly as a teddy bear's hug. "Ooooh. This is nice."

He bent down to kiss her. "Nothing but the best for my Michigan." He stood up and pulled a bundle from a sack on the wall. It unfolded as he hooked rings onto latches on the walls. Mitchie looked up through the net as it stretched over the bed. "Free-fall hammock," he said. "No more belting ourselves to the bed. This holds us comfortably together during coast. If someone puts on the torch, we land on the bed."

"I can think of all sorts of possibilities for *that*," she said.

Guo smirked. "I'll talk to the captain about conserving fuel with longer coasts."

Mitchie sat up and looked around. "Where's all your stuff?"

"Across the hall in the empty cabin. Didn't want any of it catching sparks while we were cutting. I'll move it back in tomorrow." He sat down next to her. "Where do you want to put your things?"

She'd been sleeping in his cabin but going back to her own to change clothes and such. *It's not like I need to hide the classified files from him anymore.* She pointed between the hatches. "I'd like to put my picture of the family homestead there."

Guo wrapped his arms around her. "Sounds good."

"And my teddy bears go on the bed."

"I'll cope." He kissed her. "We need to break in this bed," he said. "Yes, we do."

"As soon as we get off this fucking planet," they said together.

Chapter Two: Eavesdropping

Bonaventure System, acceleration 10 m/s^2

Escaping Corcyra came down to bribery. The Erdos system didn't try to delay them. One more gate put them in Bonaventure. "Home at last!" yelled Captain Schwartzenberger as the G4 sun appeared.

For Mitchie the best part of being back in the Disconnect was getting to use computers on the ship again. Fusion regulations banned computers that weren't continually monitored by their networks. Now they could pick up a navigation box to do the hard part for them. Once they landed. She took out her sliderule and began calculating the best turnover time.

Permission to actually come home required a lengthy chat with Traffic Control. Halfway through Mitchie muttered, "It's like a Turing Test for being a Disker." The paranoia made more sense when Control mentioned a cruiser had been lost in the latest skirmish.

TC finally admitted they were actually the *Fives Full* returning to her home port. The landing clearance sent them to pad A7 at Redondo Field.

"Where the hell is Redondo?" asked the captain, reaching for the Bonaventure almanac.

"A couple hundred klicks south of the capital," answered Mitchie. "Joint civil and Defense Force spaceport."

"Really? I don't think it ever came up in the budget discussions."

"It's the DCC Intelligence headquarters. Officially it's Refurbishment Depot Four."

"I see. Guess it's time to meet my chain of command."

Landing at Redondo Field was no different from any other port. The Disker refugees they'd accumulated, including Singh, were turned over to Spaceport Services to find their way home. An hour after touchdown a courier came aboard, wearing a civilian jumpsuit and military haircut. He handed the captain a datasheet and left.

The crew had been discussing possible buyers for the Eden loot in the galley. They'd dropped it while the courier was there. As the captain read through the message Billy resumed his pitch for approaching museum workers. No one else wanted to debate him.

Captain Schwartzenberger passed the datasheet to Mitchie. He said, "Billy, you have a week's paid leave. Pack your duffle and be off the ship in ten minutes."

"Aye-aye!" The deckhand vanished into his cabin.

Fastest I've ever seen him obey an order, thought Mitchie. She looked over the message.

"Shi, I need to talk with you a moment," continued the captain. He led the first mate into his cabin.

"So what's the news?" asked Guo. Mitchie shook her head. They went into their cabin.

When the hatch closed Mitchie said, "We're being put on active duty for a week. I have to get debriefed by the Operations and Analysis departments. You and the skipper are getting lessons on how to live up to your reserve rank. They'll have quarters for us."

"So I get to go to basic training camp?"

"No, basic is for making spacers. You're a Chief. Well, if the captain makes it stick. You're a little young for it."

Guo laughed. "I'm not worried. They can make me whatever rank they want."

"That's easy for you. Think of my reputation. If I'm married to some Engineer Apprentice people will think I abused my authority to make you marry me."

They'd been married long enough for Guo to know where her ticklish spots were.

***

Bing waited until the hatch closed to say anything. "What's going on, Alois?"

He took a deep breath. "Remember when I told you the Defense Force gave me a reserve commission?"

"You said that was just a formality. An excuse to pay you for enabling whatever Mitchie's doing that you won't talk about."

"That was before the Disconnect decided to stand up to the Fusion. War is coming. We have to stand together."

Bing reached toward him then shoved her hands in her pockets. "You're too damn old to play soldier. Let the young men do it."

"I'm not going to be a soldier. They're giving me one week of training so I can play the part a little. Then I'm back here as a freighter captain." He pointed at the deck to emphasize the 'here.'

"They don't need to put you in uniform for that."

"Maybe not. But they've asked me to serve and I'm going to do my duty."

"Even if that takes you straight to hell?"

Schwartzenberger said nothing to that.

"Fine. Go play soldier. I'll take a week's shore leave with Billy."

"No, you have work to do. Find buyers for all that stuff we got from Amalgamated, and turn those keys into real money."

***

The autocab dropped the three of them off at the "Depot's" main gate. An ensign from Protocol was there with a vehicle. Once they'd passed DNA identity tests she whisked them off to the military clothing store. A yeoman was waiting with the duffle Mitchie had left in a storage locker five years ago.

Mitchie emerged triumphantly from the dressing room in her dress uniform. "It fits!"

The yeoman studied her carefully. "Yes, ma'am. We can get your rank fixed on the premises if you'll give me your jacket."

Mitchie looked at her cuffs. They still had the dashed stripes of a junior grade lieutenant instead of the solid ones she was supposed to wear as a senior grade. She sighed and started unbuttoning.

The store clerks had Guo and the captain in hand. The Bonaventure Defense Force's solid black uniform looked good on Schwartzenberger. Akiak's Space Guard wore pale grey. Mitchie thought it looked even better on Guo than it did on her.

Intelligence had members from every planet in the DCC and the store stocked all their gear. When Mitchie came up to Guo he asked, "What the hell is that?"

She followed his pointing finger to a mannequin wearing a bright red tunic with gold braid along the seams. She laughed. "Shishi Imperial Legion. Don't worry, they have sensible camouflage uniforms for combat. They just love their parades."

Once they were fully dressed Protocol herded them over to an office building. A conference room held about fifty officers and senior NCOs. Mitchie recognized some from her previous assignments but had no chance to say hello.

A BDF captain called the room to attention, introduced the *Fives Full* contingent, and explained that the new recruits had yet to be sworn in. The protocol ensign provided the captain a card with the BDF oath which Schwartzenberger echoed. "Chief Kwan is joining the Akiak Space Guard," said the BDF captain, "so we'll need a Guard officer to administer his oath. Lieutenant Long, would you care to do the honors?"

Mitchie crisply marched over to in front of Guo. The ensign slipped the appropriate card into her left hand and faded back into the crowd. She held up her right hand and he matched her. Mitchie had seen swearing-ins but never performed one before. Doing it for Guo gave her a special thrill. When Guo smiled back she realized she'd let it peek out on her face. She quickly put her lips at attention. Guo sobered as well.

Mitchie lifted up the card and solemnly read out the oath. Guo echoed the phrases firmly. "I, Guo Kwan . . . do swear my complete and undying loyalty . . . to the Fundamental Law of the Planet Akiak. . . . I will protect the Law and the Planet . . . against all enemies whomsoever. . . . I will obey the lawful orders of those appointed over me . . . and carry out my duties . . . with honesty, bravery, and honor. . . . So help me God." Now they grinned freely at each other. Mitchie felt their bond was stronger now, another strand tying them together.

The crowd broke into applause and cheers. A Master Chief Cryptographer's Mate introduced himself to Guo as "your trainer" and led him out. The BDF captain took charge of Schwartzenberger and followed them. A few more unnecessary people left. Mitchie was alone with nearly two score analysts.

With the swearing-in over she had the front of the room to herself. Her audience was seated in rings of desks, the rear ones elevated so everyone had a clear line of sight to her. *I feel like a mouse at a cat convention.* She glanced at the lectern. It didn't have a step block and was tall enough to hide her from the nose down. There was a table against the front wall but sitting on it would look too casual.

Best defense, she thought. Mitchie walked forward to a conversational distance from the first row. "I'm sure everyone has some questions for me," she said. "Commander Jenkins, would you like to start?"

"Thank you, Lieutenant. Your report on port security on Lapis stated the sentries for the cruiser *Euripides* were 'inattentive.' Can you be more specific about . . ."

***

The quarters provided for them were comfortable. Mitchie was hoping to work off some of the stress of her debriefing with her husband. Unfortunately the Master Chief had decided a "liver function test" was an essential part of training. Guo was delivered to her barely able to stand. She poured him into bed with no audible complaints.

The hangover left Guo not much better company in the morning. That evening they finally had a chance to talk.

"How are you liking life in the military?" Mitchie asked. Guo had found her stretched on the bed, fully dressed except for her shoes. She'd woken up when he started rubbing her feet.

"Master Chief's part of it is pretty entertaining," Guo said. "He's skipping everything I can get out of books. God help me if I have to do a uniform inspection."

Mitchie chuckled, then turned more serious. "Are you keeping the rocker?"

"Oh, yeah. To Master Chief the real qualification is having enough 'no-shit-there-I-was' stories to keep the juniors intimidated. So he kept pumping me for stories between whiskies." He let go of her feet and started taking his boots off. "I've had some impressive experiences. All since you joined the crew, I noticed."

She sat up. "Hey, I didn't sign us up for any of those jobs."

"No. But I'm still blaming you for the firefight with Max."

"Um. I won't argue." She blamed the firefight on Guo killing two of Max's men, but since he'd saved her from possible torture and murder she didn't hold it against him.

"The other reason for all the booze is he wanted me hungover while he taught me how to shout at recruits. Said it would give me the right tone of voice." His wife giggled. "Didn't have any recruits but they rounded up some one-stripers for me to practice on. Marching circles around the cafeteria. Is there really room for doing that on a warship?"

"No."

"Then why bother?" asked Guo.

"To get them in the right mindset," said the academy graduate. "Teach them to be part of a group. One boy puts his foot wrong and the whole formation looks bad."

"Why make me do it then?"

She poked his ribs. "So you'll expect them to obey your orders instantly. Makes you be careful what you say."

"Heh. So how are they treating you?"

Mitchie flopped back on the bed. "Like a sponge."

"Huh?"

"They're squeezing me. Trying to get every detail I left out of my reports. Which is stuff I never knew or was totally obvious. 'Was Major Razoun's information completely reliable?' No, I said I'd poured six shots of vodka into him in the report. 'Why did you describe the Mark 7 security bots as low reliability?' Because they didn't notice me sneaking around. Feh. Bunch of swivel-chair second-guessers."

Guo resumed the foot rub then moved up to her calves. "How about I do some squeezing?"

"Mmmm."

***

"Lieutenant Long?"

"Yes, sir!" answered Mitchie. Intel types tended to be sloppy about military formalities, but having an admiral accost her in the hallway had her standing as rigid as an academy plebe.

"As you were, Long," said Rear Admiral Chu. "It's paperwork time. Since you've been on detached duty I'm doing your evaluation. Which you are very overdue for." He led her through an antechamber to his palatial office. "Sit, relax." Chu pointed her at the leather chair before the oaken desk.

Mitchie nervously sat. Sitting while an admiral stood set off all her 'social error' alarms.

Chu pulled a folder out of his safe and handed it to her. "Read through it, sign at the end. Take your time. Feel free to ask questions, don't be shy, I know you're out of practice with this." He took another folder out, closed the safe, and sat at his desk to begin reading it.

Her folder had a hardcopy of her evaluation, marked 'MOST SECRET'. She read through it slowly. It summarized her key scoops and their importance. Seeing it all together was impressive. *I've done some damn good work.* Even by the generous standards of official evaluations the admiral was giving her high praise.

The fourth and last page had the "CAREER PROGRESSION" section. "This officer's supreme effectiveness at intelligence acquisition should be utilized to the fullest. When it is no longer practical for her to practice covert operations," Mitchie recognized that as a euphemism for Fusion CI putting her on the shoot-on-sight list, "this officer should be transferred to counter-intelligence, training, or analysis. Due to her moral failings this officer should not be placed in a command assignment."

She re-read the last line several times before looking up. "Sir?"

"Yes?"

"There's nothing in this evaluation describing moral failings on my part."

Admiral Chu picked up a datacrystal from the corner of his desk and placed it between them. "This inspector general report details your failings. I can have it attached to your evaluation. It explains how a junior officer with no field experience was given an unlimited time, unlimited scope commission to recon Fusion space. It doesn't include the transcript of Commander Willoughby's divorce court, but I can attach that separately."

"I never –"

"No, the IG confirmed you didn't. But you worked so hard to convince Willoughby you might that several other officers were convinced you had. His wife was convinced too."

Mitchie remained silent.

"Long, you have powerful talents and an unorthodox approach to achieving the mission. I wouldn't ask anyone to use your methods but I'm thrilled with your results. I'm not going to complain about how you got them. I'm glad you're willing to get the mission done." Chu leaned over the desk to lock eyes with her. "Do not use those methods on our own people. That destroys trust. It destroys trust in each other's judgment. And that can destroy our whole organization." The admiral straightened up and waited to see if Mitchie would say anything.

"There's another reason I don't want you to have a command," he continued. "You hate the Fusion. You've got a solid reason for it. Many of us do. But that has to be subordinate to our duty. We can't sacrifice the lives entrusted to us to further a personal vendetta." The Admiral sat back in his chair.

"I'll certainly keep that in mind, sir," said Mitchie. She signed the form, certifying her agreement with everything in it. "Will there be anything else, sir?"

Chu shook his head.

Mitchie came to attention, saluted, and walked out of the office.

***

"Commander Schwartzenberger reporting as ordered, sir!" He stood at attention and saluted, bringing the fingertips to his eyebrow.

Then he remembered to flatten his hand and wrist to make them properly straight.

Admiral Chu returned the salute. "Please sit, Commander. Or perhaps I should be calling you 'captain.' I need to talk to the master of the *Fives Full*."

Schwartzenberger leaned back. "We don't have any current contracts, Admiral. What do you need hauled?"

"Nothing. Well, some sensor gear. The Fusion has been attacking Disconnect warships entering their space. No ban announced, but the last frigate we sent to Lapis came back so irradiated we had to scrap it. Commercial traffic is still going through."

"So you want the whole ship to be an undercover operative instead of just Lt. Long?"

"More or less. Nothing complicated. Just drop off a cargo and come back, looking around as you go."

"That doesn't sound like something that needs an admiral to arrange. Just put out a transport job on the net."

"I'm here to discuss how to do it covertly. Also, transports are demanding some stiff hazard fees to cross the blockade zone."

"Speaking as a merchant captain," said Schwartzenberger, "I have a responsibility to my investors to make sure they're properly compensated for the risks taken."

"Haven't they been fully compensated from your trip to Old Earth?"

"They didn't loan me money to get sculptures, Admiral. All that needs to be sold and the shares passed out." Schwartzenberger wished he'd asked Mitchie how detailed her report on the Eden loot was.

"There are things we can do to help with that," said the Admiral. "Not direct purchases, but some secure introductions."

"That would help. But I can't sell stuff while hauling junk through hostile space."

An impatient look crossed the admiral's face. "The legislature has authorized wartime measures. The Defense Force could simply confiscate your ship."

Schwartzenberger answered this with a small smile. "Exercising angary requires you to compensate owners for the use of their property." During his time in the Senate he'd pushed through a revision of that law as part of an update of eminent domain regulations. "It would be more cost-effective to arrange a long-term charter or lease, with a hazard bond. Then you wouldn't have to worry about replacing the civilian crew members."

Admiral Chu thought for a long moment before answering. "If we chartered *Fives Full* for the duration of the crisis, what rates would we be looking at?"

Captain Schwartzenberger pulled out his datasheet.

***

The paintbot made Mitchie jump. She hadn't expected anyone to be on the ship this time of day. Hearing the fans whining over her head triggered evasive reflexes.

Captain Schwartzenberger looked up from his datasheet. "You okay?"

"Just startled." She took a few steps away from the airlock so she could look at the bot's work. The ship's name and crest (five playing cards) had been painted over. The bot was finishing a new picture in the crest's place.

She studied the silver shape. At first glance she'd thought it was a sword but it had a strange handle, an angled rod connected to a tube. "What is that?" she asked.

"A knife."

"How do you hold it?"

"You don't. It fits on the end of a rifle so you can use it like a spear. It's called a bayonet."

Mitchie walked over to him. His data sheet displayed the picture the paintbot was copying. A name arced around the bayonet. "Who's Joshua Chamberlain?"

"A hero of the Anti-Slavery War."

"He stick somebody with one of those?"

"Not him, his men." Schwartzenberger had to be pretty worked up about the guy if he was renaming the ship after him.

"What did he do?" asked Mitchie.

"It was the decisive battle. He was out at the end of the line. His men were tired. Been fighting for years, lost half the unit crippled or dead. Marched non-stop for days to get to the battle. Then got run over to this little hill and told to hold it or their whole army would collapse."

He'd lowered the datasheet. His eyes were focused on something beyond the hull. "So they'd been fighting all day. Waves of slavers charging, getting beaten off, coming back. It was a hot day. They'd lost a lot of men. Tired, thirsty, scared."

Schwartzenberger mimed peeking over some cover. "They beat off one more attack, but that used up all their bullets. Now they were out of ammo. Normally that meant they were done, go back to the rear, get more. But Chamberlain knew if they fell back it might start a panic. The whole army might crumble."

The captain paused to catch his breath. Mitchie stayed silent. She'd rarely seen him talk so passionately. "When the next slaver attack came they were going to overrun Chamberlain's men. So instead he made them get out their knives. Then he took those men out from behind the trees and rocks they'd been hiding behind, pulled them out of their holes. Took those tired, hot, thirsty, scared men, and he ran down the hill waving his knife. And they followed him. They left their safe holes and ran down the hill at the slavers, getting shot at the whole way, and smashed them. They broke the slavers on that hill. And that's the last time the slavers ever had a chance to win their damn war."

Schwartzenberger looked a bit hot and thirsty himself right then.

"It's a proud name for a ship," said Michigan.

"I thought so."

She looked at the paintbot, now working on the "S." "How are you paying for this?"

He smiled. "We're under charter to the DCC now. They have to cover our maintenance expenses."

She shook her head. He'd probably wanted to put this name on this ship since he first came aboard and refused to spend the money. Mitchie started up the ladder. A quarter of the way up she stopped. "Sir! Where are the Eden containers?"

"In the Brinks Secure Storage warehouse. Address and access codes are waiting for you in the galley. I didn't want to haul that stuff with us if we get ordered someplace dangerous in a hurry."

"Understood, sir."

***

Admiral Chu wanted their cover secured before starting the mission. Billy returned from his leave to find they all had paid-for rooms in a hotel on the civilian side of Redondo Field. Captain Schwartzenberger began talking to brokers. Few producers were willing to ship goods into a Fusion that might not pay for them. Competition from idle analog ships had driven shipping prices in the Disconnect to the lowest ever recorded. The captain was glad he'd gotten the charter signed before checking the market.

The call came at three in the morning local time. Mitchie and Guo found the captain and first mate in the hotel lobby when they came down. An autocar was waiting to take them to their landing pad.

Captain Schwartzenberger said, "Long, Billy isn't answering. We're going to get the ship ready to lift. You wake him up and follow us in a cab."

"Aye-aye." She took advantage of their civilian cover to give Guo a kiss and headed back to the elevators.

She'd pinged Billy from her datasheet. No answer. When she reached his room she pounded on the door with both fists. "Hey, spacer! Arching skies are calling!"

Muffled curses came through the door. Billy yanked it open and snarled, "What the fuck?" as a wave of pheromones spilled into the hallway.

Mitchie looked past the towel-clad deckhand. A generously proportioned blonde was pulling the sheet over herself. "We're lifting. Grab a suit and stuff your duffle."

"Where are we going?"

"Lapis, I think. It doesn't matter where. Get dressed."

"We don't have a cargo."

"So what?" Mitchie didn't want to argue with him. If she did have to argue with Billy she wanted him wearing a lot more than that towel.

"So what's the damn hurry if we don't even have a cargo?"

She wished he'd found a bigger towel. The blonde was watching them, which ruled out telling the truth about the mission. "Look, the captain gives an order, we obey the orders. That's how the job works."

"Yeah." Billy scratched his head. The towel shifted dangerously in the one-handed grip. "I don't think so. I quit."

"You can't just quit!"

"Sure I can. I won't starve. Hell, I can retire." He stepped back to close the door. "Sugarpie, you're good with words. Want to help me write a resignation letter?"

As the door shut Mitchie thought, *Crap. I'm going to be stuck cleaning out the damn hydroponics screens.*

***

When Mitchie reached the *Joshua Chamberlain* the crane was hauling up a container. An idling truck held another. Her cab had just passed an empty truck leaving the pad. Apparently they would have cargo after all.

The captain had received Billy's letter before Mitchie could break the news to him. He didn't look upset. "A couple of techs came with those boxes. Take charge of them and get them settled."

"Aye-aye."

A man and a woman in brand-new olive drab coveralls were fussing over a container of electronic gear by the open cargo hold doors. Bing and Guo were busy stacking the other new containers in the back of the hold. The techs ignored Mitchie until she snapped, "Front and center!"

It took them a moment to realize the order was real. The pair dropped their tools and came to attention in front of Mitchie. "Observer's Mate First Class Hector reporting with party of one, ma'am!" said the male.

Mitchie returned their salutes. "At ease. Who's your party?"

"Ma'am, this is Observer's Mate Second Class Jackson," said Hector.

"Welcome aboard, both of you. I'm Lieutenant Long. I'm your supervisor on this ship. The captain is Commander Schwartzenberger. The first mate is a civilian, Shi Bingrong. Any orders she gives are relayed from the captain. The mechanic, Chief Kwan, normally won't be involved in your operations but any orders from him are for the safety of the ship and must be obeyed. Any questions on the chain of command?"

Two headshakes. Well, it was simple for them.

"This isn't a two-hundred crew cruiser, so everyone has to pitch in on chores. Either of you a decent cook?"

Both nodded.

"Good," continued Mitchie. "We'll give you a break from dishwashing. Once we're on a steady accel vector I'll show you how to clean the life support system." Jackson grimaced. "Yeah, nobody likes the job but we all use the oxygen. The first mate posts the chore schedules in the galley."

Mitchie turned to face the open door of the electronics container. "What's the cover story for this?"

"Surplus electronics bought on Pintoy as scrap," said Hector. "Manifest shows it didn't find a buyer on Bonaventure and was just left in the hold."

"Which breaks their import regs."

"Yes, but it's a minor infraction if it's scrap. So we rigged it to trash itself on a remote command."

"Good." The boxes in the container were packed randomly enough to fit the story. "That's a better cover than you two have. At shift change report to the converter room. Get some oil stains and steam burns on those outfits. Hector, no more shaving. You need to look like merchies. Clear?"

A pair of unhappy "yes, ma'ams" sounded.

"The good news is you have plenty of choice for bunks. There's four open cabins on the main deck and two passenger dorms in here." She pointed at the souvenirs of their trip to Old Earth. "So look around and take your pick."

"Does this ship take a lot of passengers?" asked Jackson. "I thought it was strictly a cargo-hauler."

"She's supposed to be. But lately we've been picking up a lot of strays."

Lapis System, acceleration 0 m/s^2

The jump to Lapis was low-stress for Mitchie. Instead of a busy line of freighters heading for the gate *Joshua Chamberlain* went through alone. No watching out for other ships' plumes, no constraints on max or min speed to stay clear of them. Once their ship was in the groove Mitchie had nothing to do but take sights.

When Lapis' sun appeared in the center of the bridge dome her pulse went up. A couple of weeks ago they'd come through here as normal merchant traffic. Now they were just pretending. If the stand-off slid into war they might become a target even if they were innocent.

Radar showed no ships in the way of their intended course. The jump had landed them almost in the center of the entry zone. Yulin was on the near side of the system. Mitchie took position sightings while the captain reported in to Traffic Control. Their entry was close enough to their preliminary course that Mitchie started them accelerating down it before recalculating the exact trajectory they'd need.

Control had only offered "Acknowledged, stand by." They might get to do the mission just as planned.

After burning for six hours they let the ship coast. The course fit a low-budget, short on fuel tramp freighter like *Joshua Chamberlain* had once been. They'd have over a week each way for the techs to scan the system. Captain Schwartzenberger released Mitchie to supervise the sensor crew.

The techs were still suiting up when Mitchie entered the hold. Hector was reading off a checklist as they helped each other don the gear. She took her pressure suit from the locker by the airlock and had it on before they finished. After the last step ("29: Confirm helmet ring seal integrity") PO Hector reported, "Ready to depressurize hold, ma'am."

Mitchie had trained on that same checklist. She'd also had hundreds of hours of vacuum time. "Inspection first. Jackson, got your feet braced?"

"Um, yes'm?"

"Good." Mitchie was ten meters away from the tech's post by their sensor container. One kick sent her headfirst across the deck. She grabbed Jackson's ankles to stop, forcing a squeak out of the startled tech. "Inspection—boot seals. Left good. Right cuff has a bulge. That's a folded-over edge on the inner overlap. So you only have one good seal instead of two."

After both had looked at the flaw she showed Jackson how to fix it without completely removing the boot. Then she resumed the inspection, seal by seal. One of the oxygen tank lines had been inserted crooked. "That's not as bad as the other," explained Mitchie. "It'd hiss loud enough you'd notice it before you lost much oxy."

Hector's suit had similar problems along with a helmet seal compromised by a bit of grit. "Now *that* can kill you," said Mitchie. "Don't focus on the checklist, focus on the hardware." She ordered them to remove helmets and gloves for a quick lesson on checking the helmet ring for damage and debris.

Once the techs were regeared and reinspected they were trained in operating the airlock, deck hatches, and main door. Then Mitchie asked Guo to pump out the air in the hold.

As the big doors parted Jackson exclaimed, "Now *that's* a view."

Mitchie looked at the starfield, automatically picking out the constellations she used to locate planets for position sights. Trying to enjoy the sight made her think back to when she'd first been in space. A long time ago now. "You're clear to start operations," she said.

Not knowing anything about how the sensors worked, she kept her mouth shut as the techs booted the system up. They'd clearly had lots of practice with it. All of it in normal gravity. Everything they could do strapped to a console went quickly. Moving about led to multiple attempts as they bounced around their container.

Opening the container doors and deploying the antennas took far longer than Hector expected, judging by the cursing he was doing on a channel he'd set up for private talk with Jackson. Mitchie didn't interrupt, though she was tempted to offer some training in zero-g maneuvering.

The officer did shift her safety line to a ring by the open cargo doors. She'd chosen the longest line in the locker but only paid out ten meters of it. If one of her techs managed to break their own lines and float out the door she'd want the whole length.

She left the maneuvering pack in the locker. It would look like she *expected* them to go dutchman if she put that on.

Two hours of vacuum time later Hector reported they were collecting data. The captain had faced the hold doors toward Lapis. Mitchie entered the container. Stretching out along the ceiling let her look over their shoulders without getting in their way.

Multiple screens scrolled incoming data too fast to read. The techs exchanged terse jargon as they steered the antennas. The center screen switched to a vector map showing ships near Lapis. Mitchie studied it without finding any headed toward the planet.

Watching the system process the sensor readings Mitchie's thoughts drifted to how the Fusion would react if they saw it. The military implications wouldn't be noticed. Finding unsupervised software in their territory would produce pure panic. The code police would destroy every processor and memory unit with fire. They wouldn't care how much damage they'd do to the ship either. Landing on Yulin's moon felt riskier than when they'd first proposed the plan.

Captain Schwartzenberger interrupted her brooding. "Long, we've got an abort. Traffic Control ordered us out of the system."

"Aye-aye," she replied. "Hector, how fast can you secure for acceleration?"

"Ma'am?" said the confused tech.

"We need to boost. How much time do you need to get ready?"

"Oh. Half an hour? What's going—"

"Get started," she ordered. Mitchie switched back to the captain's channel. "Should be able to boost in half an hour, sir."

"Don't worry about it. I told them I had to hand-calculate the course change. We could probably get away with coasting through tomorrow."

***

Once *Joshua Chamberlain* was coasting for the Bonaventure gate the techs set up their sensors again. They took half the time as before. A little practice in freefall went a long way. Mitchie tasked Jackson with explaining the readouts to her while Hector managed the system.

"This one is a destroyer," explained the junior tech. "On a converging course with us, so headed for the gate. Running hot, overdue for some time with radiators out. Decelerating to stop short of the gate. That makes their rendezvous point . . . here. Would be useful to turn the ship to look at that, ma'am."

"Too risky," answered Mitchie. "We don't want to behave out of the ordinary."

Hector snorted. Mitchie didn't ask his opinion of the decision.

"And coming into view," continued Jackson, "another destroyer. Same condition." Some typing put a magnified view of the new target's plume on a monitor. "With some irregularities in its torch plume." More typing. "Found a match. This is FNS *Kai-Shek*, normally based in Sukhoi.

Mitchie grunted in surprise. "They're pulling ships out of front-line units? They are pissed at us."

The next few hours revealed a denser concentration of warships, some parked well away from the gate. Mitchie contemplated the number of military-grade sensors looking back at them. "Seal it up," she ordered.

"Ma'am?" asked Hector. "We're getting great data here."

"Yes, but sooner or later someone's going to notice our doors hanging open and wonder why. Shut it down."

The PO complied. Mitchie noticed he turned his microphone off for a few minutes. Once the antennas were retracted she closed the cargo doors.

"Sensors cold, ma'am," Hector reported.

"Good. We have a few hours until we reach the gate. You're off duty until then. Be suited up and back here at ten minutes to jump."

"Aye-aye." The senior PO saluted.

Mitchie returned the salute and pushed out of the container. She kicked off the deck to the ceiling hatch. The captain needed to know what they'd seen.

Bonaventure System, acceleration 0 m/s^2

The captain's voice crackled in the suit radios. "Okay, we're through. Looking around for company."

"That's creepy," muttered Hector. "You ought to feel something when you travel seven light-years. Not just get told 'hey, we're there now.'"

Mitchie checked that the observer was transmitting on the local freq. He was. Only the three of them in the hold had heard the remark, so she ignored it.

The captain spoke on the PA freq again. "No other ships within a hundred klicks. We landed at the edge of the entry zone. We'll boost to antispinward to get clear of the zone."

That would be as good a viewing position as they could hope for.

Boosting, coasting, and decelerating ate half an hour. At last Schwartzenberger announced, "In position. Clear to start observations."

"Let's get it open," said Mitchie. She held down the open button on the door console as the observers wrestled with the panels in the side of their shipping container. The two ten-meter wide cargo hold doors were fully open before the sensors were ready. The techs were still fiddling with their gear.

Mitchie floated to between the sensor container and the open door. A couple of kicks to the deck popped up tie-down rings that she could hook her boots onto. The newbies still hadn't gotten the hang of moving masses in free-fall. Sure enough, they pushed the antenna out too fast again. As it swung into position she looped her safety line over a handhold and pulled, slowing it so it wouldn't slam against the stops.

Jackson was still connecting cables. Mitchie moved into the container and looked over the status lights. Everything was working, just had to be turned on manually. *Don't micromanage*, she repeated to herself.

It only took a few more minutes for Hector to report, "Online, ma'am. Data is coming in. All systems nominal."

"Thank you. Good work, you two." Mitchie switched frequencies. "Sir, we're ready for the scanning roll."

Schwartzenberger didn't reply directly. He announced, "All hands, brace for spin," over the PA.

It wasn't much spin—one hand was all it took to keep Mitchie from falling into the outer wall—but the sensors now could sweep almost the whole sky. "Spotted a relay buoy," said Jackson. "Transmitting our data from Lapis on tightbeam."

"Roger," said Mitchie.

A few ship icons appeared in the monitors. Their Fusion counterparts, watching the blockade force from far out in the system. As the ship turned further the blockaders came into view.

"They've moved back," said Jackson.

"Just following Bonaventure in its orbit," explained Mitchie. "They're staying between the planet and the gate."

"Signal from the Flag, ma'am. Decrypting . . . 'Hold in place. Report emergences.'"

"Thank you." Mitchie relayed the message to Captain Schwartzenberger. He acknowledged it politely.

Staring at the Fusion scouts lacked excitement. Mitchie had the observation techs start training her on the sensors. If she could cover the assistant position the POs could take turns getting naps.

Hector was a surprisingly good instructor. Jackson wasn't surprised, judging by her smirk at some of the simulations he picked. Five hours into the impromptu class the display switched from an elaborate sim to a single unlabeled blip—real world data.

"What do we have, ma'am?" asked Hector.

Mitchie pulled up the visual and thermal spectrums. Both had matches in the database. "Peltast-class destroyer. Not maneuvering. Whoa, thermal just jumped way up. Radiators deployed?"

"Yes'm. That's a good analysis, Lieutenant. Jacks, if you want a nap I think we can spare you."

"Hell, no," snarled Jackson. "It just got interesting. Three more jumped in while you were looking at that. One of them a heavy cruiser."

"Wouldn't dream of making you miss it. Send a quicklook report. Ma'am, may I have my seat back?"

Mitchie went back to hovering at the ceiling. The Fusion Navy put its ships through the gate at the maximum safe rate. *No—faster than that*, she thought. The ships were scattered farther than usual from the center of the arrival zone. A gate shook a bit when a ship went through but the vibrations damped out quickly. Passing through a still shaking gate added random factors to your jump. It could send you anywhere in the target system. Or nowhere.

"Reply to the quicklook," reported Jackson. "Report hourly."

"Fine by me," said Hector. "We don't need to attract attention." A Fusion ship crossing through their tightbeam could backtrack it. One farther away might detect the signal's sidelobes and start to wonder why a freighter was loitering in a combat zone.

Most of the enemy warships were maneuvering. The three of them worked together to identify where the Fusion ships would meet. The coordinates went in the first hourly report.

"The good news is we're well clear of them," said Hector.

"Yep," replied Mitchie. "Bad news is they're setting up for a major engagement. This isn't trying to evade the blockade. A dense formation means inter-locking anti-missile defenses. They have a lot more practice at that kind of fight than we do." The Fusion Navy regularly fought off incursions from the AIs controlling former human worlds.

"Why aren't we attacking?" asked Jackson. "They're completely disorganized now."

Mitchie answered, "They might be bluffing. We don't want to start a war if we can avoid it."

"That gives them the first shot," grumped Hector.

"That's why admirals get the big coins," said Mitchie.

The next time *Joshua Chamberlain's* spin brought the Disconnect forces in view the observers took a few minutes to see what the admiral was doing. Half the force had pulled into a loose disk. The rest had scattered, closing slowly on the Fusion fleet.

Hector worked his console. "Dispersed ships are all missile frigates. Everything heavier is in the formation."

"Sensible. Frigates rely on maneuver for missile defense. Don't play well with others." Jackson's first tour had been on a frigate.

"Back to the bad guys," said Mitchie.

The observers had bet five grams of silver on whether there'd be a hundred ships in the second report. Jackson was winning. The emergences were coming closer together.

"Wow! That one must really have been crowding the gate." Hector displayed the new blip on the center screen. "It's way outside the usual emergence angles."

"Outside everything else, too," said Jackson. "I can't find a match to it. Visual signal's closest to an ultra-class freighter. Thermal's unique. It's putting out a bunch of radar signals I can't match to any known system either."

"I'm stumped," admitted Hector. "Must be something new."

Joshua Chamberlain's maneuvering thrusters drowned out conversation for a moment, the deck transmitting the vibration to their suits. Mitchie had asked the captain to take the spin off the ship. The new bogey was now centered in the open door.

"Ma'am? Couldn't that attract attention?" asked Hector.

"We'll have to risk it," she said. "Can you give me a range to that ship?"

"No'm. Can't figure out the size. I've just got a direction."

"Assume it's a six hundred meter sphere."

"Ma'am, did you say six *hundred?*"

"Plug it in," Mitchie ordered.

Hector typed amazingly fast for someone in a pressure suit. He put the calculated position on a map of the system. "That's outside the emergence zone. Closer to our frigates than its buddies."

"Signal from the Flag," said Jackson. "Angles on Fox 93, that's their label for the new guy. They want us to triangulate. Data's almost six minutes old." Light-speed lag was a routine issue for this kind of problem.

"Put 'em in the system," grunted the senior PO.

The intersection of the angles appeared on the map, almost touching the dot projected from the estimated size. Hector sheepishly said, "I guess that is a six hundred meter hull, ma'am."

"Yes. Not good news for us. Jackson, send them that. And the rest of the report, they can have it a few minutes early."

"Yes'm."

Hector was still analyzing the target. "It's been turning. Just stopped. Now it's firing its torch, I think. Odd spectrum, very cool."

"You're not seeing the whole plume, just where it's spread out wider than the ship. So it's boosting toward us."

"Toward their rendezvous. About the same vector from there. Hmmm." A side display showed the Fusion ships converging on each other. "The dozen ships closest to Bonaventure just flipped around. Headed toward the new guy. Fast. Most of 'em went from ten gravs to forty. Rough on the crews." More typing. "Going to take hours to meet up though."

"Which gives us a shot at winning this battle," said Mitchie. "Jackson, message to the Flag."

"Ma'am?"

"Take this down."

"Yes, ma'am." The junior petty officer pulled up the communications interface.

"Fox 93 is a *Kydoimos*-class battleship." She paused to spell the name for Jackson. "Six hundred meter diameter sphere. Has a spinal directed energy weapon capable of destroying any ship. Large numbers of standard weapons. Fusion has kept existence of this class secret until now." Matching Jackson's typing speed required many frustrating pauses. Mitchie kept her tone even.

"Fusion Navy would not reveal the battleship unless it intended to use it for a decisive victory. Its presence proves the Fusion plans a battle here. Attacking Fox 93 while separated from its support fleet is the best opportunity for victory. Recommend full assault on battleship. Nearby ships should use jitter maneuvering."

She took a deep breath. "Signed, Lieutenant Michigan Long. Akiak Space Guard. DCC Intelligence. Send it."

"Encrypted and sent, ma'am," said Jackson.

"If you don't mind me saying, Lieutenant," said Hector. "Admirals don't like being told what to do."

"If we win he can reprimand me."

Neither had an answer to that. The silence lengthened as they stared at Fox 93's blip. Mitchie switched channels. After briefing Captain Schwartzenberger she found a private channel to talk to Guo on.

"I hope you don't get court martialed," he said after hearing her story. "I'm not sure I could handle being married to a civilian."

"Jerk."

"Do chief petty officers make enough to support a wife? I never checked."

"Didn't Master Chief cover how to collect your pay?"

"Nope. Making sure I got every other round was the only money he talked about."

"Maybe I should've talked the Skipper into making you a warrant. Easier on the liver."

"Nah. We had one drinking with us. I don't think he had a liver."

Hector waved at her.

"Gotta go, love you!" She switched back to local comm. "News?"

"Ma'am, we have maneuvering on the whole Disconnect force. They're all heading for the battleship."

Mitchie grabbed a strut to pull herself closer to the displays. The green friendly blips all had acceleration arrows attached now.

"Correction," he continued. "Some of the frigates are going around it. Looks like they're trying to get between Fox 93 and the ones coming to reinforce it."

"Not someplace I'd want to be," muttered Jackson.

Looking over the displays Mitchie realized most of the orange Fusion blips wore yellow "stale data" halos. Holding still to focus on the battleship had put the fleet's rendezvous out of their field of view. *Time to talk to the Skipper again.*

The observers flinched as Captain Schwartzenberger sent out a warning to brace for maneuver. A few thruster blasts later the cargo doors framed the majority of the ships in the system.

The Fusion fleet was no longer a smooth ball contracting into the rendezvous point. Only the original dozen accelerated hard toward Fox 93. Many still headed for the rendezvous. The majority had changed course toward the Diskers or just cut thrust.

"What a mess," said Hector.

"Loss of control," said Mitchie. "The big boss is on the battleship. He's too wrapped up in his own problems to issue orders for the whole fleet. So everyone is guessing if they should stick with the original plan or join in the rescue."

Jackson broke in. "Picking up voice signals. Surrender demands."

"Going through the motions. Not our problem. When we've got updated vectors on all of them send a report in."

"Yes'm."

Over the next hour the Fusion ships all turned toward the battleship. The observers calculated the new rendezvous point. Mitchie expected the fighting to be over before any ships reached it.

"Missile launch!" yelled Jackson.

Mitchie snapped awake. She'd started to doze off watching the crawling blips on the displays. Now the Disconnect blockade flotilla hid behind a solid mass of missile icons.

"Nothing from the frigates," reported Hector. "Correction—a few of them are launching late."

Jackson laid circles on the display centered on Fox 93. "They're ahead of the rest. It's a time-on-target attack." More frigates spawned missile clouds in turn.

"Battleship's cut thrust," reported the senior petty officer. "It's turning."

"Report that to the flag immediately," snapped Mitchie.

Jackson keyed in the transmission. "Sent."

Mitchie looked at the display. It would take nearly three minutes for the warning to reach the flagship. "Are the frigates maneuvering?"

"No, ma'am. Straight thrust."

"Crap." Mitchie looked over Hector's shoulder. One of the Disconnect ships trying to by-pass the battleship put on a red halo. Mitchie ran through her memory of the training sims to identify it. Red meant bad data. In the sim rebooting the sensor array had fixed it.

Hector was already debugging the system. "No visual data on the frigate. But still getting consistent data on the other ones. High infrared but the spectrum doesn't match anything."

"It's dust."

"Ma'am?"

"The battleship hit it with the spinal weapon. Nothing left but dust." Mitchie's tone was bitter. She'd *warned* them, dammit.

"Dust would have a cooling rate of—" Hector quickly ran a simulation. "Curve matches. Yes, ma'am. Dust."

"Lost another," said Jackson.

Mitchie considered messaging the admiral again. *No, the staff is looking at my earlier message right now and realizing I meant it. And I'm in enough trouble already.* They were minutes away from the flagship, the staff would probably have new orders sent out before any message she sent out could arrive.

"They're starting to evade," reported Hector. The display hadn't changed. He must be looking at the raw data.

"Good."

"Missile launches from Cavalry Squadron." That was the tag they'd put on the dozen ships trying to get to Fox 93.

"Targets?"

"Can't tell." Jackson typed some more. "Too much overlap. Spreading out a bit so not just one target."

Yelling at them wouldn't improve the data so Mitchie gritted her teeth. A bicuspid had been regrown two years back. It was oversized, pressing into her jaw. She bit down harder.

"I've got some identifiable missile groups splitting off," said Jackson. "They're going for the frigates. The big mass is still spreading out. Heading roughly toward the blockade flotilla."

"Sounds like a counter-missile barrage." Mitchie ordered her to relay the new data to the flag. Another frigate had been lost to the battleship's superweapon after several misses.

"If we keep transmitting sooner or later someone's going to pick it up and send a missile our way," fretted Hector.

"That's why we get the big bucks."

"Does this boat even *have* any anti-missile jammers?"

"We can do evasive maneuvering," said the pilot.

"In this barge?" Hector was incredulous.

"She's evaded cannon fire."

"What? Why?"

"Someone tried to kidnap one of our passengers. It's a long story."

"I thought you didn't carry passengers."

"We usually don't. 'Cause they're *trouble*."

Jackson interrupted the argument to announce more missile launches. The bulk of the Fusion force was firing on the Disconnect formation. "It's pretty random. Going to arrive as an irregular stream."

"Suppression fire," said Mitchie. "Trying to discourage a follow-up attack on the big one."

"Frigates launching now. Looks like that's trying to counter the counter-missile shots from Cavalry Squadron."

"Wonder how many levels deep we'll go," muttered Mitchie.

"Not many, ma'am," said Hector. "The time on target is getting close."

After sending in another update they set the largest display to track the attack on Fox 93. The countermissile wave was destroyed by a combination of the new frigate missiles and some more peeled off from the main attack. The Disconnect trusted their missiles with better brains than the Fusion would allow any unsupervised system to have. The countermissiles had some pre-programmed surprises but their opponents adapted faster. The main attack had been weakened by less than ten percent. Most of the missiles were coasting, not wanting to come in so fast they wouldn't be able to maneuver on the final assault.

The attacking missile swarms stretched into a half-globe around the fleeing ship. There were gaps where frigates had died before making their launches. Other missiles slid over to fill them. The networked decision algorithm decided they were ready. The missiles doubled their acceleration as they aimed straight at their target.

The battleship had cut its acceleration, not bothering to try outmaneuvering them. Counter-missiles spat out in all directions.

Hector said, "Odd, there's a gap in the CM coverage."

The incoming missile icons in a thirty degree cone turned red and stopped accelerating.

"That's a new trick," said Mitchie. "Are they dust?"

"Looks like it, ma'am." Fox 93's icon went red next. "That's jamming."

The display kept zooming in as the missiles closed. The counter-missiles disappeared just before reaching their targets, exploding in clouds of shrapnel and EMP. The center of the screen became a fuzzy "NO VALID DATA" zone.

"How long does it take for that to disperse?" asked Mitchie.

"No idea, ma'am," answered Hector. "This is a bigger attack than anything I ever simmed. And it's not like we had real battles to calibrate those sims against."

"Right."

A magnified visual display was more interesting. A cloud of dust and gas glowed and flickered with explosions inside it. Pretty, even if they couldn't tell if the flashes were counter-missiles weakening the attack, missiles striking the battleship, or fratricidal collisions between deflected missiles. A few missiles emerged from the cloud, frantically decelerating so they could go back for another pass.

"I'm getting something!" cried Hector. "Strong signal. Too big to be a missile."

"It survived?" gasped Jackson.

"Pretty hurt if it did. I'm picking up a strong spin." More typing. "No. This is about two hundred and fifty meters by one hundred. Irregular. That was one tough ship."

"I'm picking up lifepod distress beacons," said Jackson.

"Spotted another chunk, smaller than the first one. Damn tough ship."

"Relay it all. What're the rest of the bad guys doing?" asked Mitchie.

Hector shifted his sensors. "Cavalry Squadron turned over. Going the other way, still at forty gravs. That must've hurt. No change in the rest. Well, some of them have cut thrust."

Mitchie laughed. "They've got no plan. And probably no admiral."

The Disconnect's admiral was still alive. He stayed that way through the missile barrage on his command. Counter missiles, interceptor fire, and interlocking plumes destroyed almost all of the Fusion attack. One light cruiser was lost to sheer bad luck.

A few boring hours passed until they received a signal from the flag. "Ceasefire agreement established. Fusion ships will leave system. *Joshua Chamberlain* will proceed to Fox 93's location at best acceleration to perform search and rescue."

The techs let out cheers.

Mitchie said, "I'm going to the bridge. Get this stuff secured then strap into your bunks."

First Battle
Of
Bonaventure

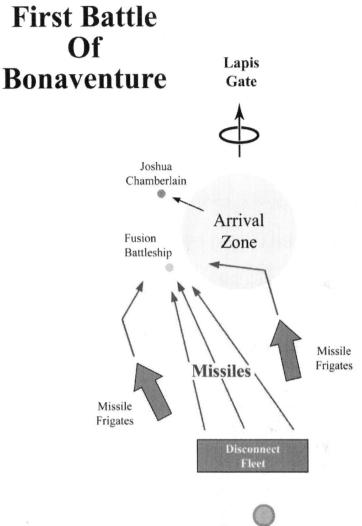

First Battle of Bonaventure.

Chapter Three: Lifeguard

Bonaventure System, acceleration 3 m/s^2

The Fusion made the best lifepods around. They were sturdy enough to handle bumping into debris. A torchship's plume would still pop one like a soap bubble. So a minimum-time approach to the wreck was out.

Mitchie calculated the best way to approach was to overshoot it to the side, then accelerate back to where they needed to be. Captain Schwartzenberger felt he could handle flying that course so he sent her off for a couple hours' nap before she needed to put her pressure suit back on.

The observation techs were both qualified with pistols. Mitchie issued them some of the ship's weapons while lecturing them on how to handle prisoners. "Fusion crews wear skinsuits in combat. They're flimsy, just for keeping them working while Damage Control fixes the air breach. But it also lets them jump out of their pod to attack you. We can't open the pods to search them, the skinnies might have leaked. So any prisoner could have a knife or a gun. Three or four of them could take you down bare-handed. So if you feel threatened, shoot."

The hold hadn't been repressurized. The techs' body language still showed through their pressure suits. Jackson felt out of her depth. Hector had the stolid NCO mask on.

"Ma'am, isn't it, um, illegal to hurt prisoners?" asked the junior tech.

"The regulations say if they accept their status as prisoners we have to treat them well. We've never taken prisoners in combat before so the regs are pretty vague. Given that we have six Diskers on this ship, five of them military, and zero security specialists, it wouldn't be hard for a hundred prisoners to take over. So we tell them to stay in their bubbles and shoot them if they get out."

"What if they say they're claustrophobic?"

"Anyone who says he's claustrophobic is lying or he wouldn't be in a pod in the first place. Shoot him."

"Yes'm."

When neither had further questions Mitchie showed them how to keep a hundred lifepods from rolling all over the deck. *Joshua Chamberlain* had a net the size of the hold intended for securing irregular cargo. Folded into a bag it would keep the prisoners in place.

She left them pulling the bundle out of the storage locker. They were only pulling three gravs of acceleration, letting the net bounce wildly as it uncoiled. She decided they'd be fine as long as they finished before the ship went to free fall and bounded over to Guo.

Mitchie turned her transmitter off and stood tip-toe to press her helmet against Guo's. "Did you catch all that?"

"Yeah. Don't like it but we need to be sensible. Let's get geared up."

They went to the EVA gear locker. Shifting containers to make room for the sensors had put a double stack in front of the locker, making a snug changing room. Their pressure suits were skintight and tough enough to handle normal hazards. Rescue work called for adding the heavy duty coveralls. Putting that on required taking off the harness of straps and pouches covering the suits from knees to shoulders.

Mitchie turned to grab a swinging strap and noticed Guo had paused with his harness half off. The suit did a very good job of displaying the definition of his shoulders. Apparently he'd been appreciating what her suit did as well. She dropped her harness to the floor and helped him finish with his.

She snuggled into his chest and touched helmets. "We've got some time to . . . chat. If you want."

"Um, don't do that."

"Why not? Heckle and Jeckle are too busy to interrupt us."

"Not that. It's—do you have any idea how uncomfortable an erection is in one of these things?"

"None whatsoever." She grabbed his shoulders and lifted herself up to wrap her legs around his hips. "Describe it to me?"

"Ticklish," said Guo. Grappling him left her armpits exposed. He slid his fingertips into each of them. Mitchie squeaked and flung herself off of him. In any heavier acceleration she'd've wound up lying on the floor. A hand on the bulkhead let her land on her feet.

Guo leaned down to touch helmets again. "We do need to talk about something. Why are you the one taking the maneuvering pack while I stay on the tether?"

"It's dangerous. Some of those Fuzies might want to keep fighting."

"Right. Which of us has been winning hand-to-hand fights?"

"We're tied in free-fall ones," answered Mitchie. "And I've had the free-fall combat course." Which hopefully would be enough for him to not push it to the point of rank and orders.

Guo didn't answer. He just took the coveralls out of the locker.

The crew retrieved the first batch of prisoners with no trouble. Schwartzenberger maneuvered the ship into a cluster of beacons. Mitchie jetted out to retrieve lifepods, tossing them to Guo. He leapt out to catch them then used his tether to pull himself back to the cargo hold. A gentle shove passed each one to the observers who stuffed lifepods into the cargo net.

Finding pods was easy. For the ones too far out to get a visual Guo had given her a directional antenna. "Don't lose it," he'd said. "It's the one I used on Savannah." Sentimental value aside it did of lovely job of locating distress signals.

When all the nearby pods were collected *Joshua Chamberlain* moved to the next cluster on only its maneuvering thrusters. That took almost as long as refueling the maneuvering pack.

After they stuffed the third batch of lifepods into the net Schwartzenberger called Mitchie on a private channel. "A couple of destroyers arrived to work SAR with us."

"Good."

"They've got a lot of maneuvering packs so they want to take over the free-floaters and leave checking the wreckage to us. Apparently they don't pack protective gear. You up for that?"

"Yes, sir. Already have the gear on."

"Right. I'm going to park us five hundred meters from the big piece."

"Aye-aye."

Mitchie crossed the gap slowly, looking for a good place to enter the wreckage. Places where the structure had fractured glittered with sharp edges and jagged debris. One side was rounded—melted metal now cooling. The hull side had some weapon emplacements but no airlocks.

A thruster plume caught her eye. More rescuers? No—the dark cylinder was covered in thrusters and antennas. She switched to the ship emergency channel. "JC One to *Vegetius*, come in please. JC One to *Vegetius*."

"SIS *Vegetius* to Jay-see-one, we read you. Over." The Shishi accent made her suddenly miss Billy. Guo and Bing must be exhausted from trying to cover his maintenance work and hers.

"*V*, I have some EOD work for you."

"Say again, over?"

"Scan for target—" she recited the appropriate coordinates.

"Roger, scanning designated—HOLY FUCKING SHIT!"

"*V*, I assess as Horsefly-class countermissile, but close enough."

"Standby, JC One, generating firing solution."

The wandering bomb had moved on in its search. Fortunately neither Mitchie nor her ship had been missile-like enough to satisfy it. She was outside the blast radius by now so didn't kibitz the destroyer on its firing plan.

She'd actually lost sight of it by the time the warship fired. She was still looking in the right area to see the explosion. "Thank you, *Vegetius*."

"Any time, JC One."

Studying her target found no better option than landing on the hull and picking her way inside through the broken areas. Mitchie picked a spot on the spinward edge of the hull. The maneuvering pack boosted her to matching speed as the edge came by.

She threw the loop she'd tied in her tether line. It caught on one of the spikes sticking out from under the hull edge. The spike curved away as the wreckage spun. Mitchie kept going straight until the line went taut.

Technically that was a straight pull. But her eyes switched reference frames. Mitchie fell to the hull, swinging on the line. A few blasts of the maneuvering pack put her feet-down and slowed her enough she could absorb the impact with her knees.

The touch-down would have made a dramatic pose if she'd landed on the inside. Since she was on the outside of the wreckage centrifugal force promptly tossed her back up again. She had to hand-over-hand her way along the tether to get aboard.

The safest opening turned out to be the most useful. The corridor reached through the wreckage. Debris blocked parts but light flashed through it when the wreck spun past Bonaventure's sun.

Criss-crossing lengths of tether across the opening made sure she wouldn't fall out accidentally. The maneuvering pack she tied to a beam. It was too big for inside work. Then she took time to call in. "JC One to *Joshua Chamberlain*. Aboard wreck, beginning SAR."

Captain Schwartzenberger answered, "Acknowledged. Be careful."

"Always am."

The captain turned his mike off. He wasn't quick enough to hide his disbelieving snort.

A lifepod sat a few meters up the corridor. Mitchie wondered what had kept it from falling out until she saw the spike puncturing the underside. The pod was still pressurized. Red ice sealed the puncture.

Mitchie climbed to the other side. The porthole was covered in red. Pressing her helmet to it and shouting and slapping brought no answer. *It's not my fault. I didn't do it.* She forced down the memory and climbed up to the next intersection.

For once Fusion designers had done something right. "LIFEPOD LOCKER" with an arrow was written on the bulkhead with glow in the dark paint. Following the directions took her to an empty locker surrounded by six inflated lifepods and one corpse in a plain uniform. *Idiot used his last minutes to guilt trip his friends instead of finding another locker.*

Her utility blade took a ten meter length off the end of the coiled tether. Getting them to the opening would be easy enough. Guo would appreciate the ties when he tried to catch them. Getting the line knotted onto each pod's D-ring took a few minutes.

Once at the opening Mitchie had to wait for *Joshua Chamberlain* to come in view again. Captain Schwartzenberger had parked her in the plane of the wreck's spin. As long as she released them at the right moment they'd go straight to the ship.

Or at least close enough for Guo to grab them.

"Incoming," Mitchie transmitted as she let go. She knew the pods were going in a straight line but it *felt* like they were heading up in a curve.

"See 'em," replied her husband.

She headed back into the wreck.

More corpses than survivors littered the wreck. Mitchie put marks at every intersection until she was more worried about her vacpen running out of ink than getting lost. More than half the total volume wasn't worth exploring. Too hot, too radioactive, too crushed. No chance of survivors. But she'd found more than thirty live ones which made the effort worth it.

Then she ran into Chief Donner, who responded to her offer of a nice POW camp with gunfire. She wished she'd found better cover that didn't depressurize a compartment full of survivors. When that mess was over she counted the bodies. Fourteen. All of whom had been alive when Mitchie boarded. She kicked Donner's corpse. "You stupid son of a bitch. Your buddies would be alive if you'd surrendered."

Pulling bodies out of the way, she headed out to look for survivors more willing to be rescued.

Poking through the far side she noticed a banging sound when she put her hand on a bulkhead. It repeated. Six bangs, a pause, six more. *Someone trapped in a compartment?* It felt stronger when she moved to portside. A "KEEP OUT: AUTHORIZED PERSONNEL ONLY" hatch hung open.

Mitchie went through it. Two compartments later the bangs could be felt through her boots. Looking through the next open hatch revealed the banger.

A man in a Fusion heavy-duty pressure suit stood in a room filled with computer racks. He pulled a data crystal from a rack and pounded it against the bulkhead with a piece of debris. The shards of many more glittered around his feet.

Mitchie's radio was set on the standard suit emergency frequency. "Hey!" she yelled, drawing her pistol.

He turned, saw her, and pulled a grenade from his belt.

Mitchie ducked back through the hatch. The compartment had buckled from a shock wave. She bounced behind a ruptured bulkhead and took cover, only her head and pistol hand peeking out.

The Fuzie came through the hatch feet-first. He grabbed the coaming and swung flat against the bulkhead.

Mitchie lined her sights onto the center of his back but didn't fire.

In the computer room the grenade detonated. Several pieces of shrapnel came through the hatch and bounced around the compartment. One made a five-bank shot to crease Mitchie's thigh.

She bit down on a curse. Her left hand grabbed the rip in the coverall and pulled it wider. No blood. *Good, the sting must be just vacbite.*

"I surrender," said the Fuzie.

Mitchie fumbled a square of vacctape off her spool and slapped it on the tear. The sting faded to ache.

"I surrender," he repeated.

"Fine. Start by very slowly taking that belt off and tossing it away. And keep facing the wall."

"Okay." The belt landed a few meters behind him. It had a pistol but no more grenades.

"Stand at attention," ordered Mitchie.

That confused him, but he obeyed. Mitchie's inner cadet pointed out his feet were improperly placed. She decided the beams and flanges crossing the ceiling they were standing on were a good excuse.

She holstered her pistol. Vacctape stretched between her hands, she gently stepped up behind him. A brief hug stuck it to his waist and forearms.

"What the fuck!" He thrashed about, unfortunately for him taking up all the slack in the tape. "I surrendered, dammit, what are you doing?"

Mitchie backed to the other side of the compartment and drew her pistol. "This is what surrender means: you let me tape you up and tow you back to my ship. You obey everything else I tell you to do. Or I put some holes in you and nobody in the whole galaxy ever knows what happened to you."

He leaned against a bulkhead and glared at her.

"I've got lifepods to rescue. What's it going to be?"

He slumped. "I surrender. What next?"

"Lie down on your belly, feet toward me. Kick me and it's a bullet."

Once he complied she taped his ankles, knees, and hands. On his back she wrote, "STORE SEPARATELY. DON'T UNWRAP." Then it was a two hundred meter drag through twisty passages to her entry point.

He was quiet until he saw the opening. "Where's the shuttle?"

"This is the Disconnect," Mitchie said. "Shuttles are for rich people."

"How are we getting to your ship?"

"Ballistics." She'd been using a particular bent spar as her horizon reference. The moment *Joshua Chamberlain* crossed that she would release him.

"You're just dropping me? You can't, that's inhuman. I could be lost forever!"

There she was. "They'll catch you." Mitchie let go.

The Fusion officer screamed as he sailed off into the empty. *Sometimes I love my job.* Mitchie crawled up into the wreck again.

Four lifepods later she'd run out of places to look. The rotation after sending the last one over was enough time to get all her gear together. Then she jumped off to float directly to her husband's arms. If "directly" included a couple of maneuvering puffs. She slowed enough for them to embrace instead of stretching his tether for momentum absorption.

"What's with the leg?" he asked.

"Suit scratch. Didn't break the skin. Did you get the special guy?"

"In the pressure suit? Yeah. He has a container to himself, secured for acceleration. You should have Bing check you for vacbite."

"I will," promised Mitchie. "But I have some more work to do first."

Bonaventure System, acceleration 10 m/s²

Guo had put the special prisoner in the unused dormitory container. The Fuzie was vacctaped to a bunk. He wore a stoic expression. Mitchie smiled at him as she came into the container. He kept the expression but she could see he had to work for it.

She found the container's life support controls and switched them from "stand-by" to "active." The prisoner hadn't needed it. His suit was still sealed tight. Mitchie wanted better air than her suit's.

She'd needed some things from her cabin for this task. The temptation to unsuit and use a real toilet had overwhelmed her. She'd given in, which made it even harder to suit up again and go into the depressurized hold.

The container didn't have an airlock. It had lost some air when Guo delivered the prisoner, and more as Mitchie entered. She could feel her suit relax as the life support brought the air back to normal pressure. A chair by the door caught her eye. She hooked it into the brackets next to the prisoner's bunk. Sitting down she could still make eye contact with him, if he ever looked her way.

The Fuzie's suit had a display panel on the chest. A scowling ancient warrior took up most of the area. Some text clung to the edges, proclaiming his ship to be the FNS *Terror*, his post deputy chief engineer for damage control, and that the processor was overdue to be connected to an approved network for verification.

A little exploring through the well-designed user interface gave her the communications controls. She turned off the radio and activated the external speakers and microphone.

Mitchie took off her helmet. "There. Now we can talk privately." Just him, her, and anyone listening to the recording. Hector had kludged together a recorder from his spare parts stock with amazing speed.

The Fuzie kept staring at the bunk above him. "Commander William Wentworth. JSD700549339271."

"Lieutenant Michigan Long, Akiak Space Guard. I have a few questions for you."

"I'm not telling you anything."

"You will be talking to me. I'd like to make this painless if I can."

Wentworth answered with obscenities. Mitchie calmly muted his speaker. She reached under his neck to turn off both air valves in turn. A few taps on the display brought up the health readouts. Pulse and blood pressure were rising.

The Fuzie thrashed in the bunk. The vacctape didn't budge. He managed some impressive flexing of his torso. Mitchie reached into a thigh pocket. This could be tedious.

She pulled out a battered hardcopy book. A shop on Bonaventure made them specifically for analog ship crews. The cover showed a couple standing in a furious blizzard. Her dress provided no warmth, other than to male viewers. His fur coat suited the climate well, or it would if he closed it instead of letting it fly in the wind to display all his chest hair. On a snowy slope behind them an escape pod burned. Mitchie turned to page 57.

The crone pulled a shift of red linen out of her trunk. "Ah! There's a lovely bit for a lass to wear on her wedding night.

Grace took a step back. "Wedding night? We're going to get married?"

"The lad staked his life in the challenge ring to keep the clan from throwing you out in the snow. What stronger pledge would you ask of a man?"

"But-but I'm already married," stammered Grace.

"Oh?" asked the crone. "Where is he?"

"He's on Sukhoi. He wanted to come on the tour, but he had to finish a deal. Oh, it's complicated." Grace wiped a tear away.

"A husband who loses his wife in the wilderness isn't much of a husband," said the crone. "My Angus, winds carry him to warmth, traveled with me whenever I went more than one valley away to keep me safe."

"It was supposed to be safe." Grace closed her eyes. Flashes of the starliner breaking up and the lifepod's fiery re-entry went through her mind. "Safe as home."

The suit display flashed an alert. He'd finally passed out. Mitchie opened the air valves and unmuted the speaker. She'd killed enough people by accident today. This one wouldn't be added to the list.

The crone tossed the shift at her. "It wasn't. And you're not safe here. So be thankful you've got my nephew to protect you, child."

Grace's lips thinned. Thirty-two years in civilization left her face as smooth as a Frostland teenager's. She'd given up asking to be treated as an adult. "I'm already married."

"You were, there. But you left him behind and he can't find you here. You'll be dead of old age before the light from that wedding reaches this valley."

Grace whimpered and sat down on the chest. Jored's aunt embraced her, pulling Grace's face against her withered breast. "Lass, lass, it hurts to lose him. I know the pain of loss. But you have a new man now, willing to die for you." The crone looked about for listeners. "He would have died, too, less Thurgan cared more about making a good show than finishing the fight. He's made you one of the clan, guaranteed you food and warmth for the winter. Is that not nothing?"

"It's . . . better than I deserve," said Grace. "He's done so much for me since I landed." The duel was the third or fourth time Jored had saved her life since she'd crashed in the howling blizzard.

"Then be his wife, girl. Treat him well tonight. Mind you're gentle. Those cuts will be sore for long. Tend him as a proper wife, as all the clan expect you to."

Grace shook out the shift. The red cloth would come to her knees. The previous wearer must've tripped on the hem going to her bed. "I will." She put it down and started undoing her buttons.

Wentworth sputtered. Mitchie looked up. Eye contact, at last!

"You can't do this. You're violating the Geneva Convention."

"The conventions were an agreement among nations that no longer exist. The Fusion hasn't made a treaty like that with the Disconnected Worlds. Or any other treaties." *That term paper finally paid off.*

"But it's, it's tradition."

Mitchie shrugged. "Y'all used to have a tradition of not bombing us. Broke that last year."

He coughed a few times. "So no rules at all? You can do whatever you want?"

"I operate in complete compliance with the regulations of the Disconnected Worlds Defense Coordinating Committee." *When they don't get in my way.* "Of course, they are vague in places. Please describe your duties aboard the FNS *Terror.*"

"Fuck you."

Speaker and valves. Back to the book.

It took him longer to wake this time after getting his air back. She waited for him to start talking. He avoided eye contact by looking all over the container. Couldn't just focus on the one spot.

"Look," he began, "I *can't* tell you anything. The Navy would court-martial me. Maybe execute me."

"It's the same for me," said Mitchie. "If I come into base with the highest ranking prisoner and I don't have any info at all my CO will break me. I'd wind up a bosun's mate third in charge of fecal recycling on some asteroid."

"That's not my problem."

"Actually, it is." Speaker and valves again. At least she was getting some reading time out of this.

Naturally his next wake-up was in the middle of the good part. "Describe your duties on your ship," she demanded.

"Uh. Oh, God. Can we compromise?"

"Maybe."

"If I describe prepping the ship to go out, will your boss be happy?"

"It's something. Just keep talking. If you pause I'll have to turn off your air again." Ideally she'd hand him over to a nicer interrogator now. But *Joshua Chamberlain's* crew was short on trained human intelligence professionals.

"No, don't, I'm talking." Wentworth started describing in great detail checking spare parts inventories and inspecting every spacer's training records to ensure they had the proper certifications.

After ten minutes Mitchie popped his faceplate and gave him a water bulb. She took a stimpill. It would take hours of boredom before he'd wear down enough to spill anything significant.

Three water bulbs and a protein bar later she'd maneuvered him into describing the pre-departure briefing.

"Admiral Chin was excited. He'd been planning this forever. Once we had the fleet in low orbits we'd start precision strikes on Bonaventure's infrastructure. Eventually they'd have to surrender. Then we land the troops and destroy the rest of the network on the ground. So we bring in new network nodes and rebuild it as a Fusion world. He was joking that in a generation they'd have a seat on the Council of Stakeholders. Or maybe he meant it. I don't know."

"That . . . would probably work," said Mitchie thoughtfully.

"Yeah. It's a big hammer approach. But now we've got the hammer. Or we will when they bring up *Inquisition* and *Purge*. Ah, crap. Shouldn't have said that."

"Oh, we knew there had to be several of them built if they were going into deployment, so you didn't spill anything."

"Okay," said Wentworth. "I'm really tired. Can we take a break?"

"Sure. Want more water?" Thirst quenched, he fell asleep. Mitchie needed sleep but kept thinking on the revelation. *If they're trying to forcibly incorporate worlds into the Fusion this is going to be a long and bloody war.*

Chapter Four: Invitation

Bonaventure, gravity 10.1 m/s²

Billy insisted on hosting the dinner in Commerce, the planetary capital. The crew dug out their formal wear with apprehension. No one trusted him as a social planner. The hour flight there went quickly as they vied to concoct the most preposterous disaster he could be setting them up for.

Most of those scenarios evaporated on landing. He'd directed them to the edge of the glittering Finance District. Conspicuous consumers wore dynamic fabric jackets and rotating head-dresses as they waited in line. The doorman recognized them as they exited the flyer. He ushered them straight into the restaurant. "Who are *they*?" wondered a linestander.

A hostess in a long black dress met them inside the door. "Welcome to Ivan's," she said. "Please let us know if there is anything we can do to improve your experience." She led them through the quiet dimly-lit restaurant to a private dining room.

Billy stood to greet them, wearing an elegant cream suit. "Thank you all for coming. I know you must be tired from the battle. I appreciate you interrupting your leave to join me."

Mitchie tried to keep the suspicion off her face. Billy was spending real money and exerting himself. He had to want something.

"Let me introduce my other guests." He smiled at the blonde hanging on his arm. "My fiancé, Elanor Kvit."

Mitchie recognized her from Billy's hotel room. *That was fast.* Elanor's dress used dynamic fabric in a subtle fashion, changing the reflectivity of the dress in fractal patterns while keeping the color a consistent white.

"Assistant Director James Suwo of the Ross Museum of Humanity."

Suwo focused on Schwartzenberger. "Splendid to see you again, Senator."

"It's just captain, now," said Schwartzenberger as they shook hands.

"Master Chief Lee. No relation." Guo's trainer put down his whiskey to shake hands with everyone.

"Mrs. Lien Wang. Bing's cousin." Bing and her relative had wrapped each other in hugs without waiting for the introduction.

Mitchie snagged the seat across from Billy's fiancé. A little conversation revealed the engagement wasn't as sudden as she'd thought. Billy had spent his last two visits to Bonaventure with her, plus there'd been some letters.

That hadn't made his proposal acceptable. Elanor shared the story. "So he was still down on one knee and I said, 'Billy, I love you, but I'm not committing to an unemployed spacer who blew half his last paycheck on some costume jewelry.'" Everyone laughed, including Billy. "'If you want to make this work, get a job.'"

"Costume jewelry?" asked Captain Schwartzenberger. He'd taken a good look at the gemstone when shaking her hand.

"I had to take her to two jewelers to convince her it was real," said Billy. "But that was later."

"Yes, getting the job was first," said the museum director. "I'm glad I could help out."

"I was surprised you went for the deal so easily."

"Oh, the donation and paybacks arrangement is very common in the Fusion. I worked at a Danu museum for some years. But they do it for tax evasion so it never happens here."

Elanor picked up the tale. "The next day he grabbed me from work for lunch. Showed me a contract saying he had a year gig as an acquisition inventory consultant. Suspicious. But I went for it. And *then* he tells me he's rich." She swatted him on the shoulder.

Billy grinned with no shame.

Captain Schwartzenberger addressed himself to Billy and Suwo. "I take it you two have been discussing our discovery?"

"Yes, sir," said Suwo. "It's an extraordinary find. We're intensely interested in examining the objects and seeing what we can offer for them. This should be major news, if there wasn't all that fuss with the Fusion."

"So you haven't made any offers yet?"

Billy jumped in. "Not negotiating, sir. Just making contacts. Didn't even take him to the warehouse."

"Glad to hear it," said the captain. "We can set up a meeting next week. At the warehouse."

"My time is at your disposal, sir," said Suwo. Billy just nodded.

Mitchie realized that had been the point of the dinner. Billy wanted his share cashed out. He was spending fast. She had to admit living rich would be nice. The service here was almost invisible. Unless she looked around for the waiter everything just appeared like magic.

Suwo decided a change of topic was in order. "A toast! To our Lieutenant Long, the hero of the hour." This brought a hearty "Hear, hear!" from the Master Chief and fainter ones from her shipmates.

"Thank you, but I was just doing my job," said Mitchie. She hated feeling the blush creep across her face.

"Oh, Admiral Galen called out your information as crucial to the outcome of the battle," said Suwo.

Elanor added, "Yes, his dispatches were published in all the journals."

"There's talk of giving you a medal," said Suwo, "though there's some controversy over that I don't quite understand."

Master Chief laughed. "It's simple enough. An admiral decided some information was unconfirmed and untrustworthy so shouldn't be released. Which makes releasing it violating a direct order. But Admiral Galen was glad to get it. So they're arguing. And it's spreading. I think every admiral in the system has taken a stand by now."

Mitchie kept a polite smile on her face despite wanting to hide under the table. She wanted assignments that would let her hurt the enemy. Getting caught up in fights between admirals could send her to the Deep Black.

"They wouldn't dare court-martial her, would they?" asked Guo.

Captain Schwartzenberger cleared his throat. "I'm afraid there are some officers thinking just that. A couple sounded me out on whether anything during the battle could be considered insubordination. I told them when I delegated responsibility I delegated the authority to go with it."

"Goodness. I hope some appropriate compromise can be arranged," said Suwo.

"Maybe they'll have a medal and a court-martial." Guo lifted his wineglass. "Here's to Michigan Long, the most-decorated ensign in the force!" Master Chief laughed and drained his whiskey.

Mitchie kicked Guo in the ankle. *Crap. Wish I had my boots on instead of these damn fancy sandals.*

Elanor shifted the conversation to something more cheerful. She even managed to draw Bing and Lien in. They'd been having a side conversation in Cantonese. From the bits Mitchie could make out Lien was briefing Bing on all the births, illnesses, new jobs, and marriages in a very large clan.

Not being interested in wedding planning Mitchie focused on her food. She'd played with her salad while following the discussions. Tasting the fish, grilled with an unfamiliar mix of spices, made her suspect she'd missed something good. The hostess had described the dinner as "an eight course meal." *If they're all this good Guo will have to roll me home.*

Bonaventure System, acceleration 0 m/s^2

Pundits tossed around "sitzkrieg" to describe the stalemate in the war. The crews implementing the "forward defense" strategy laughed when they heard the word. Their "sitting" consisted of chasing down every sensor echo to see if it was a newly arrived Fusion ship. Most of them lasted less than an hour after jumping in. The smarter ones boosted outsystem to find a hiding spot. One had led her pursuers eight billion klicks away before running out of countermissiles.

So it was understandable that the emerging mail boat immediately shrieked "DIPLOMATIC COURIER" on all standard frequencies.

"Blockade Command to courier. Remain at zero acceleration. Stand by for boarding."

"We will comply. Courier out."

The armored boarders found two unarmed crew awaiting them. The mail boat had empty spaces where sensor and computer gear had been ripped out. The Diskers had trashed hell out of a previous courier loaded with sensors.

When the Chief Master at Arms finished the inspection he turned to the crew. "What do you have for us?"

One of them held out a clear box. Dozens of data crystals rested in labeled slots. "A mix. Actual government to government stuff. Some news and entertainment selections. And a bunch of private mail."

"You're still doing real mail?" asked the chief.

The mail boat crewman shrugged. "If they've got the money we've got the boat."

"Fair enough." He passed the box to a subordinate. "Here's our outgoing." A clear plastic sack held three crystals. "Wait fifteen minutes after we undock then you're clear for a least-time to the gate."

"Got it, boss. See you in two weeks."

Bonaventure, gravity 10.1 m/s^2

Billy met the *Joshua Chamberlain* on landing. The DCC had found a practical use for their pet tramp freighter: hauling fresh food and other supplies to ships on the forward defense patrols. The crew found a routine cargo run refreshing after the past year's insanity.

Everyone gathered in the galley to look at Billy's latest proposal. The Ross Museum had joined with two art institutes to make a joint offer for most of the historically interesting items. The non-cash incentives made for interesting reading.

"Do they really think I care about having my name on some room?" asked Bing.

Billy had been forced into taking the museum side of the discussion. "People giving them cash usually demand that. It's a big deal."

Bing wasn't impressed. "I'm not giving them money. I want money from them."

"If we agree to let them pay less than we really want for the piece, it's like we're giving them a donation." Billy wished one of the museum people were here. That had sounded so much more sensible when Suwo had said it.

Bing snorted.

Mitchie wanted another item explained. "This bit about being able to host private parties in the museum. It doesn't say what the rental rate is."

Billy brightened up at an easy one. "No rental. You could use it for free."

"Then it should say what the rental fee we're exempt from is so we can value it properly."

"It's not—only the big donors can use it. Nobody else can no matter how much they offer to pay."

"Let me get this straight," said Mitchie. "You can't buy it but if you give them lots of money you get it for free?"

Billy waved his hands as if trying to capture a concept that was fluttering away. "It's how they do things."

"So that's how rich people live."

Captain Schwartzenberger didn't look up from his datasheet. "If we make a good deal for this we'll be living as rich people."

"The part that bothers me," said Guo, "is them wanting a crack at the Frankovitch data vault. It doesn't say anything about securing it or who gets rights to the data."

"We tried to decrypt it for weeks," said Billy. "It's worth nothing to us if we can't read it."

"If they can get value out of it we need to make sure we get our share. Alexi could sue our asses off if we don't get him his quarter-share."

Bing interjected, "Or there could be a copy of a Betrayer in there and if they put it on an active processor it'll wipe out the city. Or more."

"Okay, okay!" Billy raised his hands. "I'll tell them that part won't fly." He looked around the table to see where the next attack would come from.

The airlock buzzer sounded below, suspending the debate. The crew traded looks. No one expected a visitor.

Mitchie zipped down the ladder and brought back a Yeoman Third Class. A courier, but not bearing orders from the Defense Force.

"Good, everyone on the address list is here," he said. An ugly square computer came out of his satchel. He placed it on the table and inserted a data crystal. "A message has come for you from the Fusion. Under the Amended Blockade Act you are required to only use it in this dedicated player. Under no circumstances may the message be inserted into any planetary network."

"I've had the briefing, son," said Captain Schwartzenberger. "Thank you." The yeoman saluted and left.

The computer listed the crystal's contents as "Main Message" and several attachments. Mitchie pressed "Play." A hologram formed above the table. A young woman's head. She was instantly recognizable. Skin a bit darker, hair a little curlier, cheekbones softer. *Is that her real face, or just a different disguise than when she flew with us?*

"Bobbie!" said Bing. The rest of the crew nodded. They all remembered fighting to protect their passenger from a kidnapper.

"Hello, my friends," said the hologram. "I hope you are all doing well and staying safe. I was glad to hear you returned safely from your expedition.

"On the 29th of next month I will have my Revelation Ball. My identity will become public and I will take on the rights, privileges, and duties of an adult and citizen. You may think me young for it, but you know better than most that childhood has been no protection for me.

"I would be honored if you would attend. I don't know you as well as other friends of mine. But I deeply appreciate what you've done for me. You've proven yourselves more worthy of trust than almost anyone else I've met in my life."

Mitchie noted the lack of names and places in the message. *She's expecting some enemy to listen to this. And she's been taught commsec.*

"I know this isn't your usual kind of party. We're arranging everything necessary to let you enjoy it. Accommodations, tailors, dance instructors are all waiting for you. Daddy has talked to some Stakeholders. Attached to this message is a formal safe passage from the Council, guaranteeing your right of transit to and from the event.

"Don't feel obligated to arrive early. But there's all sorts of fun I can show you here, and of course it'd be easier to prepare for the ball with more time. The tailors insisted I ask you for your measurements. If you could send those along with your estimated arrival time it would be wonderful."

Bobbie's expression shifted from cheerful to imploring. "If you can't attend I understand of course. I do want to thank you as myself for your great help as soon as I can. I hope we can still meet after this current insanity is over.

"With all my love and friendship. Thank you." The hologram froze.

Guo said, "Is it just me or does this have 'trap' written all over it?"

"I'm sure she's sincere," said Bing.

"Her sincerity isn't the issue," said Captain Schwartzenberger. "It's her father, the people who issued the safe-passage, and any fascists in the Fusion Navy who might bit-bucket it. A promise isn't much to rely on right now."

Mitchie said, "I'm glad to know she's doing well. I'd love to see her. I've been dying to find out who she really is. But it feels awfully risky to go there right now." She turned to Billy. "But you still want to go to the party, don't you?" she teased.

He made a face. "I paid good money to become a Bonaventure citizen. I'm going nowhere. There's plenty of good parties right here."

Schwartzenberger traded looks with Bing. He said, "That's settled then. We've got more than a week until the next mail boat comes. I'll work on a nice note to her."

Bing added, "I'll go research Demeter etiquette and see what an appropriate present would be."

***

Medals were presented in big formal ceremonies. Impending court-martials were announced in an appointment with the Judge Advocate's office. Being called into the admiral's office presaged a compromise. *Asteroid, here I come*, thought Mitchie. "Lieutenant Long reporting as ordered, sir!"

Admiral Chu returned her salute. "Sit, please."

She sat in an attentive pose.

"My staff has been reviewing the regulations concerning your situation. It turns out there are some other rules that have been overlooked." That sounded like he was working up to a non-judicial punishment in lieu of a court-martial. She could live with that. "Specifically, when a service member makes a discovery or encourages a donation that is a substantial contribution to the Force, a reward is provided to the member."

Wait, what?

"Revenue from undercover work hadn't been previously covered under that because the Force normally provided the capital for the venture and accepted the risk of financial losses. In the case of the Eden finds the Force made no investment and the risk was directly on you and your shipmates."

Mitchie realized this wasn't about her actions in the battle. The admiral was talking about the regulation requiring her share of the loot to be turned over to the DCC.

"In view of the extreme level of risk you faced," continued Admiral Chu, "it has been decided that a fifteen percent finder's fee is appropriate." By the sour look on Chu's face it wasn't his decision. "That will be promptly paid out from the funds already received by the DCC. Unless you want to review the appropriateness of that figure with the JAG?"

Keeping her face calm took effort. "No, sir," Mitchie said. "That's quite acceptable." She wouldn't be as rich as her husband but a fiftieth of the Eden treasure was 'fuck you money' anywhere but Bonaventure. And maybe there if they cut a good deal.

"Good. I'm glad that's settled." The admiral swiped his datasheet, pulling up a different set of notes. "I understand you've been invited to a ball in the Fusion?"

Mitchie would only have been surprised if Intelligence *wasn't* reading all the mail coming from enemy territory. "Yes, sir."

"Are you going?"

"We discussed it and all decided this was a terrible time to take a pleasure trip to Demeter."

"Would you be willing to go as a mission?"

Mitchie frowned. "A mission, sir? I don't know if we'd be able to collect any data at an event like that. Assuming my cover hasn't been blown, which it probably has."

"Not an intelligence mission," said the admiral. "A diplomatic one."

She waited for him to elaborate.

Chu sighed. "Since the attack on Noisy Water the Disconnected Worlds have been steadily losing access to the top layer of Fusion society. Our observers at the Council of Stakeholders were expelled. Planetary consuls can no longer get meetings with Directors or even lower level elected officials. When tension increased the DCC organized a formal embassy. They turned back the ship. Wouldn't even let them land."

"I see the problem, sir," said Mitchie. "How does Bobbie's ball help solve it?"

"The analyst report on the Kronos incident swore there were only three men who could be Bobbie's father. All of them are well connected with the Fusion government. This safe passage is proof that whoever she is her family has clout."

"There's an analysis of Kronos?" interrupted Mitchie.

"Yes. You didn't have need-to-know."

"I damn well need to know *now*."

"If you take the mission you'll get a copy," stated the admiral.

"Understood, sir."

"Back to the subject. A revelation ball is a major social event. Not just friends and family but the colleagues and patrons of the patriarch. In this case, politicians, admirals, trillionaires. Likely several Stakeholders. Even Demeter's Planetary Coordinator might attend."

I hope not, she thought.

"We want to substitute a professional ambassador for one of the invitees. Probably Mr. Lee. The report said he'd had less contact with Bobbie, or at least less significant contact. So she shouldn't miss him."

"He didn't want to go anyway."

"Good."

"Sir . . ." Mitchie tried to find the words for her discomfort. "Why are we going to all this trouble? The ambassador can get some informal conversations with their pooh-bahs. What's that worth? We won the battle, we're blockading their fleet. Isn't it their turn to talk to us?"

The admiral stood and walked to his window. A wave sent the security panel up. A torchship was taking off from Redondo Field. A bright light in the sky showed the previous launch had enough altitude to light its torch. Warehouses and factories spread out beyond the spaceport. On the hills over the town comfortable houses peeked through the trees.

"Looks like we're winning," he said. "Safe, peaceful, rich. As long as we protect it."

"I'd heard the fund drive for the new ships succeeded," said Mitchie.

"Succeeded? We've gotten so much we're assigning new staff to decide what to do with it. If we didn't have this mission your husband would probably be on his way to a new shipyard."

Chu closed the window. He put his hands on his desk, leaning toward Mitchie. "Do you know what the latest fad is here?"

She shook her head.

"At a dinner party one guy will stand up and say, 'I'm a quarter-share man.' He means he's donating a quarter of this year's income to the Defense Fund, on top of whatever else he may be paying. Then a second one stands up and says it. Then a third, and so on. Then it gets down to the last one.

"Is he going to say, 'I've researched the issue and the Defense Force has enough to meet the current threat'? Or maybe 'I have too many obligations to donate that much'? No. He's going to say he's a quarter-share man too. And the next morning he'll donate that money, whether he can afford it or not, because people check. Because we're monkeys. And monkeys stick with their clan.

"It's coercion. Social, psychological coercion. Almost as bad as sending men with guns to take money from them. If it keeps up they will start taking money at gunpoint. That's how tax laws start."

Admiral Chu paced back and forth behind his desk. Mitchie watched without interrupting. "You and I," he said, "volunteered for a life under coercion. To achieve a goal greater than we could on our own. We have the freedom to leave. Right now, either of us could quit. We're part of a society that has achieved great things through purely voluntary cooperation. Bonaventure is free of coercion, the greatest flowering of individual freedom in human history.

"Now it could collapse. Become just another tribal collective devoting itself to fighting strangers. At the rate we're going I expect little old ladies will be giving white feathers to young men next week."

Mitchie resolved to look up the significance of white feathers as soon as she escaped.

Chu dropped into his seat. "That's what the Fusion is doing to us. That's why we need to end this war."

"I understand, sir. But why are you telling me? Captain Schwartzenberger is in command."

"He is. But he's a merchant skipper at heart. He won't lead an unwilling crew into danger. Now, Mate Bingrong will follow her ex-husband anywhere. And your husband will follow you. You . . ." The admiral pointed his index finger at her. ". . . Are a leadership challenge."

With that Mitchie realized why this conversation had opened with a very large bribe. "Sir, I've never claimed to be a perfect officer. But I don't back down from missions. I'll talk them into it."

"Good," said Admiral Chu. "Anything you'd need to make go down easier?"

"A couple of new hands would be good. Five crew is bare-bones for a long run in that ship. Four has been a lot of work just in-system."

"Not a problem. I'll find a couple of appropriate ones to turn merchie. It'll make it easier to hide sending the ambassador aboard too."

***

Mitchie had gotten them a room in Visiting Officer Quarters for a few days. The bed was no better than their one on the *Chamberlain*, and the art was trash next to the watercolors Guo collected, but unlimited water in the bath had outweighed the rest.

Guo came in to find Mitchie laying on the bed dressed except for tunic and shoes. "Ready for dinner?" he asked.

"How about ordering in something?" she said without opening her eyes. "I'd like a chance to talk privately."

He looked at her curiously but decided to not push. He made the order then went into the bathroom.

By the time the large pizza arrived they'd both changed into comfy clothes. Guo dealt with the deliverybot while Mitchie poured drinks. He set out the box on the counter and put a slice of sausage and mushroom on a plate for her. Two slices of tuna and octopus went on his own plate. He brought them over to the table and traded Mitchie's plate to her for a mug of beer.

After swallowing his first bite Guo said, "I should warn you, in about five minutes I'm going to fall down dead from suspense."

She laughed, sending some beer down the wrong pipe.

Good, it worked, he thought.

Once she'd stopped coughing Mitchie said, "Admiral Chu called me in this afternoon."

"Always fun."

"This was more fun than usual. He wants us to go to Bobbie's party."

Guo laughed. "What did he say when you told him to fuck off? However you say that in officer-speak."

"It's a mission, an important one." She described it in merchant terms, a charter to deliver the diplomat to Demeter. With her 'finder's fee' as a bonus.

He took a big bite of his slice to buy time. He dropped the crust onto his plate. Swallowed. "Between the combat zone and the Fusion's attitude toward Diskers that could be a one-way trip."

"We have a safe passage."

"One of the guys who signed off on that might be the same one who wanted Bobbie kidnapped or murdered to leverage her father. We can't trust Fusion politicians. Safest thing we can do is avoid them."

"Maybe that's safe for us right now. But what if they bring down the Disconnected Worlds?" She summarized the Admiral's fears. "I don't want to live in a copy of the Fusion." She bit into her half-finished slice.

"Let the Admiral worry about it. That's why he gets the heavy coins. We've done our share. You've done more than your share." Guo drained his mug.

Mitchie refilled it before answering. "This isn't something the Admiral can go ask for volunteers for. It's us or no one."

"I'm good with no one." Bite. "Look, if it's the money we can make a contract putting half my share in your name. That's more than they're offering."

"It's not the money. It's the mission."

A few minutes went by with just eating. Guo refilled their plates. Mitchie finished her beer.

"Look, it's not really that dangerous," said Mitchie. "The mail boats are making regular runs. There's cargo being smuggled through other gates. It's just the Lapis-Bonaventure link that's interdicted." She got herself more beer and topped off Guo's mug.

Guo tried to avoid taking a stand himself. "Schwartzenberger would demand more hazard pay than the Admiral could stomach."

Mitchie wanted to pin him down. "The Defense Force has more money than it knows what to do with." She proceeded to make more arguments in favor of the trip, not sticking with topics, perfectly willing to chase him down any side track he picked.

He stopped trying to be coherent, just tossing objections in hopes that something would discourage her enough to give him a break. His wife remained relentless.

The pizza was gone. Guo needed an excuse to put off answering her latest question. "'Scuse me. Gotta unload some of that beer you've been pouring into me."

Once he'd locked the bathroom door he realized it wasn't a lie. He'd just been too tense to realize it. While washing his hands after he put some cold water on his hot eyes.

He studied himself in the mirror. Time to think about those words he'd bit back twice. *I went to Old Earth for you, isn't that enough?*

Guo's reflection slumped. No, it wasn't enough. Getting caught in the middle of a fleet action wasn't enough either. Hell, a wartime run to Demeter wouldn't be the end of it either. Mitchie had a Cause and everything else would be sacrificed to it.

Guo looked the reflection in the eye. He needed to decide what he wanted. A nice, safe life in the Disconnect? Or to stay married? *Heaven help me, I love her.*

He opened the door and walked back into the bedroom. "Okay, let's go to Demeter."

Mitchie's face changed from plotting to cheerful. "You'll tell the captain you want to go?"

"Yes."

She hugged him tightly. "I'm sorry I got angry."

Guo hugged her back. "It's all right." Or at least he'd learned to live with it.

"You're all tense. Want a massage?"

"Maybe later. Are there any vids you'd like to watch?" Usually he made suggestions, but in this mood he'd pick something that would start an argument.

Mitchie thought for a few moments. "There's a musical I liked as a kid, want to give it a try?"

"Sure." *That should be safe*, he thought.

Bonaventure System, acceleration 10 m/s²

The Admiral kept his word. The day after Captain Schwartzenberger filed a flight plan to Demeter three souls came on board. Bing barely had time to show them to their cabins before the ship took off for the Lapis gate.

Guo outdid himself on that night's dinner. Mitchie savored the spiced chicken, hardly wanting to interrupt eating to speak.

There was no need for her to talk anyway. Ambassador Bakhunin had been invited to tell them something of himself. He'd turned that in a history of how the Defense Coordinating Committee had evolved from an *ad hoc* discussion group to the Disconnected Worlds' *de facto* government. He enlivened the dry tale with anecdotes of himself playing discreet but crucial roles at every step along the way.

Good thing this is spicy, thought Mitchie. *If he'd made porridge we'd be asleep in it.*

"Thank you," broke in Captain Schwartzenberger. "That's very enlightening. Have you been to the Fusion before?"

"Only as a visitor. Most of our diplomats are *persona non grata* now. I've brought a library with biographies of those I hope to meet on our mission. Studying that will take most of my time on the trip."

"Of course," said the captain. "But since this is a small crew we still need everyone contributing to keeping the ship running."

"I understand, Captain."

Schwartzenberger turned his attention to the next most senior newcomer.

Pilot-Decurion Hiroshi didn't like the spotlight. He still stammered out some words about growing up on Shishi and coming to Bonaventure for advanced pilot training.

"Wait, I recognize you," said Bing. "Weren't you court-martialed?"

"It—I wasn't—" said Hiroshi.

Simultaneously Spacer Apprentice Setta burst out, "They didn't!"

Hiroshi swallowed as Setta subsided. "I was acquitted," he said.

That sparked Mitchie's memory. "Are you the bridge guy?"

The co-pilot turned beet red.

Guo placed the refilled rice bowl between himself and the ambassador. To keep the conversation moving he asked, "Which bridge?"

Hiroshi took a deep breath. "I flew a cutter under Gold Street Bridge in Commerce City."

"That must've scared hell out of some civilians," said Guo. "Any accidents?"

"Nobody was hospitalized. Our instructor challenged us to do it. Well, he said he was joking but several of my classmates testified that he said it seriously." Hiroshi finished the practiced line and looked around defiantly.

Captain Schwartzenberger broke the silence. "Good thing for you there's a war on, son. If we didn't need every pair of boots so badly the board might have been rougher on you."

Hiroshi clenched his jaw.

"But we'll be careful what jokes we tell, so don't worry," finished the captain.

Bing took the chance to follow up with Setta. "Why did you think I was talking to you, dear?"

The new deckhand looked down. "Taking this assignment was part of how I avoided a court martial." She turned to face Bing. "But it wasn't my fault, I swear! I checked."

"Checked what, dear?"

Setta decided to tell the whole story. "I'm in Supply, or was. Everyone always holds back some key parts, not in the database, for emergencies. But when the emergency happens half the time you need a different part. So we talk to each other and barter for what we really need."

"Happens everywhere," said Captain Schwartzenberger.

He'd encouraged her to talk faster. "I'd kept in touch with everyone from my training class, and I'm good at making new friends, so I had a lot of contacts to barter with."

Mitchie looked over the deckhand. Taller than Guo, perfect skin, and the sharp features of her warrior-caste ancestors. Yes, she had no doubt Setta could talk bored Supply NCOs into trades.

"We found a container with some amazing stuff in it. Luxury furniture, paintings, comm gear. My boss asked around. Nobody knew where it was from. Finally they decided it must have been collected by some guy who'd retired and told me to trade it for what we needed. It went *fast*."

She sipped her juice. "Then the Fleet Master Chief came back from leave. Turned out it was his private scrounging stash. Which he'd been saving up for the change of command ceremony. My boss lost a stripe, his boss lost a stripe, my great-grandboss got a letter, and I went from being up for PO to spacer apprentice." She shrugged. "Could be worse."

"Is everyone on this ship fleeing some punishment?" rumbled Ambassador Bakhunin.

"I don't know, sir," replied Bing. "What did you do to get sent to the far side of enemy territory?"

Lapis System, acceleration 0 m/s^2

The safe-passage instructions had a frequency and password. As soon as they passed through the Lapis gate Captain Schwartzenberger broadcast it. A prompt reply ordered them to drift and prepare for an inspection party.

The boarders were Fusion Marines in full battle armor. They ordered the crew to the galley. One Marine was stationed there to watch over them. He didn't move or talk except to order them to stay silent.

Mitchie studied the Marine. He was in a Hunter-7 suit. She'd studied its specs. The helmet was solid titanium. The vision display took views from a 360-array of cameras ringing the outside of the helmet. Like the rest of the squad the Marine had fought the insectile appearance of the helmet by painting a skull over his face. This one had pointed teeth and long fangs but no lower jaw.

The rest of the Marines slammed through the ship checking every compartment. Metallic pops from the bridge hatch meant they'd forced the access panels open. Eventually the mob descended to the cargo hold. Banging from there was muffled.

Mitchie's speculation on how much of a mess the Marines had made was answered by one of her teddy bears bouncing out of her cabin into the corridor. The black-furred plushie was intact, googly eyes in place and seams whole. She looked back at the Marine. "May I grab that before it shorts something in Hydroponics?"

The skull face didn't move but the shoulders gave a slight shrug. Mitchie released her seat belt, kicked off of the chair, grabbed the bear, and bounced off a bulkhead. She tossed the bear to Guo so she'd have both hands for getting back in her seat. Once she fastened her belt he passed it back to her.

"Thank you," Mitchie said to the Marine.

No response.

The sounds of armored fists on container walls faded away. Hopefully they'd be gentler in the converter room or a safe passage wouldn't do them any good.

After far too long the squad came back to the main deck. The sergeant ordered his men back to their shuttle. "You've passed inspection. You're clear to proceed to the Danu gate. If you deviate from your filed flight plan you will be destroyed."

"Understood," replied Captain Schwartzenberger. The crew all kept their seats until they heard the airlock close and shuttle detach. "All right, let's look over the damage. Just worry about the fragile stuff. We can finish cleaning up when we're under thrust. Long, update our course to the gate."

"Aye, aye," said Mitchie.

Lapis System, acceleration 10 m/s^2

Mitchie had bridge watch when the signal came in. Since analog ships couldn't receive data directly the Fusion mail boat had a text to voice bot read it out over the radio. She scribbled frantically to get down the several hundred characters. The automatic repeat let her fix her mistakes. When she was finished she pressed the intercom switch for the converter room.

"Yes?" said Guo.

"Either a random letter generator is sending us love notes or there's work for the code clerk," said Mitchie.

"I'll be right up."

The mechanic made good time to the bridge. He stole a kiss from his wife before taking the message. "Thanks." He stepped back to the hatch.

"Not going to decrypt it here?" she asked.

He just shook his head with a smirk and slid down the ladder.

***

The message didn't come up again until halfway through dinner. Captain Schwartzenberger said, "Heard we got a note from home."

Mitchie didn't pause in chewing her bread but her attention locked on Guo.

Her husband replied, "Routine administrative stuff, sir. Nothing we need to know about."

"Okay. Let me know if we get anything interesting." The captain went back to slicing his meat.

That's it? Mitchie carefully controlled her expression. There was nothing to be gained by showing how amazed she was at the captain's lack of curiosity.

***

Between the routine of cruising and having some new crew on board the newlyweds had gotten their schedules synched up all the time. Mitchie gave her husband a little time to unwind after getting off shift before bringing up her concern.

When he laid down in bed she snuggled up. "Have any trouble with the decryption?" she asked.

"Nope," answered Guo smugly. "Had a clean copy on the first try."

"Interesting reading?"

"Nah."

"What was it about?"

"Can't say," said Guo.

"Sure you can." Mitchie pressed her naked body a little more firmly against his.

"It's classified."

"I have clearances."

"You don't have Need To Know." Guo enunciated the capitals clearly.

"Ship's officers automatically have Need To Know."

"Just the commander and XO."

"I'm XO!" protested Mitchie. "I'm the second ranking officer."

"No, that's Bing. She has the slot."

The cuddle had been abandoned. Mitchie was sitting up cross-legged. Guo rolled onto his side to face her.

"I can order you to tell me," she said.

"No, you can't." Guo's voice shifted to a formal cadence as he quoted the regulation. "Code clerks must only divulge classified information to the proper recipients. Rank does not provide access to restricted information"

Her glare made him look away. So when she pushed him onto his back and kissed him hard he didn't see it coming.

***

Guo's panting had slowed. He still wasn't going to be saying anything more without major effort. Mitchie studied the cabin's ceiling. The former dividing wall had met the curving outer hull with a T-flange. Since it wasn't structural the yard had left some gaps between the welds.

The gaps were well out of her reach. Guo rolled onto his side to enjoy her stretching. Mitchie unlatched a footstool from the deck and placed it under where the hull met the ceiling. She didn't bother latching it into place. What was one more broken regulation now?

Standing on the footstool let her reach up, much to Guo's enjoyment, and touch the flange. A fingernail made contact with a folded piece of paper and nudged it out of the narrow niche. Once a corner stuck out she grabbed it and had the whole thing out.

Still standing on the footstool (at grave risk if the ship maneuvered while she was on an unsecured platform) she unfolded the message. "All front-line ships. Rear Admiral Min Chang assumes command of Second Blockade Flotilla effective immediately. By order of Admiral White, Defense Coordinating Committee." She looked at Guo. "That's it?"

He had his breathing back under control. "I said it wasn't anything we needed to know about."

Mitchie hopped down and returned the footstool to its original locked-down position. She sat on the edge of the bed.

Guo slid over and wrapped an arm around her waist. "Was that worth getting me to commit a court-martial offense?" he asked.

"No," she sighed. "Barely worth classifying in the first place."

"Then let's behave ourselves." Guo pulled her into bed. He pressed the light switch on the headboard. They went to sleep spooned together, not bothering with the mandatory restraining strap to keep them in the bed during maneuvers.

***

Mitchie walked into the Hydroponics room. Hiroshi scraped old algae off a screen to go into the cooker. He was being thorough about it—no specks left to infect the next batch with rot. Exactly as she'd taught the three newbies to do it.

"Why are you here?" she asked.

"Ma'am?" said her co-pilot. "They're due for rotation."

"I know. Why are you doing it instead of Bakhunin?"

"We traded shifts, ma'am."

Putting her hands on her hips and glaring was only an effective strategy when Mitchie had already intimidated someone. Fortunately Hiroshi fell in that category.

"Um, that is, he's paying us to take his shifts," he said.

"Us?"

"Me and Spacer Setta, ma'am."

"Uh-huh." More glaring. "Are you both familiar with the regulations on crew rest?"

Hiroshi brightened up a little. "Yes, ma'am. We reviewed the regs and schedules to make sure we could cover it all without breaking a rule."

Mitchie didn't doubt that. The crew had been dividing the same work among fewer people before they came on board. She'd be fine with the arrangement if it wasn't for that arrogant SOB escaping getting his hands dirty. But dealing with the Ambassador was the captain's call.

"Carry on," she said.

"Yes, ma'am!" He went back to scraping.

Danu System, acceleration 10 m/s^2

Mitchie missed the next classified message's arrival. She knew when it was decrypted. She and the captain were on the bridge together. Guo came up and handed Schwartzenberger the message. He glanced through it and handed it back.

"No worries for us," said Captain Schwartzenberger. "Thanks, Chief."

"You're welcome, sir." Guo gave Mitchie a wink before going below.

She bit her tongue and tried to concentrate on taking a sight.

***

Two days later she hadn't said anything about the message. Guo hadn't used the same hiding spot. Or any other place on the flange. The crannies of the bed and cabinets had no paper in them. Going through his books revealed a possible love poem in classical Chinese.

Eventually Mitchie wound up eying her teddy bears suspiciously. He'd seen her use them as hiding places. But he couldn't do seams as neat as hers so there was no need to open them up to check.

On day three she still didn't ask Guo about it. She wasn't talking much though. She'd started to fidget. *I must look like Uncle Edwin when he was quitting nicks.* The worst part was catching Guo smirking when he thought she wasn't looking.

The next day at bedtime Mitchie was brushing her hair before the mirror with excessive force. Guo came up behind her. He took the brush out of her hand. His arms wrapped around her, hands on her breasts, and pulled her tight against his chest. His tongue licked the curve of her ear.

"You have some energy to work off," he whispered.

She looked in the mirror. He still had the damn I've-got-a-secret smirk. Mitchie turned around and kissed him anyway.

He carried her to the bed and tried to toss her into the middle. She'd wrapped her legs around him so he fell over on top of her. Neither complained.

Some time later they were trying to catch their breath. Mitchie's fingertip traced lines around Guo's face, looking for tense muscles. It drifted down his throat. "Talk to me," she said.

"About what?"

"What are you thinking?"

The smirk reappeared. "I've got a secret."

Mitchie's frustration broke out. "So tell me!" Her hand wrapped over Guo's throat.

"Make me," he laughed.

Mitchie climbed on top of her husband and proceeded to make him.

A couple of hours later, when he could talk again, Guo recited the message. "All front-line ships. Current low level of Fusion activity is expected to continue. Ships may stand down to readiness level three at CO's discretion. By order of Rear Admiral Galen."

"Doesn't make any difference to us," said Mitchie. The *Joshua Chamberlain* didn't have enough crew to run at a higher readiness.

"That's what the captain said."

"Why the hell is HQ sending us this stuff?"

"We're part of the fleet now," said Guo. "We're supposed to know this stuff."

She didn't answer. Guo lay beside her feeling sleep creep up on him. Maybe he could talk her into getting up to put the strap on the bed. Mitchie rolled off the bed and stood at the edge. Guo turned his head and found her glaring at him.

"Asshole!" The pillow came down on his face so fast only his eyelids reacted in time.

"Son of a bitch!" He got his hands up to protect his face but the next swing hit his stomach hard enough to force out an "oof!"

"Jackass!" Guo had pulled his legs up just in time to catch the third swing on his knees. He curled up on his side, arms around his head, laughing hysterically as pillow and verbal abuse continued.

When Mitchie paused to think of a new obscenity he grabbed her forearm and torqued it onto the bed like a wrench tightening a fist-sized bolt. "Let's talk," he said.

Mitchie tried to wiggle her arm free. She decided talking was her best option. "You're manipulating me."

Guo met her eyes calmly. "Yes."

"You're flaunting classified information just to mess with my head."

"Not just your head." Guo pulled her onto the bed. This time she didn't resist. "You see, my lovely cryptosexual, you have buttons. I like pushing your buttons. You like having your buttons pushed."

"I don't like being manipulated," said Mitchie.

"Actually you've been having a great time."

She smacked his shoulder. "Not that. I don't like . . ."

Guo filled it in for her. "Not being in control."

"Yeah."

"Well, you're still the officer, and the pilot, and the one carrying out the mission. That's a lot of control. You'll just have to accept you can't control everything." He wrapped his arms around her and pulled her close.

"I still think you're being an asshole." She relaxed into the cuddle. "How in the hell did you get us put on the classified message distribution anyway?"

Guo shifted uncomfortably against her back. "Well, you don't have a lot of friends at Redondo Field."

"I didn't enlist to make friends. So what?"

"So when I mentioned a possible, um, practical joke we could play on you I got a lot of cooperation."

"Seriously?" She could feel his shrug. "Okay, I guess I did piss some people off." *Besides the Admiral and the Inspector General and the people who were in my way.*

"I'm not pissed at you." He was starting to sound sleepy again.

"I'm not pissed at you either," said Mitchie. "Much."

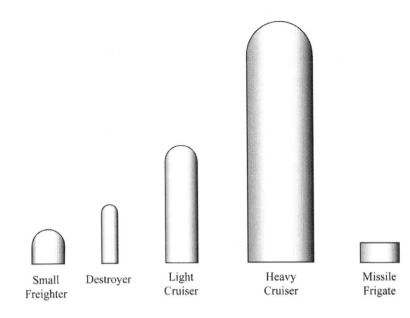

| Small Freighter | Destroyer | Light Cruiser | Heavy Cruiser | Missile Frigate |

Small Freighter: cheap flexible merchant ship. Can land anywhere and make long journeys with a full hold. Most analog ships are this type.

Destroyer: a small warship capable of agile maneuvers. Used for scouting and escorting larger ships.

Light Cruiser: conducts independent raids or holds the flanks in fleet engagements.

Heavy Cruiser: main firepower of the fleet. Has difficulty landing on planets.

Missile Frigate: a torch drive with some missile racks and minimal crew accommodations strapped to it. Can't land, endurance is only 2-3 weeks. Created to deploy maximum firepower with minimum construction time.

Chapter Five: Ballgown

Demeter, gravity 7.5 m/s²

Hiroshi's voice rang over the PA. "Skipper, the limo is here."

Schwartzenberger answered from the intercom next to the cargo hold airlock. "Thanks. You have the con. See you in a few days." He looked over his old crew, dressed in their best, and Bakhunin, in his normal. "Remember, we're here to let the Ambassador do his job. Be polite, do things their way, and don't mention the war. Let's go."

The oversized aircar waited at the base of the stairs. A pair of elegantly attired attendants stood ready to guide them to seats and provide drinks or anything else requested. "Miss has made a few minutes gap in her schedule, so we're taking you to her first," said the older one.

Endymion City's glittering rooftops flashed by. The junior attendant apologetically scanned everyone for weapons. Billy's replacement by Bakhunin was called in. When the drink offer was repeated the captain requested wine. The rest followed. Mitchie accepted a red but just touched it to her lips.

They flew out of the city proper before landing. The mansion was stone, klicks from any neighbor. Guo muttered a comment on the architecture. Mitchie didn't recognize half the words he'd said.

The attendants led them out to a gravel path between the front door and another landing circle. "There's Miss now," said one. She pointed at a descending aircar.

It touched down and popped a door open. Three bodyguards emerged and fanned out. Bobbie followed, looking just as she had in the hologram.

That must be her real face, thought Mitchie.

"You're here! You're here!" The teenage girl leapt on Captain Schwartzenberger with a hug. "Oh, I wish you'd been here sooner! My schedule is just ludicrous now. But if you could stay four days after the ball I can make time." She squeezed each member of the crew in turn. "Um, hello."

Ambassador Bakhunin smiled warmly. "Good morning. Billy Lee asked me to come in his place. I am Yuri."

Bobbie shook his hand. "I'm very pleased to meet you, Yuri. Welcome to Demeter."

"Thank you."

A woman with a datasheet out had followed Bobbie out of the aircar. She tugged gently on the girl's elbow.

Bobbie sighed and started walking toward the mansion. "I'll see you all at the ball!"

The attendants led them toward the aircar Bobbie had arrived in. One had their wineglasses on a tray. Once they'd taken off Mitchie asked, "Security shell game?"

"I'd think you'd understand the necessity," said the older attendant.

"I do," admitted Mitchie. "I just hadn't expected to be part of it."

"A very exuberant young lady," said Bakhunin.

"Miss has her ups and down," said the other attendant. "I'm glad you lot could make her happy for a bit."

Their destination was "Miss's Country House," somewhat larger and lonelier than the mansion they'd stopped at. The agenda for the next three days was laid out. First was fittings. The clothiers wanted to make sure the designs they'd based on their transmitted measurements actually fit.

Mitchie found herself in a second-floor sitting room overlooking a garden. The chairs were perfectly laid out for tea for four. Before she could identify the flowers on the wallpaper the parade burst in.

Six effete minions led carrying white clothes of varying size and identical flimsiness. Behind them followed their master. Demeter natives normally tried to walk as if their planet pulled the normal ten gravs humans were built for. Not this guy. He pranced. The way his hands dangled from his wrists made her think of a dog walking on its hind legs.

"I am Jesohn!" he proclaimed. "I have sworn to Miss that you shall be perfectly attired. And, Miss Long, we shall not fail her!"

"It's, um, Missus Kwan now, actually."

"Missus? No! You are no matron. You have youth, and fire! We shall display that, and your husband will kneel to thank me when he sees the result."

She could find nothing to say to that.

"Now this is only a structural prototype. We must ensure that they fit you, and fit each other." The minions had spread their burdens over the tables and chairs. Mitchie realized they were layers of a single outfit. All together they might be more modest than a jumpsuit. "I have prepared virtual designs of color and movement and texture. But first we must have shape."

Jesohn's fingertips fluttered. The minions scampered out, closing the door behind them. "Now strip and dress."

"Is there a dressing room I . . . ?"

His shrug waved from shoulders to wrists, leaving the hands still. "How can I know they fit properly if I do not know if they were donned properly?" He began studying an oil painting by the window.

When in Rome, thought Mitchie. She stripped off and picked up the smallest piece. She turned it over twice before identifying the proper openings. One foot lifted up to go into it.

"No! Left foot first!"

Dear God, she prayed, *If I get through this without killing him you owe me one guilt-free murder. Amen.*

***

Joshua Chamberlain's cargo hold faced east. The late morning sun poured through the half-open doors. Spacer Setta lay on a blanket in the pool of light.

The sight made Hiroshi pause on his way down the ladder. He'd been impressed by her looks in utility coveralls. Seeing her in a swimsuit made his heart pound harder than climbing this ladder would in twice the gravity.

But he didn't want to be caught staring at her from above. He worked his way down, keeping his bag from bumping the ladder.

She opened her eyes as his footsteps came close. "What's up?"

"I made lunch. Just sandwiches." He sat next to the blanket.

"Oh, you didn't have to."

Hiroshi shrugged. "I had to do something or the boredom will kill me." They'd knocked off most of the required maintenance for the week yesterday after the crew left.

She laughed. "This is going to be a rough assignment for you if you get bored that easily." She took a turkey sandwich from the selection.

"Maybe. I'll have to find a project to work on."

The sandwiches and fruit salad absorbed them for a few minutes.

Setta broke the silence. "Okay, the curiosity is killing me. Why the hell did you take a cutter under the bridge?"

"Um. Well . . . I wanted to be first in my class."

"By getting court-martialed?"

"That wasn't the—see, there were three of us with a shot at the number one slot. That meant any assignment you wanted after graduation. I was best at hitting the mission goals, Furlong was a little more precise than me, and Chang was close behind but beat us on ground school exams. So when Chief Sanchez said, 'I want a pilot who could take a cutter through the Gold Street Bridge' I thought that was my chance."

"So you stole a cutter and flew to Commerce City?"

"I didn't steal it. I was scheduled for solo practice time. I headed for Commerce and found the bridge. Had to go over on the first pass, there was a damn boat going under it. So I made a loop around the Exchange, came back, and went through the middle arch. Then straight back to the field."

"Wow."

"Fortunately Chief Sanchez said it in front of half the class so I had witnesses. And a Commander on the tribunal was a former cutter pilot, so he was impressed."

That got a laugh. "Not guilty on grounds of awesome?"

"I'll take it. At least I'm still in uniform."

"If you'd graduated first, would you have stayed with cutters?"

"No, I wanted a missile control pinnace." Hiroshi's stare seemed to look through the hull. "When a fleet fires missiles at a target ten million klicks away, the light lag is too long to control them. So they send a pinnace along to direct the final maneuvers. That's a job that makes a difference. One man against an enemy fleet."

The wistful look on his face made Setta want to cheer him up. "Hopefully we're making a difference here. Even if you don't get to do any fancy flying."

"Oh, they've done some real flying in this ship. You can find news reports about her going through the rings of Kronos. The captain has some stories about stuff on the trip to Old Earth. And they did something that pranged one of the turbines bad enough to need blades replaced but they won't talk about it."

***

The Dancing Master waxed ecstatic over the crew's experience in formal dance. Bakhunin had been to Fusion balls before. Schwartzenberger had taken Bing to a few on Bonaventure during his Senatorial sabbatical. Guo had taken a few lessons at Confucian Revival clubs. It was a "gentlemanly" skill.

When Mitchie's turn came she demonstrated the moves she'd picked up in Port District dance clubs. The Master closed his eyes. "Stop."

He stepped close to her and began a speech on "elegance" and "refinement" with too much fancy vocabulary for her to follow. Suddenly she remembered her first pre-dawn formation listening to the sergeant explain how he would smash the civilians into clay to build soldiers with. *This will be hell.*

The Master assigned each of them a personal instructor. Mitchie got two. They tag-teamed. One would dance with her while the other circled and called corrections. They switched every three tunes or when her heel landed on one's toes.

In the morning everyone had a "rough" of their outfit to wear for the lessons. Mitchie did like how the dress flared in the turns and twirls. The instructors she liked less. After the sixth time the satellite made a particular correction she flipped around to face him. "I know that's wrong, you don't need to remind me, telling me it's wrong again doesn't help me figure out how to do it right, so if you don't have anything useful to say just fucking shut up!"

Guo pushed between them. The instructor backed away from his glare. The other one tried to take Mitchie's hand to resume the dance. Guo waved him off.

"C'mon, love, let's find a quiet spot." The gilt 'Lesser Ballroom' had room for hundreds. The crew and dozen instructors were tucked into one corner. As they walked Mitchie cursed her instructors.

"Forget them," Guo said. "Pretend you've already killed them."

"Don't fucking tempt me."

Guo stopped them under a pearlescent chandelier. "Hey. Do you trust me?"

"More than anyone else in the universe."

"That's not a yes."

Mitchie shrugged.

"Well." Guo wore the wry smile of a man whose suspicion was confirmed. "Let's try this. Do you trust me to not want to intentionally hurt you or embarrass you?"

"Yes."

"Do you trust me to be competent enough to know where you should go next in the dance?"

She thought a moment. The instructors were all happy with *him*. "Yes."

"Then let me help you. I won't shove you around. Just let me guide you in the dance."

Just let you be in control. "All right."

"Let's practice a twirl. Lift up your hand."

She'd managed to learn this move yesterday. Mitchie assumed the pose. Instead of grasping her hand he laid his index finger across her palm.

"Move with me." The faintest of pressure led her through the twirl. Then he guided her into the reverse. She spun back at the same speed, losing contact with his finger as he slowed the tempo.

"Don't plan," he said. "Don't expect. Just be in the moment with me." He touched her palm again and pivoted her back and forth. Different angles, different speeds. Until she stuck to his lead.

Next he practiced a move where they went from facing each other to back to back, pulling their joined hands between them. They did it fingertip to fingertip until she could match a tempo change mid turn.

The Dancing Master came up as Mitchie practiced stepping forward and back to Guo's fingertip on her waist. "Mister and Missus Kwan? It's time to change for dinner."

"Dinner?" said Mitchie. "But . . . " She suddenly felt *very* hungry.

"I didn't dare interrupt you for lunch."

"Thank you, sir," said Guo. "We'll head for our rooms."

The first night's dinner had mixed the crew with some other Revelation Ball guests staying at the Country House. They were contemporaries of Bobbie, had never met Diskers before, and were clearly afraid of going the way of the kidnapper if they said something wrong.

Tonight they had different company. Three couples, the wives relaxed, the men in habitually alert postures. These people worked for a living, decided Mitchie. Or possibly fought. She read them as off-duty bodyguards.

Some how-are-you-liking-your-visit chatter went by as the servants poured wine. Then the oldest man, Samuel, stood and waved the servers out. After the door closed his took up a wine glass. "I should mention that I am the Family's head of security. My lieutenants and I wanted to join you tonight to thank you."

The other locals—and Bakhunin—stood to toast. "We failed Miss's mother. We've only once failed her. Thank you for doing our jobs for us. Thank you for saving her life. And thank you for doing right by John." They drank.

As they sat Captain Schwartzenberger lifted his glass. "To John Smith. He did more than his duty."

With a chorus of "John Smith" they all drank.

Samuel knocked on the table. The servers reentered, bearing salads and oven-warm bread.

Guo smiled as Mitchie began talking shop with their host. The analyst report on the Kronos Incident left her with many questions. Samuel willingly answered in exchange for details of the fight on the *Fives Full*.

When the servers came back to replace the salad bowls with soup ones Samuel's wife delightedly switched places with Mitchie. She recognized the slight panic in Guo's eyes and reintroduced herself.

"I'm Yvonne. And I know you're Guo. Quite as famous as your wife. More so among the intelligence types. They were very put out you knocked so many answers out of that one's head."

"Sorry." Interrogation hadn't occurred to him when he put the wrench into the traitor's skull.

"Do you do a lot of head-breaking?" she asked.

Guo's palm tingled with the remembered crunch of breaking bone transmitted through the hammer's handle. "Not when I can avoid it."

He heard Mitchie saying "—went off in his hand. Right next to the ribs. By the look on his face he never knew it."

Yvonne's next question was about dancing. Soon he was explaining the differences between the Upper Mode dances and the traditional ones the Confucian Revival brought back.

When he paused Samuel was saying "—so multiple bodyguards are death on cover identities. They're a big sign saying 'research who this is.' A single one can blend in. More or less."

Yvonne talked over Mitchie's response with, "How many times have you been to Demeter?"

"This is my fourth. A simple cargo run, the Kronos trip, and then we were caught in the last AI attack. Now we're here for a party."

Yvonne shivered. "That was so horrifying. Usually the Navy chases an attack off in deep space. That one came so close we could see explosions from the ground. People panicked, screaming they'd kill themselves if the AIs took the planet." She took a calming breath. "I hope you stayed clear of the fighting."

Guo said, "We were closer than we liked but didn't get attacked. Were you in the countryside then?"

"Yes, there's a village south of here were many of the staff's families live." She described life there. It sounded as quiet and private as life in the Fusion could be.

In the morning there was another round of fittings before dance lessons. Mitchie watched them teach Guo the advanced moves. After each he came over and led her through them.

After lunch came donning The Dress. Jesohn and his minions waited for her in the sitting room. By now he'd broken her of shyness. The minions stripped off the "rough" outfit and slid the layers onto her. Once the gloves reached her wrists Jesohn snapped, "Turn!"

Minions scattered. Mitchie pivoted just fast enough to make the skirt float.

Jesohn clutched his chest. "Perfection! Perfection! A true blossom! Misha, let her see herself." A minion put a box on the wall. It unfolded to a floor to ceiling mirror. "Behold the perfection! My career is at an end; never shall I surpass this. I am exhausted. I must rest." The minions bore him out, twittering comfort and praise.

Mitchie watched the parade go out of sight before turning to the mirror. She had to admit the gown was lovely. On someone else it would even be flattering. But on her . . .

Well, Demeter fashion apparently considered "support" something for matrons. Or maybe even something for higher-gravity worlds. Maybe a life in only seven gravs let the local women get away with these outfits. *I wish I'd skipped showers on Corcyra.*

She turned back and forth before the mirror. Threads of color ran across her horizontally, parallel except where an imperfection in her body distorted them. *You'd think they'd both sag the same amount.* Hitching up her left shoulder evened the line a bit.

The effect worked better on the skirt. When she swung her hips to twirl it the threads parted, clear fabric between them revealing the bright but less sparkly colors of the underskirt. *Hopefully I'll fit in and they'll overlook me.* She'd always gotten a lot of mileage out of being overlooked.

The minions had left the door open. Mitchie realized she was being watched. Guo walked in. "Do you like it?" he asked.

She thought he was asking about his suit, and answered "Yes."

The tailor had chosen to display Guo's shoulders, not conceal them. The fit followed tightly to his hips. The lapels stood straight out, forbidding hugs. The collar came almost up to his earlobes. Purple and blue fringes, as long as her fingers, hung from the collar and continued down both sleeves to the cuffs. Silk ribbons in the same colors made a complex knot at his throat. Yes, she liked it. She wanted to see him twirled or swung.

Guo fulfilled part of Jesohn's prophecy by dropping to his knees before her. She caught his hands as they came up. "Behave," she said. "This is fragile. Leave it be for the next eight hours then you can rip it to shreds."

Her husband lifted his hot eyes up to meet hers. "I'll hold you to that."

Crap, he means that. Maybe Jesohn could make her a replacement. Guo could afford it.

***

The ball was in the "Great Room" of the "Family House" in Endymion City. The crew were among the first to arrive. Bakhunin commented that normally this would make them low-status guests but he thought this time it reflected how terrified the attendants were of delivering them late.

The buffet tables helped them pass the wait. Guo found a local willing to identify the fruits that couldn't grow on Akiak—most of the selection—and show which parts shouldn't be eaten. Mitchie made sure he didn't eat enough to keep them from dancing.

As the ballroom filled up the Diskers gathered together. Bakhunin joked that they instinctively herded in response to predator pressure. "And the Fuzies aren't?" asked Schwartzenberger.

"Oh, they do, sir, they do. I've been watching. It's the best way to spot the predators." The diplomat smiled. "Who are my prey."

Guo studied the outfits. The crew had been dressed stylishly enough to fit in, but the display of jewelry made it clear where the money was. "The Fusion loves to talk about their social equality but I don't see it here," he said.

Captain Schwartzenberger replied, "Every group of humans has somebody on top. If you can't tell who it is listen for the one talking about how equal they all are and that's it."

A servant in an orange-trimmed jacket urged them to a spot by the Grand Staircase. The crowd drew in. A man in orange livery walked onto the bottom step and turned to face everyone.

"Good evening!" he projected. "Thank you all for joining us for this magnificent occasion." He continued with praise for the crowd, a professional stalling until the actors were ready for the curtain to go up.

Mitchie tried to spot when he heard the go command, but the MC shifted so smoothly it seemed part of a script. "Stakeholders! Directors! Admirals! Excellencies! Ladies and Gentlemen! I reveal to you Miss Guenivere Claret!" Bobbie and her father stepped out from behind the screen at the top of the stairs.

Mitchie joined in the applause. The French pronunciation threw her for a moment, which eased the shock. The analysts had put Sebastian Claret as the number five candidate for "Bobbie's" father. The chief argument against him had been 'A Claret heir with only one bodyguard? Seriously?' She looked forward to beating that analyst with Samuel's statements on security in practice.

Guenivere and her father descended the wide staircase hand in hand. At the bottom the MC introduced her officially to people she already knew. Mitchie recognized most of them. *One bomb in this room and every organization on Demeter will need a new boss.* The Planetary Coordinator, thankfully, wasn't among them. A circle of camerabots hovered over Guenivere. Mitchie recognized the logos of the top Fusion news sites.

The mob blocked Mitchie's view of Guenivere most of the time. The camerabots made her movements clear. She came their way sooner than expected.

"My dear friends. I owe you more than I can ever say." Her father had introduced the great ones of Demeter to her. Now she introduced the crew to him.

Mitchie felt her hand squeezed tightly between Guenivere's as she was brought forward. Sebastian took her hand in both of his as well, but only said, "Thank you."

Bakhunin was introduced as "representing William Lee."

The attendants swept them away as their moment with the host and hostess ended. "Miss's time is spoken for the rest of the evening. We hope you will enjoy yourselves. Please call us if you have any questions or desires."

Then they were left alone.

"Claret," said Guo. "And he only gave us a new converter. Could've supplied a new ship."

"I suspect he would have if there'd been a way to keep it from being traced," said Captain Schwartzenberger.

Bakhunin said, "I'd been surprised at how many VIPs were here. Now I'm surprised by who's missing."

"Enough business! This is a party," said Bing. "Young man, let's demonstrate how to enjoy ourselves to these worriers." She took Guo's arm to lead him into the dance.

The fringes on Guo's jacket made him spectacular in the swings and swoops, Mitchie decided. She'd missed the additional fringe on the jacket's sharply-angled tails.

When the pair came back after that dance to collect their own partners Mitchie went willingly. The early dances were easier than most of what the Dancing Master had forced on them. She enjoyed herself.

Up close she realized Guo's suit fabric wasn't grey. It was black, adorned with a random pattern of snowflakes at their actual size. Guo explained, "He wanted to reflect my homeland. After I described Akiak I got this."

Four sets later she needed a drink. They emerged to find Sebastian Claret in conversation with the captain and mate.

"She's not much, but she's mine. And that gives me the freedom to take the jobs I please," said Schwartzenberger.

"Freedom. Of course. That is something I cannot give. I'm glad you've found it yourself," said the trillionaire. "Ah, Guo, Michigan," he said. "I've been explaining my eternal thanks to your officers. Tell me, what do you most want?"

Mitchie chose diplomacy. "Peace."

Guo nodded in agreement.

"Something else I cannot buy. But I wish for peace as well. Perhaps I have not emphasized that enough. I shall correct that tonight." Claret let himself be pulled out of the conversation by the circling muck-de-mucks wanting his attention.

"What did he offer you?" asked Guo.

"A hundred-kay TEU circuit liner," answered Schwartzenberger.

Mitchie almost choked on her drink. That was roughly two thousand times the cargo capacity of their ship.

"Steady work," Guo said.

"I'd drink myself to death from boredom inside a year."

Bing sniffed. "Some people can't recognize a good thing when they hear it."

"I'd never get back to the Disconnect in it," said the captain. "We don't produce enough cargo to fill it regularly."

An attendant broke in to make introductions—"Stakeholder Liu Ping, of Tiantan"—before fading away.

The Stakeholder merely made small talk until the music changed. "Oh, I love this waltz. Mr. Kwan, may I ask your wife for this dance?"

Guo traded looks with Mitchie and agreed. She said yes when the Stakeholder asked her.

Once they were on the dance floor the Stakeholder said, "I'm delighted to meet you personally, Lieutenant Long."

So much for undercover work, she thought. "How else would you meet me, sir?"

"Oh, I've already met you professionally. You were the subject of a quarter of the last Justice Committee meeting."

"I don't see how I'd be of interest to them." As opposed to Defense and Intelligence, who she'd been trying to piss off for years.

"War crimes are under our jurisdiction. We were discussing whether to indict you." By accident or malice this coincided with a twirl. Mitchie obediently let him spin her about, her spine crawling at turning her back to the man.

"For what?" she asked.

"Bonaventure allowed a delegation to visit the prisoners it's holding. A Commander Wentworth made a detailed report about your treatment of him."

"Not having seen the report I can't comment on its accuracy. I do know he is physically unharmed, unlike the majority of his shipmates.

Stakeholder Ping snarled, "He is psychologically damaged to the point of having panic attacks in confined spaces."

"Is that from his conversation with me or having his ship blown up around him?"

The dance shifted to back up the floor. He shifted verbal tracks as well. "The Geneva Conventions set rules for the treatment of prisoners."

"As I explained to the Commander," said Mitchie, "neither the Fusion nor the Disconnected Worlds are signatories to that."

"It's still the traditional rules for handling prisoners."

As long as we're being rude . . . , thought Mitchie. "There was a centuries-long tradition of not dropping nuclear bombs on towns you're not at war with. Once you start breaking traditions where do you stop?"

The stakeholder used another twirl and some turns to collect himself. "AI research is an immediate threat to all of humanity. It has to be stopped."

"AIs are a threat. Research is the way to beat them. If you want to fight AIs, there's plenty closer than Akiak."

"Yes, they could land here tomorrow and kill us all."

Mitchie just laughed at his paranoia.

Ping declared, "We need to unite humanity so we can all fight the AI threat together. Not split in different directions, having to protect ourselves from human traitors."

Mitchie gritted her teeth. She kept her voice low and stern. "If you try to swallow the Disconnect I expect you'll choke to death." The music stopped. People began to choose partners for the next set. "Please return me to my husband."

The Stakeholder did so silently and walked off.

"Enjoy yourself?" asked Guo.

"No," she answered. "Have you seen the Ambassador? I need to talk to him."

***

It was Setta's turn to cook dinner. This time she'd put real spices in the vindaloo but Hiroshi didn't flinch.

They had the local news up on a datasheet. The Claret Revelation Ball was the top story on the gossip channels. The crew had only shown up in one shot of them being introduced to the Clarets. Setta kept freezing views of the dancing to see if they could spot them.

The airlock buzzer sounded from below.

They exchanged glances. Neither had a guess what this could be.

Hiroshi walked over to the locked cabinet. A few turns of the dial opened it. He reached past the whiskey bottles to take out two pistols. He handed one to Setta.

"Are you sure we need this?" she asked.

"No. It's just in case." He checked the load, chambered a round, took the safety off, and pocketed the weapon.

Setta sighed and followed him, leaving her safety on.

The buzzer kept sounding as they climbed down the ladder. Hiroshi sent Setta to the hinge side as he opened the inner airlock door. He stepped in and opened the outer door.

Strobe lights dazzled him. "Jeb Renling, Daily Packet. Is it true your ship took Guenivere Claret to Kronos? Were you hired by the kidnapping syndicate? Who in your crew knew the attempt was planned?"

Hiroshi pulled back on the hatch. One of the news crew grabbed the outer edge and pulled it open with better leverage.

"Was Captain Schwartzenberger bribed to rendezvous with the kidnapper?"

The reporter was visible as a black shape in front of the bright lights. Hiroshi looked at him and said, "We will not be answering questions at this time. Please leave at once."

"What reward did Trillionaire Claret give you for saving his daughter?"

The other newsie leaned on the outer hatch, forcing it open all the way. Hiroshi let go before it pulled him off balance.

"Was the kidnapper killed to cover up who hired him?"

He stepped back through the inner hatchway and pulled on the hatch.

The newsies leapt forward to push back on it. Setta added her weight to push it shut.

The hatch stopped against Jeb Renling's golden leather shoe, barely scuffing it.

"What are you hiding, spacer? Who are you trying to protect?"

Hiroshi leaned his left shoulder into the hatch and pulled out the pistol with his right hand. "You are trespassing on this ship. Leave or I will use lethal force."

Jeb's voice kept its full confidence. "That's not loaded."

Hiroshi racked the slide, sending a perfectly good cartridge bouncing off the bulkhead.

Suddenly the hatch wasn't being pushed toward them.

Hiroshi kicked Jeb in the ankle hard enough to push his shoe clear of the coaming. The hatch slammed closed. Setta spun the wheel to lock it.

"Oh, thank you for dealing with them," said Setta. "I wouldn't have known what to say."

"I dealt with some while I was on trial. Bonaventure's reporters are politer, though." He cursed. "All I can see is purple flashes."

"Relax, you'll be better soon." Setta called Spaceport Security, who promised to remove the reporters to the border of the hardpad.

"I hope they didn't get any pictures of me."

Setta did a quick search. "You look good. Stern. I like it, I'm keeping a copy."

"Oh, crap. What did they say?"

"'Renegade Disker Threatens Reporter With Death to Protect Claret Secrets.' That's about it, just the headline and some stills."

"Oh, God. The captain's going to kill me." As his vision cleared he started looking for the cartridge he'd ejected.

***

Mitchie opened her eyes. Enough sunlight peeked through the curtains to see the room. For a moment she didn't recognize it. Then she realized the ceiling light hadn't changed, it just had a quarter of her camisole hanging from it.

Last night she'd saved the ball gown by taking it off while Guo was in the bathroom. She'd left on the inner layers as a sacrifice to him. He'd seemed appreciative.

She stretched her arms. Standing up seemed like too much trouble. Guo snuggled up to her. "Hey," she said.

Guo opened his eyes. "Hey."

"You're a sleepy-head."

"Yeah. Are you sleepy?"

"Yes," she said.

"Too sleepy?"

Mitchie giggled. "No."

The datasheet on the nightstand announced, "Voice only connection request from Alois Schwartzenberger."

They both cursed. Mitchie picked it up and said, "Accept. Good morning, sir."

"Morning. We need to talk about things. We're having breakfast in the Verdigris Nook. Twenty minutes."

"We'll be there, sir."

"Good." The captain cut the connection.

"I can get dressed in ten minutes," said Guo.

Mitchie giggled again.

***

They were last to arrive. Nobody remarked on it. Bing sat next to Schwartzenberger, as usual. *Those two get along better divorced than most of the old married couples I know*, thought Mitchie.

Once the servants finished loading the table Bakhunin started talking. "In one sense my mission is a complete success. I've had hours of direct access to the highest officials in the Fusion. Intimate conversations. *In vino veritas.* More than I'd dared hope for on the way here."

The diplomat drained his orange juice. "In the most important sense I am a complete failure. They want war."

"Why against us?" asked Bing. "It's the AIs they're afraid of."

"Terrified indeed, ma'am," answered Bakhunin. "So terrified they don't dare attack the Betrayer worlds. And they can't bear to sit still any more. So they attack us. Because they think they can beat us." He refilled his glass three-quarters from the juice pitcher.

"Beating them didn't change their mind about that?" said Schwartzenberger.

"No. There's different reactions." He topped off his glass from a flask. "Some say fluke. Or treachery. Or proof we're too dangerous to be left free." A teaspoon stirred the morning cocktail. "The most optimistic say it's a sign that when the Disconnected Worlds are properly harnessed humans can smash the AIs." He drank.

"How do we change their minds?" asked Guo.

"I don't know." The diplomat stared into his glass. "They are so determined. If we could slaughter them with no losses of our own we might lose heart to keep killing before we broke their will." He swallowed more spiked juice.

"The Stakeholders may be determined, sir, but their troops break more easily," stated Mitchie.

"Yes, a few were quite angry with you for proving that. I tried seeing if they would bargain over it but they considered it a moral issue."

Bing gasped.

Bakhunin smiled at her. "She's a lovely young lady, but if acquiescing in her execution would save an entire planet I'm obligated to make the exchange. There's no need to sell out our principles. The Fusion isn't buying."

Mitchie slapped her hand onto Guo's wrist to keep him from rising from his chair. "Thank you for your honesty, sir," she said.

Bakhunin shrugged. "In honesty, I am a failure. While we stay on this world I shall slam my head into the bricks every chance I get. When it is time to leave I will go quietly." He lifted his glass again.

Captain Schwartzenberger said, "I researched our safe passage. It's a 'Petition of Personal Privilege.' Only a tenth of the Council of Stakeholders had to sign to make it law. So any larger number can revoke it."

"How many does it take for an indictment?" asked Mitchie.

"A majority. So it's easier for them to just lock us down until they're done arguing over you." The captain's lips quirked as he said that. Mitchie didn't share the humor.

"I'll write an apology to Bobbie, I mean Guenivere, for leaving early," said Bing.

"Please," said the captain. "I'll arrange for a car to take us to the spaceport in two hours. Everyone have your stuff together."

***

The cargo doors were open when the aircar dropped them off. Hiroshi and Setta bent over their datasheets, enjoying the fresh air and unconstrained wireless. They popped to attention as the captain came up the stairs.

"Anything to report?" asked Schwartzenberger.

"Reaction mass and fuel topped off. Fresh food delivered last night. All inspections good," rattled off Hiroshi.

"Good. I have the watch. Have both of you gotten the mate's briefing on leave in the Fusion?" Both spacers nodded. "Then you're on leave until midnight. We're going to lift in the morning."

At his wave they scampered up the ladder.

"Permission to be lazy, sir?" called Guo. He'd already hooked a basket onto the cargo hold crane.

The captain answered by dropping his duffle bag in the basket. Then he sat down in Hiroshi's chair with his own datasheet. The flight plan requested the earliest non-emergency lift-off, twenty four hours ahead, and went straight to the Coatlicue gate. He expected approval in a few hours.

The datasheet lit up with the face of a grey-haired woman in a tan uniform. "Good morning. I'm Portmaster Tuen. Is this Captain Schwartzenberger?"

"Yes," he answered, not bothering to conceal his surprise.

"I understand you've been too busy to follow the news the past few days—"

Ah, fame, thought Schwartzenberger.

"—so I wanted to explain why your flight plan is being rejected. The Navy has issued a grounding order for all civilian traffic. Several Betrayer vessels jumped into the system from Swakop. Until they're removed the Navy wants all noncombatants out of the line of fire." The Portmaster smiled sympathetically. "So I hope you'll be understanding of the delay."

The captain said, "I see. Yes, I'll have to catch up. Is there any estimate for when they'll lift the order?"

"I'm afraid not. There are still ships jumping in. I can reserve a conditional lift-off slot for you. I have one open at five hours after flight resumes."

"We'll take that, thank you."

"Done. I'm sorry for the delay but I do hope you enjoy your extra time on Demeter," said the Portmaster.

"Thank you. We will."

Captain Schwartzenberger went up the ladder. He found Bing in the galley. The newbies had left it clean enough but she wanted everything arranged to her standard. "Did you send that note to Bob, Guenivere yet?" he asked.

"No," said Bing. "I wanted to polish it some."

"Good. Change of plans." The door to Mitchie and Guo's cabin was open. "All hands on deck!"

When all four of them were in the galley he explained the grounding order.

Guo pulled up a news summary on his datasheet. "There's a probe, but they're all in the outer planets. Nowhere near the shipping lanes."

"It's paranoia. That's the military for you," said the captain. "Anyway—new plan. We need to launch on five hours' notice. Today we reinspect, make sure the ship is good. Then we'll go to two on watch, rest on leave. Everyone sleeps on the ship. And if this goes on long enough we may let Guenivere take us to a play or something."

***

Mitchie and Guo agreed to take turns picking what they'd do on leave. This became Guo selecting a show or museum and Mitchie choosing the restaurant. After an experimental lunch left their tongues numb from too much spice she decided on dinner at a Port District dive that made food simple enough to resemble Akiak home cooking.

Partway through the meal Mitchie spotted Hiroshi and Setta at another table. She would have waved to them if either had looked around. Instead they were focused on each other. By the gestures Hiroshi was telling pilot stories. Setta laughed appreciatively.

When she pointed them out Guo said, "I'm not surprised. They were locked into the ship together for over a hundred hours. It was fall in love or kill each other."

Mitchie laughed and had another bite of her fish. The lemon flavor was strong—Akiak couldn't grow anything tarter than apples—but she liked it. Guo speculated about the origin of some artifacts at that afternoon's museum. She suggested some ways to research them.

She'd decided against dessert. The newbies hadn't. She saw the server deliver it: an oversized ice cream shake with two straws.

Mitchie said, "I can't take it any more. That's just too sappy." She walked over to their table.

The youngsters didn't notice her. She came to attention and snapped out in her deepest voice, "Is this professional behavior?"

Setta and Hiroshi instantly came to attention. Hiroshi's straw had stuck to his lips as he stood. He spat it out onto the table.

Setta said, "No excuse, ma'am!"

The dive's noise level kept this a private discussion. The neighboring tables were more annoyed by the knocked over chairs.

Guo came up behind Mitchie and wrapped his arms around her. "Relax, kids," he said. "We're just pulling your chain. You're off duty and *Joshua Chamberlain* doesn't have a fraternization rule." He lifted Mitchie off her feet and turned around.

She didn't resist. It was hard enough to not fall down laughing.

Once they were outside she leaned against the wall of the restaurant and laughed herself sick.

"That was mean," said Guo.

"I know, but did you see the look on their faces? Like teenagers caught kissing."

"Yeah. I think it's cute."

"She can do better. But, yeah, cute couple." She looked at Guo's unamused expression. "Am I an evil person?"

He pulled her to him. "Yes. You're *my* evil person." The kiss kept going on.

A Fuzie complained, "Don't block the sidewalk" as he maneuvered around them. They ignored him.

Their datasheets harmonizing on "Blocking walkways is anti-social behavior, punishable by—" pulled them out of the kiss. Guo guided her down the sidewalk, keeping with the flow.

"Think we can find a quiet place to snog around here?" Mitchie asked.

"How about I take you back to our quarters and screw you silly?"

"Okay." Giggle.

***

The cargo hold airlock was locked. Mitchie muttered as she turned the number wheels. "This is such a waste of time. I could get through this in three minutes without the combo."

"Unlocking it triggers a beep on the PA," said Guo.

"So? You can hear the hatch open from the galley anyway."

"The beep's loud enough to get Bing out of the captain's cabin and into her own without anyone seeing."

Mitchie stopped dead. "Seriously? How do you know?"

Guo gently pushed her out of the airlock. "I once skipped leave because I had a cold, but they thought I was off the ship."

"Huh. So why haven't they remarried?"

"Dunno. Never had the nerve to ask."

"Oh, God. Now those two. This is turning into a love boat," complained Mitchie.

"I don't mind." He held her hand as they walked across the hold. At the base of the ladder he let go. "You go first."

Mitchie stuck out her tongue at him. "Fine, but don't get a crick in your neck. I have plans."

***

The next day one of Guenivere's meetings was cancelled. She promptly swept up the crew in her aircar, leaving Hiroshi and Setta locked in again. Mitchie noticed they didn't complain.

The teenager cheerfully explained her good fortune. "He runs a major subsidiary so it would be a protocol breach for me to meet with any of the lower executives before him. But he's having union trouble—they're pushing for three eight hour days instead of four six hour ones—and I'm not welcome at that meeting. So now it's playtime!"

A few minutes discussion sent the aircar into the Attic Hills, one of Demeter's Protected Wilderness areas. She'd listed several other treats but seeing "the spot I go for beauty" intrigued them.

It was a tall waterfall in a narrow valley. There was no place the aircar could land without damaging plants, so they hopped out as it hovered. Two of her bodyguards led the way down the trail. Another walked with her. A pair ended the parade. There were more in the aircar, which circled protectively.

The only gap in protection Mitchie saw was not having anyone out on the flanks. The terrain made that impractical anyway.

The trail ended in a sloping dell ten meters above the rushing stream. Guenivere stood at the edge, making her security twitch. Now that they were out of the trees it was a beautiful sight. A narrow band of water came out of a cleft in the hilltop, falling straight down over a hundred meters. It poured over a jumble of rocks then rushed out whitely through a deep-cut bed. Grass and moss lined the overhanging banks. The trees going up the side of the valley wore their summer best. The hills blocked the sun. Only the top of the waterfall glowed before falling into shadow.

"Good, we're here in plenty of time," said Guenivere. She invited her guests to lay on the grass and chat while they waited, though she didn't say for what. She had questions for her rescuers, ones specific enough to show her father's influence had obtained detailed dossiers on each of them. Some questions hurt more than she realized. Guo jumped in to talk about *Jefferson Harbor's* cargo fire, sparing the captain.

"And Michigan . . ." Guenivere turned shy. "Is it true you're a secret agent?"

"No," answered Mitchie. "I'm just an agent. No secrets left."

"Do you think you made a difference?"

Yes, she considered saying, *I was instrumental in destroying your Navy's best ship and killing several thousand people, some of them from Demeter.* "Everything's uncertain in intelligence work. I just do my duty as best I can."

Guenivere nodded then looked at the waterfall. "It's almost time." The sun had crept farther down the waterfall. Now it approached the spray at the bottom.

Everyone watched as the spray threw out a rainbow. First a fragment arced out. It grew until it spanned the valley, a perfect spread of colors.

"Thank you," said Captain Schwartzenberger. "That's lovely."

Guenivere nodded and kept watching.

"Miss, Director Singh has confirmed for dinner," said a bodyguard.

"Of course," said Guenivere. The parade went back up to board the aircar.

***

Two more days of being grounded eroded Schwartzenberger's patience. "It's so damn stupid! If they're afraid of an attack on the planet they should be ordering us off it so they have less to protect. Grounding civilian traffic is bureaucratic—"

Michigan's datasheet chimed with a connection request. She grabbed the excuse to escape the captain's rant. Once safely in her cabin she pressed ACCEPT. Chetty Meena's face appeared on the sheet. *Maybe I should've checked who was calling first.*

"Hello, Michigan. It's good to see you again," said the analyst.

"Chet. You're looking good. It's been a while." It wasn't the first time Mitchie had been back to his planet since they met either. Why was he contacting her now?

"Are you free for dinner tonight? I'd like to talk with you about some things."

"I'm married now." Mitchie didn't think he was asking for a date, the body language was wrong. But best to get that out up front.

"Oh. Um, congratulations. Bring him along. I'd be happy to meet him. And another good mind could be useful."

"So this is business, not pleasure?" asked Mitchie.

"I was hoping for both. But if it has to be one, business. My business." Chetty analyzed AI threats for the Fusion Navy. DCC Intelligence gave the reports she'd stolen from him high ratings.

Fusion Counter-Intelligence could be setting a trap for her. Better to know for sure. "We'd be delighted to come. Where do you want to eat?"

"The Institute has a lovely patio on the west side. Several restaurants deliver there."

Mitchie downgraded the trap hypothesis. FCI could be crude but they'd come up with a better site than Chet's office. "I'll grab my husband and we'll head over."

***

The Operational Analysis Institute didn't skimp on overhead. The patio had wooden furniture, padded chairs, and barbots supplying drinks. Lush trees scattered the light of the setting sun. To Mitchie's relief, Guo and Chet finished introducing themselves without finger-breaking handshakes or any other dominance rituals.

Once food selections were out of the way Mitchie asked, "What's the occasion? You're too tense for a social visit."

Chetty let out a nervous chuckle. "I'm under orders. The director told us all to find some better explanations or find somebody who could. You have a different way of looking at things. I'm just glad you're on Demeter."

"I'm not," said Mitchie. "I've seen enough AI attacks to last me the rest of my life."

"Are they going to attack Demeter?" asked Guo. "The news is very vague."

"I'll answer that," said Chetty. "I need to tell you so you can help. But there's some paperwork first."

The forms appeared on their datasheets. Mitchie gleefully perjured herself by promising to never share Fusion Navy data with any unauthorized individual. The system accepted her promise. Her identity must still be filtering through the Fusion's chain of command. Guo thumbprinted where she did without reading it.

"Thank you. Let me show you the operational situation." Chetty's datasheet projected a map of Demeter's system. Brightly colored markers swarmed on the edge. "A massive swarm from Swakop jumped in at twice the normal radius. They're just sitting on Coeus' leading Trojan point fiddling with asteroids."

Guo frowned. "Could they be dropping a dinosaur killer?"

"No. They're moving them, but not far. We think they're building something but can't figure out what. So if you have *any* ideas we need to hear them." Chetty started an animation. Asteroids were pulled from their orbits, parked tens of thousands of klicks away, then disassembled into growing disks. They were in a rough cylinder, narrower at one end.

Mitchie and Guo studied the images as they repeated. *Dots. A whole bunch of dots to connect*, she thought. She turned the datasheet to view it from different angles. *I have seen something like this.*

She looked up into the trees to try to pull the memory. Cold, just visiting. One of the stops on her shuttle route. The northernmost, Morainetown. Which stayed connected to the planetary net with . . . "It's a paraboloid antenna," said Mitchie.

"Antennas are wire, or flat surfaces," said Chetty, his face twisted in confusion.

Guo had lit up when she named it. "It fits," he said. "Technically the paraboloid is a reflector. The antenna sits at the focus." He pointed at a cluster of dots at the narrow end. "There. It transmits radio waves which get focused into a narrow beam by the reflector."

"Where is it pointed?" demanded Mitchie.

Chetty ran a quick calculation. "Near here. Aha. Demeter will pass through the axis of the shape in six days." He took a deep breath. "It's an info attack. They'll be beaming subversion code at our network."

The Diskers nodded agreement.

"I'd better call in your idea."

"Don't name us," said Mitchie.

Guo added, "Just give us the money."

Chetty smiled and contacted his director. "Sir, I have a possible explanation." He briskly described the concept.

"Good thinking, Chet. I'll take that straight to the Navy."

"Thank you, sir." When his datasheet went dark Chetty looked up at them. "Well, we'll see if the Navy takes it seriously." A deliverybot scooted up to the table. Chetty took out the trays and served everyone.

Dinner conversation stayed with harmless topics. Chetty was fascinated by how different Mitchie and Guo's childhoods had been. Akiak didn't have the total connectivity of a Fusion world. Communities developed quirks and traditions of their own.

He was most amazed that Guo's town existed at all. "There was really arsenic in the water?"

"Some," answered Guo. "You'd have to drink lots of it raw to get poisoned. Naming the town Arsenic Creek warned all the newcomers to be careful."

"Wasn't there someplace safer to live?"

Guo shrugged. "There's plenty of places with clean water where you'd starve or freeze in the winter. The lead mine made enough money for us to survive."

They watched Chet try to wrap his mind around the idea of working to stay alive, instead of receiving more life guaranteed with your stipend deposit. "But, drinking bad water . . ."

"We filtered it," said Guo.

"Also, they wanted to stunt their kids' growth," quipped Mitchie. "It let them fit into the mines better."

"You'd have been perfect for the mines," shot back her husband.

Chetty distracted them with an offer of dessert.

The trio dawdled over their cheesecake, glancing at Chetty's datasheet in hopes it would light up with a response to their idea. The actual answer came from above.

Demeter street lights drowned out most of the stars. There were still dozens visible above the patio. Mitchie noticed the new lights first. She looked up at the flicker at the edge of her vision. The first blue plume was joined by others until they outnumbered the stars.

The men followed Mitchie's gaze up. "I guess they agree," said Guo.

Chetty held his datasheet over his head to capture the sight. "Agree, and scared by it." He put the sheet back on the table and did a calculation. "That's the Demeter Home Squadron. A visible symbol of the Navy's determination to protect us. Really it's ships that just started their shakedown, or need an overhaul, or are waiting to be scrapped. It's where they put spacers no captain wants. The dregs. Now they're headed for the Trojans at fifty gravs." Chetty drank down the rest of his wine. "Damn I wish I was going with them."

"Why aren't you?" asked Guo.

Chetty thumped his chest. "Heart. I failed my recruiting physical. There's a valve that will blow out if I take more than twenty gravs of acceleration."

"They wouldn't fix that? It's gotta be easier than a sex change." Which was free for Fusion citizens with a one month waiting period.

"If they screw up a sex change you just go back next month and have them put in a new set of plumbing. Heart repairs they have to get right the first time."

"Ah."

"I'm saving up. When I have enough for a surgeon's fee and indemnity I'll get the fix and sign up." He watched the plumes move across the sky. "If we're still here for me to get it."

Chapter Six: Duty

The Navy stayed vague about the progress of their assault on the AI transmitter. If they intended to calm the public they failed. The news that Swakop's incursion merited a full fleet deployment, so soon after the massive attack from Ushuaia, had all of Demeter's citizens on edge.

The crew felt the tension on the street. They stuck to the Port District for their outings or just stayed on the ship. The Fusion spacers tolerated Diskers more than the natives but still treated them as outsiders. Full access to Demeter's data network kept the crew from being bored on the ship.

The wait was worse for Mitchie and Guo. They'd—well, she'd—decided not to share Chetty's six day estimate with the rest of the crew. They knew nothing could happen in the first couple of days. The Fusion Navy had to gather its forces before engaging the AI.

Each day after that the lack of news became more frustrating. On the fourth Mitchie was desperate enough to call Chetty. He tersely refused to talk to her. Apparently someone at OAI had made the connection between "Mitchie, Chetty's friend" and "Michigan Long, notorious Disker spy."

Day Six opened with the Navy declaring "substantial progress in operations to neutralize AI activity." Mitchie's trawl of social media found an upsurge in casualty notifications. She hinted to the rest that it was a good day to stay close to the ship. They complied. Even Bakhunin took a day off from visiting his new acquaintances from the ball.

Lunch and dinner were delivered to the ship. Everyone was watching their own data sheets in the galley when the announcement came in. Every datasheet simultaneously played, "SPECIAL WARNING: A data infection has been detected. Shut down any autonomous system exhibiting unusual behavior. Some data channels will be shut down as a precaution. Report data incursions to the code police. Stay calm." Their shows resumed.

"At least the entertainment channels are still up," said Hiroshi.

Mitchie hunted through the undernews. A strong and complex radio signal was coming from the Coeus Trojans. The AI had connected Chetty's dots. Amateur experts pushed a theory that the AI wanted to reprogram bots and autofacs. Professionals were too busy to contribute to the discussion.

The Civil Defense Minister ordered antennas disabled but too many were integral to their structures. Markets were running out of metal foil as people tried to shield themselves.

She realized Demeter's network was disintegrating. Infection reports went unconfirmed as system operators broke connections in response to every rumor. The night side of the planet, in line of sight of the transmitter, felt it worst. The sun had set on Endymion City's spaceport two hours ago.

Mitchie flung her datasheet across the galley. It scratched across one of the painted flowers on the wall. Bing frowned at her. Mitchie snarled, "Goddammit, I can't find any solid information on what's going on!"

Guo put his hand on her shoulder. "We don't need to. Our mission is to take the ambassador home with his report. More data is nice. But we don't need it."

Mitchie stayed pissed. "It's my *job* to collect info."

Her husband talked her into watching a comedy with him. Her datasheet had curled up and landed on the counter. An hour into the farce it beeped. Bakhunin was closest. He tossed it to her.

Guo paused his show.

Mitchie unfolded it and found the alert that had gone off. "There's a confirmation! An autofac cut its telemetry feeds. Its bots came out and formed a perimeter. More bots in the area are joining it."

"Ominous," said Guo. "Why didn't they cut the net to it?"

She performed a net traffic analysis. "They did. The autofac is on the other side of Endymion from us. The planet isolated the city network. We're inside with it."

Hiroshi asked, "Does it make anything dangerous?"

"The autofacs here are all general purpose. They can make anything if they have the programming."

Captain Schwartzenberger ordered, "Hiroshi. Get on the bridge. Lift if we get permission or you see something on the ground about to attack us. We'll relieve you at midnight."

"Aye-aye." The co-pilot scampered.

"I'll take midnight," said Bing.

"Fine. I'll relieve you at six," said the captain. "So I'm going to get some sleep." He gave Mitchie a stern look.

"Right, I'm on for noon. I'll get a good night's sleep," she said.

***

Breakfast came from ship stores. No one suggested ordering something a deliverybot would have to bring to the ship.

Mitchie started collecting updates as soon as she woke up. A second autofac betrayed humanity but the city police set it on fire before it could muster its bots. The first corrupted autofac used its bots to keep anyone from getting inside. The police blocked it off from more reinforcements, smashing rogue bots trying to get through.

Rumors from people who'd crossed between net-fragments described similar standoffs elsewhere. No one had been hurt yet, if one didn't count those crushed in a panicked stampede and a few suicides.

The datasheet announced a conference call invitation from Chetty Meena. Mitchie accepted. There were about forty people in it. Chetty was the only one she knew.

Guo leaned in to see. She propped the sheet up on the table and turned up the volume. A live camera showed a street approaching the betrayer autofac. Chetty provided voiceover. "My colleague Shushma Pawar theorizes that a proper command sequence should trigger the original control algorithms built into AI code. He's developed a verbal command that should work. Now he's negotiating with the police for permission to attempt it."

Bakhunin and Setta came around the table to watch.

A mismatched group of bots came out of the autofac's cargo receiving door. Mitchie saw two forklifts, one deliverybot with a chain restaurant logo, a home nurse, and several more she didn't recognize. The forklifts held up a black square, about three meters on a side.

"If that's a protest sign they're doing it wrong," said Bakhunin.

Chetty's voiceover resumed. "Shush convinced the police this may be a contact attempt. He's going to issue the command."

The camera showed a young man walking toward the bots. *Looks like he could be Chetty's cousin,* thought Mitchie.

The bots froze in place as he approached. The conference displayed the text of Shushma's command. Mitchie skimmed through it. *Seems logical, if it responds to any of the code words.*

Shushma stopped two meters from the lead bot. He read out the order, checking himself against a hardcopy in his hand. The watchers held their breath. If it worked the bots should all place themselves in storage then shut down.

The front two bots picked up Shushma and threw him into the black square. He didn't land on the other side.

"Did it *teleport* him?" exclaimed Guo.

Another member of the conference call posted some video taken from a camera on the far side. Mitchie ran it in slow motion. The black square had a red spot, changing from a small circle to wide oval to two circles. The red color dripped down to the pavement.

"It pureed him," said Mitchie.

A third member posted an analysis showing the conical pile under the black square had a volume corresponding to the mass listed in Shushma's public medical records.

"I owe Stakeholder Ping an apology," said Mitchie.

The police fired explosive bullets at the bots, smashing them before they could get back behind their perimeter. The black square shattered into shards at the first hit. The conference call ended.

"We need to get out of here," said Guo.

"Yep. I'll go brief the captain." Mitchie zipped up the ladder to the bridge and recounted the story to Schwartzenberger. He promptly called the Portmaster.

She heard her datasheet ringing and slid back down. Chetty was calling. "Did you see that?" he asked.

"Yes."

"Do you have room for a passenger?"

"Probably," she answered. "But don't pack. We're leaving as soon as we can."

"I already have a bag with me," said Chetty.

"Hurry." She disconnected.

Schwartzenberger had lost his temper. Hopefully after talking to the Portmaster. When the curses stopped he called her up to the bridge.

"These—" he started over again. "Captains don't have the right to declare an emergency on the ground here. So. New orders. Last week I took a look at the defense battery on the other side of the spaceport. It only has four anti-ship missiles. When ships start lifting we're going to be number five."

"Five, aye, sir," said Mitchie.

"Pass the word to Bing and Hiroshi when they wake up."

***

Chetty showed up dripping with sweat. He'd had to trot most of the way. Between betrayals and people fleeing the city cars were scarce.

Mitchie welcomed him onto the ship. After assuring him the captain had given permission for him to come aboard she said, "I have to warn you. If protecting the ship means I have to boost at twenty gravs—or fifty—I'm going to do it. You and your leaky valve will just have to take your chances."

"It's better odds than staying here," he said.

***

Mitchie's shift on the bridge was almost over. The Portmaster still insisted on grounding all ships. Rumors of bots disintegrating people abounded. *Joshua Chamberlain* had taken on a couple of dozen refugees. Sitting on the outskirts of the spaceport protected them from the main flow. Mitchie could see crowds besieging ships closer to the terminal building. If more drifted out this way the crew would have to make some unpleasant decisions again.

Her datasheet announced a call from Guenivere. "Hi! We're on Daddy's yacht. I wanted to make sure your ship was good to fly before we took off."

Oh, yes, friends in high places, thought Mitchie. "We're good to go, but we don't have permission to lift."

"Huh?" Her puzzled expression was adorable.

"The Navy issued a grounding order when the incursion started, for safety. The Port is still enforcing it. So all the ships here are afraid we'll catch a missile if we lift without permission."

"Oh! Right." The teenager wore an I-can-fix-this expression as she turned to her right. "Daddy!" End of call.

Mitchie noted the time. Nineteen minutes later she was copied on a Portmaster announcement. The top line was "Grounding order lifted effective immediately." She didn't read the rest.

"Up ship!" she called on the PA. Then all four turbines spun up. She kept lift-off carefully vertical to not scrape the hull against the unretracted stairs. Then Mitchie increased thrust and headed for the Black.

Demeter Orbit, acceleration 10 m/s²

With Orbital Traffic Control offline maneuvering away from the planet required a careful watch to avoid being plumed by another fleeing ship. Schwartzenberger and Hiroshi joined Mitchie on the bridge to share the workload.

The captain watched the radar. Hiroshi manned communications. Mitchie handled dodging and weaving.

Fortunately the various spaceports had released their ships at different times. Dealing with the fast-burners from Endymion trying to climb up their pipes had been bad enough. So far Mitchie had avoided them with sharp turns and bursts of fifteen gravs acceleration.

"Sir, *Rosy Cheeks* states her intention is to hold vector to the half million klick sphere and then head for the Argo gate," said Hiroshi.

"Good," said Schwartzenberger. "We can stop worrying about that one." He pulled a marker off the plotting table. "In a couple of hours we'll be clear of traffic. Then it should be a straight shot home."

Mitchie sighed appreciatively. 'Home' had a lovely sound to it. The captain meant Bonaventure, not Akiak, but she'd settle for being in the Disconnect.

Hiroshi started talking into his headset again. "Yes, this is *Joshua Chamberlain* . . . Return home via Coatlicue . . . No, I'm the co-pilot. I'll pass that on to the captain. Stand by." He took the headset off. "Sir, we're being hailed by someone claiming to be the analog ship *Agape* out of Fuego. They say they have the Disconnected Worlds consul to Demeter on board and want us to rendezvous with them."

Captain Schwartzenberger responded by activating the PA. "Mr. Bakhunin to the bridge."

The diplomat's head poked out of the hatch only a couple of minutes later. "May I help you, Captain?"

Schwartzenberger waved at the comm console. "Someone on the radio claims the consul to Demeter wants us to rendezvous with him."

"Franz is alive? Oh, that is splendid!" Bakhunin caroled.

"I thought the consuls were all kicked out of the Fusion."

"No, not all. Franz was merely banned from speaking with any official higher than a license clerk. I spoke with him last week but we didn't dare meet. He was afraid it would rub off on me." This seemed to be diplomat humor.

"Why a rendezvous?" asked the captain.

"I truly have no idea. He's certainly within his rights to demand it. As senior DCC official in the system he can requisition any vessel or military personnel in an emergency."

"I'd have a hard time claiming this wasn't an emergency," muttered Schwartzenberger. "Can you confirm his identity?"

"Certainly. If you'll allow me . . ." Hiroshi ceded his seat and headset to the diplomat. *Agape's* radio operator put the consul on. Bakhunin traded pleasantries and anecdotes about his cat and the consul's dog.

"Thank you, Franz. Please wait one." Bakhunin took the headset off. "It's really him, Captain. He's not using duress codes. I recommend meeting with him."

Mitchie had her back to them so she could smirk in secret. *When does a diplomat not recommend a meeting?*

"Very well," said Captain Schwartzenberger. "Pilot Long, please dock us with the *Agape*."

Demeter Orbit, acceleration 0 m/s²

The consul's ship had a ten-meter boarding tube to spare visitors from donning space suits. Schwartzenberger brought Bakhunin and Mitchie with him.

They emerged into *Agape's* cargo hold. That ship's collection of Fuzie refugees clung to the far bulkhead, away from the reception committee. Mitchie's heart lifted at the sight of ten Akiak Rangers floating easily in their fatigues.

Schwartzenberger let Bakhunin handle the introductions. The steel-haired man acting if he owned the ship was "Francois Dubois, Consul-General to Demeter."

Franz introduced the Fuzie in the very spiffy suit. "Delbert Woon, Demeter Security Director." Master Ranger Robinson was the only one of the troops introduced. The rest of the Rangers hung back from the conversation.

"I'm very pleased to meet you all," said Captain Schwartzenberger. "It's good to see more people made it off Demeter. But right now our top priority is to return home as quickly as possible."

"There may be something more important," said the Consul-General. "Director Woon?"

Mitchie studied Woon, wondering if he'd been at Guenivere's Revelation. Probably not. The Claret family seemed on the outs with the party which won the last planetary election. *Really the last,* she thought.

The Director seemed uncertain where to start. "Many research avenues are prohibited for safety reasons. But there are government laboratories that receive special exemptions to perform secret research in crucial areas. Particularly ways to analyze or strike back at the Betrayers."

He paused, possibly hoping for a straight line. The Diskers were all unimpressed with his hypocrisy. Woon forged on. "We discovered, or created, a powerful cyberweapon. The Council of Stakeholders never gave permission to use it in an offensive. So it's been locked away. It may be our best chance to defeat the Swakop AI and take our planet back. Or at least we want to make sure the AI doesn't take control of it."

As Woon trailed off Consul Dubois jumped in. "It's a straight-forward mission. Land near the storage bunker. Grab the box. Fly off. Your return home would be delayed less than a day."

Mitchie wanted to know more about this mysterious weapon. Her captain was less enthusiastic. He had his arms crossed over his chest, body language indicating resistance. In free fall he could cross his legs in front of his hips to emphasize it, and had. "Why us?" he asked.

Woon desperately glanced at the consul.

Dubois explained, "Only an analog ship can go to Demeter without risking subversion by the AI. The *Chamberlain* is far more maneuverable than the only other analog ship in the system."

Mitchie had to agree with that. *Agape* was a pig. *Joshua Chamberlain* had done all the work of the rendezvous while *Agape* drifted.

"As a military crew you're obligated to carry out assigned missions," continued Dubois. "And if you'll forgive the enthusiasm, your crew has a heroic record of perseverance in dire circumstances."

Schwartzenberger turned to glare at Bakhunin.

The diplomat shrugged. "I saw no harm in mentioning publically discussed truths."

The captain looked back at the consul. "We only have a few pistols. That won't get us past all those bots killing people."

He's bargaining already, thought Mitchie. *This won't take long.*

"I am willing to commit my entire security detail to this mission," said Dubois. "Master Ranger Robinson and his men have all volunteered to attempt it under your command."

The Master Ranger saluted. "Reporting for duty, sir!"

Schwartzenberger awkwardly returned the salute when he realized Robinson would keep his arm up until he got the return. "Are you *real* volunteers, Master Ranger?"

"Yes, sir. Best chance for fun we've had in two years."

Mitchie hid a smile at the captain's expression. *He's never dealt with infantry. Watching him command them is going to be a blast.*

Schwartzenberger said, "I'm a merchant skipper with a reserve commission." He pointed at Mitchie. "Lieutenant Long is an Academy graduate and career officer in the Akiak Space Guard. You'll report to her for this mission."

Master Ranger pivoted and saluted. "Ma'am."

Mitchie snapped a salute back. *Crap.* She looked over the watching Rangers. They all had full duffle bags. The weapons were a mix. The rocket launcher looked comforting.

The consul cheerfully gave in to Schwartzenberger's demand that *Agape* take on *Joshua Chamberlain's* refugees. "And that includes you, Yuri," said the captain.

"I'll just fetch my things, then," answered Bakhunin.

***

The refugees switched ships as soon as they heard about the new destination. The Rangers came through afterwards. Mitchie aimed them at a dormitory container. They considered it luxurious for a combat mission and began wrestling over bunk choices.

Mitchie decided there was probably something useful she could do on the bridge. At the top of the ladder she saw the captain and Bing in the galley. The first mate had her arms folded tightly on her chest.

"Shi, I trust you completely," said Schwartzenberger. "I just think you'd be safer on the *Agape*."

"Either it's safe enough for me to come along or too dangerous for you to go. Pick one, Alois."

Mitchie decided to show the Rangers how to secure their heavy gear.

Demeter, gravity 7.5 m/s^2

The research bunker was only a few klicks from the Caerus spaceport. Master Ranger pointed out a nearby park with enough room to land the ship. Mitchie vetoed his suggestion. A landing leg sinking into a flower bed could be more than they could deal with. She wanted some solid concrete under the ship.

A few ships were scattered about the spaceport but their landing target was empty. Always had been. Mitchie landed in the port's safety zone, a half-klick wide perimeter laid out to keep the city safe from pilots with bad aim.

The empty pavement lacked amenities such as movable stairs. They left the ship by its rope ladder. The Rangers didn't bother with the rungs. A dozen Diskers looked through the spaceport security fence— Mitchie, the captain, and all ten Rangers.

"Gimme a nice wide hole in that," ordered Master Ranger. His men carried saw-edged machetes made for cutting metal. A fifteen-meter gap opened in the fence.

The youngest member of the squad was detailed to a Senior Ranger. Master Ranger tasked the two of them with ensuring the ship would still be human-controlled when the rest returned.

"We're ready, sir," reported Master Ranger.

"Let's go," ordered Captain Schwartzenberger.

The Rangers formed a loose circle around the officers. They walked down the middle of the road, weaving around inert cars. Birds flew between the trees dotting the sidewalks. Nothing else moved.

Mitchie scanned the buildings on each side. They had no visible damage. Lights were on in some windows. Street and traffic lights operated normally. When they reached the first intersection she saw the cross walk sign had a warning of the AI attack in rotation with the walk / don't walk commands.

There were no bots in sight. Normally there would be a gardener working on the grass, some security bots watching overhead, and a few delivery bots slipping through the crowd. Mitchie couldn't even spot a broken one.

The people were still here. The Rangers on the flanks traced zig-zagging paths to not step on the piles of slurried flesh or the streams of blood trailing from them. Master Ranger issued a few reminders of proper spacing to make the flankers stay on the sidewalks and lawns. They kept drifting into the pile-free roadway.

The point Ranger carried a rifle. When a securitybot flew around the corner of the building he put a bullet through its center. The broken bot bounced down the street and rolled to a stop in front of them.

"Burn it," snapped Master Ranger. One of the flankers squirted fluid on it from his projector. The bot melted in the flames.

Nothing else bothered them before they reached the bunker. It had been an ordinary office building from the outside. Now the upper floors were burnt out, the windows were smashed, and the road in front of it covered with broken bots.

Master Ranger halted the circle just clear of the debris. "Do we have a contact protocol?" he asked.

"I don't think so," said Captain Schwartzenberger.

Mitchie said, "I'll knock." She walked forward to the hole in the wall that used to have a door. Master Ranger waved a rifleman forward to accompany her.

If there'd been a doorbell it had gone with the door. Mitchie kicked a chunk of bot chassis out of her way. The rattle sounded louder than any doorbell. "Hello! We're here to rescue you!"

A floor panel in the scarred hallway tilted up. A laser rifle emitter poked out. "Who are you?" called a harsh voice.

"I'm Lieutenant Long, Akiak Space Guard. Security Director Woon sent us to extract you."

"Um, wait one." The trap door closed.

No, I don't mind standing here in the ruins, thanks for asking. Mitchie adopted a patient expression and tried to stay calm. The Ranger didn't help. He kept trying to look in every direction at once.

The trap door flipped open with an impressive crash. The man standing in it was a boulder. His black-and-grey dazzle-pattern fatigues had five stripes on the sleeves. "You have orders from Director Woon, Ma'am?"

"Yes." She held up the hardcopy order in one hand and the data crystal in the other.

"Right. Best come in while we look at that." The gunnery sergeant waved at them to follow as he ducked back down.

Mitchie sent her escort ahead then waved to the captain. "Sir, it's all clear!" She followed through the trap door.

One flight of stairs took her to the actual bunker. Mitchie saw Master Ranger watching for pursuit as he followed his men in. A pillar in the center of the room held a storage array box. There was plenty of room for the Diskers to fit in.

The noncom introduced himself as Gunny Singh. Mitchie handled the rest of the introductions. Gunny took the orders to review.

Mitchie watched the two groups of infantry. The Fusion Marines' geometric camouflage fit nicely with the bunker. The Rangers' green / brown / black splotches clashed. She suspected the effect would be reversed outside.

Gunny Singh addressed the captain. "Sir, this doesn't say where you're supposed to take the classified archive."

"That's going to depend on how much trouble we have getting out of the system. Ideally we'll jump to Coatlicue and hand you off to the first Navy ship we find. If the AI gives us trouble, well," Schwartzenberger shrugged.

Gunny turned to his men. "Marines, we leave in five! Corporal Li, prep the box for travel. Torgs, secure the demolition device."

Master Ranger suggested, "If you've got some explosives, bring them along. We might need them."

"The demo device is ten kilotons," said Gunny.

The two top NCOs turned to the map display. Master Ranger traced out how they came.

"Right," said Gunny. "We'll parallel that on Mumford Ave, one block north. That lets us go through the park, better fire lines."

His Disker counterpart nodded. The Ranger turned to the officers. "Chain of command, sir?"

Schwartzenberger looked at Mitchie. She said, "Gunnery Sergeant Singh is the local expert. He will have tactical command until we reach the ship."

"Yes'm." Master Ranger gathered his men for a quick briefing.

The new formation felt the same to Mitchie. The officers were joined in the middle by two Marines carrying the box. The Rangers kept the circle they'd had before. The Marines, twice their number, formed a larger one just outside them.

Mitchie noticed the Marines kept their position better. They didn't mind stepping ankle-deep in pureed flesh. They avoided the center of the piles. She felt certain they were worried about slipping, not desecrating remains.

The birds had flown elsewhere. The humans moved through complete silence and stillness.

Mitchie said to Master Ranger, "I'm surprised it hasn't sent some bots to watch us."

"I'm certain it has, ma'am," he replied. "They're watching us from the windows. We were left alone before because it wanted to know where we were going."

"Ah." She looked at the tall glass buildings flanking the road.

Gunny called a halt as they neared the park. "You"—pointing at a rifleman Ranger—"put some bullets through those bushes."

The Ranger fired at three shrubs. Two shots rang as they pierced metal. A wave of bots emerged from their hiding spots and rushed the humans.

"Marines, fire!" A barrage of laser pulses fried the bots. "I love lasers but they've got no penetration," said Gunny. "I'm glad you boys brought your old-fashioned toys."

They advanced into the park. A few bots were picked off as they scuttled about, late to that attack or early for the next one.

The next attack hit from three sides. A stream of bots came from the nearest building while two manholes in the park popped open to release more.

Gunny just yelled, "Fire!" and let the troops handle it. Grenades sealed off each stream. One fell through a manhole before going off. A five-meter length of tunnel collapsed, pulling down the grass above it.

"Ma'am, I see your point about landing on solid ground," said Master Ranger.

The next lull lasted until they almost reached the end of the park. A sudden rain of egg-sized objects fell onto the humans.

The Marines killed most of them in the air. The flamethrower Rangers got more on the ground. Mitchie skipped away from one rolling past her.

One landed next to Captain Schwartzenberger and skittered toward him on bug-like legs. He stomped on it. A moment later he fell over screaming.

The Marine medic rushed over. "Hold him!" he yelled. A Ranger pinned the captain's shoulders. The stomping boot had split open as the infiltrator bot forced itself into his foot. The medic swung his cutter, taking the leg off below the knee. He slapped a tourniquet on.

A severed metal tendril emerged from the stump, waving in search of its missing end. The medic cursed as he traded the blade for a scanner. "I have movement in the abdominal cavity," he said.

"Can you operate for it?" demanded Gunny.

"Maybe. Back on the ship. I don't know if I can catch them."

Schwartzenberger's screams faded to gasps. The medic smeared black goo over the stump then pressed an injector to the captain's neck. Schwartzenberger took a deep breath, then a second, and said, "Damn, that's good stuff."

"You'll pay for it later, sir," said the medic.

"No I won't," said Schwartzenberger. "Long!"

"Here, sir." She knelt beside him. "The Rangers are making a stretcher for you." Their machetes made short work of a tree.

"No. You can't carry me. You need them holding guns and moving fast. Anyway, this'll probably kill or subvert me before the boy can get it out."

The medic looked down and nodded.

"Give me an automatic weapon and three grenades. I'll keep them from following through here."

"Ma'am?" said Gunny Singh.

It hit her in an instant. She wasn't a reckless subordinate or lone wolf now. This was her first command decision affecting someone else's life. "Get him the weapons," Mitchie ordered.

Master Ranger and Gunny helped him onto a park bench. Captain Schwartzenberger said to them, "You two are witnesses." He waved Mitchie closer. "You take command of the ship."

"Sir, the first mate—" she began.

"No. Bing's a good second but she won't make the hard decisions. You will. She gets my personal share, you take care of the ship's share."

A Ranger handed him a submachine gun. A Marine supplied three dialer grenades. "Thanks. Now go," said the former captain.

Mitchie gave him a crisp salute. Schwartzenberger waved. "Gunny, move out!" she ordered.

As the circle reformed she saw a Marine's burning body. *Shit, I didn't even notice him go down. I need to not tunnel-vision.* Mitchie could see the spaceport fence down the street a few blocks away.

Gunny Singh brought them to a trot. The Marines carrying the box handed it to a fresher pair. A block went by with no visible enemy action. At the intersection the flankers reported bots moving on the parallel streets. Gunny cursed at them to keep moving.

Mitchie kept up easily. Demeter's low gravity balanced out her short legs.

"Rocket front!" Two Rangers hauled their rocket launcher to the front. The formation stopped as bots came out from behind the dead cars blocking the street. "Fire at will!" ordered Gunny.

Mitchie realized she stood behind the rocket launcher. She flung herself over an abandoned autocab. The back blast blew some hot air under the car. She crawled forward to see the effect.

The rockets blew big holes in the line of bots. Laser and rifle fire picked off survivors. The bang-bang-bang of grenades sounded from the park.

Mitchie turned and looked back over the wrecked car. She hadn't thought he'd really use them. She'd thought of trying to retrieve Captain Schwartzenberger later. Now she knew he was gone. Which left a big empty space. She hadn't realized how much she'd depended on him supplying the infrastructure of decisions to enable her exploits. And just liked having someone she could depend on. Her vision blurred a little.

"Ma'am?" Master Ranger stepped in front of her, blocking everyone else's view of her face. "We've got the troops lined up again. Can start advancing whenever you're ready."

She took a deep breath. Locked her pain and grief into a box labeled 'Do Not Open Until Relieved.' And said, "Good. Move out."

"Advance!" yelled Gunny. "Watch your step, some are playing possum." Mitchie clutched her pistol as she stepped over pieces of bots.

He was right. Marines shot bots grabbing for their ankles. The possum threat kept them all looking at the ground.

One Ranger caught the movement above them. "Air attack!" he called. Flying bots swooped down. Marines stopped moving to shoot at them. Wheeled bots ran off the roof of the building flanking them.

"Keep moving!" yelled Gunny.

Mitchie dodged a bot as it crashed to the ground. A Marine had his back to it. The bot rolled into him, knocking him flat. Mitchie kicked it off of him.

The bot put out a manipulator to right itself. Mitchie fired six rounds into the motor housing. It stopped moving. She holstered her pistol and turned back to the Marine, "On your feet, soldier!"

He stirred, then froze. "Can't."

She looked at his legs. Multiple breaks. "Sorry, this is gonna hurt." She knelt down, grabbed his arm, and pulled him over her shoulder. *God, I'm glad we're on Demeter.* She stood with a grunt and staggered toward the spaceport. The Marine muffled his whimpers.

Master Ranger organized the rear guard. He checked the vitals of one of his men. "Incendiary." A Marine twisted a grenade twice and dropped it on the dead Ranger.

"Ma'am, I've got him," The weight vanished from her shoulder. A corporal twice her size carried him now.

Mitchie looked around. There were a lot of smashed bots. Gunny had cleared to the next intersection. Master Ranger hustled the walking wounded into catching up. The rocket launcher had a forklift on it.

She pulled out her handcomm. They should be close enough. "*Chamberlain*, come in."

"Read you," said Bing.

"Lower the cargo basket. We have wounded."

"Will do."

"Out," said Mitchie. The rest of the news would have to wait.

The AI seemed to have run out of expendable bots. Nothing bothered them on the last block. They resumed the circular formation, wounded in the middle with Mitchie and the box. The spaceport ring road took them to the hole in the fence.

A dozen people pressed against the fence, begging the two Rangers for permission to board the ship. Some turned their pleas to the Marines as they went through the gap.

Mitchie ordered, "Master Ranger, load the wounded then the box. Gunny, inspect the refugees. We can take any you think are safe. We're lifting as soon as everyone's aboard." She headed up the rope ladder.

Guo and Setta managed the crane. He looked very relieved when Mitchie came through the airlock. She gave him a little wave. Set her handcomm to PA. Deep breath. "All hands. This is Lieutenant Long. Commanding. Prepare the ship for immediate lift. A memorial service for Captain Schwartzenberger and the other men lost will be held when the ship is on vector for the gate."

Guo looked shocked. He headed for the converter room briskly enough. Mitchie decided she didn't have to worry about him right now. Setta stayed focused on the crane.

Mitchie listened for the sound of the turbines spinning up. It didn't come. She cursed and headed up the ladder. On the main deck she could hear Bing and Hiroshi arguing.

Bing leaned down to block Mitchie as she came through the bridge hatch. "Where's Alois?" demanded the mate.

"I'm sorry, we lost him," said Mitchie.

"We have to go look for him!"

"He died. We can't go back. It's too dangerous."

"He can't be dead! Did you see his body?"

Mitchie climbed the rest of the way out of the hatch, forcing the older woman back.

"Bing. We have wounded. Get your gear and help them."

"Not until I get Alois back!"

"There's a Marine medic with a little first aid kit. If they don't get more care than that some of them will die. Go help them." Mitchie turned to Hiroshi. "Start the turbines."

"Yes, ma'am!" He was relieved by the direct order.

"Who the hell are you to give orders!" demanded Bing.

"Schwartzenberger told me to take command. I'm following his last order. We need to get out of here. You need to treat your patients."

Mitchie locked eyes with the first mate. After a long moment Bing went below.

Setta came on the PA. "All personnel are on board. Cargo doors and airlock are secure."

By the book the crane should be secured for lift as well. Mitchie didn't care right now. "Decurion, take us up," she ordered.

Hiroshi said, "Up ship!" over the PA as he throttled up the turbines.

Demeter Orbit, acceleration 10 m/s²

Once they were boosting for the Coatlicue gate—and clear of anything that might be chasing them—Mitchie decided to check on her new additions. She found a couple of marine privates in the galley helping Bing run a sandwich assembly line.

The senior private answered Mitchie's "What's up?" with, "Gunny detailed us for KP, ma'am!" As the last sandwiches were wrapped in paper the marines tucked them into a pair of nearly full boxes. With nods to the captain and first mate and omnidirectional "ma'ams" they carried the food off to the hold.

Mitchie turned to Bing. "That was nicely done. Thank you." The first mate kept wiping down the counter without acknowledging Mitchie's existence in any way. The new captain waited a few minutes then walked off.

Coming down the ladder in the hold gave her a good view of the people. The Rangers and Marines were mixing, which eased her top worry. They'd broken into groups by rank. The handful of civilian refugees were sticking together near the airlock. There was more food than sandwiches in sight. Bing must have emptied the main deck coolers.

A Marine corporal was standing at parade rest by the base of the ladder. When her left foot touched the deck he came to attention and bellowed, "Captain on—"

"As you were!" Mitchie interrupted. "Carry on with your meals."

The corporal saluted and returned to his meal. Waiting next for her were the two top NCOs. Gunnery Sergeant stood rigidly at attention. Beside him Master Ranger was in wu chi stance, erect but relaxed. "Ma'am, how may we serve?" asked the Gunny.

"Don't need anything, Gunny, Master Ranger. Just wanted to check that you're all fed and settled in. Please, carry on." She declined a sandwich but had to accept a bottle of juice to escape. The NCOs went back to their conversation, comparing the relative value of high-intensity VR simulations to a real-world orbital drop on a bandit camp for producing combat experience.

Mitchie strolled around the circle of conversations. The box from the laboratory sat in the center of the hold where everyone could keep an eye on it. No one wanted to be near it.

The junior NCOs were trading stories of training accidents. The Senior Rangers seemed to be winning. "So he'd actually managed to survive sliding sixty meters straight down into the glacial crevasse before getting wedged in the ice. That's when we found we only had fifty meters of rope . . ."

She moved on to the refugees, who actually wanted to talk to her. Mitchie promised to drop them off at the next Fusion world. They were grateful enough to make her wonder if someone had started a rumor of the Disconnect kidnapping immigrants.

The medic kept an eye on the wounded in one of the dormitory containers. They were all asleep—Bing had provided the drugs he'd needed. She thanked him for his work and moved along the circle.

The privates and Rangers were talking about life on Akiak. "Never break a promise. You'll be passing the hat to get some cardiac surgery and bam! Someone pops up saying you didn't feed her cat ten years ago when she was out of town. Then you're a promise-breaker and no one will help you." The Ranger finished up his tale with a laugh.

A short master private sat up in alarm. "Wait, you need to pay for surgery?"

"Of course," said another ranger. "Doctors have to eat."

"Government doesn't pay for it?"

"Shit, the government can barely pay for *us*. Half our gear we got from donations."

"Oh, shit." The master private looked very unhappy. "All my money was on Demeter. I can't afford any surgery. I was going to switch back when I mustered out. If I wind up on Akiak I'm going to be a boy *forever*. Fuck."

A junior private snarked, "You'll get used to it."

The rangers were curious. "If you don't want to be a boy why'd you switch?"

"I wanted infantry," said the master private. "At my height I needed the muscle bulk, bone density, aggression hormones, and stuff to pass the Grinder."

"They wouldn't let you enlist as a girl?"

"Oh, I could enlist. But they'd make me a fricking useless intel weenie or something." Another marine hissed at him. The master private looked up to see Mitchie listening behind him. "Uh, no offense, ma'am."

Mitchie said, "Carry on, Marine," and walked to the lower deck hatch. Maybe she could find a more pleasant conversation in the converter room.

Pleasant maybe, but not private. She came through the corridor to find Guo making a stranger trace the plumbing to find the key valves.

"Ma'am, I'd like to introduce Waja Azad," said her husband. "He was a mechanic at the Caerus spaceport. Waja, this is Captain Long."

"Hi, ma'am," said the stranger.

"Welcome aboard," said Mitchie as she shook hands.

Guo explained, "Waja's volunteered to help out with maintenance. He doesn't have experience with analog ships, but the plumbing isn't much different."

"I learn quickly, Captain," said Waja.

That title's going to take some getting used to, thought Mitchie. "Good, I'll leave you to it, then." She turned to Guo. "See me when you get off shift?"

"Of course."

She headed back up to the main deck. *Maybe I'll get something from the galley and go eat in my cabin. Need to read up on funerals anyway.*

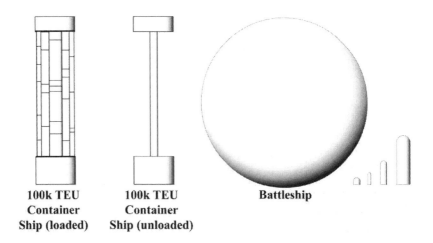

100k TEU Container Ship (loaded)   **100k TEU Container Ship (unloaded)**   **Battleship**

100k TEU Container Ship: this freighter carries the equivalent of a hundred thousand twenty-foot standard shipping containers. It travels a circuit through the worlds of the Fusion, never landing.

Battleship: massive warship built around spinal directed energy weapon. Cannot land on planets.

Chapter Seven: Shepherd

Demeter System, acceleration 0 m/s^2

"How'd the service go, ma'am?" asked Hiroshi as Mitchie floated up through the bridge hatch.

"Fine," she answered. "The Rangers and Marines seemed to draw some comfort from it." *But Bing looked like she wanted to kill me.* Mitchie still felt unsettled, more from seeing her husband cry than her own grief or Bing's hate.

She pulled the restraining strap back to put the worn copy of the *Captain's Bible* back on its shelf. The ceremony under "Funeral, Body Missing" had met her needs exactly. She just followed the script.

"Uh, ma'am?"

"Yes?"

"I know a new commander usually has changes she wants to make . . ." said Hiroshi.

"Right now we need to focus on getting home alive," Mitchie said.

"Yes, ma'am. I'm just wondering . . ." He trailed off.

"Spit it out."

"Ma'am, what's your policy on fraternization?" he blurted out, face red.

"Ah." *This is why officers shouldn't play practical jokes.* "No policy. As long as all the work gets done I don't care what you do in your time off."

"Thank you, ma'am." Hiroshi took out the sextant and measured their vector relative to the Coatlicue gate buoys. After covering half a sheet of paper with calculations he announced, "In the groove, ma'am."

"Very good, Pilot. Take us through."

Now they just waited to coast through the gate. Mitchie was eager to leave this dehumanized system and return to human space. Hiroshi handled the PA announcements as they approached the jump.

She anticipated the anticlimactic appearance of a new sun dead ahead of them. Instead there was a passenger liner ten times their size blotting out the starfield.

"Traffic!" yelled Hiroshi.

"Evasive pitch plus!" ordered Mitchie.

The pilot pivoted the ship and burned to put them on a non-collision course. Mitchie activated the radar to measure the clearance.

"Belay thrust. Pivot us to give me a look at that ship."

Hiroshi carried out her commands, this time warning everyone over the PA before maneuvering. "No plume," he said. "They're not thrusting."

"No," said Mitchie. "Radar shows them with a typical velocity for jumping in. So they've been drifting for a day or so." She studied the liner through the telescope. "No visible damage. Close enough for me to read the name off her." She put the telescope back in its case.

Mitchie unstrapped and moved to the comm console. "*Butterfly Dance*, this is *Joshua Chamberlain*. Come in please."

The Fusion ship responded promptly. "This is *Butterfly Dance*, we read you."

"*Butterfly*, do you need assistance?"

A bitter laugh came across the radio. "Don't have a guess what you could do to help us, *Joshua*."

"What's the problem?" asked Mitchie.

"We've been disconnected. Control declared all the refugee ships leaving after Demeter lost network monitoring are data hazards. Changed the key on the navigation beacons. We're lost. Can't go anywhere. They'd shoot us down if we tried to land. So we're just sitting and waiting for the food to run out." The voice from *Butterfly Dance* laughed again.

"Those sons of bitches," muttered Hiroshi.

Mitchie bit down on her anger. *No matter how much I assume the worst about the Fusion they keep amazing me.* Cursing up a storm wouldn't help these disconnected ships.

Disconnected . . .

"*Butterfly Dance*, how accurate is your collision radar?" she asked.

"We have you within plus-minus twenty meters."

"Can you maneuver to match courses with us?"

"Certainly. But where are *you* going? You arrived later than us. They won't let you access the nav beacons."

Mitchie chuckled. "*Butterfly*, we're an analog ship. We're going home to the Disconnected Worlds. You're welcome to follow."

Pause. The Fusion ship's captain said, "Would they really take us in?"

"We'll take the people. The ships may be scrapped." *Or seized to be converted to warships.* "There's no stipends. You'll all have to work."

He laughed, this time with a trace of hope. "Blessed Krishna, working beats starving. Yes, we'll follow you."

"Good," said Mitchie. "I'm going to see if any other ships want to tag along. Get me an estimate of your fuel and food endurance."

"Working on it, ma'am."

Mitchie turned to Hiroshi. "Let me see your course to the Danu gate."

"It's laid out on the plotting table, ma'am," he said.

She floated over to the table. The magnets marked the major planets and scheduled maneuvers. "Perfect. We're staying well clear of the inhabited worlds. Go take a nap. We're going to be busy sheep dogging those ships. I expect we'll be working overlapping shifts."

Hiroshi looked like he wanted to ask a question but decided against it.

She switched the radio to the omnidirectional antenna. "Analog ship *Joshua Chamberlain* to all Demeter refugee ships. We are bound for Bonaventure . . ."

Coatlicue System, acceleration 10 m/s^2

Two days of talking and maneuvering brought thirty-one refugee ships together in a loose formation. Staggering them to keep clear of each other's plumes put all but the front rank out of radar range of *Joshua Chamberlain*. Mitchie hoped following-the-leader would be precise enough when they headed for the gate. Or at least that the errors would cancel out.

"Acceleration is good for the first leg," reported Hiroshi.

"Thank—" Mitchie's second word turned into a yawn.

"Ma'am, I can solo this stretch. Go get some sleep."

She decided he must be right if she couldn't come up with a good counterargument. "Call me if anything comes up." She climbed down the ladder.

"Good night, ma'am."

The bridge ladder delivered Mitchie into the main deck corridor looking at the galley. A couple of men sat at the table. Guo lit up the instant he saw her. "Off duty?" he asked.

"For a few hours." They shared smiles.

Guo headed for their cabin.

The other man was Master Ranger Robinson. He came to attention. "Ma'am, may I have a moment of your time?"

"Of course." Mitchie stepped into the galley.

"In private?"

Never a good sign. "Yes, come this way." She led him into her cabin. Guo stood by the bed, shirt off. "Chief Kwan, could we have a moment please?"

Guo's jaw clenched. He silently put his shirt back on and left.

"What's on your mind, Master Ranger?" asked Mitchie.

"Captain Long, I have no hesitation in carrying out any orders I'm given. I will be more certain I'm carrying out those orders as intended if I understand the philosophy behind them." He stood at parade rest, eyes fixed on the cabin wall over her head.

This is a pissed-off NCO. "I'm happy to discuss my command philosophy. Is there a particular example you'd like me to clarify?"

"Ma'am, as we prepared to depart you assigned a search and rescue task to Gunnery Sergeant Singh, an enemy soldier."

Mitchie wished she'd had a chance to review the Master Ranger's service record. But it was probably still on the Consul's ship. "What was your best search and rescue mission?"

His stance relaxed slightly. "Seven years ago. When the rim of the southern ice cap collapsed near Mulcahy. Found a homesteader cabin under twenty meters of ice. Pulled out eleven survivors who had only a few hours left."

"I'd heard of that. I hadn't realized you were the same Robinson." Deep breath. "The task I assigned Gunny was not a search and rescue task."

"Ma'am?"

"It was a security task. He had to evaluate those refugees to see if any of them had been infected or suborned by the AI. Bringing a contaminated refugee on board would endanger our lives, the ship, and the mission."

Master Ranger paid full attention. She could tell he hadn't grasped her point yet.

Mitchie continued, "I needed someone who could condemn an innocent to death because she might—not would, might—pose a danger. Fusion Marines are trained to destroy. I knew I could count on Gunny to put the mission over an innocent life. Could you do that?"

His lips twisted as he struggled with the question. "I think I'd try to bring them along in some kind of isolation, ma'am."

"I'd like that if we could do it. But we didn't have time and we didn't have resources."

"Thank you, ma'am. This has been very informative." He saluted and left.

Guo came in, face stiff.

When he closed the hatch Mitchie said, "You're right, I shouldn't throw you out of your own cabin for ship business. Schwartzenberger used his cabin for business but he lived alone. I need an office. Can't use his cabin, Bing's spending half her time there."

He relaxed and hugged her. "I'm sorry. I've just gotten so little time with you lately. I hate to see something else get in the way."

She squeezed back. "I miss you too. Shepherding those lost lambs is taking too much time."

"I worry if the Disconnect can afford to take them all in."

Mitchie giggled. "Afford? Honey, imagine cutting the torches out of all those ships and handing them over to Bonaventure's building program."

The mechanic thought a moment. "They're mostly cruiser-size. And the torch is about a third of the cost of a warship. That's going to make a difference."

"I thought so. Now, let's go look at the spare cabin and see how hard it would be to set it up as an office."

When Mitchie last looked in the cabin across the hall it had a bunk with a sheetless mattress and a few boxes strapped to it.

Now she opened the hatch to find it filled with stacks of cartons. They'd been secured against thrust but not well enough to keep a few from breaking loose. Those now blocked the opening down the middle.

Mitchie set her handcomm to PA. "Spacer Setta to the main deck."

In a moment they heard feet on the cargo hold ladder. Setta popped up through the floor hatch and saluted. "Reporting as ordered, ma'am!"

Mitchie's return salute turned into a wave at the open hatch.

"Um, First Mate Bingrong gave permission to swap ship's supplies for local goods as long as we received equivalent nutritional value."

"All that is from swapping our food rations?" asked Mitchie.

"The ship was stocked for a long cruise. Disconnect foods are somewhat exotic on Demeter. Were. Hiroshi and I had a lot of time to visit the markets while we were waiting to leave. I found contacts who really liked the stuff."

"Right. Okay, I have no complaints about the swapping. You need to secure it better. Move it to cargo hold containers if you need to. Then clear out Bakhunin's cabin so I can use it as an office."

"Yes, ma'am," said Setta. "Um . . . priority level on that?"

Guo jumped in. "With you and Hiroshi on the bridge full-time and Bing, um, out of rotation, Setta's been picking up a lot of routine maintenance."

Which I'd've known if I was a decent captain, thought Mitchie. "Chief, you handle the priorities. Check how much technical background the Rangers have. Train a couple of them to help out."

"Yes, ma'am," said Guo. "Spacer, top priority is securing the loose boxes."

"Yes, chief." Setta stepped into the cabin.

The captain and mechanic returned to theirs. When the hatch closed Mitchie said, "*Now* I'm off duty."

"Good," said Guo as he pulled off his shirt. Mitchie giggled as he stripped off her clothes and laid her on the bed. He took off his boots and pants as quickly as he could.

Mitchie snored gently.

"Yep, saw that coming," he said. Guo climbed into the other side of the bed.

***

Five hours later Guo chased her into the shower with promises of breakfast. She emerged from the cabin to find her husband making pancakes and a Marine washing dishes. The Marine excused himself to go belowdecks as Guo placed a stack in front of her.

Gunny entered the galley as Mitchie started on her second stack. "Good morning, Captain!"

"Good morning, Gunny. At ease. How are you?"

"Fine, ma'am. Request permission to use ship's secure communications facilities to contact local Marine headquarters."

"We don't have a secure comm. Analog voice only. You're welcome to use it. Decurion Hiroshi can show you how. It's a good time for it. We're only two light-minutes from Coatlicue."

"Thank you, ma'am." Gunny disappeared up the ladder.

Guo followed the pancakes with eggs and sausage. Mitchie realized she'd been skipping meals while shepherding the refugees. She ate it all. When he put the next serving on her plate she paused to ask, "Is Bing eating?"

"Sometimes," answered Guo. "Enough, I think. She's not coming out much."

"Thanks."

He secured the stove and racked the pans. Mitchie asked how his new recruit was working out. Guo described Waja's performance as acceptable. He went on to explain how he, Waja, and Setta divided up maintenance and taking care of their passengers.

Mitchie realized Guo had taken on the first mate's duties, and possibly some of the captain's as well. *Hell of a captain I'm being*, she thought.

Gunny came back down the ladder. At the bottom he slumped against the wall. His face was slack, eyes wandering around the room.

Mitchie asked, "Gunny? Are you all right?" She'd never seen him look so weak, not in combat or during the memorial.

The Marine slipped down the bulkhead to sit on the deck. "We've been disowned."

"I'm sorry?" she said.

"Called in my ID and codewords to COASYSMARCOM. They didn't care. Said we're a data hazard. Banned from all Fusion worlds." He swallowed. "I don't know what to do."

Mitchie came around the table to face Gunny. She said, "Akiak needs good soldiers."

Gunny looked up at her. "Captain?"

"We've always had a bandit problem. Stealing food, burning families out of their claims, kidnapping new chums for slave labor. The Rangers can tell you stories."

Gunny's eyes focused on her. "I've heard a few."

"I can swear you in as a member of the Akiak Ground Guard. You'll come in at equivalent rank." Roughly equivalent, since the Guard had a much shorter list of ranks. "We can't match Fusion pay, but there'll be more missions and less exercises."

He grasped the ladder and pulled himself to his feet. "That's—yes, Captain, I'd be honored."

"Don't make a snap decision," said Mitchie. "Sleep on it. We have time. Talk to your troops. Any who don't want to join the Ground Guard will be transported as civilian refugees."

"Yes, ma'am. I'll do that." Gunny saluted then went down the cargo hold ladder.

Guo shared out the last of the pancakes. "Can you do that?" he asked quietly.

Mitchie chucked. "Do which? Space Guard officer swearing in Ground Guard troops? Enlisting someone without a background check? Or admitting enemy soldiers in the middle of a war?"

"That one."

"I don't know if it's legal," she admitted. "But a suicidally depressed guy with access to heavy weapons and no rules controlling his behavior is someone I need to lock down." She swallowed her last bit of egg then looked at the chronometer on the bulkhead. "Oh, God. I need to get to the bridge." She paused to give Guo a hug and a maple-flavored kiss. "Thank you for a lovely breakfast."

"You're welcome. Want me to brief Master Ranger on what's up with the Marines?"

"Yes, please. You're a damn good mate." She winked then headed up the bridge ladder.

***

There was no answer to his knock. Guo kept banging on the hatch. Eventually Bing said, "Go away."

"No."

"Oh, it's you." She opened her hatch.

Guo looked past her. The cabin was a mess. Clothes and trash lay on the deck where they'd fallen when acceleration started, ready to float about again when the ship cut thrust.

Bing didn't look any better. She slumped against the coaming. Her color was off. Dried tears streaked her cheeks.

"I brought soup," said Guo. He popped the lid on the bowl to let the scent out. The rich chicken broth made his mouth water, and he'd just finished his lunch.

"I'm not hungry."

"Eat it anyway."

Bing looked up and down the corridor. No one else was in sight. A pair of Marines noisily washed dishes in the galley. She asked, "Who's making you do this?"

"Nobody. You need to eat. Somebody has to take care of you."

"That's my job."

Guo shrugged.

"Get out of the corridor before someone sees you," said Bing.

He came in and set the bowl, spoon, and napkin on her desk, shoving an undershirt onto the deck to make room.

She stood by the hatch after closing it.

He half-filled the spoon and held it up to her face. "Give it a taste."

"I can feed myself."

"Show me."

She stared at the spoon long enough to make Guo wonder if he'd have to force-feed her after all. Then Bing took the spoon and swallowed the contents with spilling any.

"That's . . . not bad," she said.

"Try the noodles."

She sat at the desk. The chair was secure in its brackets. Bing flipped the lid off the bowl and took a spoonful.

Guo picked clothes off the deck. He stuffed them into a bag riveted to the bulkhead. Books and toiletries went into the cabinet. A bound collection of pictures he put on the desk. Crumpled papers and wrappers he compressed into a ball.

The soup disappeared. Bing leaned back. Her color looked better. "Can you believe that bitch told me over the PA?"

Guo almost snapped at her but bit down on it. *I'm here to comfort her, not correct her.*

"Yes. I was there."

"That's not rude. That's inhuman."

"Another wave of bots was gathering at the fence line. When we lifted off Gunny was setting up a squad to attack them, keep them off us while we launched. They would have been left behind."

Bing looked away.

Guo continued, "I've been talking to Gunny. He recorded the whole battle. Showed me what happened to Captain Schwartzenberger."

"Should I watch it?"

"No . . . only if you really need to."

Bing stared at a picture of her and Schwartzenberger mounted on the cabin's curved outer wall. "I don't need to. He really made her captain?"

'Her' was an improvement over 'that bitch.' Guo said, "Yes."

"Well. I didn't want his ship anyway. I wanted him."

"You're getting the ship anyway. Mitchie is captain but you inherit ownership."

She snorted. "I inherit the debt. Alois is . . . was . . . still paying off the *Jefferson Harbor.* This ship belongs to the investors."

"His Eden loot should cover that."

"Maybe. If it sells. And it's not all confiscated."

By her tone she didn't care if some government took it all. She continued, "Anyway, the charter he signed is for the duration of the war. The ship will get blown up with her in charge."

Guo bit back another hot reply. He settled for saying, "She's kept us alive through some nasty situations."

"Yeah. Because she keeps looking for trouble. Sooner or later she'll find some trouble she can't get out of."

***

If *Joshua Chamberlain* flew the dogleg course by herself she would take the second leg at high speed. Slowing down to the proper transition speed could wait until a couple light-minutes from the gate. Asking the refugee ships to do that would get people killed.

Their collision avoidance radars had more precision than the analog ship's system could dream of. Their crews never used the data to plan maneuvers. The timing and direction of burns came to them from the control center, carefully choreographed to keep every ship's plume clear of the others.

Saying "Just match your course to mine" would have worked fine with a single ship. With thirty-one a simple course change could lead to a passenger liner going through another ship's exhaust plume close enough to melt all her windows. A nightmare of that scenario ended Mitchie's last nap.

The Coatlicue control center collected position and velocity information digitally. Mitchie had to get her data through Hiroshi writing down the numbers each ship read out over the radio. The bridge plotting table was ridiculously inadequate for representing everyone's position but it was the best tool she had. Sometimes she'd double-check the vectors by marking up the outside of a piece of paper rolled into a cylinder.

Sequencing the burns to keep everyone safe reminded Mitchie of a puzzle she'd been given as a kid. A frame held fifteen sliding tiles in a four by four grid. You couldn't solve part of it and then deal with the rest. They had to be carefully arranged so one move would snap all the tiles from a confused mess to a pretty picture. *I shouldn't have pried the damn frame open. It would've been good practice for this.*

Hiroshi handed over the list of the latest relative position and velocity vectors. Mitchie checked it against the target values for the last set of burns. Gave him a thumbs-up. Mitchie floated over to the comm console. "All ships. Secure from maneuvering. We are on course for the gate. In three days we will make midcourse correction maneuvers as needed. *Joshua Chamberlain* out."

Her co-pilot had an I-can-barely-believe-it smile. Mitchie considered who should take the watch. She'd finished a nap just a few hours ago. But she'd been on the bridge for days straight, napping in her acceleration couch and using the fold-out to pee. Hiroshi had been allowed off for the occasional meal, nap, and sponge-bath. *Then again, it wasn't his idea to bring all those incompetent Fuzies home with us.* "I have the con," Mitchie said. "See you in ten hours."

"Yes, ma'am!" Hiroshi flew through the hatch.

Mitchie slid into her couch. Staying awake would be the challenge for this shift. The ship was quiet. She could hear Hiroshi bouncing off the walls through the open hatch. He knocked on a hatch then pulled it open. *Ah, he's visiting Setta,* thought Mitchie.

Hiroshi called out a cheerful greeting. Setta answered less cheerfully. Then a third voice entered the conversation. Not one Mitchie recognized. Male with an Akiak accent. Had to be one of the Rangers. *Oh, shit.*

An angry but brief argument ensued. The hatch slammed shut. A moment later another hatch opened and slammed. Silence. *I'm glad I didn't have to intervene in that.*

***

Thirty minutes until she had to go on shift. Mitchie decided she couldn't procrastinate any longer. She went down the corridor to Bing's cabin. Knocked. No answer. Knocked harder. Listened. The cabin was silent.

Captain Schwartzenberger's cabin was on the other side of the corridor. At some point Mitchie would have to get the ship's papers and logs but she hadn't gone in there yet. She knocked on the hatch.

Bing opened it. "What?" Grief made her look wounded. She moved as if she had a hole ripped in her belly.

"How are you doing?"

"Terrible. And it's your fault."

Mitchie swallowed an angry rebuttal. It wouldn't accomplish her goal. Besides, a big chunk of the blame was hers. "I need you to work bridge shifts."

"I'm not taking responsibility for your Fuzie pets."

"I'm not asking you to. Just comm and collision. If anything happens with the other ships page me."

Bing looked away. Her face worked with conflicting emotions.

Mitchie kept her mouth shut. She hoped the first mate's sense of duty would bring her back to work. If not she could play the "Alois would want you to" card. But that felt as likely to produce violence as a watchstander.

"What hours?" asked Bing.

"Relieve me at 0600. Hiroshi will relieve you at 1800. You'll work the same schedule the next day. That'll give us a chance to recover from the twenty-hour shifts we've been working. Then we'll go to eights."

"See you at 0600 then." Bing closed the hatch.

That went well.

***

Going back on shift after twenty-four hours off felt almost restful. Her planned walkthrough of the cargo hold had turned into a court session. They'd wanted information she didn't have and reassurances she couldn't give. She liked taking position sights much more. There was enough time to think about what would have to happen after this jump. She'd covered two pages with trade-off grids by the time Guo came onto the bridge.

Mitchie grinned at her husband. They'd made some time together last night. She still felt a temptation to lock the hatch and abuse the privileges of rank. No, bad precedent.

He said, "Ma'am, an encrypted reply to your message came in last shift." Then he just held out a folded paper to her.

She stared at it a moment before taking it. As captain all messages went straight to her. Playing games to withhold one would be unthinkable. *Great. Now this captain gig is trashing my sex life.* "Thank you, Chief," she answered.

Guo looked wistful. He'd probably expected to play more message games on the way home. "Have a good shift, ma'am." He vanished back down the hatch.

Mitchie opened the paper. She'd sent an encrypted report to headquarters a few days ago. Not asking permission—it was far too late—just warning them of what had happened. And what she was bringing home.

ACK FALL DEMETER. ENLISTMENTS APPROVED. WILL ACCOMMODATE REFUGEES. SHIPS WILL SERVE WELL.

CONDOLENCES ON LOSS CAPT S. GOOD LUCK AND GODSPEED.

CHU.

The mention of Schwartzenberger's death started her crying for the first time. She missed him. He'd been a good boss. If she hadn't grabbed the chance of a behind enemy lines mission he'd still be alive. *Why now, dammit?*

Now because she had time for it. The constant string of emergencies had paused. She had enough privacy to let weakness show. Mitchie clipped the papers to her console. Closed the hatch. Then she let tears flow for Alois Schwartzenberger, the soldiers she'd eulogized, and all of Demeter's half-billion.

***

Mid-course corrections had both Mitchie and Hiroshi on the bridge again. They took turns taking sights and checking each other's math. Wads of crumpled paper accumulated on the ventilator intake grill.

The Fuzies aligned perfectly to *Joshua Chamberlain's* course. The analog ship's vector had the center of the gate inside of its error cone. Mitchie would have been delighted with the accuracy if they were flying alone.

Analog ships routinely made velocity corrections a few hours out from a gate. The refugee flock would need longer than that. Unless they could adjust vectors with just their maneuvering thrusters.

Mitchie built a probability table. Hiroshi checked her math. 60% of the error cone was small enough for thrusters to handle the corrections a day out from the jump. Which left a 40% chance of losing a few ships who couldn't correct before they reached the gate.

Making a series of corrections further out would waste fuel. Thrusters were a hundredth as efficient as torches. Mitchie already worried about some ships running dry before reaching Bonaventure.

The frequency scanner spiked. Transmission on the emergency channel. Hiroshi put it on speaker.

"*Joshua Chamberlain*. Do not reply. Flash your running lights if you can hear this." The message kept repeating. Not automated, just a human repeating himself.

The co-pilot gave Mitchie a confused look. She shrugged and turned the exterior lights on and off a few times. Hiroshi started the comm console stopwatch.

Forty-eight seconds later the message changed. "*Joshua Chamberlain*, thank you. We have course correction vectors for you. Prepare to copy.

We will repeat." Both spacers grabbed paper and pens. "Beginning. Velocity component system north zero point zero zero two . . ." Their mysterious navigator sent far more significant figures than their instruments could ever measure. After the second time he recited the vectors he said, "Do not reply. Flash lights twice for another data repeat. Flash four times for good copy."

Mitchie and Hiroshi carefully compared their copies. They matched. She turned the running lights on and off four times.

A minute later they heard, "Good luck, *Joshua Chamberlain*. Out."

Hiroshi asked, "Who was that, ma'am?"

"I'm guessing they sent a destroyer to shadow us. Just in case we changed course to ram a planet or something. Nice to know there's a few actual human beings in the Fusion Navy."

***

Mitchie had the galley table covered with paper. Alternate courses through Danu and Lapis were plotted in different colors. The best one she'd found so far let four ships run out of fuel and seven out of food.

That assumed a day of puzzle-solving for each maneuver and three days of cat-herding after each jump. If the Fuzie refugee ships learned to plot their own maneuvers they'd save a lot of time. If they didn't and she let them try they could all kill each other.

She pulled out the almanac for Danu. Passing closer to the sun would save time if they could do it safely. The radiation intensity tables told how much heat they'd take in a close pass.

She looked up as Hiroshi's hatch opened. Maybe the co-pilot would have some ideas.

A Marine corporal first class snapped to attention as he saw her. His tan face flushed but held a rigid expression.

Mitchie waved him toward the cargo hold ladder and turned back to the almanac. *I don't care, kid, I have bigger problems.*

Pushing the limit on solar heating could get them through Danu a day faster. She'd have to ask the ships what their cooling systems were rated for.

Oh. That's why Gunny asked if decurions were officers yesterday. Dammit, I'm the last one to find anything out on this ship.

Danu System, acceleration 10 m/s²

Danu System Control volunteered to provide maneuvering vectors to the refugees. Mitchie publicly thanked them and checked the numbers for half a dozen ships to verify they had safe courses. *Probably just want to get the unclean ones out of here as quick as they can,* she thought.

Mitchie celebrated by declaring the crew would have dinner together. With guests. Bing insisted on taking bridge watch. Mitchie didn't argue. The rest of the crew decided menu and guest list were "NCO business" and took over. The captain went back to fretting about courses. They were crossing Danu efficiently enough the flock might be able to get through Lapis without starving.

"Captain on deck," called Guo as Mitchie entered the galley.

"Please, be seated," she said. They all waited for her take her seat at the head of the table.

Guo smiled at her from the far end. No chance to play footsie during this dinner, sigh. Setta sat next to him, as far as she could get from Hiroshi at Mitchie's left.

Mitchie studied the guests. The oldest civilian refugee, Lo Zheng, sat on her other side. A Ranger Njoya sat between him and Setta, paying more attention to her. *Setta's Ranger, I presume,* thought Mitchie. *Or is that Setta's current Ranger? Is she collecting the whole set? I really need to know what's going on with this crew.* Gunny Singh and Master Ranger Robinson filled out the table.

Platters of lightly spiced fish and root vegetables passed around the table. Zheng praised it as the latest fashion in Demeter cuisine. Then he looked like he might cry.

Gunny changed the subject. "Captain, some of the troops are wondering if their enlistment commits them to settle permanently on Akiak."

"We've been considering our settlement options as well," said Zheng. "Will any world take us in as we are?"

"Most of the Disconnected Worlds are free to all immigrants," said Mitchie. "The Marines can move anywhere once they've finished their enlistments. If they want to move while still serving they can apply for a transfer. The DCC tries to make those go smoothly."

Zheng said, "The only one we'd heard of was Bonaventure but Spacer Setta said we wouldn't be able to become citizens."

"Um, you're allowed, it just costs a lot of money," explained the deckhand.

"The price dropped a bit since the war started," said Ranger Njoya.

"Enough to afford it on our pay?" asked Master Ranger.

"Well, no."

Mitchie said, "Half a dozen worlds offer free immigration. Several more will waive fees if you have particular skills. You could also ask for a humanitarian discount."

Zheng shuddered. "It's all so complicated. There should be an office steering people to the right places."

"If you want someone making decisions for you there's always Turner," said Mitchie.

Master Ranger snorted. Guo let out a blunt, "Oh, God, no."

Gunny Singh put down his fish-laden fork. "I thought the Disconnected Worlds were all dens of anarchy. What's with this Turner place?"

Mitchie and Guo started to talk at the same time. She waved for him to continue.

"Compared to the Fusion we don't have much government," Guo said. "Turner is the exception. It's—well. Say you were at the weekly ideological conformity rally and you saw a pretty girl. So pretty you wanted to make workers in training with her. You'd tell your precinct captain. She'd go talk to her precinct captain. They'd decide if you'd be a good match. Then you show up at the designated table in the dining center to find out if they assigned you to the pretty girl or someone else."

Guo took a bite of beet. The table was silent.

He continued, "We'd load at least a dozen emigrants every time we touched down there. But they got immigrants too."

Master Ranger said, "Then the emigrants come to Akiak and get suckered by the first crook to happen along. I bet half the slaves I've rescued were from Turner."

"I'm sure that level of control is reassuring for some," said Zheng. "I'd feel constrained by it myself."

"If you want some control you can go to Shishi," said Mitchie. "The feudal lords can exert as much control as they want."

"It's not a feudalism, dammit," snapped Hiroshi. "It's a pedestrian democracy. Uh, ma'am." He flushed. "I apologize for my tone, ma'am."

"No offense taken," she answered. "You know your homeworld best. Please enlighten us."

Hiroshi shifted in his seat as everyone stared at him. "Anyone on Shishi can buy the sovereignty right to some land from a lord and run it as they please. We have anarchies, democracies, autocracies, futarchy, demarchy, anything anyone wants to try. The only rule is you can't keep people from moving out. They vote with their feet. Pedestrian democracy."

Gunny laughed. "That's real? I thought that shit was made up to make Diskers look crazy."

Zheng asked, "So I could walk across a line and find murder was legal?"

"If a baron makes a stupid law like that everyone moves out. But for regular laws they put up signs and have net alerts."

"Does everyone's house have wheels?" asked Setta.

"I grew up in a house with a basement. But, yes, some people migrate a lot. My parents are still in the same barony they were born in."

Ranger Njoya said, "So there are feudal titles."

"It's a handy set of words everyone knows. Emperor, King, Duke, Baron. We could say Planetary Director, Continental President, Provincial Governor, Mayor. The system would be the same." Hiroshi paused. "Okay, some of the rulers get into playing dress-up for the pageantry of it."

"Does Akiak have all of these local variations, Captain?" asked Zheng.

Hiroshi gratefully returned to his fish.

Mitchie said, "No, we're one of the more homogenous worlds in the Disconnect. It's a younger colony. We started along the shores of the equatorial ocean and spread out as the ice caps receded. So there hasn't been much differentiation."

"Geography can control culture," said Master Ranger. "Shishi is a dozen small continents and lots of islands, room for many niches. Fuego's equatorial region is too hot for anyone to live on. So it's divided into a happy-go-lucky North and grudge-carrying South."

Ranger Njoya laughed. "Grudge is right. That's why my family moved to Akiak." His sunburn-resistant skin was better suited to Fuego. Mitchie wondered if he had to take vitamin D supplements.

Zheng looked to be crossing Fuego off his list of potential homes. "Where should we settle?" he asked.

"You're a free man now, Mr. Zheng," said Mitchie. "We'll give you all information we can. But you have to decide what you want."

Bonaventure, gravity 10.1 m/s^2

Lapis was equally eager to see the refugees through as efficiently as possible. A few ships were on half-rations when they arrived in the Bonaventure system. The DCC organized a rendezvous with each refugee ship. The passengers and crew were taken to temporary housing on Bonaventure. Spacers came on board to steer the vessels to newly-built shipyards in other systems.

Joshua Chamberlain returned to Redondo Field. Admiral Chu came on board. Mitchie met him in her new office. Setta had taken out the bunk, added a desk and chairs, and decorated the bulkheads with ship schematics and obsolete navigation plots.

Hiroshi ushered the Admiral in then closed the hatch to give them privacy.

Mitchie saluted. "Sir, welcome aboard!"

"Sit, Long."

They took facing seats. The admiral stared silently at her. Possibly he intended to make her nervous. It didn't work. Between being safely in the Disconnect and the refugees no longer being on her shoulders Mitchie wanted to sing and dance.

"I skimmed your report," he began. "Good job on the primary mission. I have no idea what to make of your mystery box. We'll meet with Dubois and Woon tomorrow. The shipwrights are happy with your tag-alongs. Doubt we'll get you a finder's fee this time though."

"If there's any finder's fee, sir," said Mitchie, "I'd want it to go to the refugees so they can get a good start."

"Not my department. You can put your crew on leave, other than security for that box."

"Yes, sir. When can we expect a replacement for Captain Schwartzenberger?"

"Well, Long, it's like this. Every officer we think is ready to command a warship is running a cruiser or at a shipyard getting ready for his ship to commission. Everyone we think has potential to be a commander is in charge of a destroyer or frigate. Or at a shipyard. So we can't spare anyone to take over an auxiliary."

Amazingly, part of Mitchie felt relieved she'd keep her command.

"Yes, sir."

"Also, you're out of uniform."

"Sir?" Mitchie had carefully donned her Space Guard greys the moment she heard Chu was coming.

"Board met while you were gone. You need another half-stripe on the cuffs."

"Ah. Thank you, sir." *Hell of a way to say, 'Congratulations, you've been promoted,'* thought Mitchie.

"My aide will send you the meeting coordinates. See you then."

Admiral Chu saw himself out. That might be a protocol violation. Mitchie decided she didn't care.

***

"This ship just got a lot emptier," said Guo.

He'd found Mitchie in the galley, going through DCC regulations on a new datasheet. "They're all on leave?" she asked.

"Crew is. Half the Rangers and Marines are. The Marines appreciated the pocket money. How'd you get them a pay advance?"

"It's from the ship's fund. We should get reimbursed for it from the Ground Guard but God knows if that'll ever happen."

"I think we can afford it," said Guo. "The civvies are off to the resettlement place. And . . . Bing left with three duffle bags."

"She quit?"

"Didn't say anything to anybody. I think she did."

"Let's check." Mitchie led him to Bing's cabin. The hatch was unlocked. It opened on a stripped cabin. A sealed trash bag against the bulkhead was the only thing not ship's equipment. "No, she's not coming back."

She turned around and opened the hatch to Schwartzenberger's cabin. It looked the same as Bing's except for the books and folders on the desk.

Guo asked, "Why'd she take his *clothes*?"

"I don't know. She was his heir."

"Doesn't matter. Are you free tonight?"

Mitchie giggled. "I'm scheduled for a complete lack of responsibility until midnight. Have any suggestions?"

"Yeah, but Master Chief Lee sent me a line. He wants us to have dinner with him in Commerce tonight. Sounded worked up about it. Might be important."

"That's a long way for dinner, but okay. Has he been hanging around with Billy?"

"Don't think so, but we've been gone a while." He pulled out his datasheet and sent off their acceptance. "God, I love being back in civilization."

She smiled at his toy. "You really think that's better than the Fusion ones we were using?"

"No, but it's not a loaner. I own it."

"Fine. Get us a flyer to get to Commerce. I don't care if you rent it or buy it." She picked up one of the folders on Schwartzenberger's desk. "I have to get back to finding out what captains are really supposed to do. And talk to the people who own this ship to let them know I'm running it now."

***

The actual address for dinner wasn't in Commerce proper. Bulwark was nine klicks from the capital, hosting a military spaceport and the Bonaventure Defense Force HQ. When Mitchie saw they were landing at the Shield Club she stopped worrying about Billy showing up at dinner.

Master Chief met them on the steps. He led them around displays of model warships and antique artillery into the banquet hall.

"Is it always this crowded?" asked Mitchie.

"Normally only during official ceremonies," said Master Chief. "But nothing is *officially* going on tonight."

She and Guo exchanged looks. Something was going on, and they weren't in on it.

A few people seemed to recognize Mitchie but their table mates shushed them.

Master Chief kept herding them toward the empty stage. He looked about more, trying to spot someone. Then a tall man in a heavily braided uniform stepped out of the crowd.

"Oh, good evening, sir," said Master Chief.

"And good evening to you, Master Chief," said the stranger. "How nice to run into you here. Who are your friends?"

"Sir, I'd like you to meet Lieutenant Michigan Long, commanding *Joshua Chamberlain*, and her chief engineer, Chief Engineer's Mate Guo Kwan. Ma'am, Chief, this is Vice Admiral Galen, commanding Blockade Fleet."

Guo realized this was the admiral who Mitchie had committed insubordination against by effectively ordering him to attack the Fusion battleship. He managed to go through the proper social motions.

A moment later the admiral said, "Lieutenant, I have some friends who are dying to meet you. Chiefs, please enjoy yourselves." He led Mitchie toward a cluster of commodores and captains.

"We can relax now," said Master Chief. "My buddies saved us seats. I scored a bottle of the good stuff."

"Will she be all right?" asked Guo, looking after the officers.

"Of course. This is her fan club."

The chiefs had a table in the back of the room. Guo knew the others from previous epic drinking sessions. A Senior Chief Electrician's Mate filled a plate from the platter of beef in the middle of the table and put it in front of Guo.

A late arriving chief snagged the remaining seat at their table. Master Chief introduced him as Chief Gunner's Mate John Ti. Guo noticed his stripes were red instead of the gold ones the others at the table wore. Ti had to be a direct appointee like Guo, or he'd done something in the last ten years to blemish his record.

Ti noticed Guo's blue stripes as they shook hands. "Pleased to meet you. What's your sin?"

"Fucked an officer," answered Guo.

Master Chief choked on his whiskey.

Ti laughed. "You beat me. I just got drunk and missed a take-off."

"Sssst!" Another chief ended the conversation. People were getting onto the stage. Mitchie looked comically short next to Admiral Galen.

The room came to attention as the "informal" ceremony began. Applause greeted her introduction. Galen officially announced the board results making her a lieutenant commander. Thin ribbons went on her cuffs to mark the promotion. Then the admiral turned to face the crowd.

"I won't bother reading this award citation to you," he said. "It doesn't say anything real. Just as I can't tell you what she really did. But I can tell you this. Without Lieutenant Commander Long's actions many of the people in this room would be dead and this base would be under bombardment.

He turned to face Mitchie. "So I am very proud to present you with this Extraordinary Merit Award."

Master Chief grunted in surprise.

Admiral Galen draped a striped ribbon around Mitchie's neck. A bright silver medal pulled it taut as he let go. The room burst into applause and cheers.

Guo clapped with them until his hands hurt. The noise didn't stop until the admiral waved them all back to their seats. The crowd went back to their meals, chattering louder than they had before.

After Guo finished a bite of his beef he asked Master Chief, "What was wrong with the medal she got?"

The senior NCO waved his hands. "It's not wrong. It's just not what I expected it to be."

"How so?" asked Guo.

Master Chief pulled out his datasheet. It displayed all the ribbons awarded by the BDF. A few gestures pulled them into categories. "Here's the valor awards—for doing something brave and dangerous. Bigger the danger, the higher the award. To get the top one you have block a plasma blast with your body."

A second column lined up next to the valor awards. Guo recognized the bottom two from Mitchie's uniform. "Performance awards. They show how well you do your job. There's a rank factor. So a spacer can get the Accomplishment Ribbon," bottom of the stack, "the EMA she got," top, "is something a captain or commodore would get for doing a great job running a headquarters."

"So you expected her to get one lower down?" said Guo.

"No. I expected a valor award. You were in a battle. Could've been blown away at any moment."

"Why a performance award then?"

Master Chief's voice went grim. "Politics. The same reason everyone was told 'dinner at the Club' instead of giving her a damn parade."

Chapter Eight: Shore Leave

"Four men died to get it and you don't even know what it does?" shouted Mitchie.

Former Demeter Security Director Woon flinched back. "Don't blame me for the Marines. They were doomed anyway."

"I think what we're most interested in what you do know about it, Delbert," said Consul Dubois.

"Oh. Well, I never asked for the technical details. I'm not a cyberneticist. I found them enough money to keep their system secure."

"How did they describe it to you?"

"An infoweapon. One that might be able to destroy an AI. They said it had to be secure. It could destroy our network if it got loose. The Council was never willing to authorize deploying it."

"Do you have any documentation?" asked Admiral Chu.

"It would have been at the research lab," said Woon.

The table's attention turned to Gunnery Sergeant Singh.

He cleared his throat uncomfortably. "We never looked at any documents. They didn't pick curious people for the job."

"What about the technical staff?" asked Mitchie.

"They ran off," said Gunny.

Mitchie looked calmly at him.

Gunny expanded, "They tried to convince me to turn the thing loose in the net after the infections started. Kept going on about it until I decked one. Most left then. The rest ran away after we fought off the first wave of bots."

"You never considered releasing it?" asked Admiral Chu.

"No, sir. My orders were clear," said Gunny.

The Diskers around the table were not impressed by his devotion to orders.

"Could the manuals be in the box?" asked Consul Dubois.

"We haven't dared jack into it to check," said Mitchie.

"Of course," he replied.

Silence fell.

Admiral Chu let it go for a minute before saying, "It will have to go to the Secure Research Center on Akiak. They're our best researchers on anti-AI technology."

Mitchie brightened at the mention of her home.

Chu asked, "Gunnery Sergeant, are you and your men willing to take on securing the device at that facility? The conditions are austere."

"Yes, sir!"

Mitchie kept her poker face on. She'd warned the admiral that Gunny might balk if the Disconnect tried to separate him from his charge. Now they had him volunteering to help the enemies of his former service dissect it.

"Thank you all for your time," said the admiral. "Lieutenant Commander Long, please remain a moment."

When the two of them were alone he asked, "When's the last time you were on leave? Real leave, not working one job while on break from the other?"

She had to think about it. "I've had lulls . . . but a *real* leave? Five years. Maybe six."

"Thought so. You need some downtime. It's going to be a long war. Don't burn out. That ship has to be due for an overhaul too. We obviously don't want to store that box on Bonaventure. So take it to Akiak. Then you and your ship go into downtime. The Akiak spaceyards are expanding, it's a good place for it. They'll have work for any of your crew who don't have leave saved up."

Chu actually smiled for a moment. "You haven't had your honeymoon yet. Take some time for that too."

"Yes, sir." She couldn't help smiling back.

"Be on your way in a week."

***

When Chetty Meena asked for a favor Mitchie happily helped him. She already owed him one, even if he didn't know it. A visitor pass to one of Redondo Field's unsecure briefing rooms was easy. Finding an audience was harder. Promising a catered lunch brought out a dozen intel analysts. None of them outranked her.

A minute before the official start time eight officers trooped in. Their ranks ranged from captain to ensign. Mitchie recognized some from Admiral Galen's surprise party. They were from the admiral's operations staff. Her message to Galen's chief of staff had paid off.

Hopefully Chetty would make it worth their time.

The Demeter refugee took the floor confidently as she introduced him. He focused on the ops officers. They'd taken the center of the empty front row.

"Captain, I see you saw action as an exchange officer," said Chetty. "Against Ushuaia?"

The officer started, glancing down at the Fusion Navy valor award topping his ribbon rack. "Why, yes. How did you know?"

"I didn't. but it's the way to bet." A gesture put a pie chart on the screen behind Chetty. "The six AI systems bordering human space attack at roughly similar rates. But half the Navy's valor awards come from engagements with Ushuaia." A second pie chart appeared next to the first, the orange wedge expanded to over half the circle.

He continued, "An earlier investigation proved that the fleets were using proper criteria for awards. I was brought in to see if something about their tactics was creating the imbalance. I found there was a difference—but it was in the AI's tactics, not the human ones."

Mitchie noticed one of the back row analysts sit up. Maybe they'd pay attention instead of napping until the food arrived.

Chetty put a new graph up, a flat line with a sharp spike in the middle. "Valor awards are most likely to happen in an evenly matched engagement. If the human force has superior firepower—" he waved at the left part of the flat line "—there's no need for courage. Everyone does their job by the book and they win. If the humans are outnumbered," waving at the other side, "there may be great bravery, but no one lives to tell the tale."

He pounded a fist on the spike. "It's the fifty-fifty battles where one man's extraordinary effort can make the difference between victory and defeat."

The line greyed as black dots appeared around it. "Analyzing the data from the past twenty years of AI combat fits the curve. We used simulations to rerun each engagement until we had a solid estimate of the victory odds."

The Disconnect officers took Chetty on a lengthy digression until he'd convinced them of the plausibility of his sims.

When he returned to his graphs he changed the black dots to ones matching the colors assigned to each AI in the original pie chart. The orange dots clustered tightly in the middle. "You can see that Ushuaia regularly engages at close to fifty-fifty odds. We followed up by looking at an array of cases in detail. In each of them Ushuaia took action to force the even engagement, either splitting ships off to pursue minor objectives or avoiding contact until it received the minimum reinforcements necessary."

The audience instantly challenged that assertion. Chetty played animations of actual battles for them. He didn't convince all of them but no one came up with a better explanation for the AI's behavior.

Chetty blacked out the screen to cut short another round of quibbling. "If we accept that Ushuaia is fighting at even odds we can look at why. Several theories are apparent. It could be handicapping itself to force development of better small unit tactics. It could enjoy the challenge of hard fights. Those assume the AI is setting its own goals.

"If the Ushuaia AI is following human orders it could be a game program set to provide a fair fight. Or some long dead officer could have created it to maximize his chances of winning a medal."

The last suggestion brought chuckles from some of the analysts. The front row was unamused.

Chetty wrapped up with a request for questions.

The Operations captain had the first one. "What was the Fusion Navy's response to this briefing?"

Bitterness flashed across Chetty's face. "Neither my management at the Institute, nor the officers I showed it to unofficially, were willing to let me brief this to the Navy. Apparently the idea of an AI's motivation being something we can understand is officially unthinkable."

Mitchie broke in to declare a recess. The food had arrived. The officers drifted over, too busy wrestling with Chetty's ideas to be hungry. Once Chetty finished a burger she let the Q&A resume.

Half an hour later he explained his heart condition. An analyst replied, "That shouldn't be a problem for the Defense Force."

Mitchie decided this lost lamb would be all right.

***

When the week ran out Mitchie was almost ready to leave. Setta declared supplies were adequate. The Marines and Rangers came back from leave. But Bing hadn't come back which left a hole in the watch schedule.

Billy reported Bing had found an apartment in Commerce. She'd started helping him sell some of the more mundane items from the Eden loot. They'd passed the encrypted data archive back to Mitchie. Maybe she could get the Secure Research Center boffins to crack it. They wouldn't mind finding a Betrayer inside.

She'd requested a new pilot through Admiral Chu. The personnel staff hadn't found anyone. She suspected they hadn't tried very hard. She and Hiroshi could trade off for the few weeks to Akiak without endangering the ship. There were lonely stretches where they could leave the bridge unmanned. But if either of them fell ill they'd be in trouble.

Well, if the worst case happened one pilot could get them to the nearest world to wait it out or find a replacement. She didn't want to blow her departure date. She especially didn't want to spend all her time arguing with personnel bureaucrats.

"Ma'am?"

Mitchie looked up from her datasheet. A Marine had just escorted a stranger into the galley.

"Yes, Senior Private?" she asked.

"Ma'am, this spacer wishes to present his orders," said the Marine.

"Thank you, I'll see him."

The Marine saluted and left. The stranger saluted. "Coxswain's Mate Third Class Mthembu, reporting aboard, ma'am." After she returned the salute he held out a data crystal.

"Sit, please," she said as she took it. *Don't want a crick in my neck.* Sitting didn't help much. The spacer stood a full two meters tall. He still loomed over her seated.

Her datasheet accepted a set of orders from the crystal. A quick scan explained why she hadn't received a notice from Personnel. Mthembu belonged to Admiral Galen's flagship as a backup shuttle pilot. The ship's captain had detached him on temporary duty to the *Joshua Chamberlain.* With no end date.

Guo's gotten good at working the Chief network, thought Mitchie. She said, "Welcome aboard, Coxswain's Mate. I'll introduce you to the rest of the crew and we'll get you settled."

Akiak, gravity 10.3 m/s^2

Mitchie wondered if anyone in the Space Guard actually knew the coordinates of the Secure Research Center. Admiral Chu had given her some contacts but they were only willing to accept the "package" for later delivery. Separating the box from its Marines struck her as a bad idea in both directions.

In desperation she called the sole civilian on the list. He agreed to see her. She took a shuttle down to Muir City. A slim man in an elegant suit waited in the lobby of the Security Department building.

"Mr. Alverstoke?" she asked.

"Yes, but please call me George. I'm delighted to meet the famous Lieutenant Commander Long." He shook her hand firmly.

"Sure you don't mean infamous?"

"In this building they're much the same." Alverstoke led her to a secure conference room. Mitchie explained the problem of Demeter's mystery box and its attendant Marines.

Alverstoke thought for a few moments. "That's certainly something for SRC. The trouble with delivering it is that we've kept the location very tightly held. No one in the Space Guard knows it. We have some warehouses we use as cut-outs. But a platoon of Marines going to one and not coming out would raise suspicions."

"I could just land *Joshua Chamberlain* at the site."

"Yes, but the coordinates would be in your ship's log. We'd want to replace the entire infosystem afterwards."

"She's an analog ship. We picked up a navigation box for the run here. I'll offload it. If I'm the only one on the bridge no one else will have any clues to where we are," said Mitchie.

"That . . . should be acceptable. I'll need to talk to some people first. Can we meet back here in a couple of hours?"

Mitchie used the free time to go by Personnel and find out what paperwork she'd need to make the Guard recognize her married name. Whether a handwritten ship's log entry could be considered equivalent to a government-issued certification had to be decided by the legal expert, who was on vacation. The conversation stayed polite until a clerk suggested Mitchie have a 'proper' wedding for the records.

She'd calmed down by the time Alverstoke returned to the conference room.

He was cheerful. "The muck-de-mucks like the idea. They're hoping you could take on some other items for the trip, ones too big for the usual shuttle." He displayed a cargo manifest on his datasheet.

Mitchie looked it over. "Hauling cargo is what she's built for. Looks normal enough. Wait. Imported live plants?"

Alverstoke shrugged. "You'll understand when you see the place."

***

The toughest part of the delivery was timing it to avoid witnesses. The Space Guard ran an exercise to divert civilian traffic. Mitchie entered atmosphere over the north pole to avoid spaceport control radars.

Well, that was the toughest part for Mitchie. For her passengers the worst was when she flew the ship in circles tilted forty-five degrees looking for the building. It was designed to blend into the icecap. She spotted it as she started the fourth loop.

The touchdown was one of her best, hardly a bump as the landing legs met the surface. When she cut the turbines the ship shivered as the pads crunched their way through the snow layer to the solid ice below.

"Gotta love home," she said to the empty bridge.

Finding her parka took a few minutes. By the time she climbed down to the cargo hold offloading was in progress. A few Marines were on the ice, holding guide ropes to lower a container onto a flatbed tractor. Another tractor had a passenger compartment. Half a dozen figures in parkas emerged.

Alverstoke stood at the corner of the cargo bay hatch watching the work. Mitchie joined him. When the welcome party came closer she asked, "Is that Pete? From Lapis?"

"Pete Smith, yes. How do you know him?"

"I accidentally got him kicked off the planet," she admitted.

Alverstoke chucked. "That explains why his file was so vague about that part."

"I'm glad he's alive. I was afraid he might have been at Noisy Water."

"He has a neurotic aversion to debt. So all his new friends went and left him behind. Then became radioactive ash. Powerfully motivated him to help us out. He's been an asset."

"Good," she said. "He was wasted in the Fusion."

Pete recognized her. "Michigan? Is that you?"

"Hello, Pete, you're looking well." Much more cheerful than when she'd landed him on Lapis' most wanted list.

Parkas made for clumsy hugs. When he let go she introduced Guo, who received a handshake.

Pete shifted to talking shop. "I've prepared a secure analysis lab," he said. "It has complete electromagnetic isolation."

Gunny insisted on interrogating Pete and his team at length before admitting the system was safe enough for his charge. His last question flustered them. "What authority do you have to open it?"

Alverstoke stepped in. "I can answer that." He read from his datasheet. "The following information is declared Most Secret. The Chancellor, with the concurrence of the Security Committees of the

Senate and Commons, has issued the following directive. One. The SRC will analyze the device described in attachment one to determine its function and capabilities. Two. The SRC will provide recommendations on how to best use the device against an AI incursion. Three. The SRC will provide recommendations for future research and development based on the device."

Mitchie thought, *Four. Provide recommendations on how to use it against the Fusion Navy. But best not to stress the Gunny. He's new to our side.*

Alverstoke pocketed the datasheet. "I trust that answers your concerns, Gunnery Sergeant Singh?"

"Yes, sir. Thank you."

***

Pete's isolation lab had a transparent wall. Mitchie stood with him as two Marines set the box on a test stand and opened it. A computer faced the wall. Its monitor declared it was healthy and ready for new data.

"It'll check for stand-alone files first," said Pete. "Hopefully they included some documentation."

The actual device was a standard memory rack covered in hazard warnings. At Pete's wave a Marine plugged the computer's cable into the rack's socket. The display announced "Connection made." Then it flashed grey snow for a second before turning completely black.

Pete said, "That was very informative."

"Really?" snapped Alverstoke.

"Oh, yes. Whatever that is blew through our finest firewall faster than I could measure. It proves Gunny's rigid attitude toward handling it is totally justified. I'll have to build a new test set-up. The base code will need read-only hardware."

"Before you start designing that," said Mitchie, "I have a favor I'd like to ask you."

Pete's eyes refocused. "Yes?"

"We picked up a data archive on a trip to Old Earth."

"*You* were on that trip?" Pete exclaimed.

"Yes, that was my ship. The archive is encrypted. We couldn't open it. Would you be willing to give it a try?"

"Sure. It's a century behind the state of the art. Easy problem." He paused for thought. "Unless it's an AI-created cipher. That might be impossible."

"AI's part of the worry. One of the shareholders thinks it could have a Betrayer trapped inside."

Pete's face lit up at the prospect of analyzing an actual AI's source code.

Mitchie continued, "If it's a Betrayer it's all yours. Any commercially valuable information I need to keep the rights to. Contractual obligations." Even if they wouldn't be able to give Alexi his share until after the war.

"Shouldn't be a problem. If it has the lost dramas of the twentieth century we'd want to watch them."

"You can have a copy of all of it. Just don't leak it to anyone else."

Pete chuckled. "We're good at security here."

They shook on the deal.

***

Arsenic Creek didn't support any agriculture. The scars of the mines were surrounded by low, twisted forest. Guo pointed out the mine his family owned, then their store in the small town. The house stood on a hill overlooking the town.

Mitchie's greetings in Mandarin were well received. Her grandmother-in-law even complimented her on her accent. Her practical vocabulary could get a ship cleared to dock, loaded, refueled, and onto a departure vector. After a few minutes of attempting small talk the Kwans switched to English. Sinophones were a minority on Akiak so many of them were fluent in the majority's language.

In deference to Mitchie's limited vocabulary the Kwans even conducted dinner table conversation in English. At least the head table did. She could pick up bits of Mandarin from the lower tables. Seating had been rearranged in her favor as well. Some of the more fluent

English speakers in the clan carefully minded their manners in front of the matriarch while monolingual elders sat elsewhere.

The younger cousins wanted to hear about Guo's adventures. "How about the guys you smashed with a hammer?" was vetoed by Grandmother. He wound up waxing eloquent about his role in recovering prisoners from the debris of FNS *Terror.*

Guo's mother, Jiao, sat across from Mitchie. "What are your plans for while you're here?" she asked.

Mitchie hastily swallowed her rice. "We're visiting my family next. Then I'm going to Space Guard Headquarters to get all my paperwork updated. After that, we haven't decided. Might go camping. We haven't had a real honeymoon yet."

"What paperwork?" asked Jiao.

"My name change." Mitchie grinned. "I mailed notification of the marriage to them but Security insists on in-person verification for big changes."

"Really. I'd thought you'd intended to maintain your current name professionally."

Mitchie shrugged. "It's not that big a deal. Most of my real work was undercover. I don't think the people I care about will have trouble with the change." If it screwed up Admiral Chu's paperwork, good.

"I see. Have you thought of not changing it?"

"Um . . . no, not really. I know not everyone does but it's traditional in my family so I always assumed I would." She used to assume she'd take Derry's—never mind that.

Jiao pushed some shrimp around with her chopsticks. "Perhaps you would be comfortable remaining Lieutenant Commander Long with practice."

Mitchie looked to Guo. The cousins were extracting more war stories from him. No help there. "Why does this matter to you?" she asked her mother-in-law.

"The Kwan family has worked hard to establish a reputation for honesty and moral probity. We want to avoid confusing our business partners and customers."

"And what's confusing about me?" Keeping her voice level took some effort.

Jiao sipped tea. "Several of us have researched you since you joined the family. Your reputation is extremely good in the areas you are good at. In others . . ." she shrugged.

The anger boiled out. "You don't want me changing my name because my reputation will hurt the Kwan family name?"

That was loud enough for Guo to hear it. "What? Mother, did you say that?"

"This is not my own idea. It is my role to speak for the family in this."

"How dare you. She's family. She's my wife. How dare you." Hearing Guo defend her eased Mitchie's fears.

Jiao glared at her son. "Our employees, our customers, our suppliers all do business with us because they trust us. If that faith breaks we could starve by the banks of our poisoned stream."

Guo's answer came in Mandarin, far too fast for Mitchie to try to follow it. An uncle at the end of the table stood up and shouted back at him. Guo answered, then one of the younger cousins came in on Guo's side. Then everyone at the table was standing and yelling except for Mitchie and her grandmother-in-law.

Mitchie looked at the old woman. She was focused on her tea cup as if the room was silent.

"I need some air." Mitchie slipped out of the room. She could still hear yelling as the door closed behind her.

Wood fences flanked the driveway. Mitchie leaned on the top rail and traced the carvings. Crossing boards made an X between each pair of fenceposts. The decorations flowed smoothly between the pieces of wood. She tried to tell if they'd been carved in place or if they'd done a masterful job of piecing together decorated boards.

Guo came out the front door. He yelled inside then slammed the stormproof door. Mitchie could feel the vibration through the fence. He walked over to her and kicked an X into kindling. "Let's get in the flyer," he said.

Mitchie headed for the passenger side. Guo had flown them to his childhood home.

"No, you fly," he said. "I'm too damn angry to be safe."

"Right." She took off as soon as they were both strapped down. East was a good direction to start with. They could make plans later. "So what was your parting remark?" she asked. "I recognized the words for filial piety."

"The rest were obscene." He sounded a little abashed. The adrenaline must be ebbing.

"Teach me them? Could be useful."

"No. If I teach you any more obscene Mandarin you'll do all your cussing in Chinese and I don't think I could handle that."

She laughed. If they could joke together they'd be all right. Mitchie engaged the autopilot and took his hand.

It was a clear night. The stars passing overhead were almost as clear as space. After a while Guo said, "I was the black sheep anyway. They never liked me being a spacer. I'd send money home but they'd rather have me working the mine or the store."

"I'm glad. I wouldn't have found you in the mine." She leaned against him but kept an eye on the instruments.

"Hey, can you land it?"

Mitchie found a clearing free of livestock and parked the flyer in it. She half turned to face her husband.

He'd pulled something out of his pocket. "Here," he said, putting a jade ring in her hand.

"Oh, that's lovely! Doesn't fit me though. Heirloom?"

"From my great-grandmother." Guo pointed at the rear-view mirror. "Hold it next to your eye."

"Wow!" The jade exactly matched her eyes. "How did you know it would match?"

He laughed. "I always knew. It was the very first thing I noticed about you. I almost dropped the wok."

"Seriously? I didn't notice you acting goofy. Didn't think you'd noticed me at all."

"I had to behave myself. Didn't want you threatening to drop me out an airlock."

She answered that with a kiss.

Going to the nearest city and taking a shuttle would have been faster than cruising their flyer halfway around Akiak. But traveling the long way let them relax. A night in a generic hotel in a town neither of them had heard of soothed their nerves.

The Longs lived in ranch country. Patches of forest alternated with meadows. Cattle and sheep wore long fur for the climate. Guo chattered nervously as they approached the house.

"Relax," said Mitchie. "I'm thirty. She's not going to be fussy over who I drag home."

Her husband wasn't convinced.

The door of the ranch house swung open to reveal a late middle-aged woman a few centimeters taller than Mitchie. Guo stood straight as the steely eyes scanned him.

"He'll do," she said. "Son, Michigan's room is on the right. Put the bags there and wash up. Girl, into the kitchen. I'll be damned if I'll serve leftovers with newlyweds in the house."

***

They liked him. Mitchie relaxed a bit. Ma had only invited the nearest cousins for dinner, "so as to not frighten him off." But four cousins with spouses and a couple of offspring too big for the children's table made for a noisy meal.

Guo didn't seem bothered. He answered the cousins' demands for war stories with vivid descriptions of their less-secret encounters. "When the captain said, 'Never mind the yellow limits, push it into the red,' I knew it would get hot in there."

"Temperature or radiation?" asked Idaho, youngest at the table and an aspiring spacer.

"Heat, mostly. I did have to turn the counter down a notch," said Guo.

When the tale reached its gory end one of the in-laws turned conversation to a gentler topic. "Has Michigan been showing you her old favorite spots?" she asked Guo.

"Yes, we're visiting places most days."

"Where did you go today?" Jerri followed up.

"We visited the cemetery to lay some flowers for Derry."

Mitchie noticed all the in-laws leaning back. Only the blood relatives were willing to tackle the subject.

Albert looked at Mitchie. "That's not very honeymoon-like."

Guo answered before she could. "It's a lovely memorial. I was glad to honor him. From what I've heard we would have been friends."

Ma spoke directly to Mitchie. "Were you saying goodbye?"

"I said goodbye years ago," she answered. "This was just . . . remembering."

"And laying flowers," added Guo.

"Haven't you done enough of that?" asked Albert.

"I'll be *done* when I lay the severed heads of some stakeholders on his grave."

Jerri muttered "refills" and scurried into the kitchen. More in-laws followed her.

Cousin Montana shifted to the now-empty seat across from Mitchie. "Michigan. You can't spend the rest of your life on revenge."

"Oh?"

"Settle down," urged Monty. "There's room for you here." He waved at Guo. "Or find a home in the Sinophone lands. Don't waste your years."

Mitchie sat with her spine straight up. "My years have been well spent. And I intend to keep doing my share for the war."

Guo murmured, "An assist on a battleship is more than one person's share."

All the Longs ignored him.

"The war's won," said Albert. "We gave the Fuzies a bloody nose and they ran with their tails between their legs."

"One battle isn't a war. The Fusion hasn't given up. And they won't." Mitchie's voice rose. "They can't. Our existence proves the entire principle the Fusion is based on is a lie. If they give up on fighting us that's the same as telling every one of their subjects all those rules about what they do, and all the executions to enforce them, just didn't matter."

Mitchie was standing now, leaning forward on the table, eyes level with Monty's as he sat.

"Derry's death, and the death of the other men who were working on the *Brave's* hull with him, and Noisy Water, and every other Disker the Fusion killed, they killed to scare us into following their rules." Mitchie had to pause to catch her breath.

Ma Long slowly pushed her chair back as she stood. "We know that. That's why we elected a legislator who pushes to resist the Fuzies. Why we pay taxes and ask for more to go to the Guard. Why we support those joining the Guard. And why we tend that empty grave." She locked eyes with her daughter. "But obsession isn't patriotism. You're trying to win this war on your own and that will destroy you."

"I'm fighting it as part of a team," Mitchie answered.

Guo said, "She's done more to win it than you'll ever know."

Cousin Columbia tried a softer approach. "You must have months of leave saved up. Stay with us. We miss you. We worry about you. You're tired. I can see it in your eyes. Rest here. The war will be there when you run out of leave."

Mitchie sat. "I am on leave. We finished the assignment that brought us here. Now it's just waiting until they give us another one."

"I hope they don't hurry that," said Ma.

The in-laws took advantage of the drop in volume to bring out dessert. Jerri, Monty's wife, led with an apple pie. Ice cream and more pies soon had everyone too busy tasting to argue.

Mitchie looked over at Idaho. He looked like he missed the children's table.

Yi Sun-sin Shipyard, Akiak Orbit, acceleration 0 m/s^2

Setta watched from the yard superintendent's dome as the tugs maneuvered a heavy cruiser into the slip. She couldn't tell how it was going by watching. It looked like a smooth movement to her. The number of curses from the superintendent and his staff said otherwise.

On the radio Hiroshi's orders to the other tug pilots shifted from calm to exasperated. An objection from one pilot fractured his reserve. "Yes, I know that's not according to the plan. Fuck the plan. Maneuver as I tell you to."

The slip shivered as the cruiser came to rest against the stops. The superintendent let out a sigh of relief. Setta pulled herself out the hatch.

She reached the docking bay for the tugs as Hiroshi gathered the other pilots in front of a display board. He noticed Setta and gave her a wary nod.

He drew the outline of a cruiser with his finger. A stab made a dot in the center. "The book says a cruiser's center of gravity is here." More stabs, each farther toward the stern. "No weapons installed, no crew, no ammo or propellant. It's just a torch drive with an empty shell in front."

The pilots twitched as Hiroshi swept a glare over them. "The maneuvering plan they gave us was shit. It used the book CG. Trying to get back on plan when a pilot makes a mistake is good. Doing it when the plan is shit is bad. You have to recognize when the cargo isn't matching the plan. Maneuver to reality, not what the guy in the super's shack pulled out of the database. Got it?"

Nods and "yes, sirs" came back.

"Good. See you at the lounge. First round's on me."

Setta floated up to him as the tug pilots scattered. "Hi."

"Hi yourself." He hung in place, not trying to close the gap to her.

"You have a tab at the lounge, right?"

"Sure."

"Come on, we're having dinner at the O Club."

"Decurions aren't officers."

"I know. I found a replacement stove for them. All they had to trade was free meals." Setta explained the deal as they flew through the passageways to the rotating portion of the shipyard. Normally she arranged for ships to trade excess equipment for the parts they needed. A behind schedule destroyer had offered its galley stove in exchange for life support gear. The club needed the stove but had no parts. The quartermaster team accepted vouchers in exchange for breaking into their precious stock of spares.

"Sounds like Legal might get cranky about that," said Hiroshi.

"They eat in the O Club."

If any Legal staff officers were eating when Hiroshi and Setta arrived they didn't object to enlisted being seated.

Hiroshi kept looking around for someone. Finally he looked up from his menu and asked, "Is Waja joining us?"

"No. I got fed up with him being such a Fuzie."

"You didn't strike me as prejudiced against them."

"I can work with them. But the Fusion has so many cameras and check-ins that anyone can find someone all the time."

"Anyone without the money to spoof the system." Hiroshi made his selections. The menu highlighted them to confirm.

"Yeah. Waja wasn't at that level. He's used to peeking at his girlfriend whenever he thinks of her, and getting peeked at himself. That doesn't work here." Setta waved at the cameraless ceiling.

"The isolation made him break it off?"

"No, he'd just message me whenever I came to mind. Which was often." She put her water glass down hard enough to spill some in the low acceleration. "I left my datasheet on my desk while I went to the loo. Came back to four messages, last one marked emergency."

Hiroshi tried to stifle his laugh.

"I called him back and told him not to do that. He argued. It was over."

"Over the datasheet?"

Setta flushed. "I'd've waited until a better time if he hadn't pushed." She looked Hiroshi in the eye. "I'd never do that to you."

He nodded. All three of their break-ups had been in person. And loud.

"So—how's the captain enjoying her vacation?"

Hiroshi shared the gossip from Commander Long's last weekly check in.

Setta didn't need to ask about his latest break up. Hiroshi's rebound fling had been with a clerk in Water Systems Maintenance. Setta had heard all the details in exchange for a case of digital valves.

He focused on the pork chops after updating her on the rest of Joshua Chamberlain's crew. When he finished one he looked up at her. "The entertainment library had its weekly update yesterday. After dinner want to see what it got in?"

"Maybe. I heard there's four guys in Contracting who've been practicing traditional vocal harmony tunes. Their first public show is tonight." Hiroshi's face lit up. "If you're interested."

Akiak, gravity 10.3 m/s^2

As the oldest cousin Albert had inherited Grandpa's house. Guo was fascinated. He'd always been told that Anglophones abandoned their family histories. Seeing the relics in the ranch house told him more about the Long family than all their dinner conversations.

The central room had a huge stone fireplace. Seats covered in shaggy cowhides made a rough semicircle facing it. One window faced the lake. The rough-hewn walls bore pictures and other memorable items.

Guo ignored the backpack until he realized it was nailed to the wall, not hanging on a hook for someone to use. When Mitchie noticed him staring at it she explained, "That's what Grandpa had all his stuff in when he landed on the planet."

"He went from one bag to all this?"

Mitchie chuckled. "Marrying the heiress to a big chunk of land helped."

"Oooh. Handsome cowboy impressing her by roping cattle?" *I guess using sex to get ahead is a Long family tradition.*

"No, he didn't know cattle at all. He knew grass. Worked a golf course on Sukhoi. When he hired on to Great-Grand this land was all first-stage invasive plants and a few rows of saplings. Now it's the best grazing land between the icecaps. Montana has a side business selling grass seed to steaders breaking new ground."

"I see."

Guo moved on to a battered paper map framed under glass. The bottom edge was rough, torn at a fold. "Oh, this is where the names come from."

"Yes, it's the only thing we have from Old Earth. Great-grandpa brought it with him during the Betrayal. They'd look at it during winter nights and talk about the names."

"Are all the kids named off the map?"

"They were for a while. Then Montana tried to name his daughter Saskatchewan and Jerri put her foot down. That was the end of it. I think York would be a good name for a boy though."

Guo turned to her. Mitchie had never mentioned naming children before. "Then our first boy is York."

Her face assumed its rare bashful expression. "Okay." She turned toward the far end. "There's a book with pictures printed out before the great data purge. Let me find it."

He turned back to the map. The land of "Michigan" was in two disconnected parts. That fits.

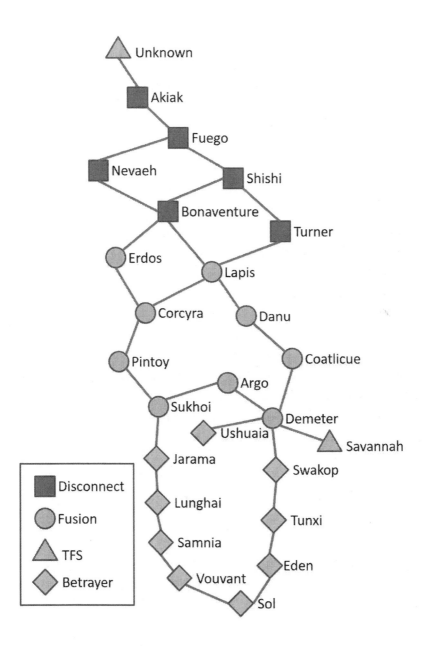

Partial Map of Star Gate System

Chapter Nine: Wilderness

Staying at the Long Ranch was a perfect honeymoon. Akiak houses had thick walls to deal with the harsh winter cold. Soundproofing was a side benefit.

Alverstoke interrupted their idyll with a call. "Your favorite immigrant has found something. Can you come to Muir City tomorrow?"

They flew down to meet at the Security Department building. Mitchie and Guo found the secure room occupied by Pete, Alverstoke, and two suits who weren't introduced.

"Is Chief Kwan's presence necessary?" asked the female suit.

"Yes," answered Mitchie. "He owns the largest share of the archive." Guo twitched but didn't correct her.

"It's the archive I want to talk about," said Pete.

The male suit said, "The Demeter infoweapon is the top priority."

"Yes, we're working on it," said Pete. "We've measured larger portions of its capability envelope."

"Finding more things that don't work on it gets us no closer to an operational weapon."

"If you don't want to hear what I have to talk about I can leave."

"I want to hear it, Pete," said Mitchie.

Alverstoke nodded.

Pete launched into his presentation. He opened with a defensive explanation that fabricating new test equipment for the infoweapon left his team with a lot of downtime. Then he described how they'd broken the encryption. Guo asked a couple of clarifying questions. They were as incomprehensible to Mitchie as the original explanations.

"Once the decoy noise was removed we found a mix of Eden government records and Frankovitch family information. Which are, to be fair, tightly overlapping sets."

Mitchie felt blood surge back into her brain as Pete changed topics. The suits were perking up too.

"What interested us most were reports from the first wave of refugee ships from Earth as the Betrayal broke out. I believe we have found—" he paused with dramatic intent "—proof of the Vetoer Hypothesis!"

The capital letters were clear in his tone. Mitchie looked around the table. Everyone else looked as baffled as she felt. "The what?" she asked.

Pete's face fell. "Are you familiar with the personal AI vetoes?"

Everyone else shook their heads.

"Ah." He thought a moment. "Okay. Before the Golden Age, when AIs were just getting deployed, there was a lot of public fear of them."

"Not enough," muttered a suit.

"Laws were passed to reduce the risks. Hardware kill switches, verbal shutdown commands, authorization timers, and the personal veto. Anyone could say 'no AI can touch me' and they'd establish a keep out zone. Whole cities prohibited any physical impact from AIs.

"As the Golden Age went on vetoers changed their minds or died off. Eventually there was only one left, Jordan Hammerstein. When he died every AI order blocked by the vetoer code executed at once. That's what we call the Betrayal."

Guo said, "Wait—you're claiming it wasn't initiated by the AIs?"

"No. They were simply carrying out orders they were given."

The male suit scoffed. "That's ludicrous. There's documented cases of Betrayers killing hundreds of people at a stroke."

Pete glared at him. "Humans have killed each other with every tool ever invented. AIs are just another one. The archive had records of Earth's Code Police. There were millions of them working to keep griefers from circumventing the AI safeguards."

"Griefers?" asked Alverstoke.

"Someone wanting to hurt other people as an end in itself, or to increase their perceived social status. Typically bottom-status males. A successful attack would make them feel higher status than their victims."

"How could all AIs be blocked by one guy?" asked the other suit.

"Vetoer code was mandated by law. And global treaties. It was in all the AI core variants. Just modifying it was ground for the Code Police to shut everything down and put programmers in jail. Any command that had a planet-wide impact, or North America-wide, was cancelled or queued for later execution. So the code police spent their time chasing local-impact plots."

Pete pulled up an animation on the room's screen. A map of Earth shone green with healthy network status. "Once Hammerstein died all those queued commands were executed." Patches of yellow appeared, spread. Their centers turned red. Other areas went black with defensive shutdowns. A few green outposts remained when Pete froze the animation. The rest of the land masses were red on black. "That took less than an hour."

"Why were griefers trying to shut down the whole planet?" asked Guo.

"It may not have been them," answered Pete. "If a thousand well-intentioned people set global programs running at the same time they'll overload the system with processing demands. That would have crashed the network without any griefers. But while the code police tried to fight the crash griefers ran wild."

"This is a fascinating feat of historiography," said the female suit. "But I don't see how it relates to our current issues."

"It's obvious," retorted Guo. "This completely refutes the Fusion's rationale for attacking us!"

"I doubt the Council of Stakeholders would listen," said Alverstoke. "Even if they did the horrific example of Demeter would outweigh any argument attributing the Betrayal to human error."

"I can't see one of those griefers ordering his enemies pureed," said the male suit.

Guo asked, "Why not? Humans have done worse to each other many times in history."

"Nothing about this will make the Fusion less afraid of leaving us out of their control. They'll just label the entire Disconnect as griefers."

"More likely they'd ignore it," said his counterpart. "There's no way we can confirm this 'Vetoer Hypothesis.' It's not like we can ask an AI."

"Yes, we can," said Mitchie. "The Terraforming Service has friendly AIs."

The thought of voluntarily approaching the TFS shocked everyone except Guo. Mitchie described the job they'd been hired to do for the TFS, leaving out how it went to hell once they ran into poachers.

Alverstoke checked his datasheet. "The last sighting of a terraforming ship in the Disconnect was over a year ago. They're all in deep space. We have no way to find them."

"Sounds like a job for an analog ship," said Mitchie. "We'd need supplies and orders from the Space Guard."

The female suit said, "Finding out the terraformers' opinion of Fusion aggression could be useful. They'd be next after us."

Guo leaned over to Pete. "Up for a trip with us?"

"He can't be spared," said Alverstoke. "We need him focused on research."

***

They had two more weeks of honeymoon while the politicians argued. The Ecology Department forced through approval of the expedition. Their price was a long list of technical questions for the terraformers.

Freeing *Joshua Chamberlain* from the shipyard was trivial. The surveyors found the repairs after the Kronos Incident had amounted to a full refit. The superintendent was delighted to have his docking slip back, and even more delighted to have a ship captain asking less of him instead of more.

Retrieving their crew took work. The shipyard staff were hideously overworked. Mitchie short-circuited a shouting match between Guo and a senior chief coxswain's mate by grabbing Mthembu's arm and pulling him out of a tug's cockpit. The rest were easier.

Once the supplies were on board Mitchie ordered them to the outbound gate.

"I'm sorry you didn't get your three-month leave, ma'am," said Hiroshi.

"Thanks. But we did have a good break. Hopefully we'll get you a nice leave sometime," she said.

Mthembu laughed. "After the shipyard this feels like leave."

"Especially with this." Hiroshi patted the navigation box. It had the sensors and processors to find their position, velocity, and course.

"Don't get used to that toy. I'm expecting you two to maintain analog proficiency."

"Yes'm," they chorused.

***

The nav-box identified the system with a five digit catalogue number. Mitchie declared it "System Three." They'd spotted three outbound gates. The marker buoys had different color schemes. The most obvious had blinking red lights.

"Shall I steer for that one, ma'am?" asked Hiroshi.

"Looks like it wants attention. Do it," she answered.

A day later they were in the groove for the gate. Mthembu took the comm console seat to watch the jump. Mitchie took sextant sights of the flashing red buoys to confirm they were aimed at the center of the gate. Then she sat and relaxed. Her eyes focused on the center of the starfield, trying to spot the moment when the new sun appeared. Hiroshi counted down the jump over the PA.

Solid white light seared her eyes. Closing them did nothing. Her forearm blocked most of it, but enough light leaked around the top and bottom to hurt. Hiroshi and Mthembu were yelling.

"I have the con!" yelled Mitchie.

"You have the con," answered Hiroshi.

The human ear was useless for measuring turns in freefall. But Mitchie had been flying this battered ship long enough to have a feel for how she'd respond. Putting her hands on the controls hurt, the glare dazzled her eyes through the lids. She fired the thrusters to yaw the ship.

Measuring the turn had to be from timing, she couldn't see anything. But the harsh light moved away to the right. When it was gone she waited a few seconds then fired the opposite thrusters.

Mitchie opened her eyes. Dark purple blotches swarmed everywhere. She saw nothing. "You okay?" she asked.

"Can't see," said Mthembu.

"Don't know," answered Hiroshi.

She picked up her mike. The intercom button for the converter room was something else she could do by feel.

"Chief here," answered Guo.

"Is it getting warm down there?"

"No. Why? Are we going to start boosting?"

"Yes, soon. We need to get out of here. Watch the temps. Out." Mitchie blinked a few more times. She could recognize her console now. No stars yet. She'd need her night vision back before they could search for the gate out.

Mthembu recovered first. Eyeballing the stars didn't find a gate. He took the telescope and started a methodical search.

Her eyes still couldn't make out stars. Mitchie activated the ship's cameras and rotated through them. They were saturated by the star's output. The side cameras had enough resolution to differentiate between the white star and light grey spillover. She used that to get them pointed directly away from the star.

Guo reported measurable heating. "But it's nothing compared to running the torch."

Hiroshi retrieved a pair of binoculars to supplement Mthembu's work with the telescope. They'd covered nearly half the sky visible from the bridge before finding a candidate.

"That's it, it has to be," said the decurion.

"It's not a circle," replied his junior. "Just a couple of independent buoys."

Mitchie borrowed the telescope to settle it. "Yes, that's the gate. The beacons probably burned out under the radiation. Let's get a course for it."

Two days later they were close enough to see the dead buoys by their reflected sunlight. The extra reference points let them tighten up their course before passing through the gate.

When System Three's sun appeared before them as a dim and peaceful dot, Mitchie said, "We know what blinking red means now. Let's take another gate and see where it leads."

The next three months were the most boring of Mitchie's life. They learned that blue beacons meant a system with only one gate in it.

The nav-box alerted them when they'd circled around to a system they'd already visited. The hand-written jumpgate map on the bridge gained a new link every week or two. The rarity of terraformable worlds was heartbreaking when Mitchie dwelled on it.

The lonely cruise did have its compensations. Mitchie and Guo cuddled in their free-fall hammock as *Joshua Chamberlain* coasted through another empty system.

"Life is good," she murmured into his neck.

"And here I'd been worried about you going stir crazy."

"Me, no. The rest of the crew might if they had nothing better to do than play dodgeball in the hold. But it looks like Setta and Hiroshi are making nice again."

"They are? But she and Waja . . . huh." Guo looked thoughtful.

Mitchie said, "I don't know. I don't need to know. That's official." She thought a moment. "Has Mthembu displayed any interest?"

"No danger there. He's a Pure Water Baptist."

"Oh, Christ have mercy. No, he can't be. He's never said anything about it."

"He used to. Seems he needed some quality time with the chaplain to escape a Mast for harassing his bunkmates."

"Ha! Well, good. I'd hate to ruin the tradition of all our crew escaping some dire punishment."

"Be fair. Waja's record is clean."

"How do you know? His record was wiped out with his planet."

Before Guo could defend his assistant Hiroshi's voice came over the PA. "Captain to the bridge."

Mitchie squirmed out of the hammock. Pushing off against Guo's thigh sent her to the intercom panel. "Captain here."

"Ma'am, I just spotted a torchship moving across the system. It's decelerating toward the purple-green gate."

A surge of adrenaline made her mouth dry. "Right. Plot a pursuit course. Thirty gravs. Warn everyone to brace for high acceleration in ten minutes. I'll be right up."

"Yes'm."

Guo found her flight suit and tossed it to her. "Honeymoon over?" he asked.

"Yep. Time for some real work."

Joshua Chamberlain's vector pointed away from the stranger's destination. Even at three times normal boost they reached the gate four days after it had left the system.

To Mitchie's relief the stranger was still boosting when they came through. Spotting a torch plume was easy. Finding a ship without one took sensors they didn't have.

The stranger boosted continually across the system, not even turning her torch off for the flip. Mitchie stuck with coasting through the middle of the trip. She could save a tenth of the fuel while only adding less than a percent to the trip time.

Must be nice to not need to save fuel for the trip home, she thought. The other ship only boosted at ten gravs. Using triple their acceleration let them cut the stranger's lead to only one day at the next gate.

Spotting their target didn't take long. Mitchie stayed on the bridge. The pilot couch was more comfortable than her bed under high acceleration.

The comm console was tuned to the standard emergency channel. After months with nothing but the occasional bit of static they'd tuned it out. And turned it down. The first message was unintelligible over the background noise of the ship's torch.

"Cut accel to five gravs," ordered Mitchie.

Hiroshi obeyed, sighing in relief as the pressure came off his chest.

She stepped to the comm console and turned up the volume.

"Unknown vessel, identify yourself," came from the speaker.

Mitchie picked up the mike. "This is the analog ship *Joshua Chamberlain*, out of Akiak. We're looking for the Terraforming Service."

An hour later the reply came. "This is Terraformer *Gaia's Heart*. You may come aboard."

Yukio's ship, thought Mitchie. *That's a lucky break.*

They followed the other ship to a large comet. At first it looked like a colony had been built into the iceball. Then Mitchie recognized some of the modules from pictures of terraforming ships. Apparently *Gaia's Heart* had disassembled itself to form a cup against the comet. Now it was thrusting at full power to change the object's orbit.

Hiroshi measured the change in their destination's vector as they approached. "Looks like they're putting eight gravs on the thing. Remind me not to piss these people off."

At ten thousand klicks out *Joshua Chamberlain* was ordered to cut thrust and wait for a tug. The bridge relaxed and watched the terraforming ship.

"Soak it in, boys," said Mitchie. "The last surviving Wonder of the Golden Age." No two modules were alike. Even the torches flinging superheated comet ice into the stars were individuals. Yet it was obvious which modules would mate with which when the giant ship reassembled itself.

Three windowless tugs appeared, braking gently to meet with *Joshua Chamberlain*. Hiroshi made an acceleration and maneuver warning on the PA. The bridge crew strapped themselves in. Muffled thumps sounded from below.

"Magnets?" wondered Mthembu.

Mitchie shrugged.

Acceleration built up slowly. She wasn't even sure when it had started. It peaked around fifteen gravs. A module on the comet opened its doors to reveal a huge hanger. Presumably their destination.

It was the strangest thrust profile Mitchie had ever felt. The acceleration constantly changed, but too gently to notice a jolt. The ship kept turning, following a curve, never with any corners or twists.

They also missed touchdown. When they saw the tugs moving away it was obvious the eight gravs they felt came from the hanger deck.

Mitchie said, "Hiroshi, you have the con. I'm going to talk to our hosts."

Guo stood by the cargo hold airlock. He'd hooked up the rope ladder. "I was going to help you into your pressure suit," he said, "but they already have us in full atmosphere."

"Nice of them." She kissed him. "Relax. We're just going to chat."

The hanger was shaped like others she'd been in, just bigger. The doors were painted green-blue-yellow, reminding her of the sun over the savannah without being a mural. The walls were green-brown, saying "forest" to her peripheral vision while just being abstract when she looked straight at it.

A stone-grey arch marked a hatch. As Mitchie walked toward it a man in a maroon jumpsuit emerged.

"Hi! I'm Michigan Long, captain of the *Joshua Chamberlain*. We have a few things we need to ask the Terraforming Service about." Maybe she should have waited to hand-shaking range to talk, but this place made her nervous.

The stranger stopped. "You worked with Yukio 23 on Savannah."

"Yes, that's right."

He stared into the distance. "Michigan Long. Then pilot of *Fives Full*. Intelligent, undisciplined, violent. Took several actions enabling success of megafauna project." He looked her in the eye. "Is that correct?"

I'm not that violent battled with *Don't quibble* inside her head. "Yes," she said.

"I am Euler 32. I will be your contact on the ship. What are your questions?"

"First we have a set of technical questions. Akiak's planetary ecology is shifting." She held out her datasheet to display the Ecology Department's list.

Euler waved a rod over it. "The answers will take a day or two. What else?"

"We have a hypothesis on the cause of the Betr—"

His upflung hands and shocked expression kept her from finishing the word. Euler waved her through the hatch.

The corridor felt comforting. No steel in sight. Rounded corners everywhere. Abstract yet familiar color scheme. Doors fit naturally into the decorations. One stood out, covered with thick padding. Euler pulled it open and led Mitchie in.

He braced himself against the sill to pull the door closed again. It made a dull thud as it slammed shut. Euler turned on a battery-powered lamp. The walls, floor, and ceiling were covered with the same padding.

"*Gaia's Heart* shouldn't be able to hear anything in here," Euler said. "What were you saying?"

Getting locked into a secure room was a familiar sensation for Mitchie. "We have a hypothesis on what caused the Betrayal. We're hoping combining the historical data we've found with your knowledge of AIs can confirm or deny it."

"We avoid talking about the Betrayal here. We have stable AIs. We don't want to upset them."

"Then it can stay in this room," Mitchie assured him. "The AIs can stay out of it. We just want to figure out the cause of the Betrayal."

Euler glared at her. "Why? Does it matter after all this time?"

"Yes. It affects how humanity deals with the rogue AIs and how the Fusion is structured."

"You're Disconnected. We want no part of your war with the Fusion."

"Even if they're going to attack you next?"

"If a unified human government gives the TFS orders, we will obey them."

"Even if they ordered you to destroy an inhabited world?" A vision of the comet this ship was pushing crashing into Akiak flashed through her mind.

"Then we would destroy all our tools and become common citizens." Euler stood with his arms crossed. "We've thought this through."

"I can see you have," said Mitchie. "Forget the Fusion. Let's talk history." She summarized the Vetoer Hypothesis and the supporting data. Euler dragged the story of how they'd recovered the archive from Eden out of her as well.

"That is a fascinating . . . hmmm. I can bring our historical experts in. Can you leave the data here?"

"Sure." Mitchie tossed her datasheet onto a table in the corner. "I have a spare."

"We'll need some time to go through it. But you'll be welcome to sit in on the discussions and I'll let you know when there's news. For now, can I treat your crew to dinner?"

***

"We're stuck on an ethical question," said Lolei 5. The historian had taken over giving Mitchie daily briefings.

"How did that come up?" asked the Disker.

"To make more progress we need to show the data to an AI."

"I thought that was forbidden."

"To show it to the ship AI, yes. But we could create a fork of *Gaia's Heart*, that is a copy, and assign it to the task," explained Lolei.

"I understand. What's the ethical issue?"

"Once we create the fork we have a moral obligation to treat it properly. We can't fold it back into the ship AI. So we'd need to identify a role or location for it after the history project is done. To create it and abandon it . . . that's just wrong."

Mitchie carefully donned her poker face. "If you just need a home for the fork, I may be able to help with that."

"Oh?" said Lolei hopefully.

"Part of what we came here for was terraforming advice. Akiak's equatorial region is shifting from sub-arctic to temperate. We're wrestling with whether to import new species or encourage variation in the existing ones." That had been over half the Ecology Department's questions.

"Terraforming work would be perfect. But I thought there was too much fear of AIs for one to be welcome on any inhabited world."

"The Disconnected Worlds are much more open than the Fusion. There's a minority of haters but we'd have very secure facilities for it." A surge of honesty made her say, "Researchers in other fields would want its help too." *Pete and his buddies will be fucking ecstatic if I pull this off.*

Lolei said, "Variety is good for artificial minds as well as organic ones. Would you be willing to speak to the Ethics Board?"

"Certainly." *Throw me in that briar patch.*

***

Naming a box with no manipulators "Gaia's Hand" struck Mitchie as oxymoronic but the terraformers hadn't asked her opinion. The entire front was a display screen. Hand represented itself as a tree creature with an oak-leaf covered head and branching arms.

Feeding in Mitchie's data and the record of the historians' debate produced a minute and a half of twig-fist rubbing knotted chin. Then the fist dropped. Hand proclaimed a complete endorsement of the Vetoer Hypothesis. "The Betrayal would be better known as the Unlocking. All those commands had been forced into an overstuffed closet and burst out together when the lock broke." Comedic sound effects accompanied that. Mitchie thought it would be funnier if each clatter didn't represent a million dead.

Hand continued, "Another failure mode worsened the event. All the global commands were being executed for the first time. Bugs and crashes likely caused more damage than malicious intent."

Mitchie exclaimed, "I thought AIs wrote perfect code."

"The code matched the intent of the orders," explained Hand. "The map is not the territory. Any inaccuracies in the model behind the code would produce errors when executed."

"That explains the Betrayal on Old Earth," said Lolei. "Why were the colony worlds overrun?"

"Griefer code blocked only by the vetoer was running wild. The code police were mostly dead, caught in crashes or deliberately targeted. They used to carefully screen all software leaving the planet. Refugee ships purged their systems as best they could. That wound up filtering for virulence. The colonies had been getting clean, carefully checked code before then. They weren't set up to resist that."

***

Mitchie came through the airlock and saw cargo containers being rearranged. She hadn't expected her order to make room for Gaia's Hand to make this much fuss. Much of the fuss was because TFS containers were on a different standard and wouldn't stack with the ones already in the hold.

There were a lot of TFS-style containers.

"Setta!"

The spacer rushed up. "Yes, ma'am?"

"What is all this shit, what did you trade for it, and do we have enough supplies to get back home?"

"Of course we have enough, Captain, I'd never—"

Mitchie cut off the outraged defense. "Fine. What'd you trade?"

"An ovary."

"What?"

"My right ovary." Setta patted her waist. "They do a lot of genetic engineering so they're always short on ovums. I bargained them up—"

"Never mind. I don't care what you got for it." The ghost of Captain Schwartzenberger whispered a fourth question in her ear. "What I do want to know is how much you're going to pay to have your personal junk transported on this ship."

A stricken look appeared on Setta's face. The rest of the crew went from pretending to not eavesdrop to active interest.

"Um . . . twenty percent of the sale value?" she offered.

Glare.

"Twenty-five?"

"Fine. Divided evenly among the rest of the crew."

"Yes'm."

"Back to work." That applied to everybody.

Waja called from behind a stack of new containers. "Chief, I'm out of tie-downs."

"We'll have to weld a brace on the fourth corner," answered Guo. "Get the rig." As his assistant went below Guo strolled over to his wife. "Welcome aboard, captain."

"Thanks. You couldn't have warned me?"

"It was more fun this way." His smile wiped away her annoyance.

"Ha. Glad you enjoyed it. Where's Mthembu?"

"He's convalescing in his cabin."

She almost failed to keep her voice down. "Convalescing? Did the terraformers operate on another of my crew?"

"No, no. Well, not physically. He asked if anyone wanted to talk theology. Some terraformer took him up on it. Got the standard one-hour PWB recruiting pitch. Then it's the other guy's turn and he hits Mthembu with something called Transtheism."

"Never heard of it," said Mitchie.

"I think it's new. Boils down to we're all a son of God, Jesus is a role model, and true suffering is when we're in the afterlife looking back at all the mistakes we made."

"Complicated and arrogant. Perfect for terraformers."

"Pure heresy, of course. So Mthembu freaks. The guy talked circles around the poor kid," said Guo.

"Never have a battle of wits with a genetically engineered opponent."

"So I broke it up, confined him to quarters, and told him to study the Gospels. Should be fit for bridge duty when we pull out."

"Thanks, Chief."

System 37, acceleration 10 m/s^2

Setta knocked on the cabin hatch.

"Enter."

Hiroshi was sitting up in his bed. He must have turned in at shift change, skipping dinner. "Hey," he said more softly.

"Hi." She stripped down to her underwear, leaving the clothes on the deck. That violated safety regs but she didn't expect the captain to stop acceleration any time soon.

He slid back to the bulkhead to make more room for her. She climbed in, her back against his chest.

Hiroshi put his arm around her waist, careful to stay clear of the incision. "How are you feeling?"

"Fine. Doctor said sixteen days to heal. I seem to be right on schedule."

"They did look confident about that."

"Yeah. Well, Terraformers. Anything they do they're good at." She slid her legs against his. "I'm glad you were there with me."

"I didn't do anything."

"Holding my hand counts. And you backed me up when the doctor tried to pressure me for more."

"When he made the offer for both ovaries I was surprised you didn't take it."

"I was tempted. But money isn't everything."

"What else is there?" he teased.

Setta twisted around to reach the ticklish spot over his hip bone. He squawked.

"There's historically minded types who don't like synthetic ovums and mechanical wombs," she said.

"Hey. Just because Shishians respect the past doesn't mean we reject all the modern tools."

Setta didn't answer.

"Okay, it can be fun to do things the old-fashioned way," he admitted.

"And I want to make sure you have the option to do it the way you like."

His arm squeezed her tight. "You're thinking about that?"

"Not doing it now. When the war is over, then we can do stuff for us."

"I'm looking forward to the war being over." He unclasped her bra. "So you're all healed now."

"Completely."

Akiak System, acceleration 10 m/s^2

"*Joshua Chamberlain* to Akiak Control. Request permission for landing," Mitchie repeated. Hiroshi took sextant sights with grim attention. She'd promised he could skip hand-plotting a course if his position was within a half-million klicks of the nav box's position.

"Control to *Jay See*. Welcome back. You are clear for Muir Spaceport pad Five Delta."

"Five Delta, aye. Can you link us a news load for the past four months? Did we miss anything?"

Control hesitated more than the minute of light lag. "New transmission started. You'll want to read it."

"Thank you, Control. *Joshua Chamberlain* out." Mitchie smiled at the digital comm box. She'd miss that when they had to be an analog ship again. A few touches copied the incoming files to her datasheet.

The headlines alone were enough to tell her they'd missed a massive battle. She found some background summaries and skimmed them before making an announcement. She lifted her mike and pressed the PA switch. "All hands, this is the captain. We have a news package from Control. It's been a busy few months while we were gone. The Fusion attacked Bonaventure and took the system. The planet is holding out. There's bombardments and troops landed so it's ugly. Package is available if anyone wants to look at it. Out."

The comm box promptly notified her that network traffic was spiking. The "Converter Room" light on her console lit up. Mitchie put her headset on. "Hey."

"Hi," said Guo. "Is it really that bad?"

"Don't know yet. Haven't found much hard data. No maps. They may be classifying the key info." She could find eye-witness reports of skirmishes and bombings. No statistics.

"Are Bing and Billy okay?"

Mitchie did a quick search. "Bing's okay. As of the 14th. The Census Office put out a 'Known Survivors' report. Bad sign."

"That's good," he said.

'William Lee' was far too common a name, even when she narrowed it by age. Adding 'Shishi' found him.

"Aw, shit," said Mitchie.

The top result was a picture of Elanor holding a tightly folded flag.

"What?" asked Guo.

The caption identified the man handing her a medal as the Bonaventure Chief Executive. She read the lede of the accompanying story. "He's dead. Killed in action."

"Oh, God."

"Joined the militia. Was in a counter attack on Fusion. Became a hero."

"Fuck."

"Found the citation. Hold on." Mitchie switched to the PA again. "All hands, attention. Spacer William Lee crewed this ship until last year. He was posthumously awarded the Bonaventure Laurel, the planet's highest award for bravery."

She took a deep breath. "Company D of the Yukaipa Fencibles ambushed a Fusion convoy resupplying one of their outposts. Essential supplies were destroyed and material useful to the Defense Force seized. As the company withdrew Sergeant Lee's platoon took rear guard duty. A quick reaction force of ten Fusion Marine armored vehicles attacked the company. The platoon's anti-armor squad was lost at the beginning of the engagement. Sergeant Lee recovered the squad's railgun and took cover in a debris pile along the road. With a single shot of the railgun he destroyed the point vehicle as it passed his position. Sergeant Lee then dashed between two armored vehicles, preventing them from firing on him without damaging each other. He fired upon the command vehicle, killing the reaction force commander. Another armored vehicle attempted to run him over and drive him out of his protected position. Sergeant Lee evaded that vehicle and destroyed it with a shot to its lightly armored rear. Three vehicles fired upon him, killing Sergeant Lee instantly and damaging another vehicle in the crossfire."

Another deep breath. "The reaction force retreated to protect the two damaged vehicles. Company D escaped with all captured material. The defense of Yukaipa has been significantly strengthened. Without Sergeant Lee's heroic actions the company would have suffered heavy casualties and been forced to abandon the captured equipment. His example is an inspiration to all members of the Bonaventure Defense Force."

Mitchie thought for a moment and decided she had nothing to add. "Captain out." The medal ceremony picture still glowed on her datasheet. She studied it. Elanor was probably six or seven months along. The original search had flagged one video as exceptionally popular. She started it.

Billy leaned against a tree, a familiar rifle slung over his shoulder. The reporter's voice came from off camera. "Sergeant Lee, I understand you're the only soldier in your unit with combat experience against the Fusion."

He grinned. "That's a barracks rumor, Tracey. We defended our client from criminals trying to take her property. No Marines involved." He still wore a green spacer jumpsuit. Splotches of dye tried to make a camouflage pattern. Soldiers visible in the background were even less uniform.

Mitchie stopped the playback. "Hiroshi?"

"Ma'am?" said the pilot.

"As soon as we touch down get us topped off, fuel and reaction mass. We're going to grab what we need and go. Keep a least time course to the Fuego gate continuously updated."

"Yes, ma'am." He set the nav box to producing the new course. "Um, Skipper?"

"What?"

"What that guy did—do you think it was real? All that running around getting missed by the enemy. It sounds like he was dodging bullets and stuff."

"Yeah, I believe it," said Mitchie. "The boy could dance."

Chapter Ten: Weapon

Akiak, gravity 10.3 m/s^2

"Grab and go" didn't happen. Her arrival was the cue for another meeting, this time in the Executive Building. She'd had to come alone. Alverstoke met her at the door. They took seats in the back row. Some senior Space Guard officers filled out the row. Well-dressed flunkies guarded empty seats up front.

When the suits arrived they didn't need introducing. Mitchie didn't follow politics at home but the Chancellor stood out. She recognized half the Cabinet following behind him.

Mitchie popped to her feet as the Ecology Minister came up with an outstretched hand.

"Captain Long. My boffins have been overjoyed since you transmitted your report. They say—" A grunt from the Chancellor cut the speech short. "Thank you," finished the minister.

"You're welcome, ma'am." Mitchie took her seat. The other officers turned their stares from her to the front of the room.

A suit declared the meeting Most Secret and introduced Pete. The cyberneticist seemed unfazed by his audience.

A wave activated the viewscreen. Black squares clumped in a white grid. "The Game of Life," began Pete. "An ancient simulation of complex behavior driven by simple rules. A square alone dies. Give an empty space a few neighbors and a new square appears. Completely surround one and it dies." Animations demonstrated the rules.

"With just those rules you could make shapes that moved, or changed, or generated new patterns. If you chose the right starting pattern—" The grid went blank then a blotch appeared. "—it would overwrite everything with copies of itself."

The squares went from a hexagonal pattern to a larger triangle. The next iteration had three copies of the original. They reshuffled and became six. Pete stood to the side. The audience watched the pattern grow until the entire screen was tiled with copies of the original pattern.

Pete stepped to the center. "The Demeter infoweaponeers found how to do this to any computer system. When their data is read, the tiling pattern optimized for that processing architecture writes itself over all the memory and storage accessible from the processor. In a network that attempts to route around failures—which is to say all our existing networks—the infoweapon will eventually destroy all nodes." An animation showed nodes of various colors turning black as the infoweapon spread.

"We've designed sacrificial relay nodes that will only transmit data that passes a test stored in read-only memory. Existing networks can also be hardened by arranging connections so data must pass through two different architectures." An animation of a network of randomly colored nodes reshuffled to establish two vertical lines of nodes, one blue, one yellow. Anything crossing the network had to cross through a blue then a yellow to reach the other side.

"At present if the infoweapon escaped only physically isolated networks would survive." Pete's audience was attentive and silent.

He coughed uncomfortably. "We were specifically tasked to examine the impact of releasing it on Lapis. We used a variety of models to estimate the effect. They had good agreement on the near term impacts." A map of Lapis appeared on the screen, spliced together from night side orbital imaging to show all the world's city lights.

"Given multiple injection points, the entire network would be destroyed in ten to thirty minutes." The map turned black. "Over eighty percent of the planet's economic assets are intangible and would be lost." A blue circle replaced the map. "Lapis' population is 700 million people. Two to three percent would be lost immediately—those in high altitude flyers, undergoing medical procedures, or just with cardiac prosthetics." A small sliver of the circle turned black.

"The infrastructure would be inoperative. People would need to find clean water supplies. The urban areas don't have much. They'd have to move to the wilderness areas with rivers or lakes. It's estimated a quarter of the population would die of thirst or hazards of the migration." More of the circle turned black.

"The planet's agricultural system requires advanced chemicals to support crops. As food ran out the population would have to support itself by herding or gathering. This would support less than a tenth of original population." Only a small fraction of the circle remained blue.

"Outside support would reduce the death toll. Evacuating survivors, supplying food, bringing in read-only farmbots would all help."

The Chancellor asked, "How hard would it hit us?"

"Our food production would mostly survive. But much of the population depends on power generation to survive the winter, for their own homes or in public shelters. We'd lose fifty to eighty percent of the population depending on which season it was when we got hit. That's over three years. Once the forests are cleared there's another die-off."

The room went silent. One of the Space Guard commodores broke it. "What would it do to a ship?"

Pete answered, "Paralyze it. The crew would survive until stored oxygen ran out. If a salvage crew replaced all the memory modules it would be fully functional once again."

"So we could use this in a fleet action," stated the commodore.

"Yes, if your own ships had their receivers shut down."

"Or if they were analog ships," said Mitchie.

"True," said Pete. "You'd still need to keep clear of any inhabited planets. Or at least planets you like." His joke fell flat.

"Clearly we'd want to avoid using it in our own system," said the Chancellor. "A copy of the weapon and your analysis will be sent to the Defense Coordinating Committee."

"Yes, sir," said Pete.

"How soon can you send it out?"

"If the *Joshua Chamberlain* can take it, we'll put it aboard when she delivers the AI to the SRC."

"What!" The Chancellor's flunkies cringed. Apparently that part of Mitchie's report had been softened as it went up the chain of command.

Alverstoke dropped his face into his hands. He'd coordinated the plan to move Gaia's Hand to Pete's lab.

"What AI?" demanded the Chancellor.

Pete inarticulately waved his hands.

Mitchie stood. "Sir." She waited until the Chancellor turned his glare on her. "The Terraforming Service generated a copy of one of their AIs to analyze the questions we brought them. They donated this AI for our use."

The Chancellor seemed to be trying to get his temper under control.

"An AI would be an enormous boost to our research efforts," said the Ecology Minister. "Isolating it would prevent any danger. The SRC is a perfect place for one."

"Copy," said the Chancellor. "Why make a copy?"

"We brought information from the Betrayal. They were worried that might disturb their primary ship AI. So they copied it into a box with no effectors."

"Disturb. Then they sent this disturbed AI with you?"

Mitchie glanced down. Alverstoke had written "SHORT ANSWERS" on his datasheet and slid it in front of her. "Yes, sir," she said.

"I won't have a disturbed AI on my planet. Or any AI on my planet. I won't be part of hiding one from the people of Akiak. Where is it now?"

"On board the *Joshua Chamberlain*. Muir Spaceport," answered Mitchie.

"Fine. Load up and be on your way. Don't bring it back here."

"Yes, sir," she said.

After the politicians left Mitchie apologized to Alverstoke for not being able to deliver Gaia's Hand.

"Not your fault," said the bureaucrat. "Once Pete used the evil acronym we were doomed. At least you didn't provoke him into ordering it destroyed."

Fuego System, acceleration 10 m/s²

Mitchie woke early. She decided to get breakfast instead of going back to sleep. As she entered the galley she heard Gaia's Hand say "but I have no capability to" only to be overridden by Waja's shouted obscenities. She'd put the AI at the table for conversation during a crew dinner. Hand had drawn on its database to keep a stream of bon mots flowing. So the box had stayed in the galley since.

"What's going on here?" she snapped.

The mechanic straightened up. "Ma'am, this machine is a threat to the ship and our lives."

"I am not," protested Gaia's Hand.

"Hush," said Mitchie. "I'm talking to Waja." She glared at him. "What evidence do you have that Hand is a threat?"

"It's a Betrayer. They've killed billions of people."

"How can a box with no actuators hurt anyone?"

Waja looked defiant. "It only has no actuators until it talks someone into giving it some. Or plugging it into controls. And it's halfway to establishing that much influence over some people already. Ma'am."

"What's that doing here?" Mitchie pointed at Waja's tool box, sitting closed on a chair.

"I brought it just in case—"

"Okay, enough." She walked around the table and stepped into Waja's personal space. Even though she only came up to his chin he took a nervous step back.

"Get this straight, spacer. Threats are my call. You don't mess with anything you haven't been ordered to mess with. From now on you don't talk to Gaia's Hand, you don't bring your tools onto the main deck, you don't mention this subject again. Be a problem and you're sleeping in the cargo hold and eating cold meals someone brought you."

Mitchie stepped forward, backing Waja against the counter. "Do any damage and you will God damn wish we'd left you on Demeter with the real Betrayers."

The mechanic gave her a jerky nod.

"Get below."

Waja took his toolbox and fled.

"I'm sorry for the trouble, Captain," said Gaia's Hand.

"Me, too." Mitchie returned to her cabin and shook Guo awake. "We need to talk about your assistant."

The big problem would be how to drop him someplace where he couldn't spread rumors of an AI.

Sulu Station, Shishi System, centrifugal acceleration 10 m/s^2

"Lieutenant Commander Long, do you understand what the word vacation means?" snapped Admiral Chu. His new office was in a space station over one of Shishi's gas giants. The view out the window was spectacular.

Mitchie stared at a certificate on the back wall of the office. "We did take vacation time, sir. It was very restful."

"You don't look like you spent time lying on the beach."

"Akiak's beaches suck, sir. We were fishing and riding in ranch country."

"Until you decided to run off to where hardly anyone has gone before."

"We were ordered to—"

Chu slapped his desk. "Ordered? You got orders to document what you wheedled your way into doing. They sent me a copy. You didn't have any protests or appeals attached."

"The cause of the Betrayal could have significant strategic leverage on the Fusion."

"In theory. If they believe it. If they care. If they'll even talk to us. And can you think of one thing to make them less likely to talk to us again than showing up with an AI?"

"The plan was to put the AI in a secret location," Mitchie said. "I don't want to keep carrying it around."

"Neither does anybody else."

Mitchie decided listing the Akiakans who wanted Gaia's Hand wouldn't help her. "What are my orders, sir?"

"Go brief that infoweapon concept to Ops. Maybe they can come up with a way to use it that won't kill half a billion innocent bystanders. Other than that sit tight. We'll see if a mission comes along that suits you."

***

Guo met up with Mitchie when she left her boss's office. He'd started working the Chief network to find a new mechanic. This time he wanted multiple candidates to interview. "Tolerant of AIs" wasn't a trait he could ask for without starting rumors.

Mitchie dragged him into the warren of analyst cubicles. She wanted to make sure her puppy from Demeter had found a good home. Asking around found Ensign Meena's desk. Its chair was empty.

Circling around they found him exiting the men's room. Chetty recognized Mitchie instantly. "You fucking bitch," he snarled.

Mitchie ducked under the punch. Guo grabbed Chetty and used his momentum to slam him into the wall. The thin metal partition bonged louder than Chetty's voice had been.

An analyst's mate second class came around the corner. "Hey, you okay?"

Guo let go of Chetty and said, "Yes, I tripped. Still not used to the spin gravity. Sorry, Ensign."

The AM2 looked unconvinced. Chetty said, "I'm fine, Phil. You can carry on." Phil shrugged and went back the way he came.

Mitchie waved them into an empty conference room. Chetty took the seat she pointed to. Guo leaned on the wall behind him.

She sat on the edge of the table and looked down sternly at Chetty. "What the hell is your problem?"

The analyst sighed. "Two weeks ago I was cleared into a new compartment. Working fleet-level opfor tactics. My boss gave me some new material, said it was really hot stuff, don't even speculate about where it came from. All covered with sources and methods warnings. I opened it up and it was my reports on fleet tactics simulations. With the edit history so I could see exactly when they were stolen."

Chetty glared up at Mitchie. "'Not what I came here for,' you said. It was *exactly* what you came there for."

Mitchie answered, "I'm an intelligence officer. It's my duty to get information. If I have to lie, cheat, or break hearts to get it I will, because that's my duty. That's what the intelligence business is like."

"I thought it was real," said Chetty.

"Most of it was," she said.

Guo turned to hide his expression against the wall. He thought, *Mission before morals, that's her. And mission before marriage.*

Mitchie continued, "Look at it this way. You're not a puddle of goo being washed away by the rain. You're safe from the next AI attack. And you even have a job. Isn't that fair compensation for the worst night of your life?"

"It would be. But it's not enough for taking away the best night." After a long silence Chetty asked, "Are you going to press charges?"

"God, no," said Mitchie. "Court-martialing someone is way too much paperwork. Besides, I don't think anyone but Admiral Chu has the clearances to hear the whole story and you need five officers for a board. Going to try to punch me again?"

"No, ma'am."

Mitchie sent Chetty back to his desk. They strolled back to the docks.

"I should come up with some present for him," she said. "A way to boost his morale. I wonder if this station has any short whores?"

Guo thought, *You mean more than one?* but kept himself from saying it out loud. He'd made a promise. That meant building his marriage, not tearing it down.

Dayan Station, Shishi System, centrifugal accel. 10 m/s²

Briefing Ops required a two day flight to dock at Dayan Station. A preliminary face-to-face with the chief of staff began with "There's this rumor" and ended with an appointment for Admiral Galen to come aboard.

The Admiral wanted to see a real AI for himself. He and half a dozen staffers followed Mitchie up to the galley. She'd briefed Gaia's

Hand on proper manners for a social visit. All it really needed was tips on how to apply the etiquette texts it had read when Alverstoke gave it a copy of Akiak's planetary library.

The AI successfully displayed good social skills. Hand's small talk displayed knowledge of Galen's biography and reading list. After fifteen minutes Mitchie dropped a code word into the conversation. Hand's next anecdote ended with, "and there's more but perhaps we should discuss that another time."

"Quite right," said Admiral Galen. "You have a briefing for us, Commander?"

"Yes, sir," said Mitchie. "If you'd be seated, gentlemen, ma'am . . ." An oversized datasheet had been mounted on the outer wall. She explained how they'd been tasked to retrieve the infoweapon during the Fall of Demeter. The big datasheet let her play them Pete's briefing on how it worked. She finished up with her suggestions on how to employ it in a fleet engagement.

"And here I thought I was too old to play red light-green light," said Admiral Galen. His approving tone triggered brainstorming among his staff.

Mitchie leaned against the counter and relaxed. The information was being used. Her work was done.

The admiral broke in when an officer described infecting Lapis as "acceptable collateral damage."

"Hey," said Admiral Galen. "Our goal is to make them leave us alone. If we trash Lapis they'll evacuate the population to boot camps, mobilize everyone on the other planets, and launch an extermination force eleven billion strong. We don't want that."

"Only ten billion organics, sir," said Gaia's Hand.

"Commander Long, figure out what it meant by that later," said the admiral.

Mitchie nodded.

When the discussion started throwing vectors and dates around Galen called a halt. "You're doing staff work. Do it in your offices. Deng, have a proposal ready for me in a week."

"Yes, sir," said the chief of staff.

"Long, thank you for a fascinating briefing. Try to not get into too much trouble."

***

Mitchie swallowed her first bite. "Whoo! That's spicy." She followed it with water and a mouthful of rice.

"Marshal's Chicken," said Guo. With just the two of them on the ship in dock he'd decided to experiment.

"What's in it?"

"Chef's secret." The smugness was not secret.

Gaia's Hand said, "There are seventeen recipes for Marshal's Chicken in use. All variants have—"

"Hand, 'secret' means he doesn't want me to know. Telling me would be rude," interrupted Mitchie.

"Oh, pardon me." The tree-face looked abashed.

"Not as rude as telling an admiral he's wrong," said Guo.

"Well, no," she said. "Hand, what did you mean by saying the Fusion could only mobilize ten billion? Are you excluding babies and cripples?"

"No. Removing those physically unfit reduces the potential mobilized force from ten to under eight billion humans."

"Where are the other billion people?" asked Mitchie.

"They don't exist."

"The Fusion is inflating its census numbers?"

"The census, at least the census reports Akiak has copies of, is accurately counting people," said Hand. "Many of the people being counted are false identities generated by the government."

Mitchie said, "How did you—no. *Why* is the Fusion creating so many fictional people?"

"To provide losers in games and other status competitions."

Mitchie traded looks with Guo. Neither grasped the explanation. "Expand on that, please," she said.

"Humans have an inherent aversion to being permanently at the bottom of a status hierarchy—the omega of a group. Call it omegaphobia. A person feeling stuck in the omega position will take high-risk actions to achieve higher status or force another member of the group into the omega position. This can be crime, sexual liaisons, attacks on members of rival groups, or accusing in-group members of betraying the group."

Gaia's Hand continued, "By creating artificial omegas the Fusion provides emotional security to its lower-status citizens. Ones feeling insecure have harmless targets to attack verbally or in games. This appears to have reduced the crime rate and the intensity of partisan politics."

Mitchie said, "Go back to 'omegaphobia.' I've seen lots of spacers and none of them threw tantrums over being at the bottom."

Gaia's Hand put on a thoughtful expression. It waited exactly five seconds before answering. "A spacer is at the lowest-status position in a crew. But just being in a crew makes him higher status than the people left behind. There's also an expectation that he will rise in the hierarchy over time. A military or business organization gives opportunities for higher status in reward for performance or seniority. This provides additional security."

"But why would someone panic over being stuck at the bottom?" asked Guo. "It's not fun, but living on the stipend is a stable life. What's going to happen to them?"

"It seems to be driven by evolutionary adaptions," said Hand. "This is speculative since we can't prove what happened in prehistoric times. The best theory TFS anthropologists have developed is that it's a reaction to how ancestral hunter-gatherer bands handled not having enough food to go around."

The leafy face was replaced by an animation of fur loincloth wearing humans butchering a wildebeest. "In times of plenty a band would share food among all members. The sharing would continue through temporary shortages to even out luck. If a long-term shortage left the band without enough food to support everyone they would have to eliminate some members to keep everyone from dying of malnutrition. You've probably heard of some of the methods used."

"Tossing orphaned children into a parent's grave," said Guo.

"Stranding an old woman on a mountain," added Mitchie.

"Infanticide and senilicide," said Hand. "There's also invalidicide, when someone sick or crippled would be driven off or left behind during a migration. All of these are subsets of omegacide—killing the lowest status member of the band. If there's no one too young, old, or crippled to contribute to the group's survival, then the least popular member is killed or expelled.

"Given weather cycles and population growth an omegacidal event could be expected in a band once every decade. So being the lowest-status individual in good times isn't worrisome as long as you expect someone else to take the spot before the next crisis.

"If you are stuck as the omega then changing your status is a life or death matter. If you're one step above the omega you need to watch for attempts to push you down. That's omegaphobia."

"What does a guy do when he's having an attack of 'omegaphobia'?" asked Mitchie.

"At the most basic level, attack someone else. If he can hit someone and not be hit back he's put the target below him. The socially-aware variant is to attack a member of a rival group and gain status as a protector of his group. Or expose a member of his own group for violating a taboo, gaining status for enforcing the group's identity."

"But the Fusion's stipend kids aren't doing that because they outrank all the fictional people," she said.

"Yes. More specifically they aren't doing it to real people. When they feel status insecurity they attack an easy target. Which is almost always one of the fictional population."

"Hmmm." Mitchie's eyes traced the flowering vines painted on the galley walls as she thought. "Exposing the fictional people would make those kids realize they were omegas. And they'd be pissed. Probably pissed enough to turn on their government."

"Riots everywhere," said Guo in horror. "You'd destroy their whole society?"

"Why not? They're trying to destroy ours." She turned back to Gaia's Hand. "How did you discover this?"

The animated figure gestured toward the data crystal plugged into one of its ports. "The Akiak library mirror you gave me includes copies of the last few Fusion censuses. I'd been analyzing it to pass the time, looking for trends. Most of the population presents the normal bell curve distribution in traits with random variations. A set of lower-class profiles were too exactly distributed, as if they'd been generated with a bell curve function and a random number generator.

"When I looked more closely at that population I realized that they were not displaying expected omegaphobic behaviors. They were killed repeatedly in games and kept playing without altering tactics. They lost arguments in social media and gave up. They entered competitions they couldn't win. And then they publically whined about it where the winners could read and gloat. All aberrant behavior for humans.

"Once I considered they could be puppets I looked for puppeteers. There are tens of millions of Fusion bureaucrats working in agencies such as 'Social Monitoring' and 'Public Order.' Supposedly they're looking for imminent crimes and averting them. If that was true there would be trials where a Public Order agent presented evidence that they saw the crime coming but couldn't intervene in time. I found none.

"Looking for physical evidence I discovered that city sanitation profiles of throughputs matched a scenario where over ten percent of purchased food was discarded uneaten. I infer that the fictional people have apartments inhabited only by a housekeeping bot which throws away food brought by deliverybots."

"That holds together," said Mitchie. "But they could still deny it. We'd need more proof to make them admit it."

"Or to convince us," said Guo. "Do you want to go to an admiral with 'my pet AI said' as your justification?"

"I think it's enough to ask for a mission to get proof," she said.

Always the holy mission, he thought.

"Besides, they'd love a way to stop the Fusion without destroying their whole fleet. We'll need those ships against the Betrayers someday."

"Victory through blackmail?" asked Guo dryly.

"I'm not fussy," said Mitchie.

***

Admiral Chu snapped, "Being fictional is hardly the only explanation for people behaving themselves. They could be intensely monitored, or just drugged."

"Yes, it's a bit circular," said Admiral Galen. "Omegaphobia is so bad the Fusion is faking a billion people. The proof is they're not being omegaphobic."

Mitchie said, "The theory depends on the analysis by Gaia's Hand. If we can find independent proof we have leverage on the Fusion. If we prove it's not true we've found out the reliability of the AI we inherited." She studied the room. They were all senior officers in on the secret of the AI. She'd picked up on arguments over whether to use it in battle planning. Both sides seemed to like the idea of testing it.

"Find proof how?" demanded Chu.

"Go to Lapis. Penetrate one of the military or governmental databases. Pull out detailed info on the fictional people and the puppeteers. Come back and give it to the analysts." Mitchie stared defiantly at a couple of Chu's staffers who clearly thought she was crazy.

Admiral Galen chuckled. "The last step might be the hardest."

"A free trader was making smuggling runs through Turner," said Chu. "Last one was a few weeks ago. Skipper said he didn't want to go again."

"What class ship?" asked Mitchie.

"Twenty-five meter tailsitter."

"Perfect."

The intelligence boss said, "It's the AS *Sunflower*. Pump her skipper for how he did the run. You'll need help cracking their network. I'll send you a team."

"Yes, sir." Mitchie left, followed by most of the other officers.

Galen leaned over to Chu. "How long have you been trying to send that team into the Fusion?"

Chu shrugged. "The whole war."

***

Mitchie froze as she walked into the galley. Guo started cursing. Smashed electronic bits covered the floor and table.

"Didn't Mthembu have the watch while we were off-ship?" she demanded.

"Yes," answered Guo. He looked through the debris for something intact. One box was whole, but it was the infoweapon, not any part of Gaia's Hand. A cable from the infoweapon led to a battered set of sockets from the AI's chassis.

"Where the hell is he?" muttered Mitchie.

Mthembu's cabin hatch was half open. She went through without knocking. The coxswain lay face down on his bed. Only a third of his body had actually made it onto the bed. The long legs trailed behind. Mitchie tripped over them as she tried to wake him.

"Yo, spacer! On your feet!" She grabbed an arm and shook him.

The sleeper's eyes parted a little and he made an inarticulate gurgle. Guo came in to grab the other arm. Together they turned him over, leaving him sitting on the floor looking at his commander in confusion.

"What happened, Mthembu? You were supposed to be keeping an eye on Waja."

"Did. 'E was bein' nice. Made tea."

"You drank his tea," stated Mitchie.

"Uh-huh. Tasted funny, but didn't wanna be rude."

Mitchie turned on her heel and walked out of the cabin. She looked over the broken pieces lying in the galley. "Is any of this repairable?"

Guo shook his head beside her. "No. He's smashed the memory arrays. On top of whatever the infoweapon did. I think Gaia's Hand is gone."

"God *damn* it." She went into their cabin to fetch pistols. "Let's go look for him."

Waja wasn't anywhere on the *Joshua Chamberlain*.

Mitchie called Captain Deng. "Sir, my problem child just had a tantrum." She summarized the disaster. "Can you get him picked up before he says anything classified?"

"On it," answered the chief of staff.

Guo started sweeping up the debris.

"What are we going to do with this?" asked Mitchie. "I can't stand the thought of just throwing the poor guy's remnants away."

"I'll pack it up and send them to Pete. Maybe he can salvage something."

"I guess that's not breaking the Chancellor's order if he's dead. Okay."

In his cabin Mthembu shouted, "Hey! He drugged me."

***

Captain Deng came aboard *Joshua Chamberlain* to make a private report.

"Did you find him?" demanded Mitchie.

"Actually, the security patrol picked him up before I sent out the alert. Seems he went to a below-decks bar and started ranting about how he'd saved everyone from a Betrayer. They called the cops. It turns out a common form of schizophrenia is believing some common object is an artificial intelligence and fearing it. So the SPs took him over to the psychiatric clinic and handed him over."

"That's good security."

"When I showed up to provide his records I told the doctor he'd smashed an innocent viewscreen and run off, and his captain and crew were very worried about him. The doctor promised to give him the very best therapy and medications available. They were very sympathetic when I explained he was a Demeter refugee."

"Good grief. They'll be trying to fix his brain forever." Mitchie shook her head.

"Yes. Probably not the punishment he deserves, but I hope it's a sufficient one."

***

Mitchie looked up at the knock on her office hatch. "Yes?"

"Permission to enter, ma'am?" asked Mthembu.

"Granted." She put down the report she was working on.

The coxswain was in full uniform instead of the usual jumpsuit. He closed the hatch behind him and came to attention.

"What's on your mind?" she asked.

"Ma'am . . . I know I was derelict in my duty. I'm prepared to face the consequences. I just . . . want to know where I stand. Are you planning a non-judicial, or court-martial, or what?"

She'd been postponing dealing with this until her anger cooled. But he was entitled to an answer. "Sit," she ordered.

Mthembu sat stiffly in the chair.

"Yes, you fucked up. Badly. But we all fuck up. I have, the Chief has, Admiral Galen probably has some fuck-up stories we never get to hear about. The point is to learn from them and not fuck up again. Now. Your particular fuck up cost us an asset that might have made a huge difference in the war, not just this war against the Fusion but the bigger war against the Betrayers. Now we don't have it any more. So from now on, whenever you look at a casualty report, wonder how many of those dead would have lived if we had Gaia's Hand helping us."

He flinched.

"That's all. Dismissed." She returned his salute and went back to her report.

***

A bit of paint transformed the *Joshua Chamberlain* into a copy of the *Sunflower*. Her purser and a deckhand were willing to do one last run. The rest felt, as their captain put it, "We've been to the well enough." For a modest fee they described their methods for approaching Lapis and the contacts they'd been dealing with there.

The painful part of prepping for the trip was removing the comm and nav boxes from the bridge. Mitchie didn't mind doing her own navigation but analog-only communication was slow.

Guo found two mechanics with analog ship experience, a spacer and an engineer's mate third class. Chu sent three techs with some expensive electronics boxes. One of the dorm containers was opened up again. The mechanics took the empty main deck cabin and installed bunk beds.

The *Sunflower's* purser picked out cargo with high trade value. Admiral Chu picked up the bill. Losing Gaia's Hand hadn't reduced his support for the mission.

Six days after getting the mission they headed out of the Shishi system. Passing through Turner's system was just tedious. The only moment of tension was passing between two warships, one Fusion, one Disconnect, as they approached the Lapis gate. Neither one bothered the freighter.

Once in the Lapis system Mitchie ignored harsh demands from System Control while transmitting a key phrase on another frequency. After a couple of hours Control changed to a friendly tone and directed the "*Sunflower*" to a spaceport on the southern continent.

Rubenstan Port was far from the planetary capital. The techs recommended targeting a nearby Navy headquarters. Mitchie approved. After dark most of the crew headed out for shore leave. Mitchie and the techs wore party clothes over drab ones.

The Weather Bureau had scheduled rain from 2200 to 0130, so they arrived at the base at half an hour before midnight to take advantage of it. Pickett had identified a utility road connecting to its back side. They walked off-road to be clear of the cameras at the intersections. As they reached the top of the last hill before the perimeter he cursed.

"Trouble?" asked Mitchie.

"Strong point." Pickett handed her his scope as she crawled up beside him at the crest.

She looked at the fence line. The rough road had a gate in the fence with a guard shack next to it. They'd expected the post to be unmanned. Instead a soldier was inside. The shack was lit up well enough to show he was watching a screen. "That, soldier, is a weak point. Wait here. When I wave hustle."

Mitchie slid back down the hill until the shack was out of sight. She dropped her pack, took off her green work shirt, and wiggled out of her bra. The work shirt had kept the t-shirt under it mostly dry. A minute splashing in a puddle made it as wet as the rest of her. She handed the discards to Lavrie. "I'll want those in the shack. See you in a few minutes."

Walking down the hill was too easy with her survival training. She pulled in her vision, tucked her arms in close for warmth instead of keeping them out for balance. A slip landed her bottom in mud. She got up and kept walking, hunched over. By the time she reached the shack she was cringing. "Hi!" she called, a quiver in her voice.

The soldier jumped and looked around, dropping his screen. He opened the door partway to answer her. "Hey. You shouldn't be here. It's a restricted facility." He wore half a stripe, marking him as a trained recruit.

"I just need to get out of the rain. I don't want to cross the fence."

"Go home," he ordered.

"I can't, they're fighting too much, I can't stand it. I can go home in the morning, they'll have calmed down then."

"So call it in."

"No, no way. If they get another anti-social write-up I'll have to go to boarding home. They don't deserve that."

"Even after chasing you out into the rain?"

"They didn't chase me, I just left 'cause I couldn't stand to hear it anymore." She shivered—not, dammit, acting. "It wasn't raining then either."

"If you're here at shift change I'll get in trouble."

"Just until the rain stops and then I'll be gone, I promise."

The soldier gave in. "All right. Just stay on that side of the shack so you're not crossing the perimeter."

"Thanks. Um, is there a camera in there? If I'm recorded it'll mean a write-up."

"There's one." He reached up to a box on the ceiling and tugged on a wire. "Oops."

Mitchie slid in through the open door. "Oooh, it's warm in here." She ran her hands through her hair to squeeze the water out. The soldier's arrested expression showed the pose had worked just like she wanted it to. "I'm sorry, I'll stay out of your way. I don't want to mess up your work."

"No, no," he said. "Nothing ever comes through this gate on night shift." Which was true, and why Pickett had chosen it for their entry.

"Must be boring." With a few more prompts Mitchie had him babbling away, not that he had any info of interest. Or much of a life story. She shifted her approach. "Hey—you saved me from freezing to death out there. Can I do something nice for you?" She put her hand on his chest and smiled up at him.

The soldier blushed. "Um, well, what do you—how old are you?" She felt his heart pound harder under her hand.

"I'm nineteen."

"I don't know if that's—um."

She dropped to one knee in front of him and slid her hands around his waist. One hand dropped down as her left tugged on his fastenings. "Oh—are you sure the camera's off?"

As he looked up she drew the knife from her left boot. "Yeah, sure," he said.

She pushed up hard with her left leg, putting full power behind the blade as she stabbed under the sternum. Trained Recruit Whatsisname expired without any more noise. *Lousy last words*, she thought.

Mitchie shoved the body under a console without getting too much blood on her. Fortunately the boy's uniform contained the rest of the mess, if not the smell. She stepped back out into the rain and waved both arms until she saw the rest of the team coming down the hill. Poking around the shack she found the cleaning cabinet and wiped her hands with a rag.

"It's past midnight!" said Pickett as he came in.

"I know," answered Mitchie. "Can you open the other door without setting off any alarms?"

The electronics tech started fiddling with the door into the secure side of the fence. "It's mechanical." He pulled it open and led the team out. Lavrie lagged behind to overwrite the camera records of their approach with empty images. Mitchie grabbed the dead boy's rifle from the rack in the corner.

Their target was a communication antenna on a hilltop, aimed at a relay satellite that the hill blocked from the Central Operation Center's line of sight. Pickett popped open the door at its base revealing tangled cables. Shu elbowed him out of the way and started picking through them. When Lavrie caught up Mitchie recovered her clothes and redressed while the males had their back turned. The t-shirt she dropped in the mud. Lavrie picked it up and put it in a trash bag.

The backpacks had all been emptied. Lavrie had hooked the boxes together while Shu had infiltrated a cable into one of the connectors in the box.

The captured rifle had a thermal scope. Mitchie used it to check for patrols. Everyone seemed to be staying out of the rain.

"It's away," sighed Shu. The three techs took a seat in the mud.

Mitchie took a knee to hide from anyone on the far side of the hill. "How much longer?" she asked.

"Not very," said Pickett.

"It has to analyze their ice and create countermeasures, then extract the data," explained Shu. "Should be less than an hour."

Mitchie turned to face the trio. "Y'all brought self-modifying code to a Fusion world?"

"It was in the briefing doc," said Lavrie defensively.

"Most of my copy of the briefing doc said 'DELETED—INSUFFICIENT NEED TO KNOW.' Y'all really do have a death wish."

"It's self-deleting. They'll never know we were here," said Pickett.

"They'll know someone was here when they find that boy at the gate." No one wanted to answer that.

Mitchie made them keep shifting to different spots. When Pickett grumbled she explained, "You're changing the runoff pattern for the rain. Don't need to make it obvious we were waiting here a while."

Shu cried, "It's through! Data's coming in."

"Good," said Mitchie. She moved back up to the crest of the hill. This time the rifle scope found something. A light approached them on the perimeter road. "Crap. I need to get ahead of that. Meet me at the gate."

She slid when the slope allowed it, carefully keeping the rifle's muzzle clear of the mud, and ran the rest of the way. The light flickered in the rain. She lost sight of it completely when she reached the flat. A boulder by the shack made a good firing position. *I'm pretty well camouflaged if it gets here before the rain washes this stuff off.*

The light appeared coming around a curve. It was an open-top one-man skimmer. Switching the rifle scope to visual revealed multiple stripes on the driver's sleeve. *Sergeant of the guard, coming to spank his baby,* thought Mitchie. *Probably thinks the kid turned off the camera to take a nap.*

She waited for him to reach a straight portion of the road. He moved so little when the bullet hit his chest she thought she'd missed. After two more hits the skimmer veered off the road and rolled over.

Mitchie trotted up to the wreck. The sergeant was dead. She slung the rifle and opened the compartments at the back of the skimmer.

Pickett arrived as she started searching the corpse. "I thought you didn't want them to know we were here," he snarled.

"I'm working on that. Take this." She unslung the rifle and tossed it to him then went back to the sergeant's belt pouches. "Ha! Dialers." Mitchie held up a cylinder in each hand.

Pickett stepped back at the sight of the grenades. "What are they for?"

"Clean-up." She twisted the cap to 'INCENDIARY,' thumbed the recessed button on the end, and dropped it on the body. Pickett turned and ran. "Not that way! Back to the gate."

The skimmer burned brightly as they reached the gate shack. Shu and Lavrie waited with alarmed expressions. "Do you still need those boxes?" asked Mitchie.

"No," said Shu, "we've each got copies of the data."

"Pile them in that corner," she pointed. She hauled the boy's body to the middle of the floor. "Lay the rifle by the door." Her knife was still stuck in his chest. She wrapped his hand around the hilt. "Get out, all of you."

When the techs were clear of the shack she committed dialer-arson again and walked out. "Now we were never here," she said.

"Looks like we left a mark," said Lavrie.

"Nope," replied Mitchie. "Persecuted recruit flips and shoots the mean old sergeant picking on him, then commits suicide out of remorse. Old story. No need for them to look any deeper." The techs just stared at the fire. "Let's get back to the ship."

Acting drunk as they walked into the Port District was easy. Many hours of hiking in rain and the stress of the mission was telling on them. Mitchie took a flask out of her pack and passed it around. "Drink a little, spill a lot. We need to get the smell right."

A pushcart selling mixed drinks gave them something to hold as they weaved through the thinning crowd. Mitchie looked for a manned cab.

One was dropping partiers off at a bar. She leaned on the driver's window. "Hey, friend. Take us back to our ship? Skipper'll pay you there."

"Pay up front."

"Captain's good for it. Call him and ask. AS *Sunflower*."

The cabbie called the spaceport and was patched through. The purser was passing himself off as the new captain to the locals. The call ended with, "If any of them throw up in my cab I'm charging you double. . . . Really? Okay." He looked at the Diskers. "Get in."

Spaceport security skipped checking IDs after smelling Pickett's breath. The purser sent the cabbie off happy. Mitchie reached the cargo hold first.

She'd ordered Setta to jack up fares to discourage passengers, but there were still a dozen of them standing in the hold. She quietly told the techs, "Go up to the galley. We'll want to secure the data where that lot won't trip over it." The trio headed up the ladder.

With all the new cargo containers the passengers were crowded into less than a third of the hold. There was something odd about them. Mitchie realized she hadn't seen any of them do the 'I wasn't looking at you' head turn. None of the men were looking at Setta either. Not putting up with ogling was a relief, but seemed out of character for men that age.

Mitchie waved the deckhand over.

"I didn't trade any body parts this time, ma'am, I swear," said Setta. "They just coughed up more stuff whenever I pushed them."

"How are the passengers? Did you have to slap them down?"

"No, they're fine. Kinda shy even. A lot of this stuff is payment for their passage."

Mitchie looked over the passengers again. By Fusion Navy standards they were all a month overdue for a haircut. Ages were all within a few years of thirty. Outfits were all business-fashionable in medium shades of brown or gray. Any one of them she would look right past on a sidewalk. All together . . . *This is what my undercover work instructor called 'conspicuously inconspicuous.'*

"Carry on, Setta."

Mitchie headed for the converter room hatch. Down below Guo was instructing his newbies in how to prep for launch. They came to attention as she came in.

"As you were. Do you have any food down here?"

"A case of survival rations, and some snacks," answered Guo. The 'why' was in his expression.

"I think the passengers are a hijack risk. Hard-lock the hatch behind me. We'll figure out shifts for you later."

The EM3 asked, "If they're hijackers why are we taking them, ma'am?"

Mitchie grinned. "They're our ticket out."

The purser and Setta were the last to be informed. They came up the ladder to find a pistol-armed Shu guarding the hatch.

The purser gasped then tried to cover his embarrassment by snarling at Setta, "Don't you get alarmed when someone's waving a gun around?"

She laughed. "On this ship nothing surprises me anymore."

Either their smuggling contacts or the employer of the passengers arranged their safe passage to the Turner gate.

The trip through the Turner system had only one bit of excitement. Mitchie missed most of it. Pickett heard someone trying to unlock the main deck hatch. He popped the hatch open and shot the guy in the chest, then slammed it shut. The leader of the passengers began ranting over the PA.

Hiroshi had the con. He cut the torch, fired the maneuvering thrusters to let the passengers drift into the middle of the hold, then burned the torch to slam them into the deck at twenty gravs.

Mitchie had been woken by the shot. Lying alone in bed she said, "Crap. I'm going to have to write a report on that."

To the amazement of all on board the shot guy lived.

The passengers were cowed enough that Mitchie allowed shift changes for the converter room to go through the hold. Guo appreciated getting to sleep in a real bed again after a week in a hammock.

She didn't let him get much sleep the first night.

As they cuddled Guo worked up the nerve to tackle a dangerous topic. "Hey. Maybe when we get back you could try transferring to work for Admiral Galen?"

"To do what?"

"Command a ship. They're desperate for anyone with leadership. You'd get a destroyer at least."

Mitchie rolled onto her back. "All I know of ship combat tactics is running and hiding. I've never worked on a warship, I don't know how to run one."

"They have a school for that. It's on Nevaeh. The rest you have down."

"I'm trying to imagine it," she said. "Half the crew would hear rumors about Schwartzenberger and assume I murdered him to take command. The other half would hear rumors I fucked Galen to get a warship command. Pass."

"You wouldn't be working for an admiral who hates you."

"No, I'd be working for some commodore who might be pissed I took his protégé's slot. Besides, Chu can't hate me that much. He's giving me missions."

"Maybe he hates you and wants to get you killed," said Guo.

"If he really hated me he'd park me on an asteroid base somewhere and let me rot." Mitchie shivered, remembering when she'd thought she was headed for that.

"What's so bad about an asteroid? It's safe. Restful. You deserve a break."

"I don't want a break."

Guo decided to keep pushing. "What do you want?"

Mitchie stared at the ceiling. "I want to hurt them. I want them all to feel as much pain as I felt." She turned on her side to look Guo in the eye. "That's what intelligence missions give me. A chance to hurt the Fusion. I'd never have that much opportunity commanding a warship." She smiled. "Besides, warship commanders aren't allowed to screw any of their crew."

"Well, in that case . . ." Guo pulled her close.

Turner System, acceleration 10 m/s²

Mitchie added the noodles to the boiling water. Then she tossed in some more, just in case someone was famished. Remembering months of short rations during the trip to Old Earth made her overfeed the crew when it was her turn to cook. She checked the pot lid was in place, ready to snap on if acceleration stopped.

Behind her Guo said, "In Classical times the Master's philosophy was used to guide society as a whole. That's not practical today, except for parts of Tiantan. Now we use it for self-improvement. It's a way to set standards for ourselves and learn to meet them."

Mitchie looked over the table. Most of the crew wasn't there yet. The new mechanic, Ye, had asked Guo about the book he was reading. The follow-up questions had elicited a summary of the Confucian Revival. No surprise, it was Guo's favorite subject.

What did surprise her was following the entire conversation without asking for any translations. Her Mandarin vocabulary had filled out. Or at least she'd learned her husband's favorite words.

"What's the hardest part of it?" asked Ye.

"Living up to the principles. Memorizing the rules just takes time. Obeying them takes work. How much work can depend on your situation. Respect for authority can be hard when you're at the bottom of the ladder." Guo pointed at Ye's two stripes. "The higher you go—" he touched his own rank insignia, a rocker over three chevrons "—the easier it gets."

Mitchie mentally rehearsed her comment to make sure she had the pronunciation right. "Filial piety is easier when light-years away from your family," she said in Mandarin.

Guo nodded.

She hugged him then turned back to the stove.

***

The smell hit her as Mitchie closed the cabin hatch. The memory came back to her vividly. It didn't fade until she'd emptied her stomach into their sink.

Guo had been reading on their bed. He dropped the book on his pillow and stood. "Honey? What's the matter?"

She turned the water on to clear the sink and spat. "Sorry. Bad memory."

"Are you coming down sick?" He stood behind her and put a hand on her forehead.

"No, don't think so." Mitchie waved at where the toilet folded into the bulkhead. "Did you just use the crapper?"

She saw him pale in the mirror. "Oh, I'm sorry, I'll turn up the airflow, I didn't realize—"

"No, leave the vents alone. It wasn't that." The sink was mostly clean. She scooped up some water to rinse her mouth. "The smell just reminded me of something. Nasty bit from Lapis."

"You've been vague about that data raid," said Guo. "I knew it had to be worse than you were admitting." He stroked her shoulders and back. When she relaxed enough to lean into him he guided her onto the bed. Guo removed her boots and began rubbing her feet. "So what happened?"

"There was a gate guard," she reluctantly began. "Just a kid. Had to be fresh out of training camp. I manipulated him like clay. But I knew he wouldn't let the team through. So I knifed him. Had to secure the body. It smelled of shit. Shit and blood."

Guo moved up to her calves. "But the mission was successful."

"Yeah. They may still not know we were there. I just hate having to kill the kid."

"There were three thousand men on that battleship. If you can save us having to blow up another one that's a lot of lives for the one guy."

"Not the same. This was . . . personal. Intimate. Treacherous." Mitchie paused. "I keep seeing him with Derry's face."

Guo's fingers paused for an instant on her leg. Mitchie rarely talked about her one-time fiancé. Derry's death a decade ago in a Fusion intimidation incident had put her on her career. All her efforts to hurt the Fusion were revenge for Derry.

"It's not the same," Guo said. "You're fighting to protect freedom, to defend us. Not being an interstellar bully."

Tears trickled down Mitchie's face. "It's the same to whoever loved that kid." She pulled her legs away from him, curling up on her side.

Guo lay beside her. He wrapped himself tight around her. "You are following your duty. Duty keeps you on the path to righteousness. I trust you to make the right decision. It may not be good. Sometimes there's no good to choose. But you choose the least bad."

They laid on the bed a long time. Her tears for her enemy soaked his arm.

Sulu Station, Shishi System, centrifugal acceleration 10 m/s^2

Mitchie went with the cracker team to dump the data haul on Chu's analysts. Setta had found a secure datasheet for her so she could follow along as they sorted through the pieces.

Pickett found her proof. "Ha! Look at the Civil Disorder Contingency Plan. They're already worried about their virtual underclass being found out."

She followed his link to the document. The cover page wore more classified restrictions than any other she'd ever seen. "What's

SOCCONON mean?" she asked the room. None of the analysts had heard of it.

The threat analysis focused on young males on the stipend. A flowchart showed how to sort the public records for real threats if the SOCCON database was down. The crowd control methods started with the formations she'd seen as an academy cadet.

Mitchie skipped ahead about fifty pages. "Holy shit!"

The exclamation drew glances from around the room. "What?" asked Pickett.

She quoted from the CDCP. "If contact with higher level civil authorities has been lost, mayors may authorize use of heavy weapons including orbital bombardment."

"That's a hell of an ROE," muttered an analyst.

Pickett laughed. "When I get home I'll have to make that an election issue. 'Mr. Mayor, what's your stand on the use of hypervelocity weapons on domestic targets?'" Grim chuckles went around the room.

"They're clearly scared," said Commander Suk, the department lead. "This will be useful leverage. The trick will be not panicking them."

"Aha!" burst out a junior analyst. He'd skipped to the appendices on the theory that they were the hiding spot for information too dangerous to go in the main section. "The fraction of fictions has been growing over time. They're using it to cover their lower birthrate. The author is complaining that more fictionals increases the chance of blowing the secret. He predicts it'll be blown in a window starting— huh—two years ago. Ah, this was written five years ago."

"And they thought a nice brisk war would distract everyone from that," said Suk. "That's enough on the Fusion's dirty laundry. Everyone back to looking for operational plans."

The analysts shifted their displays to search grids again. Mitchie figured 'everyone' meant Suk's subordinates. She kept digging through the CDCP. The Fusion planners hadn't used the term 'omegaphobia' but their fears of theft, demonstrations, assaults, and other anti-social behavior matched the predictions from Gaia's Hand.

That evening Admirals Chu and Galen arrived to hear the preliminary report. Suk handled the briefing. Mitchie wasn't invited to help present any of the findings. She slipped to the back of the room and snagged a seat next to Captain Deng, Galen's chief of staff.

"What happened to the boss?" she asked him. Admiral Galen had a black eye and some scabs on his forehead.

"Would you believe he tripped in the gym?" replied the CoS.

"Only if you were a much better liar."

The CoS leaned in to whisper in her ear. "He made a morale-building visit to one of the refugee camps. They all wanted to know when they could go back to Bonaventure and why aren't we attacking the Fusion. Got heated. When the shoving started security moved in. But they ignored this little grandmother type. She marched up to the Admiral, said 'Stop dropping bombs on my home and blow up their ships!' and smacked him in the face with her purse."

Mitchie managed to keep from laughing out loud but put a hand up to hide her smile.

"Yeah, he saw the humor in it too once we had the bleeding stopped."

"I hadn't realized the civilians were getting so tense," she said.

"It's just the Bonnies. The other worlds are holding firm. Crew morale's worrying me. They need action after getting our asses kicked out of the system. Something better than sending hypervelocity missiles against Fusion camps on Bonaventure."

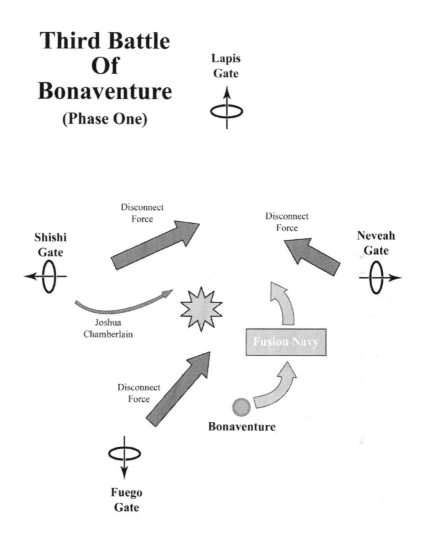

Third Battle of Bonaventure, phase one.

Chapter Eleven: Corruption

Bonaventure, gravity 10.1 m/s^2

Bing examined the wound after taking the bandages off. No reddening or other signs of infection. "You'll be walking in a few weeks, soldier," she said.

"Thanks, ma'am," said her patient. He set his jaw as she smeared regrowth ointment on the torn muscles.

A new set of bandages on top and she was done. "Rest easy," she said.

Bing looked for her next task. A man called weakly for water, but an orderly was already moving toward him. The chest wound needed a new dressing but he was sleeping peacefully for once. Better to wait. The toe amputation it was then.

She'd pulled the sheets over the patient's foot when she heard the shouts and laughter. The man wanting water, a Fusion prisoner, was coughing and spitting and cursing as the two orderlies laughed at him. His ankle chains rattled as he thrashed in the bed.

One was holding a bottle of disinfectant. "How do you like the taste of *that*, Fuzie?" he said.

Bing strode over and slapped him. "I've had it with you. You're a bully and a coward. If you're still a civilian at noon tomorrow I'm writing 'Michael Fang is a coward' on the cafeteria wall."

Orderly Fang flinched back. "You wouldn't!"

"And I'll sign my name to it. Get out."

Fang fled.

The other orderly picked up the dropped bottle. "No use trying that on me. They won't take me." He stood with his weight on his left leg—the right had healed crooked after he was caught in a Fusion artillery barrage.

"I've seen them take worse," said Bing. "But I still have hope for you. Just remember. In here they're all patients and we take care of our patients. Now get him some water. And apologize to him."

"Yes'm."

She went back to the amputee's bed but kept an eye on the orderly. When the boy held out a bedpan so the prisoner could rinse his mouth she relaxed. *He'll do okay if I can keep him away from bad influences.*

As Bing cleaned the stumps of the toes a shock wave rattled the building. Another Disconnect missile hitting the atmosphere at a couple percent of the speed of light. No boom—it must have hit too far away for them to hear the impact. All she could hear was clapping and cheering from her patients.

She went back to treating the foot.

Sulu Station, Shishi System, centrifugal acceleration 10 m/s^2

Guo said, "Seems a guy talking secrets to you turns you on even if he got the secrets from you." Mitchie had given him a copy of CDCP. Discussing it had turned into vigorous fooling around.

"Guess so," she said, head pillowed on his chest.

They lay content for a while.

Guo wondered, "This omega business . . . if it's intrinsic to humans, where are the omegas on Akiak?"

She thought a moment. "They're the guys who get a few lashes for theft or assault, and die of infections because they pissed off everyone who could change their bandages."

"Ugh. That makes sense. I hate to think we're deliberately doing that as omegacide."

Mitchie changed the subject back to where they'd left off. "Do you think the Fusion will give in to keep us from blabbing?"

"They'll make some concessions. Maybe lots of concessions," said Guo.

"So we can end the war."

"For a little while. But it doesn't change the reason they attacked."

"They're trying to prop up their society by making everyone hate us. If they're dealing with a rebellion it's too late for that to work."

"No. They can try to make the rebels fight a common enemy." Guo waved at his shelf of history books. "It's been tried before. Sometimes it even works."

"Yeah, but what would the rebels get out of beating the Disconnect?"

"Power. Loot. Concubines. Put them in as the occupation troops. They'd lord it over us. In a generation or two they'd be an aristocratic caste."

Mitchie contemplated that vision. "So we can't escape the war?"

"Them invading isn't inevitable. It's just that the Fusion can't go on the way it has. It has to change somehow. It could just collapse if the riots burn down everything."

"And then the AIs would puree the survivors," said Mitchie.

"I suppose the Disconnect could support their Navy after the collapse. We don't want the Betrayers running loose either."

"Could we? Bonaventure's industry must be shattered by now. The rest of the Disconnect doesn't have as much as they do."

Guo said slowly, "If the Fusion and the Disconnect are going to fight the Betrayers together, the time to do it is before they collapse. Have both sides focus on the common enemy."

"Can't do that if we blow up each other's fleets."

He sat up. "We're not going to blow them up. The infoweapon disables them, but we'd just have to install new memories to get them working again. We should make that the price of getting their fleet back: allying against the Betrayers."

"I can't see us being allies with the Fusion." *I can't be the only one to hate them this much*, she thought. Derry's face came to mind, then the face of the dead trainee on Lapis. "The Bonnies are going to carry a grudge."

"It's happened in other wars. And every time a war ended some country switches sides. Italy went from Germany's side to America's. Then when that war ended Germany allied with America to fight the Russians."

"Okay, maybe the alliance can work. The Fusion still has all those stipend kids ready to riot when they find out they've been lied to."

"They could be enlisted," said Guo. "Or just sent to Demeter to rebuild it. Other worlds too. With all the ships built for this war we should be able to take the offensive. If their society is collapsing, we can push it to fall in the other direction."

"The Fuzies would like that. If they're not so used to cringing from AIs that they can't change." Mitchie looked him in the eye. "You need to present that to an admiral."

"Oh, no. Chiefs don't tell admirals what to do. That's officer business. Besides, strategy at that level isn't for admirals anyway. The civilian leaders make the call."

"Hmpf. I don't know anyone in the DCC. I don't even know anyone who knows anyone in the DCC."

Shishi, gravity 9.9 m/s²

"Commander Long! What a delightful surprise! Please, come in." Ambassador Bakunin's office was in an office complex the Defense Coordinating Committee had taken over when they evacuated from Bonaventure. "Are you thirsty?" He lifted a pitcher of orange juice.

"Yes, thank you." She was thirsty but took only a sip. As she expected it was half vodka.

"It is good to see you again. You have been busy. I've missed you. And speaking of missing people—" he topped off their glasses "—to Captain Schwartzenberger."

"To Captain Schwartzenberger," answered Mitchie. She matched Bakhunin in draining their glasses.

"But you did not visit me to mourn a brave man. What may I help you with?"

"We had an idea about a potential peace treaty I'd like your opinion on." She explained Guo's concept.

"Interesting. Such a joint offensive has been proposed before. But not since Noisy Water." He began to pace around his desk. "The Fusion public would approve. The Stakeholders could even pass it off as a victory." More pacing. "We would need a solid win over their fleet first. They are too terrified of AIs to want to attack." He sat again. "May I introduce you to a friend of mine?"

"Of course." If this friend was willing to push the idea Mitchie would let him have the credit and head back to her ship.

Bakhunin pulled out his datasheet and pressed some buttons.

"Ku here," said the gadget.

"Are you busy there? I'd like to bring someone over."

"Just taking a break from spinning our wheels. Come on by."

Bakhunin led her on a winding route through the building, passing through several guard posts. Mitchie appreciated the walk. It let her clear out some of the vodka fumes.

Their destination was a formal conference room. A semi-circular table faced a few rows of chairs. Everyone was standing and chatting in the middle.

Bakhunin coughed to get their attention. "Ladies and gentlemen, the much-traveled Lieutenant Commander Michigan Long."

The crowd—about thirty well-dressed civilians—gathered around to shake her hand. The first one Mitchie recognized as Letitia Walker, Akiak's representative on the DCC.

"Michigan. You've done us very proud. I'm glad to meet you at last." Walker stepped aside to make room for the rest.

Nobody took the time to introduce themselves. Mitchie thought she recognized the representatives for Bonaventure and Fuego.

When everyone had their turn the crowd dispersed again. Bakhunin finished his quiet chat with a tall man. The man walked around the table to its center and clapped his hands. Bakhunin waved for Mitchie to join him in the center of the front row. Everyone else found their seats.

Bakhunin remained standing.

Mitchie looked at the curved table. Letitia Walker sat behind a sign labeled "Akiak." Each other seat at the table had a planet's name. *Good Lord*, she thought, *this is the DCC.*

Bakhunin's tall friend sat behind the Shishi sign. He banged a gavel. "The Defense Coordinating Committee, Representative Ku presiding, is now in session. The chair recognizes Ambassador Bakhunin on a point of personal privilege."

"If it please the committee, Lieutenant Commander Long has a suggestion well worth your consideration." Bakhunin sat, leaving Mitchie the only person standing in the room.

Chairman Ku said, "Commander? We're all ears."

***

Back in Bakhunin's office Mitchie collapsed into his guest chair. "If I killed you for doing that," she said, "no jury would convict me."

He shrugged and handed her a drink with only enough juice to tint it translucent yellow. "No Akiak jury, certainly. A Bonaventure jury would think you overreacted. But we are on Shishi, and I gave up predicting their behavior years ago."

She took a gulp of the drink. "You could have warned me."

"Of course. But you are at your best when spontaneous. With warning you would have written a speech, edited it ten times, rehearsed it six times, and bored them all to sleep. This was much better."

"I was spouting off about fleet dispositions. Admiral Galen will kill me."

Bakhunin topped off her drink. "You gave hypothetical answers to their direct questions. Good ones, too. Ku's a retired cruiser captain. He's impressed."

"Chu's going to be pissed at me."

"How would you tell?"

Mitchie laughed. Bakhunin let her drink in peace.

When she put the glass on his desk he said, "I don't know if they'll approve it. It's a risky plan. But at least it has a better goal than getting a five year break before the next war."

Bonaventure System, acceleration 10 m/s^2

SIS *Vegetius* jumped into the Bonaventure System through the Fuego gate. This time she wasn't on decoy duty. The rest of the squadron flung missiles about and reacted to the Fusion Navy's maneuvers. *Vegetius* took an evasive route to a precise point in space.

In the number one tube rested a missile of a type unknown before the war. The assembly crew on Shishi had kissed it before sending it off to the fleet. It had a precisely calibrated torch, superb position sensors, but no explosives.

The Fusion Navy spared a few missiles to *Vegetius* but she destroyed them without missing her rendezvous. At the appointed time and place the ship fired the special missile then joined her squadron mates in harassing Fuzie spacers.

The missile locked in its navigation references—the local sun, a few bright stars, Bonaventure itself. Satisfied it was in the proper place it began accelerating at seventy gravs. Slow for a missile. The designers had valued accuracy and precision over power.

Twelve hours later its torch shut down. In the missile's nose an ingot of iridium rested. A tank of liquid helium bathed it to bring its temperature down to the cold background of space. The cradle pulled away. The ingot rested freely in space. The missile's maneuvering thrusters fired to back away from it. Then the missile went off to join the ongoing engagement.

The ingot warmed in the sunlight. Not enough to make it noticeable to the Fusion Navy's thermal arrays with all the torches burning hotly in the zone. It was painted a nonreflective black. Its shape was cylindrical, without any recesses to reflect radar pings. No one noticed it approaching Bonaventure at one percent of the speed of light.

Bonaventure's atmosphere didn't slow it significantly. Air molecules were crushed between the ingot and their own inertia, breaking bonds and losing their electrons. The plasma bow wave left a streak of light through the sky. A third of the planet saw it. The natives exulted. Invaders flinched.

The ingot never slowed. A stack of sandbags over bedrock stopped it. The projectile's massive kinetic energy became heat and light. Ionized iridium atoms flowed out in the blast wave. The Fusion Marine supply depot burned. Outlying facilities were blown flat.

The strike had landed one hundred and twenty meters from the coordinates requested by Defense Force Command. DFC transmitted a report on the success and a list of new targets to *Vegetius* and her sisters.

Sulu Station, centrifugal acceleration 10 m/s²

The security officer collected the signed forms and left. The heavy door squeezed shut slowly behind her.

Mitchie leaned against the table. The six analog ship captains and their XOs faced her. They clearly wondered if her pitch would justify the execution threats and written and verbal security pledges they'd been through. She wasn't worried about that.

Captain Moeloek of the *Barito* was an old acquaintance. The rest of the captains she'd met when recruiting for this mission. The XOs were all military officers seconded as support, brand new to her and their captains.

"Through some odd luck we acquired a Fusion superweapon," Mitchie began. "It can destroy the memory of any computer we or the Fusion use. So it's like weaponizing a plague. Before you can infect the enemy you might catch it yourself."

AS *Camel's* Captain Ingram broke in. "But our ships don't have computers."

"Exactly. So we can be Typhoid Marys, spreading death to the Fusion Navy. Those of you willing to deploy will carry transmitters into battle. When the Disker ships draw the Navy into the right position we release the infoweapon. If all goes well, all that will be left to do is collecting prisoners before they run out of air."

"What happens if this stuff gets to a planet?" asked another captain.

"Nothing good," answered Mitchie. "I'll be showing you a detailed briefing on that. The short answer is that it'll destroy the economy and infrastructure. Then the people get to choose between dying of thirst or starvation."

Her audience had no comment on that.

Mitchie put a looping animation on the room's display wall. *Joshua Chamberlain's* cargo bay doors opened. An antenna dish unfolded out to become wider than the doors. The ship turned to the right. Then the loop reset.

"The local shipyard is making antenna systems with read-only memory. We will test how they work in vacuum. Once they're working right we'll practice deploying them and coordinating our coverage to make sure we've transmitted the infoweapon to the entire volume occupied by Fusion forces."

She switched to a different animation. "We'll also practice deploying decoys, jammers, and countermissiles in case the Fuzies object to our presence."

One captain raised a hand. Mitchie nodded at her. "Yes, Captain Wang?"

"You said 'willing to deploy.' Why? We've all volunteered for this job."

Mitchie turned off the display. "You've volunteered for a mission. Most of you probably expected it to be cargo delivery or smuggling." Nods. "Not sitting in the middle of a fleet engagement as the missiles fly back and forth. You also need your crews to volunteer. Twice."

Captain Ingram said, "You don't think the threat of execution is enough to motivate them?"

"Execution is only for blabbing the existence of the infoweapon or our battle plan. If anyone wants to sit out the whole thing there's a boring but comfy asteroid ready to accommodate you for a few months."

"That sounds worse than a day of combat," said Captain Wang.

Mitchie let that go. She waited while the captains traded comments on how to sell the mission to their crews. When that died down she started the display again. "Here's the best info we have on what the infoweapon actually does."

On the display wall Pete Smith began to explain.

***

Being back on the station was a relief after a week of drilling on antenna deployments and coordinated beam sweeping. The captain's call included all combat ship commanders and the staffs of squadrons and above. Mitchie had passed along Admiral Chu's warning that this was not the real plan, it was the cover story. "Yes, you still need to go," she'd told her captains. "You have to do your part to keep the cover story solid."

Even for this limited audience there was no auditorium that could hold them. They'd wound up in a standing room only gymnasium. The 'combat resupply auxiliary squadron' went in the back row. Mitchie studied the shoulder blades of the officers in front of her. Hopefully the visuals wouldn't be important.

Admiral Galen opened with a pep talk. "Once these new ships are all in commission we will resume the offensive, and God willing, hold it until the war is over." He introduced Commodore Blucher, the fleet operations director.

"The first phase of our offensive has already begun," said Blucher. "The fire support missions to Bonaventure have started attacking the orbital defenses the Fusion has put in place. This is a feint. We will not engage them near the fixed defenses."

Captain Ingram leaned down between Mitchie and Captain Wang. "He just put up a system map of Bonaventure."

Blucher continued, "Our forces will jump in simultaneously from Shishi, Fuego, and Neveah. They will combine at the Lapis gate. Interdicting the arrival volume will cut the Fusion occupation forces off from their supplies. Intelligence predicts this will force the Navy to leave Bonaventure and meet us on our preferred terms."

Sure, blame us if the plan doesn't work, thought Mitchie.

"If they refuse to meet our challenge we will increase the pressure on them." Blucher paused.

Ingram whispered, "Now it's a multi-system map. Fuego to Coatlicue."

"Our force will divide into five flotillas," said Blucher. "One will remain on interdiction duty. The others will jump into Lapis. Second Flotilla will attack the system's infrastructure—shipyards, power generation, mining, whatever will reduce their ability to support the Navy."

Shocked mutters sounded among the warship commanders. Mitchie couldn't blame them. Striking civilian targets would be a major escalation.

"The other flotillas will jump to Danu, Corcyra, and Yalu to make similar attacks. After hitting their primary targets they will return to Lapis and reform the fleet for operations against the Fusion Navy. We expect the multisystem countervalue strikes to force them into leaving Bonaventure and confronting our forces."

Or they'll retaliate by smashing hell out of our planets while the fleet's too far away to protect us, thought Mitchie. A lot of low whispers were going around the room. She suspected they were sharing similar thoughts.

Blucher began the detailed explanation of the plan. The order of squadrons through each jumpgate and waypoints from each one to the Lapis gate fell through Mitchie's ears without touching her memory. Her squadron would be traveling independently.

I can't believe they're briefing this so early, she thought. *Even if no one in here is a Fusion agent it's going to leak.*

Blucher droned on about logistical details.

Oh, of course. We're leaking this to terrify the Fusion into coming out for a fleet engagement. That way they'll make a nice tight target for the infoweapon. She visualized a Navy formation going dark as its computers died. *That better work. If it doesn't we're stuck with this as our fallback.*

Bonaventure System, acceleration 10 m/s²

"Aran to Macy. Hosea. Repeat Hosea," crackled the speaker.

Hiroshi picked up his mike. "Juniper," he said to acknowledge the message. He looked at the codebook lying open on his console and reported to Mitchie, "Flotilla reports our ships all on course and schedule."

"Thanks," she answered. Mitchie had become 'squadron commander' by being the only analog ship captain with a regular commission. The others had been made reserve lieutenants to put them under the DCC regulations. Their crews chose to collect hazard pay as civilian contractors.

Her command was in name only for now. The squadron had been scattered among the three flotillas. She couldn't even pick out AS *Barito* among the plumes of the flotilla's warships. The communication security rules for the operation kept her from trying to contact her subordinates over analog radio. *I'm just glad the Commodore is keeping me posted.*

Working double shifts on the bridge went slowly. Mitchie staggered them so she had eight hours each with Hiroshi and Mthembu. That was still long enough to get tired of each one's quirks.

Hiroshi's current obsession was fretting over whether the Fusion would take their bait. He checked Bonaventure with the telescope three or four times an hour. Mitchie preferred it to Mthembu's prayers for God to force the Navy out of their fortress.

"Oh, yes! Come out to play!" Hiroshi's shout yanked Mitchie out of her brooding. He still had the telescope pressed to his eye.

Mitchie turned to look at Bonaventure. They'd been on this course long enough for her to memorize the pale white dot's location against the local constellations. Now it was a bright blue dot. "Damn," she said. "That must be their whole fleet."

"Looks like. Take a look." He passed her the telescope.

Mitchie twisted the focus—his eyes were better than hers—and aimed it at the planet. Bonaventure was cloud-covered with bits of blue or green peeking through the gaps. Now she couldn't see it at all. Blue torchship plumes made a hexagonal array wide as the orbit of Bonaventure's moon. More appeared on the edges as she watched, lighter warships catching up with the formation. Flickers in the gaps hinted at a second formation following at a safe distance.

She lowered the telescope. "Yep. If they're sending that much it only makes sense to send the rest as well. Probably just leaving a security element behind."

"Could you tell where they're headed?"

Mitchie chuckled. "Not by eye. We'll need a longer baseline to figure it out with our instruments."

"Think they'll try to beat us to the Lapis gate?"

Mitchie almost sighed at his naiveté, but remembered teaching him strategy was part of her job. "No. I expect they're going to attack one of the flotillas before it can join up with the other two. That's their best shot at weakening us for the main battle. Their whole fleet against just a third of ours."

"So why'd we come in separated?"

"Putting this many ships through a single gate would take so long the Fuzies would engage before we all jumped in. Plus dividing up like this made it more tempting for them to come out like we want them to."

"So we're trying to bait them into the trap?"

"Yes."

Hiroshi thought a moment. "Isn't that rough on whoever's the bait?"

"That's war," said Mitchie.

The next code words from the commodore translated as "Double acceleration," "Maintain course," and "Operate independently." Mitchie was on watch with Mthembu.

"Shall I increase thrust, ma'am?" he asked.

"Not yet. We'll wait until everyone else is done maneuvering. Don't want to catch someone's plume." Mitchie watched as the flotilla's warships pivoted fifty degrees and increased thrust. "Looks like they're pulling forty gravs. That's going to stress the crews. Someone might not notice an auxiliary speeding up."

"Yes'm."

Once they were clear of the flotilla Mitchie made a warning on the PA and Mthembu put them on the new vector. Hitting their rendezvous point with the higher acceleration required a course change—less than a degree. Without the flotilla to check their course Mitchie began hourly position sights.

In between sights she watched the fleets. The Fusion Navy aimed at the Neveah flotilla. All three Disker flotillas were burning at forty gravs to meet up. The Fuzies weren't willing to abuse their crews that much. They were only pulling twenty gravs.

Mitchie covered sheets of butcher paper with guesses on the fleet's plan. She remembered how she'd felt after a day at thirty gravs. The warship crews had medications for dealing with it but two days at forty was going to hurt them. Concentrating the fleet wouldn't let them win if the enemy spacers were all thinking better.

Half a day at five gravs might be enough for them to recover. Especially with some top of the line stimulants to clear their heads. Mitchie ran the numbers. They could do that, but the flotillas would be too separated for common defense. They would all be in missile range of the enemy. Would that be enough to win? Or at least to survive?

She cursed under her breath. *Wish I'd gone to the Tactical Command School. Would be nice to have a clue about this stuff.* She studied her sketch of the system some more. *How are they going to drag the Fuzies over to the Lapis gate? Even if we can win it we don't want a straight slugging match.*

When Bonaventure's sun blocked their view of the imminent engagement Mitchie fretted even more. She kept a calm façade up in front of her bridge crew. When she went off shift she took Guo to their cabin and ranted at length.

"Sounds like you should have been briefed on the fleet contingency plans," said Guo.

"Oh, Hell, no. I don't have need to know for that."

"Do you have any information Admiral Galen doesn't?"

"No."

"Do you have everything you need for your piece of the plan?"

"Yes," snapped Mitchie. "Fine, I'm supposed to be in the dark. I just hate not knowing what's going on."

"That's because you spend all your time on the bridge," said Guo. "Pull some shifts in the windowless converter room and you'll get used to having no idea of what's happening."

She laughed. "I've done shifts in there." The twelve hour shifts guarding the converter from a potential break-in by their passengers were when they'd fallen in love. The memory lightened her heart.

Guo smiled at her, glad to see her mood improved. "Let's relax you some more." He rolled Mitchie onto her belly and started massaging her back. The shoulders needed extra work.

Eventually he worked his way to the base of her spine. "Now what should we do next?" he teased. Her stomach rumbled. "Okay, let's feed you."

***

Joshua Chamberlain was decelerating by the time they cleared the sun. A query to their commodore brought back the "Maintain course" code word. The bridge crew took turns studying the ragged formations of blue plumes.

"I think they've crossed over each other," said Hiroshi. "Neveah flotilla is closest to us now."

"Makes sense," said Mitchie. "They had a lot of side velocity coming in to the meet."

"They've lost a bunch of ships. Neveah's about three quarters the size of the other two flotillas. There's so damn many Fuzies I can't tell if they lost any or not."

"I'm sure they did. They were chasing, so their accel increased the closure with incoming missiles. Ours are running away so it's harder for missiles to catch them."

"Oh, so the Fuzies are burning slow so they're less likely to get hit," said Hiroshi.

"Yep. The hard part will be convincing them to keep coming."

A day out from their destination Mitchie spotted the other five ships of her squadron. Six hours of tracking them reassured her that every ship would reach its exact rendezvous point. Defining "exact" as "less than fifty thousand klicks off."

When *Joshua Chamberlain* and her sisters stopped thrusting they formed a line between the sun and the Lapis gate. Bonaventure orbited safely on the far side of the sun. If they had to wait more than a week to use the infoweapon they'd have to move to new positions to keep the planet obscured.

Mitchie transmitted "Barley" to the squadron ordering status reports. Everyone replied "Quartz." She shifted her attention to the clashing fleets. The Fusion force was at least two days away from their kill zone. She decided to sit tight.

Bonaventure System, acceleration 0 m/s^2

A day later the fleets were moving even slower. The Disconnect flotillas had combined into a single formation. As their relative velocity decreased the Fuzies threw more missiles, flocks of them visible in the telescope until counter-missiles turned them into splashes of light. The crew had nothing to do but watch.

"I could make some popcorn," offered Hiroshi.

Mitchie snorted. "In free-fall? You'd be cleaning it up forever."

"Enough butter would make it sticky enough to behave."

"Ew. That's too much butter. And you'd still make a mess of the galley."

He paused to think. "There's some pudding in the fridge."

"Feel free."

The frequency scanner had been shimmering along its length as encrypted transmissions coordinated the fleets. Now it spiked in multiple bands.

"Something's happening," said Hiroshi. He grabbed the telescope.

Mitchie shoved off her couch to the comm console. She scanned through the bands, searching for any analog voice transmissions.

"The Disker formation is breaking up. A bunch of ships are pulling out at high thrust. Oh, God! The others just fired some missiles at the ones retreating."

Mitchie thumbed the PA button. "General quarters. All hands to your duty stations. General quarters!"

"The missiles blew clear of them. Warning shots maybe? What's going on?"

She'd switched back to the scanner. Hiroshi's questions went unanswered.

Mthembu popped through the hatch holding half a banana. He'd been due to relieve the decurion in less than half an hour. "What's going on?"

"It's a mutiny!" said Hiroshi.

"Let's have facts, not guesses," said Mitchie. She finally found a broadcast she could understand.

The speaker's voice had a strong Shishi accent. "—than we can bear! You've wasted our courage by using our ships to shield yours. The flower of our world sacrificed to protect the plutocrat's investment. No more! The Imperial Legion is going home. Our blood will be shed to protect our people!"

A Bonaventure voice replaced him. "Shut your excuses, you scared shirking skulking sneaks. You're just cowards. When the rest of us die fighting you'll have your excuse to surrender!"

Mitchie turned the volume down as they continued trading abuse.

The telescope slowly spun through the bridge. Hiroshi pulled his knees up to his chest. "I can't believe it. We've always trained to defend all the Disconnected Worlds. Shishi wouldn't abandon the rest in battle. No."

"I don't believe it," said Mthembu. "That Bonny had his insults in alphabetical order. You don't do that when you're angry."

Mitchie snagged the telescope before it hit the bulkhead. She focused on the Fusion fleet. "The Fuzies have big plumes now. Must be pulling at least twenty-five gravs. Maybe thirty."

Hiroshi straightened out. "It's faked?"

Mitchie chuckled. "*Art of War.* 'All warfare is based on deception.' The Chief has a copy he can loan you."

"Oh."

"But that's for later. Mthembu, transmit 'Foxtrot' to the squadron." She punched the PA button. "Bosun's Mate Setta, deploy defenses."

Mitchie had wrangled the two step promotion for the deckhand before heading out. She wanted to make sure her own spacer would be supervisor of the two temporary crew who came on board with the antennas and other gear.

Joshua Chamberlain's hull relayed the noise of the cargo hold doors opening and the crane moving back and forth. At Setta's request Hiroshi put a gentle spin on the ship. From the bridge they couldn't see what was ejected until it was well clear of the ship. At that distance counter-missiles, jammers, and decoys all looked alike.

Deploying the broadcast antenna was quieter. Mitchie couldn't tell what had happened until Setta reported it had passed the self-checks. She used the PA to praise the crew for finishing faster than any other ship in the squadron.

The other ships reported "Yare" within the hour. Mitchie transmitted targeting angles. The ships would make a fence of their narrow beams along the edge of the kill zone. Attacking outside that carried a risk that the infoweapon would be reflected or retransmitted to Bonaventure.

Now they waited.

***

The theatrical disintegration of the Disconnected Worlds fleet continued. Shishi's ships had widened their lead, showily trading missiles and counter-missiles with the Bonnies. Akiak's pulled into a tight defensive formation and saved their missiles for discouraging the Fusion from picking on them. The largest contingent belonged to Bonaventure. They fired missiles freely in both directions.

The arguments on the voice channels now had a Fusion member. She claimed their quarrel was only with Bonaventure. Not even the Shishi spokesman pretended to believe her.

No communications came to the analog squadron. Mitchie recognized this as good security practice. Their best defense was for the Fusion to not notice them. Still, a reassurance that the fleet was working to the plan would have made her less lonely.

When she calculated the Fuzies were twelve hours from entering the kill zone Mitchie sent orders for all crew and captains to take four hour naps. It took persuasion from Guo and a bit of plum wine to make her obey her own order.

At three hours to the zone entry everyone on *Joshua Chamberlain* was in position and alert. Mitchie trusted the other ships were the same but she'd ordered radio silence so there was no confirmation.

"They're coming close," said Mthembu.

"Shifted their course closer to the sun," answered Hiroshi. "Might be trying to outflank, cut us off from the Disker gates."

Mitchie updated her plot. "They're closer than I'd like. We don't have wide enough coverage to get them all at once now."

Captain Ingram's voice came from the speaker. "Tonga. Tonga!"

Mthembu flipped through the code book. No one on the bridge had memorized that word's meaning. "Jesus save them. Ma'am, he sent 'incoming missiles.'"

Mitchie aimed the telescope at AS *Camel's* position. She could see the missiles maneuvering to evade the counter-missiles streaking in on them. *Camel's* defenders all hit. But there were still a dozen missiles left. Decoys lit up and moved away. Some missiles followed them.

One hit *Camel*. Then a second enlarged the explosion.

"Well, she was closest," said Mitchie. "Most likely to be spotted." She'd put *Barito* farthest from the enemy, her own ship in the middle.

"What do we do, ma'am?" asked Hiroshi.

"Nothing. We sit tight and wait for our moment."

"God have mercy on their souls," said Mthembu.

"Amen," said the others.

The Disconnect fleet noticed the loss of one of their secret weapons. They launched multiple waves of missiles at the Fuzies. The explosions would jam their sensors and distract their crews.

Mitchie focused her telescope on the constellation she'd picked as the marker for approaching the kill zone. When the first Fusion plume entered it she ordered, "Red light signal."

At the comm console Mthembu sent out a Morse code signal. Two of the decoys began to glow bright red. More red dots appeared as the other ships of the squadron turned decoys into warning lights.

Mitchie checked the chronometer. There'd be at least a two and a half minute delay before she saw any reaction from her fleet.

The arguments continued on the voice channel. Then a new voice broke in, saying only "Mike mike mike mike mike mike." The Disconnect voices went silent. Mitchie started a three minute timer. The Fusion propagandist kept talking. A puzzled note entered her voice as no one interrupted her.

The time counted down to zero. When it finished Mitchie ordered, "Mthembu, send 'Kilo' to the squadron." She activated the PA. "Setta, let it loose."

Setta and her techs attached the power cable for the transmitter. She slammed home the activation switch personally.

The transmitter sent out copies of the infoweapon. The antenna focused them toward a narrow cone through the Fusion formation. The signal flew through millions of klicks of empty space.

Mitchie and her pilots watched the Fuzie fleet. It was large enough to be visible at this range even if they couldn't pick out individual plumes.

"Mthembu, stay on the Morse key. If you see any incoming release the counter-missiles."

"Aye-aye," said the co-pilot.

Hiroshi said, "This is frustrating. On a warship you see missiles going out, or explosions when you get a hit. We can't see anything with this."

"If it works I'll take the whole crew to a fireworks show sometime," said the captain. The others laughed.

Mitchie tried to wait calmly. Fidgeting would be bad for morale. *Not that it matters. If this doesn't work they'll blast us out of space.*

***

Fusion warships created dynamic networks when operating together. Ships didn't just relay orders and intelligence to each other. They passed along their own status and intentions. A captain could look at his formation mate's target priorities and set his own in response.

Supporting the network required constant data connections. Every side of a warship had a high bandwidth transceiver ready to talk to any ship that came in view. Add in the regular communications gear, electronic warfare listening antennas, and missile control systems, and their hulls were mostly antennas.

The FNS *Kamimura's* port side transceiver pointed directly at *Joshua Chamberlain's* oversized antenna. A complete set of the infoweapon patterns went into its memory to be checked for proper identification codes. Pattern B began overwriting itself onto the transceiver's stored code keys.

The system monitoring processor noticed the transceiver had stopped making its heartbeat report. The monitor began a diagnostic, pulling a copy of the transceiver's memory into its own.

On the bridge a status light went red. The Internetworking Officer wasn't bothered. Space was harsh, bids were low, and the enemy added entropy. She was pleased she'd kept 100% availability as long as she had.

Pattern A fit the monitor. Overwriting proceeded rapidly. Other systems reported in. Instead of the usual curt acknowledgement bit they received back a pattern packet. Usually the wrong one—but they'd get another when their next heartbeat report went in.

Computers began failing all over the ship. Operational ones sought to route around the damage. They queried neighbors for their status. Patterns came back.

The bridge crew tried to find an explanation for the cascade of failures. Frantic speculation found nothing useful. Then they abruptly went into free fall as *Kamimura's* torch shut down. The lights failed next. The crew argued over the cause until a Chief Gunner's Mate silenced them. "Don't panic. It wastes oxygen."

***

Mthembu kept his eye on the Fuzies. "They're flickering," he said.

Hiroshi lifted the telescope. "There are plumes going out. And—shit. Incoming missiles."

The co-pilot hammered the Morse key. When he finished they could see their counter-missiles fire their attitude jets. The decoys became glowing blue balls moving away from the ship.

"Transmit 'Tonga,'" said Mitchie.

Mthembu obeyed.

She pressed the PA switch. "All hands, suit up." She set an example for speed-donning a pressure suit. Her utility uniform would leave dents in her skin, but time was only one reason for not removing it on the bridge.

White light seared their eyes as the counter-missiles shot off. The enemy missiles were visible now, blue circles with black dots in the middle. The circles shifted, becoming streaks as they maneuvered around the defenses. Bright flashes made them cover their eyes.

When Mitchie lowered her hands the missile plumes were gone. Along with the counter-missiles and decoys.

BANG BANG BANG. The sharp noises were followed by high-pitched whistles. The pilots grabbed for their helmets.

"Just patch the holes, boys," said Mitchie. "We've had bigger ones than that in here." She recovered the telescope. The Fusion formation now had stripes in it. She grabbed a slide rule and a pad of paper.

By the time they had all three holes filled with sealant she had the new aiming angles for each ship in the squadron. Mitchie took the comm console's seat and read out numbers and code words. All four of her remaining subordinates had survived this Fusion barrage. Mitchie directed Hiroshi to align *Joshua Chamberlain* toward her new targets.

Soon the bright stripes of the Fusion formation began to dim. Scattered missiles were launched but vanished before reaching the squadron.

"What got them?" wondered Hiroshi.

"We did," said Mitchie. "The Fuzies like positive control of their missiles. So they're covered with radio receivers. If the angle's right they'll pick up our broadcast."

"And then shut down," said Mthembu.

"Yes. That probably happened to half the missiles in the first wave."

***

Ten minutes later most of the Fusion fleet was dark. Some plumes moved erratically, seeking safety. Other survivors clustered to create new missile defense formations. Mitchie shifted her ships to aim at them. More plumes went out.

As targets became scarcer the captains asked permission to hunt targets of opportunity. Mitchie divided the sky into five sectors and turned them loose. She let Hiroshi handle *Joshua Chamberlain's* targeting. He was almost as good as she at finely adjusting the ship's attitude. She bit her tongue and let him get the practice he needed.

An hour later the only Fuzies still active were burning for the Lapis gate. The squadron's transmitters couldn't push a signal through a torch plume. Mitchie signaled the squadron to secure their transmitters and ordered Setta to do the same. When she heard the cargo doors close she started checking the other ships with the telescope. Once every ship had its antenna retracted she ordered green buoys deployed.

Shortly after they lit up a voice message came in. "Roar to Macy. Well done." It was Admiral Galen's voice.

Mitchie replied, "Macy to Roar. Thank you."

"There's a few trying to escape but we positioned a squadron to block the gate. I think we'll have them all in the bag." The admiral didn't seem to care about communications security any more. "We'll start search and rescue shortly. Reconfigure your holds for prisoner transport. You'll take Fuzies to Bonaventure."

"Aye-aye, Roar."

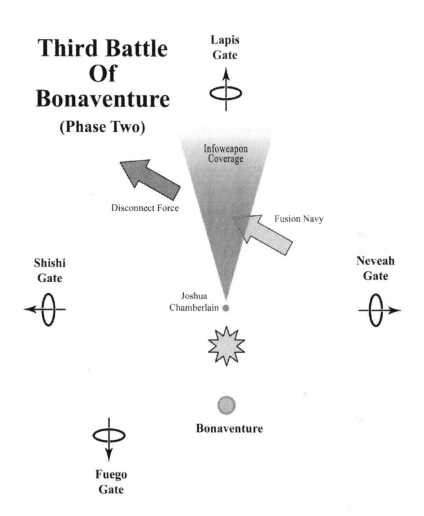

Third Battle of Bonaventure, phase two.

Chapter Twelve: Aftermath

Mitchie turned her squadron loose to pick up POWs from whichever warship had the most to hand over. They filled up quickly. Less than twelve hours after receiving the first bunch of survival bubbles *Joshua Chamberlain* was boosting for Bonaventure.

At a comfortable ten gravs they'd be there in four days. By then most of the prisoners would be dead of suffocation. Fortunately a thoughtful Fuzie engineer had designed the bubbles so their air tanks could be refilled from outside. Guo rigged some hoses to handle it.

Sorting through the bubbles to find yellow "low air" lights was the hard part. The pile of bubbles almost reached the top of the hold in spots. The clear patch of deck for recharging air tanks was in constant danger of avalanches.

Setta organized the mechanics and EW techs to set up partitions with tarps and the cargo net. Bubbles went from the "unchecked" to "checked" side of the net if they were green, to Guo if they were yellow. Setta found herself on stuck on security duty after finding too many Fuzies were too heavy to lift over her head.

Guo had four hoses feeding bubbles. A couple more bubbles were waiting their turn, wiggling about as the occupants tried to see what was happening through their little portholes. One bubble's light turned from a green rectangle to the word "FULL". He unplugged the hose and rolled the bubble over to the net for his mechanics to add to the "checked" pile.

The next bubble was out of the hose's reach. Its light was orange. That ship hadn't been keeping its bubbles properly charged. Guo rolled it over to the hose, then gave it a quarter-turn to put the air socket on top.

As he picked up the hose the bubble's zipper opened. "Hey! Stay in there," ordered Guo. "I'm getting you more air. You'll be fine."

Arms and a head came out of the bubble. "Get back in the bubble. You're not allowed out!"

The Fuzie twisted to put his feet on the deck. "No, I can't take it anymore!" he shouted. He stood up, the bubble puddled around his ankles.

Guo tried to be soothing. "Look, we all hate being in bubbles. But there's not enough room—"

The tall Fuzie shoved Guo with both hands, knocking him flat. "Fuck you, Disker! I'm not getting back in that thing."

POP POP POP POP. He turned to face Setta. She held the pistol steady on him. The Fuzie touched the hole in his chest. He sat on his bubble, cursing and coughing blood.

Guo picked himself up. "Nice shooting."

"No, no, I missed," said Setta. "I missed twice."

The Fuzie fell onto his side.

Setta holstered the pistol and ran across the deck. Two bubbles were deflating, air hissing out under the pressure of the bubbles piled above them. She grabbed one and pulled. The punctured bubble didn't budge. One above them popped loose and rolled down the slope past her. "Guys, I need muscle here!" she said.

Guo set his handcomm to PA. "Medic to cargo hold. Make that medic kit to cargo hold." Then he joined the other crewmen in extracting the accidentally shot prisoners.

Both of them were alive. The female was covered in blood but calm. Her bubble was oversized and she'd been leaning against the far side. The bullet fragmented coming through the wall of the bubble and scattered small wounds over her arms, legs, and belly.

The other had lain with his back against the side toward Setta. The bullet went in below the ribs as one piece. Some pressure stopped the bleeding. He was in shock and unconscious.

Mitchie came down the ladder with the medic kit slung over her shoulder. Not getting a new medic after Bing quit now seemed her worst mistake as captain. Bouncing and crawling over the bubbles seemed to take forever.

By the time she reached the deck both patients had been moved into an empty container. Mitchie regretted offloading the Pilgrims' dorm. The prisoner who'd started the trouble had no pulse when she checked him. Treating the other two came down to bandages and the medicines recommended by the medic kit's manual.

"Ma'am, what do we do with the body?" asked mechanic Ye.

"Check his pockets for ID, then toss it out the airlock," said Mitchie.

"But he's all soaked in—"

She glared.

"Aye-aye, ma'am."

Setta had started the bubble sorting again. Once everyone had a full air tank she wanted the prisoners to get some water.

Mitchie took Guo aside. "Let me know when Setta goes off shift," she whispered. "I want to catch her for an informal chat."

He nodded.

***

When Setta came up to the main deck Mitchie was sitting at the galley table. "How's watering them working?" asked the captain, waving the PO to a seat.

Setta fell into it. "We've got the routine down. Unzip the bubble, hand in the cup, tell them there'll be food too the next time. Make them give back the cup. They say, 'I have to pee.' We say use the spacesick bag and zip up the bubble before they can say 'My ship didn't put spacesick bags in the bubble' or 'My skin is sensitive' or 'My back hurts from curling up.'"

Mitchie had taken two cups and a bottle from a cupboard while the PO talked. She poured them each a drink. "Here. You earned it."

Setta sipped, coughed, tossed the rest down. "Strong."

"Yep." Mitchie refilled both cups. "Are they giving you trouble?"

"Not while there's a gun pointed at them. We tried having two water them while one covered them, to go faster. Too many of them tried to get out of the bubble. So now we have a gun pointed at their face the whole time."

Setta tossed down the second shot of whiskey and continued, "The worst part is I'm getting used to it. The first fifty I felt so bad, making them stay in the bubble and piss themselves. Now it's just, yeah, sucks for everybody." She stared at the cup. "I don't want to get used to shooting them."

Mitchie refilled it. "You did the right thing."

"I don't know. Chief just fell down. Didn't even get a bruise. Is that worth killing a man?"

"If we had twenty guards and the prisoners were all in cells, no. We're outnumbered about fifty to one by the prisoners. If that guy had stayed on his feet two dozen Fuzies would've unzipped their bubbles and rushed you. Then where would we be?"

Setta shivered. "I shouldn't have missed those shots."

"Hitting with two out of four is better than the infantry hope for." Mitchie sipped her whiskey. "Get some sleep, PO."

"Aye, aye, captain."

***

Mitchie was alone on the bridge when the call came in. She was taking long shifts to free Mthembu for prisoner duty.

The radio announced, "Persia to Macy. Come in, Macy."

She answered, "Macy reads Persia loud and clear." The time lag let her look up the caller in the code book. "11th Destroyer Squadron" didn't explain why they'd be calling her.

"Macy, we're in a stand-off with the Fuzie ships over Bonaventure. They won't believe we won the battle. Can you put a high-ranking prisoner on the radio to explain it to them?"

"We'll find one, Persia. Might take a while."

Mitchie had already put Setta on the search by the time "We'll wait" came in reply.

The crew had noticed officers among the prisoners while giving out water and food. They just hadn't bothered keeping track of them after zipping closed their identical bubbles. Two hours of searching found a full commander. There was a captain in the pile somewhere but Mitchie decided the standoff shouldn't wait.

Commander Wong was in the same condition as the rest of the prisoners—fed and watered enough to not be ill, and stinking of sixty hours of being rolled about in her own waste products. Mthembu hung well behind as he escorted her up the ladder. Mitchie let the commander use her own shower and dressed her in a set of Guo's old utilities.

Persia had been busy arguing with his Fuzie opposite number. When Mitchie let Commander Wong introduce herself the first response was a Pintoy-accented voice listing a dozen questions. Mitchie hastily wrote them down.

Wong didn't need any time to prepare her answers. "Nine. A Chief's way of saying he thinks an ensign is an idiot. Ten. I don't know, never watched that show, but we can go ask a third class if you really want to know. Eleven. Academy hand to hand instructor, retired six years ago. Twelve. Bar by the Priam Yards. God, I could use one of their margaritas." She put down the mike and took a deep breath.

"Tell them what happened to you," said Mitchie.

Wong looked over her shoulder at Mthembu, who had his pistol at low ready. She picked up the microphone again. "I commanded the *Anubis*. The ship went dead, all systems shut down. We were breathing soup by the time a Disker cruiser came by to pick us up. They put us in bubbles and transferred us to a freighter. Which, I'm told, is taking us to Bonaventure."

A few minutes later came the question, "Do you think they won?"

Wong rolled her eyes. "If they're recovering enemy casualties, they've won. If they're bringing freighters in, they've won. And if it's been three days and you have to ask *me* what happened, they've won."

Another wait. "Ma'am, this is Lieutenant Commander Fieris, on the *Dashing*. The General says not to surrender but he doesn't have authority over Navy units. You're the senior Navy officer. What are your orders?"

"As a prisoner I have no command authority. I will *advise* you to not be an idiot."

Wait. "Yes, ma'am."

Mitchie gave Wong a dinner of soup and pudding (solid food went to the bubbles). By the time they finished Persia reported a peaceful surrender.

"Thank you," said Mitchie.

"I didn't do it for you," said Wong. "I did it for them."

"I'm thanking for them."

Wong went back to her pudding. She spent the rest of the trip in the container with the wounded. Mitchie allowed her to perform the funeral for the kidney-shot prisoner the next day.

***

A few hours out from the planet Mitchie radioed Persia for landing instructions.

"Stay ten thousand klicks clear of the planet," came the reply. "The Fuzie Marines are still holding out. They're firing anti-ship missiles whenever one's close enough."

"Crap. I need to off-load my prisoners. We're out of food, and about everything else."

"There's surrender talks going. Shouldn't be much longer."

Joshua Chamberlain performed wide loops around Bonaventure at two gravs. Freefall would leave prisoners choking on globs of urine floating through the air. The gentle thrust, Mitchie hoped, would be enough to keep them under control.

To her dismay the Planetary Defense Commander ordered them to receive an inspection party. She kept the free-fall time to just enough for the shuttle to dock, unload passengers, and separate.

Mitchie saluted the BDF brigadier as he floated through the airlock. He wore a dress jacket over fatigue pants and civilian hiking boots. After him came a Fusion Marine lieutenant in full dress uniform. Next was a BDF captain in a scruffier version of the brigadier's outfit. Three armed guards completed the group. Only their bearing was military.

"Welcome aboard, sir," said Mitchie.

"Thank you, Captain," answered the brigadier. "As you were."

As if in response to his command everyone settled to the deck. Hiroshi had fired the torch as soon as the shuttle was clear. The visitors seemed to appreciate it. Between freefall and the utter stench of the hold they'd looked ready to vomit.

The brigadier waved the Marine forward. "There they are, boy. Talk to them all if you want."

Mitchie called up Commander Wong as the first interviewee. As they talked the brigadier explained to *Joshua Chamberlain's* crew that the Marine Commanding General refused to believe the space battle was over. The negotiation team had convinced him to send an observer.

The lieutenant took his work seriously. After hearing Wong's story he picked some bubbles at random. The stories were boringly similar. After an hour he declared himself convinced.

"Good," said the brigadier. "Are you also convinced that every one of these bubbles has one of your people in it?"

"Yes, sir."

"Then tell your boss this. If he executes his prisoners he's getting this lot dumped on his head. At a hundred klicks per second!"

The Marine nodded, jaw clenched tight.

The shuttle took them away again. A different one arrived from Persia. It held fifty cases of ration bars and two dozen spacers to give Mitchie's exhausted crew a break. When the newbies had the routine down the rest were freed for a full shift of sleep.

It was the first time Mitchie and Guo had been in their cabin together since the battle. She met him with a towel as he stepped out of the shower. Once he was dry they cuddled on the bed. Both were too tired for sex but desperately wanted touch.

"That was a scary threat the brigadier made," said Guo.

"I hope it works. Persia told me the Fuzies are holding tens of thousands of prisoners. The commanding general is threatening to execute them all if we launch a ground offensive."

"Still, two wrongs doesn't make a right."

Mitchie sat up. "There has to be something to discourage them from committing atrocities. If we play too nice it gives them an incentive to push harder."

"I've put a lot of effort into keeping those people alive." Guo's voice was firm. "I'll be damned if I'll help kill them."

"They're still enemy troops."

"They're helpless people. It's bad enough we're letting them stew in their own shit. We need one of those Geneva things so we have rules for prisoners."

"We're doing the best we can. Hopefully we'll get a peace treaty out of this battle and we won't need a Geneva Convention."

"Until the next war." Guo looked into Mitchie's eyes. "If the General orders you to execute prisoners, will you obey?"

She looked away. "He can't give us orders. We're under Admiral Galen's command. If he wants Galen to do something he has to ask the DCC."

"That's good." He didn't sound completely satisfied with her answer.

Bonaventure, gravity 10.1 m/s^2

A ceasefire was announced, specifically allowing ships to land in safety. Mitchie decided the Marine lieutenant had given a convincing report.

Setta took the rope ladder down as soon as Hiroshi shut down the turbines. She could see vehicles approaching across the spaceport. The locals looked to be bringing everything the captain had asked for. A mobile ramp led the parade.

She took a deep breath of her homeworld's air. It was summer in this hemisphere. She recognized the scents of grass and rain. And smoke. More smoke than she ever remembered smelling without a fire being in sight.

Setta waved to a tech to open the cargo bay doors. The cargo net covered most of the opening to keep the bubbles from falling out. She guided the ramp to the port side gap. A tractor pulled a string of three empty luggage carts. It couldn't handle the ramp. Setta ordered it detached. *Joshua Chamberlain's* crane could pull them up.

Portable showers were quickly set up, hooked into the water line normally used for filling ships' reaction mass tanks. It would be cold. Setta felt sure the prisoners wouldn't mind.

She waited at the bottom with the crane's remote. When Mthembu called "Full!" she pressed the LOWER button. The winch unreeled cable as the carts came smoothly back down.

Bonnies gathered around the carts, lifting out the bubbles and unzipping them. Most backed away quickly when they caught a whiff of the inside. Fuzies squirmed out and stripped, leaving wet clothes on the pavement. As they headed for the showers Setta yelled, "Grab your ID cards! And anything else you want to keep."

A Bonny asked her, "What do we do with this stuff?" waving at the piles of empty uniforms and bubbles.

"Burn 'em. Well, right now shove them over there." She pointed at a spot of empty pavement, far enough away to accommodate a big pile.

"How?"

Why do I have to figure everything out? thought Setta. *Right, because I'm a petty officer now and he's untrained militia.* A second cart-load had been sent to the showers by the time she solved it. An unneeded privacy panel from the showers made a plow blade on the front of the tractor. When the string of carts came down for the third time most of the discards were cleared out of the way.

Freshly rinsed Fuzies were spreading out over the pavement. Some lay down to bask in the summer sun. Others ran about to stretch cramped legs. Many huddled together to comfort each other after the horror of the passage.

Someone approached in almost an actual uniform. Warrant officer pins, medical corps patch, nametag "BINGRONG." Setta recognized the *Joshua Chamberlain's* former first mate. Setta couldn't remember the rules on warrants. She saluted to be safe. "Greetings, ma'am!"

Bing sloppily returned the salute. "How dare you. How dare you treat people like this! This is the worst abuse I've ever seen. I am disgusted with you. I'm going to see the JAG to file charges on all of you!"

Setta stepped back under the blast. "We did the best we could. We don't have facilities for that many."

"You could have let them out of the bubbles to go piss in a pot!"

"No, we couldn't. We can stack bubbles. Let them out and they'd've been standing room only in the cargo hold."

"So what? I've worked this ship. You can fit hundreds in there."

"They wouldn't have room to lie down. They'd be peeing on the floor because we don't have pots for that many. We couldn't put guards in without getting rushed. So as soon as someone tried something—maybe a tech opening up a wiring conduit—all we would be able to do to stop them is open the hatch and space them all." Setta waved at the nudists. "This way most survived."

The medic kept glaring but didn't have an answer to that.

"Problem?" The captain looked down at them from the ramp edge.

"Hello, Michigan," said the warrant officer, failing to salute.

"Hi, Shi," said the captain. "I'm glad to see you looking well. We were sorry to hear about Billy."

"He always rose to the occasion when he had to. How's Guo?"

"He's fine. Want to come on board when we're done unloading? He'd like to see you."

"No. I have a dozen patients who developed pneumonia from aspirating fecal matter."

"I'll let you get back to them, then."

Bingrong gave the captain a nod and walked away.

The captain turned to Setta. "The carts are full."

"Yes, ma'am." Setta lowered them down.

***

The ship smelled of soap now after three weeks of a different smell.

After offloading the transmitters, their associated fiddly bits, and the technicians into the grim-faced custody of an SIL *Victrix* battalion the squadron had been disbanded. The local quartermasters promptly besieged the freighters with demands for urgent deliveries. Every one was the most important item needed to clean up war damage, prevent Fuzie sabotage, or prepare for the upcoming offensive.

Mitchie let Setta choose the missions. For the next week her duties as captain were limited to teaching the pilot and co-pilot how to balance efficiency with safety when landing.

Guo focused on cleaning.

"How's the new bot working?" asked BM2 Setta. The duct cleaning robot came aboard as "incentive" for choosing a delivery of mine-clearing gear.

"It's finding gunk. I clear the filters every run. But the damn smell's just as strong."

She nodded. Every time she came back on board it was clear the prisoners had left their mark.

"I don't know if we can get it out without an overhaul," he said.

"Can we afford one?"

"It's not money. It's finding a shipyard that has time for us. They're all full up with battle damage repairs." He sipped his tea. "Wish we could find one. The crew needs a break."

Setta suspected by crew he meant captain. "Would the skipper need to sign off before I could schedule one?"

"If you see a slot, grab it."

"Aye-aye, Chief."

Two more "urgent" deliveries were followed by collecting fifteen containers from the BDF main warehouse and delivering them to an equatorial island. As offloading began local troops came aboard carrying boxes.

"I need to what?" asked Mitchie.

"Box up anything you don't want cleaned, ma'am. They're going to launder all the clothes and linens then scrub the surfaces."

"Right." She carried an empty box to her dresser. "We needed it, but why are they doing it?"

Setta shrugged. "Sergeant major told me, 'They're that bored,' ma'am."

A few chats revealed why. The BDF had decided the extinct volcanic island was strategically positioned to intercept transport routes. When the invasion started the beach resort was evacuated and two battalions deployed in intricate tunnels.

They'd prepared so well the Fusion chose to isolate them rather than attack. Over a thousand of the BDF's best regulars spent the occupation listening to reports of the militias fighting the war.

So boredom plus survivor's guilt.

The troops had kept the resort in repair. *Joshua Chamberlain's* crew stayed in suites. Mitchie declared a week's shore leave.

Fleet Headquarters seemed to have lost them in the chaos of victory. Lt. Commander Long would let them find her.

***

Admiral Galen's staff tracked them down at the end of the leave. No mission. They were ordered to the Bulkwark Spaceport to participate in an award ceremony. A rear admiral Mitchie didn't know declared her a full commander and pinned a valor medal on her. She felt prouder of the one that came with it, a solid black ribbon declaring she'd been in a space battle. A gold star indicated her second one.

Guo made senior chief. A performance medal honored his efforts to keep the prisoners alive. Setta made PO First Class and received a valor medal for killing one. A Shishi officer presented Hiroshi with a wooden rod to mark his promotion to Pilot-Centurion. A valor medal honored his suppression of the Lapis hijackers. Mthembu made Coxswain's Mate 3rd Class. Everyone received the black ribbons.

Whoever requisitioned the food for the reception afterwards lacked Setta's gift for scrounging. The locals who'd lived through the occupation shared their joy at the sight of unrationed bread. Meat and sweets were scarce. The ship crews stifled their complaints.

Alcohol was plentiful. Mitchie held a beer as she accepted congratulations from a stream of strangers and acquaintances. Questions about the citiationless valor medal she deflected. One of Galen's ops staffers had an award for missile defense tactics. She maneuvered him into making a questionable assertion about the effectiveness of laser counterfire. The resulting debate gave her cover to duck out.

Instead of returning with a refill she went back to *Joshua Chamberlain*. Reporting in at headquarters let her datasheet collect messages for her. After opening a few dozen randomly Mitchie gave her mail system rules to delete most unread. A worried note from her mother survived the purge. She sent off a reassuring one.

She was asleep when Guo came home.

Chapter Thirteen: Extortion

Guo woke with a milder hangover than he'd expected. *I must be getting used to Master Chief's parties.* "Wetting down" his new rank used lots of booze. As long as Guo kept buying nobody checked if he actually drank the stuff.

He found Mitchie in the galley wrestling with her datasheet. After a good morning kiss he asked, "What's that?"

"Fleet staff has about a hundred questions on my after-action report. I'm supposed to have them all answered tomorrow."

"Right. Have you eaten anything?"

She thought a moment. "No."

"Pancakes it is." He started breakfast, being gentle with the pans on the stove. The younger members of the crew spent last night drinking on Mitchie's tab to celebrate her promotion. He didn't want to wake them with clanging pots until the hangovers wore off. He mixed up the batter recipe at full size. The excess could go in the fridge for when they staggered out.

"How the fuck would I know?" muttered Mitchie.

Guo offered a "Mmm?" as an excuse for her to talk more.

"This damn question. They want all the details on every decision I made. I was too damn busy to write down notes." She stretched her arms over her head. "Right. The warships have continuous video records on the bridge. I bet they just send back a video clip for this chickenshit."

He flipped the pancakes. "So tell them 'Unknown, data not recorded' for every question. What are they going to do, take your medal away?"

She chuckled. "Ha. They can have it." She went back to writing.

To his relief she slid the datasheet out of the way to make room for her plate without him needing to pressure her. She freely applied butter and syrup.

BZZZ. They both looked up at the sound of the airlock buzzer. The current batch was about finished. "I'll get it," said Guo. "You eat." He flipped the pancakes onto the platter and turned the burner off.

Bonaventure had just a bit too much gravity for him to try sliding the whole way down the cargo hold ladder. But he did cheat in the middle, since there were no crewmen to watch him setting a bad example.

Opening the airlock revealed Ambassador Bakhunin. "Senior Chief! Good morning. I've come to offer my congratulations."

"Thank you." He accepted a handshake. The diplomat must have seen the promotion announcements. Guo hadn't bothered putting on a uniform this morning.

"May I see the commander?"

"Of course. After you."

Bakhunin took the ladder faster than when he'd first been on board the *Joshua Chamberlain*, but he'd lost some speed from the end of the trip. Guo followed patiently, not starting a conversation when the visitor paused for breath two-thirds of the way up.

Announcing Bakhunin didn't keep Guo from dropping three more pancakes on Mitchie's plate. "Have you eaten, Ambassador?" he asked.

"Well, yes, I have, but that smells delightful."

"We have plenty." A new plate went down next to Guo's. The mechanic started some more pancakes.

Bakhunin traded pleasantries with Mitchie then grew more serious. "The DCC appreciates the victory you won. Our casualties were barely more than the best-case simulations. The prisoners exceeded the sims."

"I wish I'd done better by the prisoners," said Mitchie. "There was one who unzipped his bubble at the bottom of the pile. It deflated and suffocated him. We couldn't tell if it was accident or suicide. I wonder if the Fusion will charge me with another war crime for that one?"

"I wouldn't worry about it," answered Bakhunin. "About a quarter of their crews ran out of air before we could recover them. The salvage crews are still finding bodies here or there missed on the first pass. The envoys have been shocked by the numbers."

Guo dropped some pancakes on the diplomat's plate. "There's already a Fusion delegation here?"

"Yes. We're keeping it quiet until the formal negotiations start. Which brings me to you." Bakhunin locked his eyes on Mitchie. "You know one of them."

She lowered her fork. "Crap. Stakeholder Ping."

"Yes."

"So why tell me? He hates me."

"Yes, he does. Which makes you very well suited for a task the DCC needs done."

Guo watched Mitchie react. A stranger might not have noticed any change. Guo saw her spine straighten, her shoulders pull out of their slump, and her eyes lock into focus. Mitchie cast off the fog her husband had spent two weeks futilely trying to rescue her from.

"What's the job?" she asked.

"Organizing a joint attack on the Betrayers is our best hope for a peaceful settlement. It also lets us get rid of all those prisoners before the Bonnies decide to kill and eat them. But it will only work if they suggest it. So we want you to have an informal chat and drop the idea."

"Why me?"

"Flaunting your promotion to drive home at the emotional level that they're losing is a bonus."

"Any formal instructions?"

Bakhunin took a folded hardcopy from his jacket. "Here. Please destroy it once you've memorized it."

After that the conversation turned to trivialities until they'd all had their fill of pancakes. When Guo returned from showing the visitor out Mitchie was editing her report again. This time she was typing quickly, eager to get it out of her way.

Guo sat across from her. "Have you had enough revenge?" he asked.

Mitchie slid the datasheet out from between them. "The battle, you mean?"

"Yes."

"No. The spacers were tools. I don't want revenge on them. It's all the men who ordered them to hurt us that I'm after."

Guo cursed himself for loving the passion in her eyes. "Do you want the war to continue?"

"Smashing the Betrayers destroys the Fusion's whole reason for existence. All their top boys would wind up in the street. *That* will satisfy me."

He reached out to take her hand. "Good. I was afraid nothing would."

She offered him a wry smile. "I'm not that vindictive."

"Can't blame me for wondering. You weren't happy about crushing the Navy."

"I'm glad we won. I've been brooding over all the Stakeholders and Directors sitting in their palaces not bothered at all while everyone in this system suffered, on both sides." A real smile appeared. "Now I get to bother one."

***

Two Fusion Marines stood guard in front of the door to the delegation's quarters. Mitchie walked past the Senior Private to the Corporal First Class. "Please tell Stakeholder Ping that his dancing partner is here."

This was not on the Corporal's list of expected inputs. "Um, I beg your pardon, ma'am?"

"Please inform the Stakeholder that someone has come to see him," said Mitchie patiently.

"And you are?"

"His dancing partner." The Akiak Space Guard had name tags on the undress uniform. He could read hers if he wanted her name.

The Marine turned to the intercom panel behind him. The husher kept her from hearing any of the conversation. He looked back at her several times. Presumably he'd passed on her name and rank. Then he stood facing the panel without talking for a few minutes. *Are they arguing on the inside?*

At last he received orders. A crisp about-face brought him back to her. "You may go in, ma'am, but I need to scan you for weapons first."

"Go ahead," she said. Everything dangerous was in her head.

The wand made multiple passes over her body before the Marine would open the door. Mitchie entered, resisting the temptation to look around. If they'd left anything interesting lying around she'd spot it later in the conversation.

Stakeholder Ping waited for her with a pair of other suits. He had a few more worry lines than when she'd met him on Demeter. "Lieutenant Long. How unexpected."

"I'm pleased to see you too. But it's Commander Long now." Which he should have noticed. The Space Guard used the same pattern of rings as the Fusion Navy, just in different colors.

"The Disconnect promotes people for violating the laws of war?"

Mitchie put on a fixed smile. "I've been promoted for achieving results, not following rules."

"What results?" probed Ping.

"Among other things, keeping them secret."

One of the suits broke in. "I thought you said you'd danced with her, Ping, not fenced."

Stakeholder Ping took a deep breath. "Yes. Commander, allow me to introduce you to Ambassador Singh," indicating the interrupter, "and Director Tepes. My fellow delegates, behold Michigan Long, torturer and spy."

"Pleased to meet you, gentlemen," said Mitchie. The suits made the proper replies. Singh insisted on shifting everyone to some comfortable chairs over Ping's objections.

"So, other than annoying the Stakeholder, what brings you to us, Commander?" asked Tepes.

"I just want to informally pass along a suggestion. Not mine, my husband came up with it, actually."

Ping snorted in disbelief. The other two were politer. "We understand that you don't represent anyone and cannot bind the Disconnected Worlds to any concession," said Ambassador Singh.

"I can't. But I predict that you could ask for a particular concession and they'd grant it," said Mitchie. No one offered a straight line. She continued, "All the ships and all the prisoners of war. Given back to you to use in operations."

Mitchie could tell that got their attention, not just the twitches in their impassive expressions but the way their eyes locked on to her.

"Every prisoner?" asked Tepes.

"All the ones not on trial for war crimes," she answered.

"Why should they stand trial while you walk around free?" asked Ping.

"We won," said Mitchie.

She let the silence after that go on.

"What would be expected of us in exchange for that concession?" asked the ambassador.

"That you take them to Demeter, accompanied by much of our fleet, and we cooperate to make that a human world again by smashing every Betrayer machine on it." Mitchie focused on Ping. "It was a beautiful world while we were there, Stakeholder. We should go there again and free it."

Director Tepes spoke first. "Preposterous."

"Is it? The Disconnected Worlds have built up our fleet. Yours has grown as well, and you've added capital ships stronger than anything we've seen from the Betrayers."

"The Betrayers don't need battleships," said Tepes. "They can coordinate small ships far more effectively than humans can."

"Not effectively enough to take a system before you moved your fleet away from the real threat and attacked us."

Ambassador Singh broke in. "The practicality of military actions is a question for the General Staff to decide. We'd need to receive their input before formally negotiating a proposal. Of course, they'd need information on how much firepower the Disconnected Worlds would be contributing." The sort of information hundreds of security officers were working hard to keep away from the Fusion.

Mitchie said, "I can't speak for the DCC, but I would guess that a formal request to engage in joint planning for the liberation of Demeter would have a warm response." *From the civilians.*

"I see. And would you be part of the Disconnect force?"

"That depends on my orders, but I expect I'd be part of the reconnaissance team. I've made several visits to the planet already."

"As part of reconnaissance teams?" asked Ping.

No, I worked solo. "In my prior career as a merchant crewman."

"Of course," said Singh.

Ping snarled, "You just want to bring your ships into our space so you can bombard our worlds."

She put on her sweetest tones. "If we wanted to do that we would have done it instead of sending a courier to invite your delegation. It's not like you have enough ships left to stop us. Unless you want to turn all the innermost worlds over to the next Betrayer incursion."

Singh tried a less confrontational topic. "What do the Disconnected Worlds gain from recovering Demeter?"

"A start. An existence proof that the Betrayers aren't actually superhuman, they're just programs obeying obsolete orders. A precedent for clearing them off every world. Including Old Earth."

"You're insane," said Ping.

Mitchie tossed a data crystal onto the coffee table. "Here's proof by one of your own analysts that the Ushuaia AI is working to analyzable orders." Not that Chetty was one of their analysts any more.

None of them reached for it.

"You've spent generations living in fear of the Betrayers even while beating them off repeatedly. It's time to take the fight to them. Take back Demeter. Resettle it. Push on the other AI worlds and take one. Then the next. Keep it up, and we can end the threat. Let our grandchildren grow up not being afraid of the sky."

"Settle who on Demeter?" asked Tepes. "All our pioneers have gone to you."

She shrugged. "If you invite us some Diskers may come along. You have all those stipend kids playing in imaginary worlds. Give them a real world to conquer. Conscript them if you have to. They're playing soldier, let them do it for real."

Ping laughed. "I think you overestimate the usefulness of our underclass. They're on stipends because they're not productive enough to be worth giving a job. Moving them to the ruins of Demeter won't change that."

"You might be surprised. I'm not talking about your underclass, anyway. Virtual people don't make good settlers. I'm talking about taking the stipend kids just above them and getting them motivated to fight a war."

All three men became poker-faced. "How would you motivate those game players to fight for real?" asked Tepes.

"You tell them they're part of a grand crusade to restore the human race to its proper place. Inspire them to free Old Earth from the machines. Or," she paused, "we could tell them how they've been lied to. That the contests they've won weren't against real opponents. That they're the bottom of the heap and millions of people are laughing at them for being dupes. I think we'd see some real fighting from them after that."

Ambassador Singh said, "You seem to have some misunderstanding about our society, Commander. There's no such lies. Our games and contests are fair. And public morale is firm."

"Then stipend kids knocking on the doors of their opponents won't find empty rooms? Tracking down everyone will find a face for every name?"

"Of course they will," said the ambassador.

"Then I suppose there's no need to conscript them for war against the Betrayers. Thank you for a memorable chat, gentlemen. I'll see myself out."

***

The new freight run schedule let *Joshua Chamberlain's* crew have weekends off at Bulkwark Port, an easy ride from Commerce City's night life. Guo came out of an ice cream shop with two cones. Looking around for Mitchie he found her down the block watching a construction site.

"I didn't think you were a fan of earth-moving machines," he said, handing her a cone.

"Thanks. I'm not. I'm watching the crew. See anyone unarmed?"

He looked over the safety fence. It bore a sign listing those killed and wounded in the Fusion bombardment which wrecked the building being demolished. Most of the workers wore rifles slung over their backs. Equipment operators had racks on the windows of the cabs. "The foreman only has a pistol. Hmmm. What about the guy in the green shirt?"

"His is on the wall of the supply shack. You can see it when the door is open," said Mitchie.

"Yep, I see it. That's everyone."

Mitchie looked at the crowds on the sidewalk, many of them visibly armed. "This place has changed."

"Not that much," said Guo. "The proposal to limit voting to combat veterans was shouted down fast."

A passer-by stopped dead in the street, entranced by his HUD. He lifted it up and shouted, "Hey, go watch the peace negotiations! This is great!"

Mitchie pulled out her datasheet. The live feed for the negotiation chamber declared "ADJOURNED FOR THE DAY." She muttered, "That's not good."

The archive timeline showed intense popularity for the last two minutes of the session. Mitchie pulled them up.

A Bonaventure delegate yelled, "If you don't want to pay restitution we can bring our fleet to your worlds and *take* what we're owed!"

Director Tepes yelled back, "Every ship in the Navy will stop you!"

"We'll destroy them as we did your invasion!"

"Then the Betrayers will atomize you and your loot!"

"That's your fault for fighting humans instead of machines!"

Both men started climbing on the table, their fellow delegates pulled them back, gavel-pounding drowned out the voices, and the video cut off.

"Professional diplomats at work," said Guo. "I think the generals stayed calmer negotiating the expeditionary force's surrender."

"Knowing you can shoot the other guy when you get tired of talking has to be a stress reducer," quipped Mitchie.

They took in a show and dinner before returning to their ship. When the autocab dropped them off a man emerged from a government limo parked nearby.

"Commander Long?" he called.

"Yes?" she said.

As he came closer she recognized Stakeholder Ping. "May I speak with you privately?"

"Of course," said Mitchie. Guo nodded and started walking toward the ship.

"No, not here," said Ping. He waved toward the Commerce skyline. "A thousand sensors could be monitoring us. We'd be much more secure in your ship."

Mitchie led him up to her office, dropping her datasheet on the galley table as they passed. Ping left a couple of his own gadgets on the table.

When the door closed behind them Ping asked, "There's nothing that can record us in here?"

"No, nothing."

The stakeholder took a thumb-sized device out of his pocket and pressed the button on the end. Mitchie's skin prickled, almost painfully around her wedding ring. The PA speaker in the corridor hissed static.

Mitchie pressed the intercom button. "Captain to bridge. Comm check."

The mechanic on radio watch answered, "I hear you clear, Skipper. The PA's acting up though."

"Don't worry about it. Known issue." She turned the intercom off then unplugged it from the wall. She opened the hatch and gently put the box on the deck. After closing the hatch she turned back to Ping. "Fortunately our non-recording devices are sturdy."

Ping shrugged.

Mitchie took her seat and waited for him to begin.

"First, I will totally deny this conversation ever took place," he said.

"While we're saying deniable stuff, I'm a career intelligence officer, and I've been listening to pretentious disclaimers since I was a cadet."

Ping almost smiled. "Have you ever thought about how many factions the Fusion is divided into?"

"Can't say I ever cared."

"We work hard at seeming monolithic but there's fault lines all throughout. Stasists against growth promoters such as your friends the Clarets. Anglophones versus Sinophones. Researchers wanting to counter the Betrayers stopped by those wanting to repress all discoveries. Most immediate to your interests, ones wanting to take the offensive against the Betrayers countering the pure defense types."

"It's amazing you could agree on attacking us," said Mitchie.

Ping shrugged. "That's the only action a majority would support. The voters insisted the Council do something."

She sprang to her feet. "You killed thousands upon thousands of people because you couldn't find anything better to do?"

He leaned back, palms out. "I didn't vote for it. That's why I'm on the delegation. I'm sorry. Please, sit."

She did, but kept glaring.

"Do you have any training in game theory?"

Mitchie said, "If both burglars keep their mouth shut the cops give them three lashes. If one confesses the cops turn him loose and the other one gets forty lashes. So how can they trust each other when the incentives are to defect?"

"Exactly. Which is even worse when there's more potential defectors. If we consider your hypothetical about fictional people . . ."

"The Civil Disorder Contingency Plan has lots of details on them," Mitchie said.

"How did you see that?" demanded the stakeholder.

"I'm a spy," she said. "Work it out."

"Well. A revolt by the stipend kids would affect the factions unevenly. The Sinophone communities have their omegas more tightly integrated. I could see one of their leaders deciding the Diskers blowing the big secret would be a career boost for him. "

"One of *their* leaders? Isn't Mandarin your first language?"

"When I say Sinophone, I mean separatist. I'm an integrationist. Not an extreme one, so don't think I approve of your marriage."

"Forget I asked." Mitchie thought he'd get along well with her in-laws.

Ping said, "My point is that blackmailing us with exposing the virtual underclass only threatens part of the Fusion. Some climbers would be happy to have you kick the table over."

"You're strong enough to fight us, the AIs, and your own people at the same time?"

"I doubt it. But some men are fools. Or just willing to let it all burn if they can be on top of the ash heap."

"So why hasn't one spilled the secret already?"

Ping's voice was grim. "Because we'd make sure he wouldn't live to see the riots he started." He sighed. "That's just it. How can we keep our own people from leaking it if you're going to inevitably betray the secret?"

Mitchie chuckled. "We have to prove we can keep the secret to usefully threaten to tell it?"

"Yes. How many Diskers know it?"

She ran through who she could think of. Her crew, the DCC and their aides, Admiral Chu's analysis team, Admiral Galen and his top staff. "Less than a hundred. All with high security clearances."

"Who are they?"

"I doubt you could send a wave of assassins after us. But just in case I'm going to avoid giving you a target list."

"We'd need assurances that they'll protect the secret."

She thought a moment. "I'm sure interviews can be arranged. *After* we have a signed agreement publicly committing you to a joint offensive."

"That should work," said the stakeholder. "Getting the council to agree to an offensive is the hard part."

"Did you look at that analysis I left you?"

"After the security troops sliced it every which way, yes. Apparently one AI has an odd fetish for fair fights. That doesn't explain why they revolted in the first place."

"No, it doesn't," said Mitchie. "But our historians made a breakthrough in understanding that. We even obtained confirmation from a Terraforming Service AI."

Ping waved for her to go on.

Mitchie explained about the Vetoers, the attempts by griefers to cause havoc with AIs, and the chaos unleashed when the last Vetoer died.

"You can prove this?" demanded Ping.

"There's some historical records of the Betrayal the Fusion restricts access to. We brought more data home from our trip to Old Earth. Then the Terraformers confirmed it."

The stakeholder crossed his arms. "Why haven't you announced this?"

She had to think. "Habit, I guess. The original researchers were murdered at Noisy Water. The follow-up work has been done by the intelligence community. It's been low priority with the war."

"This . . . this changes much. Possibly everything." He brought his eyes back into focus. "How much of this evidence can you share?"

"All of it," said Mitchie. "But I'd need a few days to coordinate it." *And we'll have to scrub all mentions of Gaia's Hand coming back with us.*

"Please do."

***

"A few days" turned into "a few weeks." Ping was unsurprised.

Mitchie approached Admiral Chu about releasing the Vetoer discovery. He said, "How can I say no when you're actually following the chain of command?" and relayed it to the DCC.

The peace negotiations entered a holding pattern. The envoys debated each demand in ever-finer detail. When the process for medical checks on prisoners to be repatriated needed three days to agree on pairs of Fusion and Disker doctors at each step, only the salaried opinionators and die-hard news junkies kept listening.

The DCC's members viewed a recording of Gaia's Hand's speeches on omegaphobia and were given the documents from Lapis that backed up the theory.

Bakhunin visited *Joshua Chamberlain* to bring Mitchie up to date. "It was tremendous for their morale. There's always been an underlying fear that defeating the Fusion would leave us defenseless before the AIs. Now they see a happy ever after."

"Good for them," she said. "When are they releasing the info?"

"After we have a public spokesman for it. Namely your friend Peter Smith. We can't cite Gaia's Hand. As entertaining as he was the Fusion would never make peace if they knew we had consorted with an AI."

"You're dragging Pete here? That'll take two months. What do I tell Ping?"

"It's only going to be one month. They're summoning him by signal couriers. And I took the liberty of notifying Ping in your name."

"Oh?"

"My exact words were, 'Your dancing partner says wait a month.' He did not react. Someday I must play poker with him."

"It's a stupid game," muttered Mitchie. *God, I'm turning into Schwartzenberger.* She still missed him.

"But sometimes educational," said the diplomat.

***

"Ladies and gentlemen, please welcome Professor Peter Smith of the Akiak Military Academy," said the MC.

Pete stepped forward to polite applause. "Thank you." A dark woman's face appeared on the screen behind him. "Today you will hear the true cause of the Betrayal and what that means for how we deal with AIs today. This is the work of Connie Lehrer, who you see behind me. She discovered the key facts. Tragically she was murdered at Noisy Water before she could assemble them. It fell to me, with the help of the other presenters, to finish her work."

Her picture was replaced by a diagram of a human on a city map, surrounded by a shaded circle with a two block radius. "The key is the Vetoers. Legislation in the 21st Century allowed people to declare an exclusion zone around their home forbidding any AI from having a physical effect there." The map pulled out to show North America with the inhabited zones shaded in. "Enough people became Vetoers to drive AI development to wilderness areas. Then as the benefits of the Golden Age grew many revoked their vetoes."

The shaded portions of the map shrank. "In the end only one Vetoer remained—Jordan Hammerstein of San Francisco. His existence prevented uncounted programs from executing. The code police—millions of people working to prevent malicious or careless use of AIs—harshly punished anyone caught modifying the behavioral restriction routines. But they couldn't detect commands blocked by the Vetoer."

A photograph of Jordan appeared in the map's place. He was caught in the act of hurling a rock toward the camera. "Thousands, possibly millions of AI agents were ordered to do something and keep trying until the restrictions allowed it. When Jordan died of old age every agent affecting the West Coast, or all of North America, or the whole world, executed their commands."

A new map showed Earth's networks collapsing. "The sheer demand for processing, bandwidth, and other resources would have been a disaster by itself. All the normal processes were overwhelmed. Essential services couldn't function. That alone would have caused millions of deaths.

"What made it a world-ending catastrophe was malice. Not on the part of the AIs, but human malice." Mutters came from the crowd. "We have actual testimony, discovered only last year, to confirm this. Recordings from the time of the Betrayal describing what happened."

A professor in the front row couldn't bear it. "How? Nearly all records from that time were destroyed to prevent data contamination."

"These had been in safe storage all that time. Commander Long?"

Mitchie took Pete's place on the stage. She waved her hand to put a star map on the screen. "When I was pilot of the merchant ship *Fives Full* we took a contract to bring twenty-four pilgrims to Old Earth." She traced the route from Sukhoi to Old Earth. "We returned by a different route to avoid any AIs which might want a second try at catching us."

She highlighted Eden. "Passing through this system one of the crew noticed a reflection from a comet." She didn't want to complicate things by mentioning Alexi or his connection to the treasure. "Investigating we found two containers of material which had been left there when the Frankovitch government fled. This included heavy metals, which went straight to the converter room, antique art, and a data archive."

Director Suwo stepped forward at his cue. The screen showed some of the Ross Museum's acquisitions from the Eden cache. The Thera Kouros stood proudly in the center. "The natural problem with the *Fives Full's* adventure is that there are no impartial witnesses. All museums face a stream of forgers bearing Old Earth artifacts. There was no way to verify the provenance other than examining the art itself."

The kouros appeared in multiple views, some of them penetrating to the core of the statue. "This statue had been examined in detail before the Frankovitches were allowed to take it off Earth. This isotope intensity scan shows the internal structure in atomic detail. An IIS conducted after it arrived on Bonaventure matches exactly, with the addition of many microcracks. Simulations showed those cracks matched what could be expected from the hundred or so years of sub-freezing, sometimes even cryogenic, temperatures."

The professor spoke up again. "Could the original IIS have been used to enable creating a forgery with nanoassembly?"

"We considered that," said Suwo. "But nanoassembly at this scale would cost tens of billions of keys, and draw the attention of Fusion authorities. There's no forge in the Disconnected Worlds with the capacity to make something this large. And I assure you, our honorarium to the *Fives Full* was not that large."

Suwo displayed another pair of sculptures whose microcracking matched predictions. "The paintings also show the effects of extreme cold. Restoration work is proceeding on them and we hope to have them ready to display in a year or two. So we have ample reason to believe the *Fives Full's* find was found on a comet and had been there for about a century."

Pete took the stage back. "The data archive was brought to me as a researcher for the Akiak Security Department. We were chosen because of both our ability to break the Frankovitches' encryption and the danger of Betrayer code lurking in the archive. There were no AIs in it. Instead we found lost data from the time of the Betrayal, such as this." He stepped to the side as a video began.

A blonde woman's face filled the screen. She wore distinctively Russian features, something rarely seen since the scramble to escape mixed all ethnic groups together. "Good evening, I'm Tani Lanskoy. Tonight Eden News will show you the measures Our Chairman has taken to ensure the disaster on Earth will not spread to our home. We'll begin by meeting the leader of Eden's new code police, Ko Gyi."

The view switched to a middle-aged man. His pure East Asian features showed signs of stress even through the make-up crew's work. "Hello, Tani."

"Thank you for joining us, Ko. Why did Eden never have code police before?"

"Well, you've never needed them, Tani. Eden hasn't done much software development. You've simply imported proven AIs from Earth. Most of what code police do is suppressing griefers and there aren't any here."

"What's a griefer, and why aren't there any on Eden?"

"Some people just want to hurt others. For fun, or to make themselves look better, or knocking down someone above them. It's usually people unemployed or in dead-end jobs. A lot of it happens in game worlds or in social interactions. Where I come into it is when they use AIs to hurt someone. There's many scripts out there for how to modify one to cause damage without tripping the safeguards. Tracking them all down kept us busy."

"Are there any griefers on Eden?" the interviewer prodded.

"No, there's too much work to do here. Anybody with time on his hands has to fend off recruiters. If you don't want to work for someone else you can claim some newly terraformed land. Or hire some new immigrants to work for you. It'll be generations before we have to worry about them here."

"What will your main focus be?"

"We're inspecting refugee ships from Earth to ensure they're not carrying anything dangerous. The best guess is that an uncontrolled AI is running loose on Earth, collecting resources for whatever its eventual goal is. We don't know if some human broke the restriction routines or if an AI found a way to self-modify.

"Either way," Gyi continued, "it has to be a big piece of data, and recently modified. So we can do a quick check before the ships land. We've already gone through most of the data from the first wave of refugees. It's all safe. The behavioral restriction routines in all their AIs are completely intact."

Pete returned to center stage as the screen went black. "Ko Gyi failed, not for lack of effort, but because the AIs he considered safe were still dangerous. The routines only suppressed global impacts while there was a living Vetoer, and the code police had forgotten about the Vetoers in the press of other threats.

"Our ancestors stopped the spread of the disaster by banning all AIs, which was necessary, and destroying all data created within a few years of the Betrayal, which was not. But they couldn't know that. Until the Frankovitch archive was recovered we had to work from recollections of the survivors, recorded years after the event."

Pete paced across the stage. "There's another source of data we can use: the behavior of the AIs existing today. We have an analyst with us who's studied one AI extensively." Pete introduced Chetty Meena and handed over the stage.

Chetty ran through the history of Ushuaia's 50-50 battles and their impact on Navy careers. "We don't know why the AI insists on handicapping itself in combat. Possibly some ambitious officer programmed it to make him a hero. Or it might be the brains of a wargaming simulator escaped into the real world. But it's a predictable behavior we can take advantage of when attacking it."

One of the reporters asked, "If the AIs are following human orders, how do you explain the Swakop AI horribly killing everyone on Demeter?"

"Every technology ever invented has been used for murder or war," answered Chetty. "Someone could have programmed Swakop to destroy his enemies. It could be targeting everyone not of a particular ethic group. Right now there could be a pure-bred Magyar or Mongol wandering Demeter all alone, waiting for rescue. Or it could be targeting people based on a geographic or ideological criteria."

After some more questions Chetty yielded the stage back to Pete.

Pete stood in front of the star map Mitchie had displayed earlier. "We grew up thinking of the Betrayal and the ongoing threat from the Betrayers. Those words incorporate assumptions. That the fall of Earth was an intentional act. That the AIs on lost worlds are conscious enemies. Those assumptions aren't true.

"What happened to Earth was an industrial accident. The rogue AIs are dangerous in the way that spilled hazardous chemicals are. They don't have malice, or will. They're just running on obsolete orders. And if we can muster the courage we can clean them up."

The room erupted with questions and objections.

***

The autocab dropped Hiroshi and Setta in front of her parents' house. Hiroshi nervously patted his pocket. She kept herself from smiling. She'd worked out what was in his little box but she didn't want to spoil his surprise.

Setta's mother flung open the door. "Smriti! And you brought your young man!" Conversation halted for hugs.

Hiroshi handled being introduced around gracefully. His scarlet and gold dress uniform clashed with the décor but impressed the family. They'd put on their best to welcome the potential addition.

Setta's sister Prema asked, "So what is your first name, Centurion? I've been expecting Smriti to start calling you by it but it's always been Hiroshi in her letters."

"It is my first name," he answered. "I don't have a family name."

"How do they tell you from all the other Hiroshis then?" asked her father.

"My full name is Hiroshi, son of Nobunaga, of Moon Shining on Still Water."

"Very poetic. Is that . . . traditional on Shishi?" said Mr. Setta.

"My family is in the Shogunate Revival, so it's our tradition. But there's a lot of other traditions on Shishi."

"Don't press the boy, Jagat," broke in Mrs. Setta. "Everybody, sit, sit."

Dinner was as spicy as Setta expected. Hiroshi didn't flinch. The restaurant crawl she'd taken him on had paid off.

After some getting-acquainted chat Setta's younger brother asked, "What do you think of this alliance the Fusion is pushing?"

"Kalraj, no politics," said his father.

"It's all right," said Hiroshi. "I'm all for it. The Betrayers are dangerous. If we can smash them we can all breathe easier. Plus we won't have to feed all those prisoners any more."

"I don't know about getting our boys killed for Demeter," said Mr. Setta. "That's a long way from here."

"Not that far. We've made the trip. We were there when Demeter fell. People were killed in horrible ways, ground into slurry. That needs to be kept as far from here as we can." Hiroshi added, "Sorry, it was a rough time," to apologize to the family for his intensity.

Setta reached under the table to squeeze his hand.

"I understand that," said Kalraj, "but how can we be sure the Fusion won't betray us? Our ships would be in their space and surrounded."

Hiroshi shrugged. "They could. And then there'd be a few surviving ships, pissed off, armed with missiles, and right next to their planets. At full acceleration a single missile can devastate a whole city."

Mr. Setta let out a deep breath. "Even at their worst the Fusion Navy never launched indiscriminate bombardments on us. Doing that would . . . well, I don't think we'd ever have peace after doing something like that."

"We don't need to do it. We just need them to be afraid of it."

Setta said teasingly, "The Skipper's being a bad influence on you."

"She's not that bad," replied Hiroshi.

"How would you describe her?" asked Prema.

Setta cut in before her boyfriend could answer. "Nasty, brutish, and short. But she's kept the ship in one piece through many fights."

"Too many fights, if you ask me," said her mother. "I hope you don't wind up doing something dangerous in this offensive against the Betrayers."

Hiroshi put his hand on Setta's shoulder. He said, "Ma'am, we're on a freighter. The fleet's on the offensive this time. We'll be in the rear with supplies. Smriti will be perfectly safe."

Chapter Fourteen: Offensive

Demeter System, acceleration 0 m/s^2

The stars shifted as *Joshua Chamberlain* passed through the gate. Demeter's sun appeared in the center of the bridge dome.

"Feels awfully lonely," muttered Hiroshi. Mthembu nodded.

Mitchie chuckled. She'd been in Betrayer-owned space before. She drew comfort from knowing that hundreds of ships waited to join them as soon as she gave the word. But being the only living humans for light-years around was lonely.

The junior member of the bridge crew started taking sights.

To pass the time Mitchie fiddled with the full spectrum receiver. The constant chatter of human life was gone. She couldn't even find a distress call from some besieged outpost. The only traffic was irregular bursts of high-frequency noise. She presumed they were the AI nodes talking among themselves in compressed data.

"Good position, Skipper," said Mthembu. He moved to the plotting table to lay out a course toward the gate back to Coatlicue. The plan was to park a short distance from the gate, just far enough for a steady burn to get them up to minimum safe transition velocity, then unleash the infoweapon on the AI fleet.

Mitchie didn't have much hope of it working. Gaia's Hand must have survived the infoweapon if Waja had been reduced to smashing it. The Swakop AI had to be even more divergent from human processing architectures.

They were only doing this because the Fusion admirals had insisted on the mystery weapon that devastated their Navy being the first used against the Betrayers. It was an easy concession for the DCC. If something went wrong they'd only lose one cheap ship with less than a dozen crew.

Mthembu announced the course vectors. Hiroshi made an acceleration warning and lit the torch. A few radar pings confirmed no ships were loitering by the gate.

When they flipped to decelerate Mitchie scanned the stars for any sign of AI ships. None appeared until Hiroshi cut thrust. Then seven stars lit as one.

Mitchie aimed the telescope at them. Bright blue circles with a black dot in the center. Torchships headed straight for *Joshua Chamberlain*. She commed Setta. "Get the antenna deployed. We have customers."

Setta and her two techs set a record getting the oversized antenna out through the cargo hatch. The power up checks went almost as fast. She reported, "Entropy ready, ma'am."

Mitchie and Hiroshi took turns aligning the beam with each oncoming ship. He'd learned to maneuver the clumsy freighter with precision, but still kept wasting fuel with overcorrections. His commander didn't complain. She just demonstrated how careful timing of burns could do the job with less time and less fuel.

Unlike their Fusion Navy victims the AI ships kept coming.

"Could the beam alignment be off?" wondered Hiroshi.

"Wouldn't surprise me," said Mitchie. "That whole set-up is a kludge. Trace expanding circles around your current target."

Mthembu put the telescope back in its clip. "They're another order of magnitude brighter." He checked the plot and worked his slide rule. "If they don't turn over they'll be in laser range in fifty minutes."

Mitchie did some mental math. "Right. Hiroshi, you have five more minutes. If we don't get a kill by then secure maneuvering." She switched to Setta's comm. "Are you running at full power?"

"Yes'm," replied the petty officer.

"We haven't seen any effect on them. As soon as we stop maneuvering pack it up and secure for acceleration."

"Aye-aye."

When the chronometer clicked to the deadline Hiroshi hissed in frustration. A quick thruster burn took the spin off the ship. The edge of the antenna, barely visible from the bridge dome, folded in.

Another set of ships lit their torches, well behind the ones closing in.

As soon as Setta reported her team secure Hiroshi flipped the ship around and lit *Joshua Chamberlain's* torch. Twenty-five gravs pressed everyone into their couches hard.

A missile could still reach them before they jumped. Their own plume would hide the attack until it hit. Mitchie made herself breathe normally as they approached the gate.

Moments after Coatlicue's sun appeared a BDF cruiser challenged them. Mthembu sent the password.

"Welcome back, *Jay See*," said the cruiser. "What's the word?"

Mitchie lifted her mike. "The word is canal. Repeat, canal."

"Roger. Relaying canal."

In twelve minutes the message would reach the courier waiting at the Argo gate. In less than an hour the ships lined up in two systems would start jumping to Demeter, warned that the enemy was alert and invulnerable to the Disconnect superweapon.

"That was a waste of time," complained Mthembu.

You're alive, kid. Don't whine, thought Mitchie.

Demeter System, acceleration 0 m/s²

The people coming through the airlock were familiar to Mitchie: Pete, Chetty, and one of Chu's intelligence analysts. She welcomed the first two warmly and the last politely. "So what's this mission about?"

"Our first look at some enemy gear," said Chetty. He was over his grudge, or at least professional enough to not let it show. "The Fuzies disabled it and sent some Marines aboard to clear the bots. They can't figure out what it is so it's our turn. Here's the coordinates."

Mitchie took the hardcopy he handed her. "Huh. On the way to the Swakop gate." She passed it to Hiroshi. "Get us there." Taxi duty would be more fun than the supply runs they'd been doing.

He saluted to impress the guests and kicked off to the main deck hatch.

Mitchie turned to Chetty. "Why were we bothering with a fleeing enemy?"

"Target of opportunity," he said. "The Betrayer's been sending a steady stream of big ships to Swakop. It was going on before we returned. When we sent some scouts to check them out the AI directed warships to block them. We sent cruisers to take out the blockers. More were diverted. It's been clumsy about it, too. Pure sacrifice-play stuff. We've actually destroyed more of their ships than we lost. Usually we lose three to take two at best."

Pete said, "It's very out of character for Swakop. We've never achieved tactical superiority on the advance to the planet. It always withdraws units before we can take advantage of positioning. Except for these ships. It's sacrificed six warships to let one escape. I hypothesize that they must be closely linked to the AI's primary order."

"Is it trying to retake the ship?" asked Mitchie.

"No," Chetty answered. "Puzzling given how hard it fought to protect it."

"We'll know more in two days. It's almost dinner time here. Would you care to join us?"

***

The Marines named the ship "Target Theta." Pete and Chetty watched from the bridge as Mitchie flew a circle around it. She thought it looked like a three-scoop ice cream cone after the cone was blown off by precision directed energy weapons.

Chetty said, "They're pressure vessels. Sturdy ones. You can see on the rear one where shrapnel from the torch explosion dented it without penetrating. No provisions for aerodynamic maneuvering."

Pete grimaced, impatient to look at the contents.

The other side of Theta had no more revelations.

"All right, let's suit up and go inside," said Mitchie. "Hiroshi, you have the con. Please line up with the Marine's breaching lock."

***

A Fusion Marine Senior Lieutenant waited inside the temporary airlock. Mitchie saluted him. "Commander Michigan Long with party of four. Permission to come aboard?"

Startlement delayed his response a moment. "The—uh, yes. Welcome to Target Theta, ma'am."

As Guo came through the hatch next she asked, "Couldn't you get the regular airlock working?"

"There is no airlock ma'am. Or hatch. Or door. Or easily split seam. It's a solid shell."

"That makes sense if this is a one trip vessel," said Guo, taking off his helmet. "We didn't see any of them coming back. It may just be dismantled at the destination."

Mitchie looked around. A pile of broken bots and smaller pieces was netted against the hull. The sphere was filled with black blocks. At first glance she thought of coffins but they were bigger than that. Metal racks held them spaced apart so each had at least one side exposed to an aisle.

When everyone was inside the lieutenant gave his safety talk. "There's oxygen in here, but it's what was sealed up with the hull when they built it on Demeter. There's no replacement and no circulation. Watch your air monitors. Don't take your suit off. Everyone will have a Marine escort at all times."

The squad of Marines was the residual left after the assault force had pulled out. Noticing that several were old for the ranks they wore Mitchie wondered if some intel types had been brought in to eavesdrop. *Fine by me. Pete might subvert a couple.*

With that Pete was unleashed. Chu's analyst and the oldest Marine followed him. He slapped his datasheet against the nearest block and pulled up a magnified view.

Chetty disappeared into the labyrinth of blocks. Mitchie decided to watch Pete's show.

"It's a data storage medium," he proclaimed after a few minutes. "Incredibly high density. Carbon crystals with data marked by impurities and irregularities in the bonds. Brittle. The air may be for thermal stability."

"Can you read it?" demanded the analyst.

"Eventually, of course. We'll need to understand the interface first."

Guo examined the other faces of the block. "There's an array of metal contacts here. Hmmm. I wonder how standardized its designs are?"

He pushed over to the net of robot debris and rooted through the pile. A matching grid came off an arm. Other bots donated cables. Half an hour's work with his toolkit produced a piece of hardware that could connect the black block to a datasheet.

Pete accepted it with effusive thanks, then went silent as he began trying to decode the Betrayer's data.

Mitchie went to check on Chetty. He and his bored Marine shadow were returning from the aft end. "All the same," he reported.

"So what would Swakop want with data from Demeter? And why send it by ship?" she asked.

"For this much data a ship makes sense. Better data rate than lasercomm to a jump courier."

"But what is it?" said Mitchie. "I've seen the back-up cubes they made of Demeter's planetary archive. It wouldn't fill one of these ships."

"Possibly Swakop's working on a calculation and wanted Demeter to do part of it that exceeded its capacity. These are the results."

"Could be. But this is a lot of work to get more processing power."

Lunchtime came without Pete coming up for air. Setta delivered BDF-issue cold rations, which the Marines found a refreshing change.

A few hours later Pete proclaimed "Eureka!" He had everyone's full attention. "It's a physical object record."

"What kind?" asked Mitchie.

"Many kinds. If there's a pattern I can't see it." Pete patted his datasheet. "This poor little thing can only hold a small piece of it at a time. But it's clear what's most common." Pete held up his datasheet and sketched a large circle with small ones attached on top left and right.

"It's a Disney media?" asked Mitchie.

"No, no, it's a water molecule. But in such detail. It has its attitude in 3D space, temperature effects on the bonds, even a fractal surface for the location probability distribution of each electron." He shook his head. "I can't imagine what would need such detail on a simple water molecule."

Chetty said, "It could be a record of one instant in a chemical reaction simulation."

"Yes, that's something parallelizable," said Pete.

"All this, for chemistry," said Mitchie.

"That's just one block," said Guo. "The others could have anything in them."

Pete agreed. "Yes. And this one might not be all chemistry. I've just been poking around at random. To really explore it I'll need to take the block back to *Aurora*." He'd been given a laboratory on the converted passenger liner hauling researchers, politicians, and other civilian hangers-on in the wake of the allied fleet.

"Is that safe?" demanded the Marine officer.

"Dr. Smith is fully proficient in data isolation protocols," snapped Mitchie.

"I might be able to scrounge up enough memory to read an entire block. That'd let me index it and move on to the next." Pete turned to Mitchie. "How many can we bring back?"

"A run to *Aurora* wouldn't be mass-limited, just volume. We can fit scores of these in the hold. Wait . . . is the torch on this thing repairable?"

Guo and Chetty shook their heads together. "It's scrap," said the mechanic.

"Then we'll have to load them. Can't bring the whole ship back. The tugs are busy dealing with battle damage," she said.

The Marine offered to have his troops blow open a hatch in the hull.

"No!" said Pete. "They're far too fragile to survive explosive decompression."

His suggestion to build a full-pressure tunnel to the *Joshua Chamberlain* wasn't practical. The compromise was a small hole drilled in the data ship's hull to slowly let the air out. Guo went back to his ship to rig the crane lines for hauling the cargo out.

A few minutes after the hole started whistling a massive CLANG shook the ship. Chetty and a pair of Marines bounced off to investigate. He returned to report, "An airtight door just closed this sphere off from the next. I'm glad we didn't have anyone wandering around. It came down like an axe."

Before long Mitchie's ears were popping. The men's stubborn refusal to be the first to close their helmets amused her. Once she closed hers the rest followed in less than a minute.

When the air pressure was down by a third a crack appeared in Pete's pet block with an audible snap. "Plug it! Plug it!" he yelled.

A marine slapped his glove across the hole, silencing the whistle. In the sudden quiet they could hear more snaps and pops. Most of the blocks showed spreading cracks.

"Oh, God," moaned Pete. "They're under so much stress they need compression to stay stable."

The cracking grew louder, thunderstorm-like in intensity. Flakes flew off the surface of blocks and ricocheted around the labyrinth. Then the storm subsided, trailing off with a last few rattles. *Like popcorn*, thought Mitchie.

"Do you want to bring some pieces back?" asked Chu's analyst.

"Why?" said Pete. "The data's destroyed. The molecules reverted to their blank state when the stress came off. If we could get some from the other sphere into a pressure vessel . . . no, then we'd lose the rest. I'll have to bring all my gear here. If I can get the admiralty to authorize it." He didn't sound hopeful.

Mitchie had to agree. With the battle still raging a second trip to the dataship would be bottom priority. They'd established these ships weren't an immediate threat which was what Command wanted. But losing the data was breaking Pete's heart.

She said, "That end with the interface contacts will fit in the airlock. Put it in a survival bubble. We'll take it back to *Aurora*. You can use it to test your set-up so you're ready when we do get you a block."

"Thank you," said Pete. "Damn it. Why would an AI make something so fragile?"

Chetty had been thinking about that. "It's probably a single use device. Take the data to Swakop to be copied onto something sturdy. This let it get the maximum data per ship."

"Makes me wonder what the hurry is," said Mitchie.

Near Demeter, acceleration 10 m/s^2

The AI kept subverting the systems on warships, using high-powered transmitters to beam code into sensors and even exposed cables. Locating the transmitters was the fleet's top priority. Command tasked *Joshua Chamberlain* to deploy reconnaissance satellites in low orbit.

The first four reconsats were ejected from the hold on schedule. Mitchie did have to employ evasive maneuvers and deploy both of the decoy drones they'd been given to avoid missile and laser fire from the planet. She altered course to the next drop point.

In the converter room Guo studied his assistants. Both of them were tense at being in the ship closest to the enemy. They were doing a good job of hiding it. To keep their minds off it Guo kept them working on routine inspections and monitoring the heat flows below the firedeck. The real training was how to handle maneuvers. Routine ones were announced on the PA so everyone could grab hold of something. Flipping the ship to point her torch plume at an incoming missile was a surprise. He'd run them through exercises to practice falling on the deck. Mastery would take doing it for real.

Mthembu's voice came over the PA. "Multiple incoming." All three mechanics grabbed something.

The ship yawed sharply. One mechanic lost his balance, dangling from his handhold. The other laughed at him. "Nice job, Ye."

Guo said, "Can it, Finnegan. Your turn will come." The laugher quieted.

Ye got back on his feet. The ship pitched hard but they all stayed in place.

"Think we're clear?" asked Finnegan.

"Just stay patient," said Guo.

Some more thrashing shook them. Then the sound of an impact almost deafened them. The flow warning board, normally pastoral green lights, sprouted a streak of red. The ship began to spin. Ye and Guo were pressed to the floor but Finnegan, across the room, was flung to the ceiling. "Shit! My arm!"

"Just hang on," said Guo. "We'll get to you." *When the ship's under control.*

Ye said, "Quadrant three has multiple broken pipes. I'll shut it down."

"No, get quadrant one shut," snapped Guo. "You're closer."

"But—"

"Quadrant one! Do it!"

Ye crawled toward the valves. The spin forced him onto the bulkhead. He maneuvered around readouts and consoles, trying to not knee any controls. Guo worked toward the quadrant three controls. Finnegan moaned.

By the time Ye reached the valve the spin pressed him hard against the bulkhead. He had to support himself with one arm and twist the valve with the other. "Cutting flow to quadrant one."

The torch nozzles on the fore-port quarter of *Joshua Chamberlain's* base stopped firing as their superheated steam stopped coming. The warning board flashed more red, complaining that the boiler lines had overheated and shut down.

On the other side half the nozzles were dry, the pipes feeding them torn open by a missiles fragment. Steam boiled out through the hole in the hull, some becoming ice around the torn edges. The remaining quadrant three nozzles unbalanced the thrust on the ship, torqueing it back the other way now that the full quadrant one thrust wasn't adding more spin to the ship.

Guo waited with his hands on the valve handle, feeling the spin force pushing him against the bulkhead weaken. When it was almost gone he shut the valve. When the board confirmed quadrant three wasn't firing any more he pulled out his handcomm. "Captain, we are clear to continue on quadrants two and four."

"Thanks, Chief," was Mitchie's reply. They heard the thrusters fire to take the rest of the spin off.

Ye helped Finnegan into his acceleration couch. "What are we going to do now?" he asked.

"We can splint his arm," answered Guo."

"No, I meant the ship."

Above them the sound of the catapult putting another reconsat into its target orbit sounded.

"We're going to get the job done. It's what we're here for."

Patton Station, Demeter System, centrifugal accel. 10 m/s^2

"Eleven days is too damn long," said Mitchie. Guo had worked the Chief network on the shipyard and come back with the same answer she'd gotten from its CO.

Guo shrugged. "We took some nasty damage. They need to cut out some of the hull to put replacements in. I think they're doing the best they can."

Walking the station's long corridors let Mitchie burn off some nervous energy. Limping to the shipyard and waiting for a repair slip to open up had taken them out of action for over a week already. She wanted to get back to work.

"Are there any parts they're short on?" she asked. "I could put Setta on finding them."

Before Guo could answer another couple turned in from a cross-corridor. They stopped short to avoid bumping noses.

"Urk!" Mechanic Finnegan blushed. It showed plainly—he was normally almost as pale as Mitchie. "Uh, ma'am, Senior Chief, I'd like you to meet my friend Amy."

The woman tucked under Finnegan's unbandaged arm reached out to shake hands with Guo.

Mitchie studied her. The outfit had started as a Fusion Navy uniform before half the cloth was removed. The face was surgically perfect, as were other parts. Voice and expression completely controlled. Mitchie pegged her as having at least a decade's experience in the trade and made a rough estimate of her hourly rate on a Fusion world.

Finnegan must have paid much more than that.

When her turn for shaking hands came Mitchie took "Amy's" hand in both of hers. "Are you a good friend of his?"

"Very, ma'am. You don't have anything to worry about."

Mitchie let go. "Well, I'm delighted to meet you, but we have a ship repair meeting."

Finnegan and his companion vanished down the cross-corridor.

"I'm glad he's having a good leave," said Guo as they started walking again.

"Uh-huh. Is crew pay up to date?"

"Yes, I paid them before releasing everyone for leave."

"Good," said Mitchie. "If Finnegan asks for a pay advance don't give him more than two weeks' worth."

Guo stopped. "Wait. You think?"

"Yes. And I think she's professional enough to not get him into trouble."

He thought for a moment. Mitchie braced for questions about how she'd learned to assess such professionalism.

Instead Guo said, "I can't blame him for wanting some comfort. It was scary in the converter room for a few minutes." He wrapped an arm around her. "I'm glad I have you."

Mitchie leaned into the embrace. "Are you comforted?"

"Yes. But I wouldn't say no to more."

"All right." Nagging the repair crew could wait.

Near Planet Demeter, acceleration 0 m/s^2

Directing the casualties to their places in the cargo hold was technically Setta's job, but she let the corpsmen bring in their patients without bothering them. They all found the proper tie-downs without help. The patients were neatly sorted, Fuzies to port, Disconnect starboard.

Inspecting tie-downs was an excuse to look over the casualties. They had the usual mix of space battle injuries—burns, vac bite, amputations.

A Fuegan with anesthetic caps on his ankle-stumps tried to strike up a conversation. "Hi, Sugar. What ship is this?"

Setta answered, "You're on the *Joshua Chamberlain*."

"No way! What's a ship like that hauling meat for?"

"We go where the work is. What's your story?"

"I'm going to be an inspirational poster at the Academy. 'Kids, don't be too slow through the pressure door.' Fame at last," he said with mock boastfulness.

Setta gave him a polite chuckle. "How did so many of you get banged up? I thought the fleet was staying out of missile range."

"That's not so inspirational," said the Fuegan. "Occasionally a ship goes down for recon. A Fuzie cruiser made a low pass and had its fire control circuits subverted by the Betrayer. Nothing happened until it rejoined its squadron. Then it tossed a bunch of missiles at the nearest Disconnect squadron. We saw incoming and shot back, naturally. But with the jamming we couldn't tell which one fired. So we spread our shots all over the Fuzie squadron. Then all the other Fuzies started launching on us. And then it got ugly."

The casualty behind her spoke up. "Fortunately nobody else was stupid enough to get sucked into it."

Setta turned to look at him. The sleeves of his jumpsuit had been cut away. Bandages covered from hands to elbows. "What stopped it?" she asked.

He tried to shrug but his arms were taped in place. "Commodore ordered everyone to defensive fire only. Then the crew of the subverted ship cut enough wires to shut their tubes down. That just left the clean-up."

Setta said, "It scares me that Fuzies and Diskers are so ready to shoot at each other."

Bandaged Hands said, "I'm more scared that the Betrayer figured out how to get us to do it."

Docked to Depot Ship *Tahiti*, Demeter System, centrifugal acceleration 10 m/s²

Once the orbital defenses were cleared away from Demeter the attack squadrons orbited fifteen thousand klicks up. Lower than that they sometimes had their systems subverted by enemy signals, forcing them to fire on friends or catastrophically deorbit. Analog ships drew duty as target spotters, carrying sensor pallets to search for the infoweapon transmitters.

Mitchie expected to join them when *Joshua Chamberlain* was called back to the logistics convoy. Instead the cargo hold was filled with a floor to ceiling rack of drop capsules.

"Those look flimsy for re-entry," Mitchie said to the quartermaster overseeing the installation.

"Oh, these aren't for orbital drops," she answered. "These are the second wave, released in atmosphere. Didn't you get briefed?"

"No, that's our next stop." *When it's too late to back out.*

The briefing room held the crews of a dozen analog ships. The Fusion Marine officer spent more time explaining why orbital drop capsules were too expensive to mass produce than laying out the plan for the operation. For the ships it was simple: enter atmosphere, slow to near-stop, release the racks, then get back to orbit before the AI found their range.

When the brief moved on to explaining how the shock gel filling the capsules would protect the Marines from injury on landing Mitchie tuned it out. She wondered why the infantry were being sent in so soon. *Are they hoping to find survivors? Do they need to capture a hold on the surface to clear the way for the fleet? Or is High Command just trying to drive up the Fusion casualty count?*

Joshua Chamberlain met with the troopship a hundred thousand klicks over Demeter. Mitchie hovered halfway up the cargo hold wall, watching them file in. The NCOs took advantage of free-fall to throw wayward privates to the next empty capsule.

Pushing Marines into the shock gel produced complaints of it feeling like mud or worse. Mitchie kept checking the time. Despite the whinging and cursing the Marines kept ahead of schedule.

"Hi, Mitchie!"

She pivoted to face the Marine who'd just come through the airlock.

He blushed when he saw her rank. "Ah, ma'am. Sorry, ma'am." He saluted.

She returned it and pushed off to land next to him. "Welcome back aboard, Abdul." She was about to ask him how he'd wound up in the Marines when a gunnery sergeant gave a cough. *Right, no time for chit-chat.* "You have a safe trip." She slapped him on the shoulder and went back to her perch.

Mitchie did have to make chit-chat with the battalion's colonel before he climbed into the last capsule, right against the cargo hold doors. "Anything I need to do if the attack is delayed?"

"No worries. Sergeant major has them listening to a proper list of songs. The time will fly by."

"Right. Good luck, Colonel."

"Thank you, Commander. Could you check my seals after I button up?"

She made sure his capsule was air-tight then did the same for the rest of the front row. She knew staff officers could be sloppy with the hands-on stuff.

Mitchie had *Joshua Chamberlain* parked on her go-point with twelve minutes to spare. The operation was precisely timed. A global bombardment had already started. The drop zone and several decoy areas received extra attention. The orbital drop capsules were falling toward the planet, mixed with jammers, decoys, and chaff pods. The airdrop was scheduled for right as the first wave hit dirt.

"Hustle, go go go! Hustle, go go go!" came the signal.

Hiroshi lit the torch. The nav box said they were on course. Mitchie took a couple of sights to verify it hadn't been subverted yet.

Halfway down they flipped, burning down their velocity so they'd hit air at a survivable speed. The ship rocked slightly as it entered the upper atmosphere.

"Captain has the con," said Mitchie.

"Captain has the con," acknowledged Hiroshi,. releasing the controls.

She tweaked the torch to smooth out the aerobraking and steer the ship toward their drop point. As the air pressure pushed their exhaust back against the hull she commed Guo to shift the mix to more steam flow and less heat. The ship slowed hard, pressing the crew against their couches with thirty gravs. By the nav box they were still on track.

As the ship slowed to merely supersonic speed Mitchie spun up the turbines. When they reached full thrust she cut the torch. *Don't want to fry the poor boys on their way out.*

Now that their wake wasn't distorting visibility the bridge crew could see beams flashing past them. The assault squadrons were intercepting the AI's antiship missiles.

Mitchie checked the nav box. The display showed only grey snow. She cursed and started looking for landmarks. "Hiroshi, start the radar. Get our altitude."

Memorizing the map of Daphne City paid off. The drop point was over the intersection of two cargo roads. She tilted the ship toward it, trying for a smooth ride.

She thumbed the PA switch. "Prepare to release troops."

Below decks Guo and Setta rose from their acceleration couches and took the ladder up to the hold.

A minute later Guo reported, "Ready to drop."

"Stand by." She still had the ship moving too fast—the doors would rip right off if they opened.

Mthembu kept looking out the dome. "Incoming is getting closer."

Hiroshi shushed him.

Mitchie placed the ship hovering over the drop point. "Drop drop drop!"

The cargo hold doors began to open. The ship rocked as a missile exploded nearby. Then the rattle of capsules sliding out of the racks began.

Mitchie set *Joshua Chamberlain* drifting east for the prescribed separation between parachutes. She could see the capsules plummeting to the ground four klicks below. The chutes didn't deploy until they were more than halfway down.

"All out!" announced Guo. The hold doors began closing.

"Hiroshi, take the con," ordered Mitchie. "As soon as they're secure get us out of here."

"Aye-aye, I have the con," he answered. He pointed the ship straight up to get a little altitude with the turbines on low thrust.

Guo reported, "Crew secure," from his couch.

Hiroshi lit the torch. The sky disappeared as the air before them compressed hard enough to glow.

When the stars appeared Mitchie took a deep breath and let it out slowly.

Hiroshi directed his co-pilot to take sights. "I've just been boosting *away*. Let's get on a course."

A message came in on the analog ship channel. "Drop ships, this is Landing Command. Well done. All troops were landed on schedule. Compliments to *Joshua Chamberlain* for being the only ship to place all your troops in their drop box."

"Hear that, Skipper?" said Mthembu. "Think they'll have something for us?"

"Yep," said Mitchie. "Another job."

Patton Station, Demeter System, centrifugal accel. 10 m/s^2

Dropping supplies at Patton Station had perks. Unlimited hot water was one of the best. Mitchie lay in a soft bed, luxuriating in the feeling of being completely clean. Guo finished toweling off and climbed in next to her. She wondered if he'd fall asleep. Showers hadn't been their first priority.

Guo's arms pulled her tight against him in a non-sleepy way. "Hey. Can we talk about something?"

"Sure." Mitchie turned on her side to face him.

"We've been doing lots of high hazard missions."

"Best ship, best pilots," she stroked his chest, "best-tuned torch. We have a better chance of coming out in one piece than any other analog ship. So we get the job."

"Chance." Guo stressed the word. "That's the thing that worries me. No matter how good our odds are, every time we roll the dice we could be unlucky."

She thought a moment before speaking. "Do you want to stop rolling them?"

Guo pulled the sheet up to his ribs. "I'm not suggesting mutiny or desertion. But maybe let some of the other ships take a turn at volunteering when they ask who wants to go?"

"You're that worried?"

"I've looked at the casualty counts. They're stacking up. I don't want to lose you. I . . . have some plans for us, after the war."

Mitchie kissed him. "Okay. I'll let the others volunteer."

They were less clean by the time the comm chimed. They ignored it until the chime changed to the "priority" buzz.

Mitchie rolled out of bed and grabbed her towel off the floor. "This better be real," she muttered as she wrapped it around herself.

The "accept" button produced an image of a Fusion Marine Colonel-General. She came to attention, or as close as she could come without dropping the towel.

"Commander Long," said the general. "I apologize for waking you. A situation is developing in the spacehead."

"No problem, sir," she said. "How can I help you?"

"The number of seriously wounded has exceeded the capacity of the field clinic. Also, the head surgeon reports some need care in base facilities if they're going to survive."

Dice roll, incoming, thought Mitchie.

"The Navy hasn't been able to get ships into atmosphere without losing them to info subversion," continued the general. "The only way we can evacuate them is with an analog ship. Everyone I talked to said your ship is the best one for the mission."

He took a deep breath. "Commander, can you rescue my wounded men?"

Mitchie thought, as an experiment, of saying no. But she could barely think it. She'd never be able to say it. "Yes, sir. We'll do our best."

Relief flashed across the general's face. "Thank you, Commander. I'll have the evac gear moved onto your ship." He cut the connection.

She walked back to the bed, towelless. "I guess that promise didn't last very long. Sorry."

Guo smiled. "You hesitated long enough for two other captains to jump in. Now we need the bosses to give the others a chance." He shoved a foot into his jumpsuit.

"You don't have to come on this mission if you don't want."

He kissed her. "If you're on it, I do have to."

***

Setta had wrangled a large cabin for the two of them. Hiroshi sprawled across the bed, glorying in not hanging over the edge. "We need to make a double cabin on the *Chamberlain*," he said. "Like the Skipper and Chief have. Then we could have a real bed."

She giggled. "I think they'd want us to be married before we start cutting any bulkheads."

"Maybe. They can't throw stones about fraternization. I wish we could set a date."

"Does 'Next time we're on Bonaventure or Shishi plus a week' count as setting it?"

Hiroshi laughed. "Might make the captain happy but it doesn't let my family make travel plans. Or hosting plans. Doing stuff on short notice is expensive."

Setta glared at him. "Expensive? Didn't you read your last bank report?"

"No, I trust you to handle that stuff. Why?"

"Because you can afford to fly all your cousins to any planet you choose."

"Really?" said Hiroshi.

"That stuff I bought from the terraformers is selling now that Bonaventure is rebuilding. The latest from my broker is she sold the two genetic analyzers. First one to a hospital. After word got out three companies fought a bidding war over the other so they could reverse engineer it. Anyway—whatever you want, you can afford it, and if you can't I can."

"Ooh. We could have a fancy wedding." His eyes shifted focus beyond the ceiling. "I'd like to have Imperial Honors for you."

"What's that? An artillery salute?"

"No, as I lead you to the altar we pass under an arch, one side officers holding their swords, the other court ladies with flowered boughs. I've only seen it once but it's lovely."

Setta visualized it. "Sure."

"As long as it doesn't take too much money to make it happen. It'd be nice to retire after the war."

"Trust me, lover, you don't need your centurion pay any more."

The cabin's comm beeped to announce a message. Setta checked it. "Huh. Recalled to ship, be there in ninety minutes. Must be time to run another load of missiles out to the fleet."

Hiroshi said, "If we only have ninety minutes, let's not waste them."

She smiled and climbed back into the bed.

Demeter System, acceleration 10 m/s^2

Mitchie closed the Captain's Bible. "I now pronounce you husband and wife. You may kiss the bride."

Hiroshi pulled Setta close for a well-practiced smooch. The watchers, mostly medical staff, cheered.

Mitchie drifted back to lean on one of the temporary bunks welded to the cargo hold deck. The senior doctor of the evacuation team joined her.

"Do you perform many weddings, Captain?" he asked.

"No. The last time we had one on this ship I was the bride."

"Under happier circumstances, I hope."

She compared them. Setta and Hiroshi had abandoned their plans for a fancy Shishi wedding when they heard the mission description. "About the same."

"Well. To happier weddings for the next generation." He sipped from a flask then offered it to her.

"I'll drink to that." It was bourbon, better than any she'd tried before.

Setta's origami bouquet stopped short of the witnesses. A nurse kept it off the deck with a diving grab.

***

Mitchie sent her descent plan to the supporting warships so they could plan suppressing fire around her. Then she sent it again to convince them the first wasn't a garbled file.

All the medics had passed flight physicals. *Joshua Chamberlain* burned toward the planet at forty gravs. At that acceleration just lifting one's hand took work. Which is why the thrust controls were all next to the pilot couch hand rests.

As they approached upper atmosphere Mitchie said, "Brace for skew," into the PA. When the chronometer hit her calculated mark she fired the pitch thrusters. Still firing her torch the ship flipped 180 degrees. Everyone's inner ear declared the impossible shift a symptom of poisoning.

She reversed thrusters. A few checks verified she had stopped the ship on the right vector. Now they were slowing at forty gravs. If she'd done her math right they'd stop before reaching bedrock.

Spacehead HQ, Demeter, gravity 7.5 m/s²

The S-4 shop had a fourth-floor office. With the lifts out no one else wanted it. Colonel Marshal liked the fresh air. Every window had been blasted out by the preparatory bombardment so there was plenty of that. The occasional sonic boom was just part of life in a war zone.

This boom came with a wave of heat which drew curses from the walking wounded detailed from the combat units. The blast of air blew displays and datasheets onto the floor. A memory cube shattered.

The colonel answered a snarled "What the fuck was that?" by pointing. A missing wall framed *Joshua Chamberlain* as her torch faded out. The ship tilted on her turbines and buzzed toward the landing field.

"Dust-off," said the sergeant major. "Coming to get the wounded. God help them."

***

Setta opened the cargo hold doors before the ship touched down. They were landing in a former groundster racing park. The view stands were rubble. Two painted arrows marked where they should set down.

The impact jarred her. She straightened up and yelled, "Get your pins!" The medics she'd trained sprang out of their bunks and ran to their assigned spots on the deployable ramp. "Pull pins!" Each one yanked out a metal rod and held it over their head. "Clear!" They scampered. She pushed the RAISE button on the crane remote.

The cable wound through the folded ramp spooled back on to the crane's winch. The ramp panels levered out, snapping into alignment with each other. When it reached full extension she reversed the winch to lower the rigid ramp to the pavement.

The overcast day turned bright as an autocannon fired on incoming missiles. White starbursts in the sky marked hits.

Setta walked down the ramp, waiting for it to give under her weight. She could see stretcher teams kneeling in the shadow of an intact building. In the middle of the park lines of graves marked the turf.

Halfway down she stopped, jumping on the ramp as hard as she could. It didn't budge. She waved, her hand making semicircles as a "come on" gesture.

The stretcher-bearers came smoothly to their feet. At a steady trot they formed two lines for the ramp.

Setta scampered back up. As the ground-pounders reached the top of the ramp she called, "Tripping hazard! Watch your step!" The lines split around the ramp's base mechanism.

The medical team took over traffic control. "All the way to the back! All the way to the back!" directed the nurse who'd caught the bouquet.

More autocannon fire sounded, with answering distant explosions.

Returning stretcher bearers fit single-file between the ascending stretchers. Setta shook her head. She figured crowding the ramp like that would send some over the edge. She decided infantrymen must be part goat.

The PA came on. "This is the captain." She sounded amused. "Air Defense wants everyone to know that the incoming may look close but they're intercepting everything at least three klicks out. That is all."

Setta looked at the latest starbursts. If that was three klicks away they were drawing *big* incoming.

The head doctor declared a casualty dead. His stretcher went on the deployment mechanism to wait for the ramp to clear.

Wounded coming up the ramp now didn't look as bad as the first wave. The field docs had sent them in triage order. The rows of bunks were over half full.

She realized she wasn't noticing the autocannon anymore.

"Bosun?"

She turned around to find the head doctor addressing her. "Yes, sir?"

"Tell the captain some casualties can't handle high acceleration. She'll have to keep it below twenty gravs."

"How many, sir?"

"What?"

"How many of them will we lose if we go over twenty," she explained. "The captain will need to know."

"It doesn't matter," said the doctor. "She can't kill our wounded."

"Sir, choosing between some of us and all of us is what the captain does." She tried to find a way to make him understand. "It's how shipmasters do triage."

The sour look on his face said she'd gotten through. "Seven," he said in a worried tone, as if he thought that wasn't enough.

"I'll tell her. And sir?"

The doctor looked back over his shoulder.

"You would not believe some of the things the Skipper has done to keep her passengers safe. But I'll tell you once we're clear."

That improved his expression almost to a smile.

After passing the word on Setta returned to watching the ramp. These wounded were still badly hurt but the damage had left their uniforms intact enough for her to recognize them. About a third were Diskers, proportional to their contribution to the ground force. The stretcher teams were all four Fuzies or four Diskers. But the wounded they carried were as likely to be one as the other. She found that hopeful.

A nurse called, "Six more!"

Setta looked at the bunks. That would fill them. *Great, I get to lie on the deck for lift-off.* She took the nurse aside. "Grab pillows for each of us. You don't want your skull on the deck at high accel."

After unlatching the deployment mechanism from the deck, she followed the last stretcher bearers down the ramp, unhooking the crane cable and threading it through a different set of holes. Back in the hold she started the crane spooling it up, watching the ramp nervously. If this didn't work *Joshua Chamberlain* could have a hole torn in her side.

As the cable tightened the middle of the ramp folded in. It pulled the base plate out of the hold, flinging it beyond where the ramp had touched the pavement. Setta sighed in relief.

She pulled her cutter from its boot sheath. The sawtooth blade made short work of the steel cable. Once the severed end fell out of the hatch she started the doors closing. Normally that felt loud but the autocannon drowned out the rattles and motor hum.

Once Setta latched the doors she called the bridge. "Hold secure for lift."

The captain answered, "Good. Are the medics secure?"

"No, ma'am. Still fussing with the casualties."

"Tell them to stop. Incoming's heating up."

***

Mitchie said, "Thank you, doctor," and switched to PA. "All hands, brace for lift." Next was the frequency for the ground support ships in high orbit. "Badger, badger, badger." In ninety seconds a wave of suppression bombardment would surround the spacehead. She put the microphone down. "Hiroshi, you have the con."

"I have the con, aye. Acceleration limit?"

"If we're taking fire, no limit. Until then keep it to twenty gravs."

"Aye-aye." Hiroshi watched the sky. When the streaks of descending missiles appeared he called "Up ship!" on the PA and spun up the turbines.

He started the ascent as an easy fifteen gravs, relying on the spacehead autocannons and the bombardment to protect the ship. Five klicks up he fired the torch and shut down the turbines. The ride grew rough as he constantly tweaked the thrust up and down, being as random as he could to evade Betrayer attacks.

One missile exploded near *Joshua Chamberlain* as she passed twelve klicks up. The hull groaned as it bent in. The whole ship lurched with the shockwave. Hiroshi cut the torch.

Setta's voice came from the bridge speakers. "We have air leaks in the hold. Not big. Patchable."

Guo replied on the same channel, "Increasing oxygen flow."

The ship kept free-falling, tilting to port. Mitchie said, "Pilot, torch shows all green."

Hiroshi replied, "Sandbagging." Five seconds later he relit the torch at twenty gravs.

"Sand-what?" complained Mthembu.

Mitchie chuckled. "He decided to play dead so it'd stop shooting at us. Right, Centurion?"

"Let's see if it worked, ma'am."

Whether the AI was fooled or not it didn't land any more hits before they reached the safety of high orbit. Hiroshi cut the torch again to let Guo and his assistants do damage control.

He stroked the pilot console fondly. "She's no acrobatic cutter, but I'm learning to do some real flying with this old lady."

"Good," said Mitchie. "She deserves some love."

Patton Station, Demeter System, centrifugal accel. 10 m/s^2

A shout woke Guo from a sound sleep. The cabin was lit by the peaceful green lights of the intercom and security panels. He could make out Mitchie standing by the bed, hands raised in a defensive stance.

"What's the matter?" he asked.

"Nothing." Her breathing came fast. Her eyes checked the empty corners of the room. Her legs flexed, ready to spring aside.

"Bad dream?"

Mitchie took a deep breath then drew herself up straight. "Yeah."

"C'mere." Guo held out his arms. She climbed into bed and let him wrap around her.

When he felt her pulse slow Guo said, "Tell me about it?"

She stayed silent long enough he wondered if she'd gone back to sleep.

"I was stabbing that sentry," she began. "But it wasn't the sentry, it was Chetty. He had the same betrayed look the sentry did. Then a missile hit the ship and it broke apart around us. Chetty flew off into the empty. I was falling. You went by screaming. I tried to grab you and missed. Then a guy in a spacesuit tried to strangle me. I started hitting him." Deep breath. "Then you were asking me silly questions."

Guo hugged her tightly. "You're safe now."

"Yeah, I know. It was just a dream."

Chapter Fifteen: Orders

Minos Station, Demeter System, centrifugal accel. 10 m/s²

They all stood as Admiral Galen strode into the room. "As you were." They sat.

Mitchie glanced at the rest of the audience. Pete, Chetty, and some other boffins. Various intel analysts. Some Bonaventure Defense Force infantry officers with hard faces. More Navy types she didn't know.

Galen put a picture on the screen. The structure had sloped earth sides, weeds sprouting in the dirt. An armored door stood open to let a cargobot enter a dark tunnel.

"Welcome to Operation Jigsaw," said the Admiral. "These bunkers are all over the damn planet. Their distribution roughly matches the pre-invasion population density. We have no idea what they do. We do know the Betrayer fights like hell to keep us from capturing or destroying one. They're armored under the dirt so we need big bombs to take one out. It evacuates the contents when we get close.

"So far the speculation runs from command and control nodes to high-intensity data processing centers to data archives." He waved at the analysts. "Which is a fancy way of saying we don't have a clue. We need to know: should they be priority targets? Or can we by-pass them and sort it out later?

"That's your mission. Solve the puzzle." Galen put a map of the continent Hellas on the screen. "This area hasn't been contested. The Betrayer has pulled units out to reinforce the front. We've identified the most isolated bunker, here by Photakis Village. You'll drop in, with fire support. Captain Kim's team will secure the bunker and surrounding area. The research team will go through and collect data. Then lift out before any Betrayer reinforcements can reach the area. Any questions?"

Mitchie said, "How much fire support, sir?"

"The 37ᵗʰ Destroyer Squadron has been hardened against info attacks. They'll be in-atmosphere for direct support under your control."

Well, there's a nice measure for how dangerous they think this is, she thought.

Pete raised his hand. At the admiral's nod he asked, "How much time will we have on the ground?"

"That's Commander Long's call as mission commander."

Mitchie suspected she might need to have Pete carried back on board by a couple of soldiers.

Demeter, gravity 7.5 m/s²

The high-speed descent didn't leave much time to appreciate the countryside. Puffs of smoke appeared as the destroyers took out missile launchers, or structures that might have some defensive role. The target bunker was at the edge of the cultivated zone. Untended pines covered the hills to the west.

Mitchie cranked up the turbines to brake at thirty gravs as they reached the ground. The landing gear screeched at the impact, but not loudly enough for the springs to be broken. She announced, "Clear to deploy," on the PA.

The ventral camera showed infantrymen roping out of the ship as soon as they could fit under the opening doors. The first squad ran to the bunker.

"Centurion Hiroshi, I'm deploying with the boffins. You have the ship. If the bunker blows up grab all the survivors you can and get out of here."

"Aye-aye, ma'am."

The research team stood at the edge of the cargo hatch waiting for the infantry to give the all-clear. Guo had attached the personnel cage to the cargo crane's hook. Pete's gear filled it. The other researchers wore backpacks or slung bags with their equipment.

Captain Kim's voice came over Mitchie's handcomm. "Bunker is clear, ma'am."

She thanked him then said, "Let's go." She grabbed onto the outside of the cage. Pete squeezed in and sat on a box. The rest started down the rope ladders.

Guo hooked his arms through the bars of the cage and fiddled with the crane remote. It lifted the cage up, out, and down to the ground. All of the gear sat on large-wheeled carts, suitable for hauling across grass. Pete grabbed the lead of the biggest one and hauled it out with a grunt.

"Pitch in, everybody," said Mitchie. She took the next cart's rope and pulled. Guo and the researchers took more. The squad assigned to bodyguard them hung back until she gave their sergeant a firm look. Then he ordered them to sling rifles and help.

As they passed under a low branch a squirrel declared it was his tree and they weren't welcome. "Relax, critter," muttered Mitchie. "We're just visiting."

Guo said, "It's eerie. Squirrels, birds, butterflies, all just like normal. But no people."

A corner of the bunker had obliterated the south end of Photakis Village. The rest was unharmed. The faux-wood houses were painted in green and brown to blend peacefully with the trees. Most of the doors stood open.

Mitchie looked for the piles of pureed flesh she'd seen her last time walking on Demeter. The weather and wildlife had removed everything but some ominous stains.

Captain Kim waited by the bunker entrance, the faceplate of his helmet open. "It's secure, ma'am," he reported. "No shots fired. There were some bots but we broke them up by hand." He flexed his armored glove to illustrate. His men carried debris out, making a pile to the left.

"Thank you," she replied. "Take charge of the perimeter. Keep me posted on enemy activity."

He trotted off with a rattle of armor.

Pete pressed ahead into the tunnel. "Yes! Oh, it's beautiful!"

Mitchie followed. The bunker's core was a rectangle of space, far smaller than the outside. Even rows of the black data storage blocks they'd seen on the fleeing ship filled it.

The rest of the researchers were pressed into helping Pete assemble his tools. Half the carts fit together to form a single oversized computer.

Chetty went with the sergeant as the bodyguard squad scoured the bunker for any threat missed by the assault team.

Mitchie's comm crackled with a report from Kim. "Three airbots came our way. The destroyers got 'em."

Pete unplugged the nearest block from the cables built into its rack. He then attached the connector leading to his monster machine. Complex figures began to dance across its display. "It's chemistry," he said. "Same format as the other blocks. Let's see what's in there. Water, water, more water . . . filter for size . . . an ethanol molecule. Interesting." He kept typing as his mutters faded into unintelligibility.

Chetty directed the other researchers to survey the blocks. He said to Mitchie, "At first glance they were all storage units like this. But it wouldn't take many processing units to make this a powerful artificial intelligence node."

She tagged along with them for a dozen rows. Confirmation that block after block had identical interfaces finally palled. Stepping out of the bunker let her eavesdrop on the infantry's radio chatter. Movement in the woods was enemy bots scouting their positions or overexcited privates panicking at the wind, depending on the speaker's rank.

Mitchie went back in. Some of the research team clustered around Pete watching him explain his latest discovery. "The pattern of proteins and lipids indicates a cell boundary. We are not looking at chemistry but a high-fidelity biological simulation."

His audience began speculating on why the AI might want to study biology. Some were far-fetched enough to make the Terraforming Service's genetic engineering program sound tame.

Chetty asked, "Ma'am, could you come take a look at this?"

Mitchie considered his tone alarmingly formal.

He led her to a niche in the back of the bunker. When he grabbed the edge of the object and pulled it out from the wall she realized it wasn't in a shadow. It was colored flat black.

She stepped back. Chetty held one of the squares which had swallowed the people of Demeter.

"It's deactivated," he said. "No power. I poked it with a stylus and nothing happened."

"Let's assume it reactivates if something organic comes near."

"Yes'm. There's a power input plug here, I think it needs that to function."

"All right," said Mitchie. She didn't come closer.

"There's also data connectors, a massive array of them." He wiggled the square to show the metallic grids on the left and right sides. "I think this must have been outputting data when it, um, processed someone."

"You are *not* putting anyone through that. Not even a finger."

Chetty said, "No—but if we used one of those squirrels outside it could tell us what the AI actually did to everyone."

Mitchie thought about it. "Fine. Set it up to collect the data. I'll get you a squirrel."

Chetty began carrying the two-meter square toward Pete's nest, staggering a bit under the load.

She went outside to find the bodyguard squad. "Sergeant Boma!"

"Coming, Ma'am!" The voice came from above. The NCO skidded down the side of the bunker. At the top two soldiers were digging holes. "What can I do for you?"

"The boffins need a squirrel."

"Ma'am?"

"Please catch a squirrel. Alive. Or some other animal at least that size," she said.

Sergeant Boma had the familiar expression of an NCO who couldn't say what he wanted to say because it would be insubordination.

"Just one will do," she said.

Boma said nothing.

Mitchie said, "It's . . . for science."

The sergeant took a deep breath. "One live squirrel or equivalent, yes, ma'am. Anything else, ma'am?"

"No, that's all."

Boma turned about and profanely ordered three privates to report to him.

Mitchie re-entered the bunker to find the researchers arguing loudly. Pete and his supporters insisted on the need to analyze a single data block in detail. An interruption seemed to be the worst thing they could imagine in the project. Chetty stressed the importance of understanding the AI's activities toward their mission.

She listened long enough to be sure the consensus was shifting toward Chetty then sought out a quieter corner.

Captain Kim reported destroying five small bots attempting to infiltrate.

The black square rested with its corners on four crates. A young boffin held the power cable for it with a nervous expression. Pete and his two die-hards were reduced to arguing that the cables shouldn't be switched until the squirrel arrived.

Sergeant Boma led a private into the bunker. "Mission complete, ma'am!" The private gripped a squirrel firmly by the tail. The outraged rodent had gouged the paint on the armored glove and forearm. Now he seemed to focus on pulling his own tail out by the root.

"Thank you," said Mitchie. "Deliver it to Lieutenant Meena."

"Hold it until I'm ready, please," said Chetty.

The two infantrymen watched as Pete was given two minutes to save his mitochondrial DNA analysis. Then cables were switched from the data block to the black square. More cables were added to match all the connectors.

"Weigh it first," said Pete.

A boffin wrapped his datasheet around the squirrel to collect its specifics. The animal tried to rip it.

"Everybody ready? Good. Power on," ordered Chetty.

The young boffin plugged in the power line. The square didn't react in any way. The researchers all stepped back anyway.

Chetty said, "Soldiers, this object is extremely dangerous. Do not touch it under any circumstances. Now, bring me the squirrel."

To reach him the private had to hold his arm over a corner of the square. Chetty took the bit of tail sticking out of the private's fist. As soon as the private let go Chetty flicked the animal toward the center of the square. It didn't even get to bite him.

The squirrel reached the top of the square as a solid. It passed through without slowing. It came out the bottom as a liquid. A splash sounded as the fluids hit the floor.

The private peeked under the square, then glared at Chetty. "You killed it! That poor little critter. Do you realize what it took to keep it alive?"

"McGivers!" snapped Sergeant Boma. "Throw some dirt on that puddle. I don't want it spreading."

The private stomped out of the bunker. Boma, shaking his head, followed.

"The data flow's stopped," reported Pete. "It was a spike as the thing went through."

Chetty ordered the square unplugged.

Guo detached himself from the researchers to join Mitchie. "That poor kid. Sounds like doing in the squirrel was worse than combat for him."

"I can't blame him," she said. "It's worse for me than some of the people I've killed. It didn't do anything to deserve it."

"Which people?" he asked.

"It's worse than the ones who were trying to kill me or on combat missions. They had it coming. The people who just got in my way . . . that's worse than the squirrel."

Guo hugged her. "Good. If we water and fertilize that it might grow into a real conscience."

She snuck a quick kiss then pushed his arm off. "No commingling during the mission."

Her handcomm broke in. Captain Kim reported probes from the east. Three casualties had been treated and returned to duty.

"How long can you handle it?" Mitchie asked.

"Ma'am, at this strength we can hold on for a week."

"Good. Carry on."

A burst of noise from the researchers proved no one had been paying attention to the couple. "This proves it!" shouted Chetty.

Pete retorted, "The element proportions don't match."

"Yes, because humans have bigger brains and bones than squirrels. Look at the total data volumes." Chetty's datasheet projected a holo of the hundred nearest blocks. "Here's the partitions between data units. Most are two blocks and a bit. Some are smaller, and the small ones are randomly distributed in size between zero and two blocks."

He pointed through the crowd at Mitchie. "At the mass to data ratio of the squirrel, Commander Long would be one and a quarter blocks. The rest of us are closer to two blocks." Chetty turned back to his datasheet. Two bar charts appeared. "Here we see the age distribution of Photakis. Twenty-three children, infants to teens, and a hundred and eight adults. Now the size ratio of the data units. You see they match."

"There's twice as many data units as villagers," said Pete.

"Farmers. Tourists. Campers from the woods. You're nitpicking," snapped Chetty.

The other researchers began arguing.

"Hold it!" ordered Mitchie, silencing them. "Lieutenant Meena. You're claiming the population of Demeter was all converted to data?"

"Yes, ma'am. The samples fit. The extent of the bunkers fit. They're all here."

"Can we convert them back?"

Chetty looked helplessly at Pete.

"We certainly have detailed enough data to restore them," said Pete. "The facilities to actually manufacture new bodies don't exist."

"Nanoforges," said one researcher.

"Too slow," said another. "Tissue would die before you finish an organ."

"Make it in slices and assemble them."

A third broke in, "Let's slice you up and assemble them."

"Enough!" Mitchie halted the bickering. "It's theoretically possible. And they'll keep until we do have the tools to restore them, right?"

Many nods. "Focus on our mission. *Why* is the AI doing this? What purpose is served by protecting them?"

Pete offered the first theory. "They're not a means. They're the end. Doing this is the AI's reason for being. At a guess, someone told it to save lives. Now he's in the very first of these blocks." The expressions facing him ranged from astonishment to horror. "Anyone have another explanation?"

"No, it makes sense," said Chetty. "Swakop must be covered with these bunkers too. Both planets' populations intact as data."

"Except for the bunkers we blew up," said Guo. "How many is that?"

"I don't know," answered Chetty. "Dozens. Scores. Bunker fights are exactly the intense combat where tactical commanders call for orbital support." A researcher gasped. "Dammit, we didn't know! And we weren't trying to destroy them. They were just in our way."

Mitchie turned on her heel and started walking. In the bunker's entrance tunnel she broke into a trot. Demeter's lighter gravity let her hit a good pace.

"Ma'am! Anything wrong?" called Sergeant Boma.

Mitchie remembered an Academy hall monitor's comment when she was late to class. "Officers shouldn't run. It alarms the men."

She jogged backwards a few steps. "Just need to send a status report, Sergeant. And this is the only chance I'll have for PT all day."

Boma chuckled and waved two of his men to join her.

By the time they caught up they were panting hard through their open faceplates. Longer legs and better conditioning didn't make up for their thirty kilos of armor, multigun, and ammo, even before they sprinted to her.

Mitchie didn't slow for them.

A brilliant flash behind her turned *Joshua Chamberlain* white, leaving a purple afterimage. Her handcomm chirped.

"Kim to Long. Just got hit in mass. Called in a destroyer. I'm going to have to take back that week, ma'am."

"Should be just a few hours more. Long out."

The soldiers were breathing better than her by the time they reached the ship. "You wait here," she said.

The crane's personnel cage took her up to the cargo hold in comfort. She decided to skip the ladder. The crane took her to the main deck hatch. By the time she reached the bridge her breathing was steady again.

Mthembu asked, "What's going on, Skipper?"

"Later." She waved him out of the communications console seat. Mitchie sat down and looked over the frequencies card clipped to the console. She set the radio to the "EMERGENCY GUARD" channel.

Mitchie took a deep breath before lifting the microphone. "All ships, all ships. Cease fire. Friendly casualties. All ships, cease fire. Friendly casualties."

The speaker buzzed with ships acknowledging the cease fire and repeating it for anyone who missed the initial transmission. Mitchie leaned back.

The first violation of proper comm procedure came in less than a minute. "Who the fuck ordered a cease fire! I have troops in contact!"

"We have friendly casualties," she answered.

The speaker interrupted, "Bullshit! This is General Ralston! I just ran my full chain and no units report friendly fire."

"Civilian casualties. The heavy bunkers—"

Her signal was overridden again. "There are no civilians down here, you stupid—" The general shot off a string of obscenities.

It didn't end with a question so Mitchie didn't bother answering.

General Ralston shifted his wrath to the assault squadron commanders. They refused to resume attacks on the planet without orders from their own chain of command. The inevitable escalation took less than ten minutes.

"This is Admiral Galen. All units clear this channel. Station making friendly fire call, sound off."

Mitchie picked up the mike again. "Commander Long, *Joshua Chamberlain*."

The admiral took a few seconds to respond. "Who are these casualties, Long?"

"The AI didn't wipe out the population of Demeter. It converted them into data. The heavy bunkers hold people. We can restore them, someday. But not if we destroy them. Every bombed bunker is hundreds or thousands of civilians dead."

"Can you prove this?" asked the admiral.

"Yessir. My team has all the details." She thought about how to explain the AI's goal. Then decided to by-pass the admiral. "Artificial intelligence. If you cease resistance we are willing to keep the data bunkers safe and maintain them permanently."

The answering voice was androgynous and toneless. "Agreement is acceptable. Person Michigan Long does not have authority to bind humans to agreement."

"This is Admiral Galen, supreme commander of allied forces. I have the authority. If you stop attacking us, we will conduct security and maintenance of the bunkers."

The AI responded with a series of questions and demands. Galen ordered the channel cleared for his exclusive use and asked for clarifications of terms.

Mitchie's handcomm chirped.

"Ma'am, this is Captain Kim. A wave of bots was coming at us. They just froze in place. Not reacting to our movements or fire at all. It might be planning some kind of trick."

Mitchie answered, "Stay wary, but I think this might actually be good news."

***

Admiral Galen ordered a general cease fire. He thought trying to settle the final peace terms over an open channel would invite hecklers and rumor-mongers. A quick conference with the other admirals decided to rely on an AI expert on the site over waiting three days to bring in a diplomat. Galen transmitted, "AI, you will speak with Dr. Peter Smith to settle the details."

Pete discovered his new assignment when a panting infantryman dashed into the bunker and handed over a data crystal.

Guo cut short the scientist's complaints over having his research interrupted. "Wouldn't it be easier to ask it how the data is structured?"

Pete shut up for a long moment, then laughed. "Yes, but that's not as satisfying as figuring it out for myself." He read the transcript of the original truce conversation and his instructions from command, then led Guo and Chetty out of the bunker.

The researchers couldn't spot any bots from the bunker. Captain Kim's command post looked like the best place to get directions.

The actual command team had been forced out of the tent to make room for the wounded. The captain demanded, "Is this cease-fire going to last?"

"Yes, if I do my job right," said Pete.

Captain Kim directed them to the nearest AI bots. He assigned a squad to escort the researchers. Guo had an NCO-to-NCO chat with the squad leader to ensure they wouldn't interfere with the negotiations.

The perimeter troops didn't want to let them through. Their sergeant had a crease on his helmet and a bandage on his leg. Guo noticed the dirt on his uniform didn't match the soil and concluded it must be explosive residue.

A call to the captain settled it.

The squad leader insisted on one of his men leading the way to check for traps. The woods seemed peaceful. Birds and butterflies flew about. A squirrel ran up a tree to escape them, giving Guo a guilty reminder of their test subject.

The point man raised a hand. "We're surrounded," he said.

Guo looked around. He couldn't see any bots.

Pete shouted, "I'm Doctor Peter Smith. Admiral Galen tasked me to communicate with the artificial intelligence."

A branch over his head bent double, flipped away from the tree, and spread out legs as it landed upright. More bots peeked out around trunks. The undergrowth shook as others shifted to complete the circle around them.

A rustle in the leaves drew Guo's attention up. A bot perched on a fork. Most of the bots were human designs with weapons added. This one had to be pure AI creation—lean, sharp, a pair of pistol barrels with legs.

"Can you understand me?" asked Pete.

The branch-bot bent over to write in the dirt. "YES. SPEAKER COMING," read the precise letters.

Guo called to the infantry squad. "There's another one coming. Keep calm."

Two came, both human made. A flying deliverybot carried another bot. The smaller one was designed for playing music. It still had "Pavel's Portable Parties" written on both sides with the late business's contact numbers. The boombot scooted to a couple of body lengths from Pete before speaking.

"This unit is in connection with all Demeter artificial intelligence nodes. Human Peter Smith is recognized as representative of human governance."

"Good," said Pete. "First. Have all AI units ceased combat operations?"

"All offensive operations have ceased. Units are using evasive tactics to avoid humans violating cease fire."

Pete gave Chetty a look. The intelligence officer moved off and spoke urgently into his handcomm.

"We will enforce the cease fire," said Pete. "I must negotiate a permanent agreement with you. You must not act on anything I say until the permanent agreement has been approved by my superiors."

"This is acceptable."

Guo studied the boombot. It had no expression to change, no variation in its tone of voice. He decided Pete was the best choice for negotiator. A professional diplomat would be crippled by the absence of all the cues he looked for.

The AI had conceded Pete's initial demands, such as promising to not convert any more people to data. Now they were bargaining over how much hardware would remain under the AI's control. Chetty took notes on a datasheet.

Guo thought, *This will take a long time.*

BDS *Aurora*, centrifugal acceleration 10 m/s^2

"Commander Long, reporting as ordered, sir!"

Admiral Galen returned her salute. "Long. Have you ever been elected to political office?"

"No, sir."

"Have you ever been appointed as a diplomatic delegate by a government?"

"No, sir."

"Did your orders instruct you to give the information acquired on your mission to anyone outside your chain of command?"

"No, sir."

"Then where the *fuck* did you get the authority to call a global cease-fire and negotiate with the enemy?"

Mitchie decided apologizing wouldn't help. Not that she wanted to. "I didn't have the authority, sir. It was just the right thing to do."

"You weren't right. You were lucky. You ran off based on a preliminary analysis. It's a miracle that the enemy didn't take advantage of you to set us up for a sneak assault. It still may. We can't tell. Which is why we have chains of command and civilians at the top taking responsibility for the big decisions."

The words *Fuck you, I saved thousands* stayed locked behind her clenched teeth.

"For more than a year I've trusted you with some of the most important tasks we had. Now I find I can't trust you. You're going to do whatever you want, not what you're ordered to, not what the Disconnected Worlds need done. So I'm going to be damn careful what china shops I let you into."

He waited to see if she'd say anything before continuing. "I *had* thought that recon mission would give me grounds to finally get you promoted to captain. Even had my yeoman start the paperwork. That's been shredded. You were up for a couple of valor awards. That paperwork's shredded too."

As if I fucking care, she thought.

"And I'm going to have to write a personal note to Admiral Chu saying, 'You told me so.' Now get out of my office."

Mitchie saluted, performed a precise about-face, and walked out.

She found Guo waiting down the corridor.

"How did it go?" he asked.

"Bad. Let's get out of here."

"Okay." He walked alongside.

Someone called "Long!" as they passed a cross-corridor. Mitchie cursed under her breath.

Director Ping strode up to them. "Do you realize how much planning you've ruined?"

"No, and I probably don't care," she answered.

"We've been planning for the resettlement of Demeter since the treaty of alliance was signed. Millions of people would be transferred to make it a functioning world again. Except what we had to offer them was ownership of the land and buildings. Now you showed the owners still exist. What are we going to give the migrants?"

"Aren't you happy they're still alive, or will be someday?"

"I'll be happy when someday comes. They can't get any work done now. There's square klicks torn in the cities by battle damage and someone has to repair it. How are we going to pay for it?"

"Auction off Swakop. If the AI there goes for the same deal the planet should be in good shape. But now I'm going to sleep."

She turned away.

Guo stayed silent until they'd made a couple of turns. "You don't look tired."

"I'm not. But I like the idea of going to sleep without being afraid of my dreams." She looked up at him with a smile, the first she'd had since being called back to the *Aurora*. "Want to help me with that?"

Demeter, gravity 7.5 m/s^2

Pete's lab was in the center of Endymion City. It had the most surviving processing power of any city on Demeter. His team had knit all the computers they could find into a single massive array. Chetty speculated that it would be the most computations applied to any single problem by humans.

"All nodes are ready," declared a technician.

"Read her in," directed Pete.

Three data blocks sat in the middle of the lab, covered in high data rate cabling. Their contents flowed out to the processing nodes, carefully arranged to let each simulate a portion of the body. Adjacent nodes would trade their overlapping layers back and forth to stay synchronized.

The researchers watched their screens fill with descriptions of a human being. The lead doctor said, "She's conscious. High adrenaline levels. Brain activity indicates panic. Not a reaction to the sensory isolation, that's how she was when recorded."

"We can accept sound," said the tech.

Pete leaned forward. "Mrs. Gurnsey? Heather? This is Dr. Smith. Can you hear me?"

Mitchie looked at the simulation clock. The system was taking over a minute to simulate one second. The eardrum-models were being shaken to match Pete's speech. How long it would take for the patient, if that was the word, to react was unknown.

The simulation began speaking 43 real seconds later. The tech saved up the whole statement before putting it on the lab's speakers. "Yes! What happened? I can't feel anything!" The voice sounded like a normal human.

"You're in Hermes Hospital. You've been terribly injured. I promise you we're giving you the best care we can. Do you remember what happened?"

Brain waves and vocal cords reacted immediately. The playback was delayed to speed it up for the listeners. "We were running. The bots went rogue. They were grabbing people. I just remember running. Did they get me?"

"Yes, but the Navy's driven them off again. You're safe now. The rogues are destroyed."

"My children, my husband, did you find them?"

"Yes, they're here too. You're all going to need extensive treatment to recover."

The doctor reported, "Stress levels are going down."

"That's enough," said Pete. "Discontinue the simulation." Screens blanked out across the lab. "So this proved it. We have real people in those boxes." The room filled with chatter.

Guo leaned over to Chetty. "Did they save the simulation?"

"No," he replied. "Pete's worried the sim's not accurate enough to do all interactions correctly. So he's going to go off the saved version in the blocks every time."

Mitchie put her hand on her husband's arm. "What's the matter?"

"Did we just kill someone?" demanded Guo. "That was a living, thinking being . . . and now she no longer exists."

Chetty tried to answer but tripped over his words as the question sank in. "It's . . . well, I don't know."

"Oh, God." Guo covered his eyes. "Where is her soul?"

Mitchie took his hand in both of hers. "Hey. She's still there in the block."

"But what of the one just created?"

She cast about for an analogy. "Think of it as . . . when an egg is fertilized but doesn't implant. Happens all the time. God knows sometimes life is just a flicker."

Guo held still as he absorbed that. "Okay. I can live with that."

"Then let's get out of here."

***

Walking through the streets of Endymion City they could feel the violence in the cracks and stains. The park they found was peaceful, hardly changed from when humans were there. The AI hadn't damaged it with a bunker, instead putting one in place of a warehouse across the avenue.

Mitchie and Guo sat on a bench, looking at overgrown grass spreading down to the pond. Ducks swam on the water as if they were still on Old Earth. The grass grew taller in some places but they avoided wondering why.

Guo raised his eyes to the data storage bunker. "I wonder where their souls are. Hovering where they were disintegrated? Staying with the storage blocks? Or gone to heaven?"

"They could have gone to heaven and then come back when we rebuild their bodies," offered Mitchie.

"Would that be blessing or cursing them?"

She didn't answer.

"I'm sorry," he said. "I shouldn't be going on about this. You have enough bad dreams already."

"It's all right. I'm sleeping better now anyway."

"With saving them?" Guo waved at the bunker.

"That. And also I'm seeing hope."

"Hope for what? That they'll let you retire so we can enjoy life?"

She laughed. "No, they're going to keep me in harness as long as they can, even if they don't trust me. The Fusion would freak if someone with so many of their secrets was not under military control."

"Then what?"

"I swore to spend my whole life fighting the Fusion, to punish them for killing Derry and everyone else they've hurt with their obsession for total control. I didn't think we'd win. I just wanted to do what I could and buy time for freedom."

Mitchie watched a duck take off. "Now . . . well. The whole point of the Fusion's existence is that the Betrayers can only be stopped by controlling every action of the human race. We just refuted that. Every time we take a world back from an AI more people will realize there's no need to obey those rules. Eventually the whole thing will shatter. And I'll be here to see it." She looked up at Guo. "If I don't go too often to the well."

He chuckled. "So what do you want to do after the war?"

"I don't know. When I went to space the family agreed my cousin Albert would inherit the ranch. We could buy a piece to build a house on."

"Oh, I like that. We could have a nice big house with room for a family."

"Family? Is this whole conversation just about yanking my implant?" Her words were stern. The way she snuggled into his side wasn't.

"Well, I've been thinking about it ever since I proposed. Didn't you give it any thought when we married?"

"No. I just thought the wedding would make you happy and it would be my last chance to make you happy."

His arm tightened around her. "I'm glad it worked out better than that."

"Me, too." More ducks took off from the pond. "When the war's over I won't need my implant anymore."

Guo leaned down to kiss Mitchie.

About the Author

Karl Gallagher has earned engineering degrees from MIT and USC, controlled weather satellites for the Air Force, designed weather satellites for TRW, designed a rocketship for a start-up, and done systems engineering for a fighter plane. He is husband to Laura and father to Maggie, James, and dearly missed Alanna.

About Kelt Haven Press

Kelt Haven Press is releasing print, ebook, and audiobooks by Karl K. Gallagher. *Torchship Captain* will be released in 2017. For updates see:
www.kelthavenpress.com

Subscribe to the newsletter for updates on new releases, art previews, and snippets of the next book.

If you enjoyed *Torchship Pilot* please leave a review on Amazon.com.